MINDPLANT
Trimorphia

JILL THRUSSELL

CONTENTS

1 THE CONSULTATION 1

2 CONNIE'S MINDPLANT 47

3 QUORN'S MINDPLANT 92

4 MIND OVER MATTER 143

5 TRAPPED 197

6 CROSSING PATHS 247

7 FINDING MAVERICK 283

8 ESCAPE ROUTES 339

9 CONSEQUENTIAL DILEMMAS 394

10 TOMORROW OR YESTERDAY 444

THE CONSULTATION

Connie was taut with nerves as she sat and waited in the clinical waiting room to be seen. It was unenticing with matt almost grubby, dull, cloudy, beige walls and the dark brown, wooden furniture inside the room was very simplistic. When she'd signed up, she'd expected something more visually appealing to represent this high tech program, something more lavish, luxurious and sophisticated, yet her expectations unmet, now sat now firmly situated in the tips of her toes as she absorbed the reality of the environment she was now in with sheer disappointment at its lacking. She quickly reminded herself in an attempt to relieve her disappointment that she wasn't actually there to analyse the interior decorator's aptitude and then tried to distract her mind as she thought about something else. She coughed slightly as nerves trickled through her body and tickled her throat which grated as she swallowed, it was dry and parched like the desert sands under the hot, burning sun as she longed for some moisture with which to lubricate it as she waited anxiously to start experiencing her dream vacation.

The nature of the experimental technologies she was going to be engaging in had sounded exciting when she'd first read the website and she'd imagined wonderful, high tech surroundings that would match the captivating and mind blowing descriptive of the technology she'd signed up to participate in. Although the waiting room was an utter, visual disappointment, Connie attempted to resign herself to the comforting thought that at least there was a refreshments table situated at one end of the room that seemed to be laden with drinks and snacks of various kinds. She decided to distract herself by sampling some of its offerings as she waited.

Connie stood up and eagerly approached it, however when she arrived at the table she found only very slim pickings as she cast her eyes quickly over the top. She prepared to help herself as she accepted that even the snacks looked drab and unenticing but attempted to line her stomach anyway, dull snacks were better than no snacks at all. The dullness of the snacks added to the overall dullness of the environment she was currently situated inside as a glum expression crossed her face. Whoever had picked out the colour scheme for the interior surroundings and the furniture she thought, hadn't chosen well. Perhaps it was because the program was partially financed by the government, perhaps the interior decor was simply a reflection of the limited resources the organisation actually had available for unnecessary expenditure. Whatever the reason was for the obvious lacking, her surroundings sure weren't pretty.

Connie finally choose a small packet of plain, digestive biscuits and then poured herself a murky looking coffee from the battered looking coffee machine nearby. She sighed for a moment, unsure that the vacation was actually going to live up to her initial expectations, if the waiting room was anything to go by it certainly wouldn't. The advertisement and invitation she'd been sent had been interesting enough to captivate her and seduce her desires for an exotic, unusual vacation and her curiosity had been immediately aroused. She'd been lured to participate by the enticing prospect of actually taking a vacation inside someone else's body and she'd had fancied the distraction from the monotony of her daily grind job, a job which often made life quite tedious and rather boring, yet the waiting room appeared to be almost as boring and dull as her real life actually was.

The holiday was a low cost affair which had totally suited her budget and appealed to her at the time as she'd jumped at the chance to enjoy a bargain and throughout the month in the run up to the start date of her vacation, she'd browed the various profiles she'd been sent for hours as she reviewed the various alternative bodies and lifestyles on offer to actually vacation inside. She hadn't been pressured to make a decision or final selection regarding which body she wished to actually vacation inside prior to her appointment, but had simply spent some time as she'd meandered through the many profiles and didn't actually commit to any, although she did have a few firm favourites. She'd even stood inside her bedroom on several occasions and glanced into the long mirror nearby with photos of the profiles she'd had preferences on her laptop as she'd held it up to face the mirror and envisaged what living inside each persona might be like as she'd imagined herself within each of the bodies she felt more drawn to. Today however was the final day of reckoning and now she knew she had to make a final choice and actually commit to one of the profiles she'd actually been sent.

The waiting room was empty besides herself and that surprised her as she'd expected it to be brimming with activity, vibrant bodies and life. A unique vacation opportunity such as this one, should have in Connie's mind, attracted a lot of attention but the absence of people around her simply couldn't be explained as it confused her slightly. Perhaps the company didn't advertise widely she finally concluded, the website had been very impressive however with photos of the founder and C.E.O. Barbelo Rodriquez clearly displayed upon it and she couldn't understand why they actually wouldn't. The founder Barbelo had looked confident, youthful, beautiful and elegant and although Connie estimated she had to be in her late thirties or early forties, she actually looked quite a bit younger. Her olive skin had glistened and sparkled and her auburn hair had reminded Connie somewhat of autumn leaves, Barbelo's piercing aqua green eyes had seemed to shine like an ocean surrounding a tropical island and almost shimmered like the waves that rippled and lapped gently against the golden sands they greeted each morning.

The small packet of biscuits kept Connie company as she sat back down and crunched on them hungrily and then sipped on the cup of hot, bitter coffee. The clock on the wall nearby changed every now and again to indicate each second and minute as they passed, before they disappeared never to return again. Just like the rest of the room however the clock was also very plain much like the walls it clung too. It was square, small and black and adorned with white digits which barely even broke the monotony and plainness of wall it was actually situated upon. The clock was drab just like the rest of the room and it paled into significance as Connie glanced around anxiously and started to become impatient. She'd dressed up for the occasion in one of her smartest dresses, a knee length, black, figure hugging number with a stylish white top that clung to her cleavage, it had hardly been worth the effort.

Fifteen minutes had passed by since her scheduled appointment was actually due to start and there was absolutely no sign of anyone entering inside the room to assist her as she shook her head and became slightly agitated. The lengthy wait further reinforced in her mind that this was definitely some kind of government sponsored program as no private outfit, that was well financed and had been well lubricated with abundant financial resources would keep a client waiting in that manner. Connie began to become perplexed, the long wait was a manifestation of the low cost holiday and that translated into the provision of skeleton customer services.

Five minutes later however, much to Connie's relief, a female coordinator actually finally stepped inside the room as Connie sighed and smiled appreciatively. The female coordinator made her way straight over towards the chair upon which Connie was seated and Connie immediately stood up expectantly.

"Connie Kingston?" The woman asked as she broke the silence and stretched a hand out towards her.

Connie nodded and smiled politely as she reciprocated her gesture and the two women shook hands. The coordinator appeared to be in her late forties and was extremely attractive and very well-manicured. There were a few fine lines of wear and tear upon her face, that clearly indicated she was a mature woman on the whole, but much like Barbelo she was well maintained and pedicured and presented an extremely glamorous, professional image. The white uniform she wore had black, shiny, jewel shaped buttons that ran down the front of it, which made it look slightly more extravagant and just a little better quality than the type usually worn by nurses in government funded hospitals and actually reminded Connie somewhat of the type of clothing often worn by beauticians.

"Take a seat for a few minutes please. I just have to pop down to the front desk for a minute before we start." The woman insisted.

The coordinator disappeared a few seconds later, almost as abruptly as she'd arrived as she left Connie alone in the waiting room once more. Her sudden disappearance irritated Connie even further as the thought of having to wait again prickled her mind and she sat back down. She'd be back soon hopefully Connie insisted to herself and then her wait would finally be over. It wasn't quite the perfect vacation she'd hoped for, not yet anyway.

A sudden urge teased Connie's body as she felt a desperate need to visit the ladies room. She quickly stood up and then realized that she had absolutely no idea where the restroom was actually situated. A search would definitely have to be conducted she decided as she briskly walked towards the waiting room door or she might actually urinate right there inside the waiting room. There was no way she could actually risk waiting for the female coordinator to return to ask her that could take ages.

The doorway led out into a narrow, beige hallway and as she walked towards it, she quickly glanced down at her phone for a moment, distracted by the time and the reality that she was still indeed waiting to be seen and participate in her vacation. A few seconds later, Connie suddenly felt a solid bump as she quickly diverted her attention back towards her path and looked up sharply. Connie had actually bumped into someone, a man. Surprized by his presence she quickly stepped back and then glanced up at his face apologetically as she rebuked herself internally, she totally hadn't been paying any attention at all to where she was going.

"I'm so sorry. I wasn't looking where I was going." Connie muttered quickly as she apologized.

The man smiled gently in response.

He looked a little older than Connie, at least ten years older she quickly estimated as she analysed him and he seemed to possess a quite serious disposition that was instantly apparent. Unlike the female coordinator that Connie had just met, he wasn't actually wearing a uniform and she quickly assumed that like her, he too must be a client attending the Mindplant Centre for a vacation. Connie quickly averted her gaze away from his face as she rapidly realized that she had actually been staring at him and that to do so could perhaps be interpreted as slightly rude.

"I'm sorry too. I wasn't really paying attention either." He replied as he smiled and glanced into her eyes. He coughed gently as he attempted to clear his throat. "I was probably slightly distracted by the excitement of it all."

"No really it was totally my fault." Connie insisted. "I was doing something on my phone and wasn't paying attention to where I was walking."

"You here for the vacation program?" He asked curiously.

"Yes and you?" Connie replied enthusiastically as she nodded.

"Yeah but my Mindplant vacation doesn't actually begin for another few days." He verified.

"Mine starts today. Well it's supposed to start today, when I'm actually seen that is. I'm waiting for it to begin at the moment." Connie explained as she smiled at him and relaxed a little. "I fancied a bit of a change from myself, so I decided to give it a go."

The air between the two was taut with anticipation and excitement as their presence validated each other's participation in the actual vacation program and reassured them that there were actually other human beings involved in the experimental holiday they had actually signed up for. Their expectations were high as they clung to the particles of air between them, unvoiced and unspoken and nestled gently against the pores of their skin.

"I'm Quorn." The man said as he quickly plucked a business card out of his black, suit jacket pocket and handed it to her. "Well if I don't see you on the other side, stay in touch." He invited as he smiled a little flirtatiously. "And I hope you have a great vacation."

Connie accepted the business card politely and smiled as she read it silently. 'Quorn' what an unusual name, wasn't that the name of a type of food? How strange. She politely tucked his business card away in one of the pockets inside her handbag and then glanced back up at his face once more. "I'm Connie." She said politely as she bit her tongue and kept her thoughts surrounding the strangeness of his name to herself, locked away firmly inside her mind and mouth. It wasn't helpful to appear rude the very first time you actually met someone. "It's nice to meet you Quorn." She added playfully.

"I just signed up a couple of days ago. I had some unused vacation time from work and someone emailed me this offer. I just couldn't resist it. It sounds great and it came along at just the right time." Quorn explained to her as he took advantage of Connie's willingness to indulge in a slightly longer conversation and participated fully. "Besides if I don't take my vacation time now I'll lose it altogether, so it was a bit last minute but isn't life more exciting that way sometimes?"

"That's very daring of you. It actually took me months to decide on this vacation. I was a little nervous about it myself." Connie replied.

"Perhaps we'll see each other again whilst we're on our vacations." Quorn suggested. "Wouldn't that be fun?"

Connie smiled and nodded politely as she glanced at his face and observed him a little more closely for a moment. Overall, he appeared to be quite attractive with dark brown, almost black hair and seemed to be in his mid-forties, the rugged smile that adorned his face was rough but still slightly charming somehow. His teeth flashed through his lips as he spoke and shone, they were a crisp, shiny, ivory white and they somehow reminded her of the teeth one would see in people's mouths on toothpaste commercials.

The two began to feel slightly more comfortable with each other and were about to embark on a deeper discussion, when the female coordinator returned abruptly and interrupted them both. She smiled at them politely as she approached and nodded her head enthusiastically at Connie as she touched her arm gently.

"Ready Connie?" She asked politely.

The return of the coordinator and the question she posed totally stunned Connie for a moment as she glanced at her face completely surprised and slightly confused. Her question seemed highly illogical and completely contradictory as Connie had actually been waiting for her, not the other way round. She decided not to furnish it with a response and to simply ignore it as she quickly smiled at Quorn politely and prepared to depart. Perhaps she'd stay in touch with Quorn she thought, it might be beneficial to them both and provide them with some kind of comfort. It would perhaps be nice to retain contact with someone who had shared a similar experience and participated in this strange vacation program like she had.

The female coordinator gently held Connie's arm and led her down the hallway as the two women parted and left Quorn in the hallway alone once more. Just as they approached the corner at the bottom of the hallway however, Connie quickly turned back for a moment and glanced at Quorn as she gave him one last smile before the two completely disappeared from sight.

"I'm Mena." The female coordinator explained to Connie as they entered inside another long hallway and started to walk down it. "I'll be looking after you whilst you're on your Mindplant vacation." Mena insisted as she walked a step or two in front of Connie and then stopped as they arrived outside a door which she quickly opened. "This is my consultation room. Please come inside." She invited as she stepped into the room and held the door open for Connie politely as she waited for her to enter inside.

Beads of sweat suddenly started to gather on Connie's palms and forehead as she stepped inside the room, for some reason she suddenly felt very nervous but also very excited about the prospect of actually going on her pending vacation. The consultation room provided further verification to her that the Mindplant trip was really actually going to happen now as she started to prepare herself mentally for the adventure ahead. The thought of entering inside another body that she would actually select, fully occupied her mind as she accepted she was now about to actually indulge in the mind blowing vacation she had actually signed up for.

Luckily for Connie the consultation room actually seemed to be much brighter than the dull beige waiting room and the hallway outside and that lifted her spirits significantly as she absorbed her new surroundings. The hallway had simply been an extension of the dull waiting room and the sudden change in decor encouraged her as she glanced around Mena's consultation room which actually looked clean, bright, smart and simple. The walls were a crisp, brilliant white and the furniture was a dark, shiny black which gave the room an almost elegant feel. A large computer screen was situated in one corner of the room and a large, black, leather examination sofa sat firmly leant against one of the walls.

Mena quickly invited Connie to sit down on one of the large, black, leather chairs that were scattered around in front of the computer screen and Connie participated with her request enthusiastically. Once Mena was satisfied that Connie was comfortably seated, she quickly touched the screen in front of her and loaded some profiles onto it. The screen quickly filled with potential bodies that Connie could inhibit whilst on her vacation and Connie smiled as she immediately recognized some of them. They were the same profiles that Connie had already been sent, prior to her attendance at Mindplant and hence were all relatively familiar to her, even though she hadn't made an official selection yet.

The body stats, details of each profile's personality, characters traits and lifestyles appeared on the screen beside each one as Connie started to inspect them more closely. Every profile in front of her belonged to a female as Connie had specified that preference explicitly prior to her actual appointment as she had absolutely no desire at all to walk around in a man's body for ten days, especially not when she was on vacation. The vacation for Connie was enough of an adventure and she had absolutely no desire to deviate that far from familiarity and actually change genders at the same time as that would definitely take her a little too far outside her comfort zone and detract from her enjoyment of the whole experience. Connie wanted her vacation to simply be fun and not be clouded with the complexities of exploring life as a man.

Mena turned to face Connie for a moment and smiled. "Any ideas what kind of body you'd like to inhibit from the initial profiles we sent you?" She asked politely. "The list I sent you was based on the preferences you specified when you made your initial booking."

Connie glanced at Mena's face quietly for a moment as she considered her reply thoughtfully. She wanted to have a vacation that would be lively and interesting as her life right now was rather dull. "Someone very interesting." Connie replied enthusiastically after a short pause. "Someone like, like a high tech vigilante."

Mena smiled at her response. "Sure I can do that." She insisted as she nodded.

"And preferably someone stunningly beautiful." Connie insisted. "I don't want to look drab. It's a dream vacation right?"

Mena smiled. "That can be organized too." She confirmed quickly. "We'll make sure you look stunning."

The large, wafer thin screen in front of the two women began to change as Mena quickly flicked through each profile almost as if she was reading the pages of a book. She quickly scanned around twenty profiles and inspected them a little more closely as she sought to match Connie's preferences precisely. After some deliberations the two women finally managed to narrow down the twenty to ten and then finally five as Connie rejected some completely and accepted others. There were two profiles that definitely appealed to Connie slightly more than others as Mena continued to navigate through the remaining five profiles and observed them quietly. Mena started to explain the precise implications of the five remaining profiles and what Connie should actually expect to do each day if she selected each one as the two women examined them more closely on the screen in front of them.

Connie listened attentively to Mena as she spoke, she seemed exceptionally thorough and very good at her job and Connie was instantly reassured by her professionalism. After a few minutes of further internal deliberation, Connie finally made a decision as she picked out one of the two profiles she felt the most drawn to, a slightly younger, very attractive female named Skylar. From what Connie could see having a vacation inside Skylar's body would provide her with the most fun and from her profile details she definitely appeared to be the most interesting.

Inside Skylar's body Connie would definitely have her ideal vacation she quickly decided as she pointed towards her profile and confirmed her selection to Mena.

"I'd really like to be Skylar for ten days." Connie insisted. "What happens to our bodies whilst we're on vacation?" She continued curiously as she turned to face Mena. This was a very important question Connie mused as even though her face wasn't as pretty as Skylar's was, she definitely wanted it back when her vacation was actually over.

"Your body will be stored inside a personal chamber in the Body Preservation Dormitory." Mena explained as she touched the screen in front of her again and it suddenly changed. A room filled the screen in front of them that appeared to be filled with thirty life size, transparent body capsules that were situated inside small alcoves that lined each of the walls. "If you'd like to actually see it in person, I can take you there." Mena quickly invited as she stood up and smiled.

"Can you that would be great." Connie replied enthusiastically as she stood up also. "I'd love to see it. Since my body is actually going to be there for ten days." She remarked playfully, inwardly pleased by Mena's transparency.

Mena nodded and smiled. "The dormitory is manned twenty four hours a day by medical staff and your body will be kept in prime condition whilst you participate in your Mindplant vacation." Mena continued. "It's perfectly safe."

The two women quickly left the consultation room as Mena led Connie back out into the hallway and they made their way back towards the waiting room, this time however they walked straight past it as Connie glanced curiously inside and quickly observed that it was now indeed very empty. Quorn had vacated the room and would now perhaps she thought be situated inside a consultation room with a coordinator somewhere else in the building. She smiled as she thought about Quorn quietly, he was definitely more daring than she was and had only signed up for his vacation a few days before and then he'd taken an immediate flight to the nearest city to actually participate. She was definitely less impulsive, it had taken her a few months to actually commit to this vacation and even now it was due to start, she still had some nagging doubts about it.

Her doubts swirled around the passageways of her mind chaotically as the two women walked quietly towards the Body Preservation Dormitory. Perhaps the sight of the Body Preservation

MINDPLANT: TRIMORPHIA

Dormitory would put those doubts at ease and provide her with the final reassurance she actually required Connie speculated, that the Mindplant vacations were indeed totally safe. It was a huge step for Connie and seeing where her body would actually be situated for the duration of her holiday she hoped would provide her with some grains of comfort. This vacation was the most risky, daring thing she'd ever done in her entire life and Quorn's quick decision to participate in such a program she mused, possibly verged on being slightly reckless.

The two women entered inside another hallway which led towards the back of the building as they continued to make their way towards the Body Preservation Dormitory and Mena started to discuss some of the more intricate procedures of the Mindplant vacations as they walked. Her voice soothed and appeased Connie somewhat as it calmed her and the doubts and fears began to flee as they vacated her thoughts and excitement began to accumulate inside her once more. Hundreds of people had participated in the Mindplant vacations and Connie had absolutely nothing to worry about she insisted internally, she would have ten days of fun and then return to her body once more and her dull, dreary life.

Even though Connie's life was completely dreary, drab and dull and no matter how dissatisfied she actually was with it, there was one thing she knew for sure, she definitely needed it back when her vacation actually ended. Her body would be placed in a state of paralysis for the next ten days and Connie wanted to ensure that it would actually be well maintained so that she could actually return to it when the fun was over.

"What happens when we return to our bodies?" Connie probed Mena curiously as they continued to walk down the long, beige hallway.

"You simply wake up back inside your body after your vacation." Mena explained. "It usually takes most people a few days to adapt back to the real world and their own lifestyles however so don't be alarmed by that. Sometimes it's difficult for people to readjust once their vacation is actually over. Some people get very used to the bodies their minds have been implanted into and then find it slightly disappointing when they actually return to their everyday lives. Some people find it difficult to adjust back to their own reality." She continued. "How do you feel about that?"

"That won't be a problem for me." Connie replied as she mulled the question over in her mind slightly confused by it. "Why wouldn't someone want to return to their real life after a vacation?" She ventured.

"I'm not completely sure." Mena replied. "Sometimes, some people even become slightly depressed." She explained.

Connie nodded in understanding. "Depression is not something I suffer from." She replied reassuringly. "That definitely won't be an issue for me."

The two women arrived outside the Body Preservation Dormitory as Mena paused for a moment, smiled at Connie and then stepped inside the large doorway of the vast, stone walled room. The huge space intrigued Connie as she followed her inside, totally fascinated as she absorbed every intricate detail of the interior curiously. It was a strange looking room with not only stone walls but also a stone floor and it looked very much like a high tech, futuristic, luxury science lab.

The personal chambers situated inside the alcoves dotted around the room were made of some kind of transparent glass or plastic and she could see straight through them as Connie peered into each one. The human bodies contained inside them were fully visible as she stepped closer to one of the capsules and inspected it a little more closely. The human face of the occupant seemed peaceful as they lay perfectly still and appeared to be fast asleep. They breathed in and out rhythmically as Connie stared at their face silently for a few minutes.

Next to each pod like vessel, situated upon the walls of the room was a small monitoring system that seemed to monitor the vital signs of each body situated inside the capsules. The only noise that emanated from inside the room came from these small monitoring devices as they beeped every few seconds and breached the silence that surrounded her. The sounds comforted and reassured Connie somewhat as she listened to their rhythm and smiled. A man was seated behind a desk, situated at the top of the room and he seemed to be watching over the pods inside it and that comforted Connie immensely as he stared at a screen in front of him and focused intently upon his task without even flinching once.

"That's the medical guard." Mena explained. "There's a medical guard present in the Body Preservation Dormitory at all times."

Mena nodded and smiled at him as he stopped watching his screens for a few seconds and glanced quickly up at the two women in front of him. He nodded his head politely to acknowledge their presence and then turned his gaze back towards the large screen in front of him. The two women continued their discussion as Mena turned her attention back towards Connie once more and sought to reassure her more fully.

"Each life support system monitors your blood pressure, sugar levels and temperature constantly." Mena mentioned. "That way your body is never in any real, physical danger." She reassured Connie as she led her towards one of three empty personal chambers situated nearby and smiled at her. "Throughout your vacation your body will be right over here."

"How do we actually eat? Do we actually eat anything?" Connie asked Mena curiously as she glanced inside a nearby pod that was fully occupied. The woman situated inside it appeared to be just a few years older than Connie was and looked peaceful and calm, but the fine lines around her mouth had immediately drawn Connie's attention towards the issue of food consumption. "I mean our bodies still need food right?"

"We feed your body every day with a liquid, food formula that is administered through a tube. The food provision composes of a special blend of nutrients, vitamins and proteins that are specifically designed to meet all your nutritional needs." Mena explained.

"Really does that actually work?" Connie enquired, not quite satisfied or convinced that an injection of fluid into a tube could possibly replace the intake of real, physical food. "Or do we lose weight?"

"It actually does work, it gives you everything you need whilst you are on your vacation. We've expended a lot of resources in order to find the perfect formula required to sustain people's bodies completely and thoroughly, whilst they engage in their vacation." Mena insisted. "It's very well researched and we've actually used it for the past two years very successfully and over three hundred participants have had absolutely no problems at all."

"How are our bodies actually kept clean?" Connie enquired as she walked towards a nearby capsule and peered into it as she inspected the woman's body situated inside it more closely.

"Oh the personal chambers are regulated by a hygiene maintenance module, which releases particles from an antibacterial module into the air that surrounds your body every day. Those

particles cleanse your pores and skin thoroughly."
Mena explained.

Some of the explanations provided by Mena
sounded rather technical, scientific and
complicated but as Connie glanced around the
room one final time and observed the bodies that
faced her, which stood upright in their respective
pods she was completely reassured. The human
bodies looked clean, each person's hair seemed
shiny and there was no signs of hunger or lack of
hygiene at all. The back walls of the personal
chambers inside the room appeared to be
cushioned with a white, pillow like bedding that
seemed to provide a bed like backing for each
body they housed and they looked very
sophisticated, very high tech and more importantly
relatively comfortable. She was completely
satisfied.

"Each night we position the personal chambers
horizontally." Mena explained as she quickly
demonstrated on a nearby unoccupied personal
chamber how each pod could be moved around
easily into various positions. "It's almost as if
you're actually sleeping on a bed. We do that to
assist with blood circulation and to maintain the
physical stance that your body is most
accustomed too."

Connie nodded as she listened and smiled. "Great I'm ready to go on my vacation now." She clarified as she indicated and confirmed to Mena that she was now actually ready to proceed. The dormitory had been interesting to see but somehow it had also made Connie feel slightly out of her depth, due to the scientific complexity that surrounded her. Everyone inside the capsules looked peaceful, well fed, clean and healthy and to Connie that was the clearest indication she could possibly have, that her body would indeed be perfectly safe. She smiled at Mena as her eyes shone with excitement. "It's very exciting."

Mena smiled and nodded enthusiastically.

The two women walked back towards the Body Preservation Dormitory doorway and Mena nodded at the medical guard just before they exited. They walked down the long hallway that led back towards Mena's consultation room as Connie prepared her mind for her pending vacation quietly. When they arrived back inside the consultation room a few minutes later, Mena led Connie straight over towards the black, leather examination couch that leant up against the far away wall and nodded politely at her. Mena quickly pulled a screen around the couch and then handed Connie a white, gown like outfit that she plucked out of a wall cupboard nearby as she smiled.

"Just pop that on and then jump up on the sofa and I'll get your Mindplant vacation started." Mena urged. "I'll have you inside Skylar's body and on your vacation in no time."

Connie obediently followed Mena's instructions as she changed her clothes, climbed on top of the sofa and then quickly lay down. The couch was unlike the traditional sofas usually found inside people's homes in that this couch was long, flat, black and cushioned and somehow it reminded her of the type often found inside therapy rooms. A few seconds later, Mena pulled back the screen and then quickly made her way over towards the computer screen situated at the other side of the room as Connie waited expectantly for what might actually happen next. Connie could hardly breathe as excitement gripped her body and it began to tingle all over as Mena sat down in front of the screen and began to touch it. She focused her gaze intently upon Mena as she watched her quietly. Connie didn't have to wait very long.

After just a few seconds Connie noticed that her body's exterior appeared on the screen in front of Mena as she leant forward and touched the screen several times. A program immediately started to analyse her internal organs and excitement gathered and swirled around inside Connie rapidly as she watched. Connie simply couldn't wait to actually be Skylar and Skylar's profile had actually been one of her favourites when she'd reviewed the profiles on offer at home, prior to her attendance that day. Mena had insisted that Connie should review more profiles and had presented her with a variety of options and questions as they'd eliminated each one, but Connie had still come back to Skylar's, which for some reason was the most suitable choice and ultimately her favourite. Mena seemed to be very professional in her approach and Connie appreciated that professionalism immensely and although the wait inside the waiting room had irritated her initially, at least when Mena had shown up she'd performed her job very thoroughly indeed.

Connie waited for her Mindplant vacation to actually start and for Mena to complete the necessary tasks as her mind wandered for a moment. In some ways she envied Mena as she had such an interesting job in comparison to her own. Perhaps her job had made her life boring, perhaps that was why she'd found Quorn's behaviour so impulsive and perhaps it was really

MINDPLANT: TRIMORPHIA

Connie who was more risk averse and cautious than most other people. Barbelo the Mindplant founder had an even more interesting job than Mena's in that she'd actually started her own organisation from her own life's work, Mindplant was truly her baby, her vocation and her life's passion. She had a background in medical research, science and technology and she'd utilized all of her skills to form something very unique and amazingly interesting. It seemed so much more romantic and fulfilling than Connie's own job which was dull in comparison, she was simply a Customer Liaison Account Manager for a technology company. Perhaps when she was actually on her Mindplant vacation she would have an opportunity to be wildly adventurous and perhaps then she would be able to explore that suppressed side of herself more fully as she indulged in Skylar's life and perhaps that would fulfil her slightly more than her own life she quickly determined.

Her wait ended as Mena stood up and returned to the side of the couch where Connie lay, she picked up a mask that was connected to a machine beside it and held it in her hands, neither of which Connie had actually noticed until that precise moment in time. Mena switched on the machine beside her as she smiled at Connie.

"Lie back, relax, shut your eyes and I'll take care of the rest." Mena instructed as she leant over Connie's body. "When you wake up, you'll be on your vacation and you'll actually be Skylar."

Comforted by the thought that for the next ten days she would not have to worry about cooking meals, taking a shower, laundering clothes or even throwing out the garbage, Connie closed her eyes immediately in compliance with Mena's instructions. For ten days Connie would actually be free from the daily humdrum of routine tasks and there would be absolutely no work and no difficult clients to deal with. She sighed with relief.

Her job was utterly boring and nowhere near what she'd hoped to do as a young woman after she'd graduated from college. The client list she maintained was completely stagnant and brutal as Hugh her boss had decided that Connie was the patient, nurturing, caring type and over the years he'd dumped all the difficult clients onto her list. Clients that no one else liked and that other staff struggled to cope with, client's people hated. She'd simply become a dumping ground for tricky clients and the undesirable customers no one else wanted to look after. Work had now deviated far from the enjoyable experience it had once actually been and become a tedious drag. Her clients were contentious and her daily workload had become an unbearable weight that now bore heavily down upon her slender shoulders, Connie had quite simply become the company doormat.

The mask was slipped over Connie's mouth and nostrils gently as she inhaled deeply and gases swirled around inside it as the mask filled it up. Her mind continued to jump in and out of her thoughts regarding her current job as she lay perfectly still and relaxed as she prepared to be taken upon the vacation of a lifetime.

"Connie you're such a great help." Hugh had said to her one day reassuringly as he'd assigned another client to her that one of her colleagues simply could not handle. "I don't know where we would be without you. No-one else can handle these people. Only you! Only you can handle these tricky customers. We'd lose a lot of money if we didn't have your tremendous people skills Connie." He'd insisted. "You're absolutely amazing."

Whether Hugh had actually meant the words he'd spoken to her or whether they were simply an attempt to flatter Connie so that she would accept the situation, she was unsure. He was a confident but stubborn man in his mid-forties who had actually started his business himself ten years beforehand and the company had grown to a reasonable size under his stewardship, it had even been publicly floated and Connie knew once Hugh made a decision, there was quite simply no moving him at all. Hugh had somehow resigned himself to the conclusion that Connie being a dumping ground was the best solution for his business and unfortunately he'd stuck to that decision. Assignment of these difficult clients to Connie had saved Hugh time and money and saving money was good for his business, regardless of how Connie actually felt about it herself.

A minute or two later Connie drifted off peacefully as her thoughts about Hugh and work melted away into the distance and her mind emptied. The mystery surrounding where she would actually wake up lay dormant in her thoughts as Connie had absolutely no idea what to expect when she did actually reopen her eyes and was too drowsy to even consider it further. She was ready and more than willing to explore the invigorating adventure that lay waiting for her as she slowly slipped into the depths of slumber and sleep embraced her. Her mind quickly began to lose consciousness as her thoughts became a blur and disappeared quietly as the sedation process of the sleeping gas kicked in.

Once Connie was fully sedated, Mena called for some porters as she paged them through the internal messaging system on her computer and two men arrived outside her consultation room door approximately two minutes later. Mena nodded at them as she permitted them to enter inside the room and they quickly wheeled in an empty, body trolley as they approached the couch where Connie lay. The two men gently picked up Connie's sleeping body and placed it upon the body trolley they'd brought along with them as Mena sat by her desk and watched them quietly. Once Connie had been placed securely on top of it, they wheeled the body trolley back out of the room and headed towards the Body Preservation Dormitory quietly as Connie continued to sleep, totally oblivious to the fact that her body was actually being moved around, or to anything else that was actually going on around her.

The consultation room was peaceful and quiet once the porters left as Mena sighed and prepared for the remainder of her day which she knew would now be consumed with paperwork. Unfortunately the enjoyable part of her job which was actually interacting with clients, for that day was well and truly over and she was slightly less enthusiastic about the other more monotonous duties that waited impatiently for her attention. Compulsory tasks which quite simply had to be completed that very same day before she actually departed and headed home when the evening presented itself. Quite often luckily however she was not entirely alone in the humdrummery of routine and the bureaucratic processes she had to perform each day, quite often she was actually accompanied by Gavin Franks the managing director who often worked alongside her. Technically, Gavin Franks was actually her line manager, even though they had both actually joined Mindplant as Vacation Coordinators upon its official formation at the same recruitment intake. Gavin usually split his time between the Body Preservation Dormitory and his office and for a couple of hours a day Mena would usually join him as they tackled some tasks together.

His promotion had actually irritated Mena who had felt totally slighted by it and utterly hurt when it happened. Barbelo, due to a significant rise in the number of clients Mindplant serviced and an increase in funding, just over a year ago had created a new, senior, management position, a post which both Gavin and Mena had actually applied for. She had been anxious to free up some of her own time so that she could focus on her ideas for growth, expansion and development, all of which required significant financial resources and an increase in engagement with potential financers. The need to romance more investors had been identified by Barbelo as a more effective use of her own time and there were technical aspects, experimental areas and elements actually inside the Mindplant program itself, she wanted to explore and lavish more attention upon.

Mena and Gavin had been the only two internal candidates for the management position and the post hadn't even been advertised externally. The appointment of Gavin and Barbelo's subsequent rejection of Mena, had dented her emotions and whilst she didn't begrudge Gavin the additional paperwork that accompanied the job, she did envy his participation in the more scientific aspects of his role which she was in her opinion, better suited to and even though just over a year had actually passed since Gavin had been appointed, Mena still felt quite resentful about it. Rejection for some reason seemed to inflict a deep pain that cut into the heart and engraved itself onto the mind and although time usually healed the pain of most wounds, somehow the bitterness of rejection was a much tougher pill to swallow.

The Mindplant Vacation Centre which Barbelo had built from scratch had been started five years beforehand. For the first two years, throughout what she often referred to as the 'Trimorphia Stage' no vacations had actually occurred as she'd rolled out the implementation of her original concept. Physical vacations had only actually started to occur after that two year period and had actually required a more substantial outlay of resources than Barbelo had originally anticipated, resources that she simply didn't have access too. She'd romanced politicians, government officials, scientific leaders and a host of other businesses in order to secure enough investment to realize her goals and finally the Mindplant Centre had been opened. Support from politicians and government officials, although it verged on being slightly political was good for Barbelo as it ultimately led to more funding and Barbelo absolutely loved more funding.

Barbelo's realization of her desires and her achievements over the years was enviable to many, even those within the scientific community as she had created a unique vacation experience and utilized her scientific knowledge in a manner that was commercially appealing. She had actually realized her research in reality which was something many scientists often yearned to do with research they had committed their lives too, but usually fell short of actually achieving.

She was a strong, driven woman who was completely dedicated and devoted to her work which quite often meant people found Barbelo slightly intimidating. Mena at times, actually craved to be slightly more like Barbelo herself as she felt Barbelo was very assertive and highly competent, unlike Mena who was slightly more thoughtful and cautious and over the years the two vacation coordinators, Gavin and Mena had become close friends as they worked closely alongside each other. Throughout the first four years that they'd worked together, prior to Gavin's promotion, they'd bonded in some respects as they'd often shared jokes about Barbelo's total dedication to her work, even though Gavin was around fifteen years younger than Mena and they had very little else in common asides from work. Barbelo's deep, unwavering dedication to Mindplant had become a regular source of their jokes as they'd often wondered why they'd never actually seen her leave the building in the evenings even once and they'd absolutely never,

ever seen her arrive each morning. Barbelo just always seemed to be there.

"Do you think Barbelo has a boyfriend?" Gavin had asked Mena playfully one day. "When does she see him if she does? She's always here."

Mena had shaken her head. "I doubt it. Who could be more of a man for Barbelo, than she is for herself?"

"Perhaps she has a girlfriend." Gavin had suggested.

"I doubt it." Mena had replied. "Seriously, women like attention and Barbelo just doesn't give anyone any attention besides her work. They'd get fed up in no time."

The two had giggled as they'd playfully analysed Barbelo's dedication to her work, her personal relationships and the lack of them, but behind all the jokes they both knew, Barbelo's dedication to her work was unfaltering as they'd both seen her fail time and time again and carry on regardless. Barbelo's relentless devotion had kept the Mindplant Centre alive, kept them both employed and had ensured they enjoyed a comfortable lifestyle. Despite their jokes, her dedication was actually one of the main things both Gavin and Mena actually respected the most about her character.

Luckily when Gavin had been promoted, he hadn't actually lorded his promotion over Mena's head and had stayed pretty much the same ever since it actually happened, which made him at least bearable to work alongside and the rejection slightly easier to cope with. Mena had been reluctant to leave Mindplant afterwards as Barbelo despite her failings, actually treated her staff extremely well and paid them very generously. Their workload was not overly burdensome and they usually had daily, intimate briefings with Barbelo who kept her hand firmly on the pulse of her business operations as she engaged regularly with each member of staff. Mena felt valued in a way that she hadn't experienced anywhere else and there was an unspoken loyalty that seemed to exist amongst all the Mindplant employees that Mena had simply never seen anywhere else she'd worked.

Mena spent two hours inside Gavin's office as they discussed and processed some acquisitions for the Body Preservation Dormitory and then returned to her consultation room quietly. She quickly reviewed her system client notes on the Mindplant Client System and realized that she was actually due to meet with Quorn in a few days and that he'd booked a seven day vacation. One of two other Vacation Consultants had actually attended to Quorn that day, but were unable to actually perform his actual Mindplant Vacation Implant as they were fully booked up for the next few weeks and hence he was a last minute booking on Mena's list.

His system profile confused Mena slightly as she inspected it more closely and noticed that Quorn had only actually been booked in two days before which seemed unusual as most clients usually signed up months before they were actually due to go on an actual vacation. For some reason however, Quorn had been signed up in a rush and the usual one or two month sign up process which appealed to Mena as she felt it actually gave clients more time to consider their participation with Barbelo's Mindplant Vacation program more thoroughly, had been completely ignored. The Mindplant Vacation program required a huge degree of mutual trust, it was a huge commitment and it was something most participants would only ever actually do once in their lifetime, which meant it wasn't usually a decision that could be made lightly or jumped into overnight. Quorn had paid quite a large sum of money for his vacation and Mena noticed that as she read his profile and smiled, Barbelo had obviously rushed through his application just to ensure he didn't get cold feet so that she could collect the generous premium he'd offered her. Barbelo loved premiums.

She quickly checked that his vacation had been authorized by Gavin and that his medical approval had been attained and was satisfied to find everything in order. The Mindplant vacation authorization process was quite stringent in that clients had to have their medical records checked thoroughly before they were actually allowed to participate on the program and at times some clients were not even actually allowed to participate at all due to delicate heart conditions or other potentially hazardous, life threatening ailments. Occasionally however, even some of the people who actually failed their medical checks would still be authorized to vacation by Gavin for other reasons that superseded their medical conditions.

Once a client who had been terminally ill, had simply wanted an escape from the pain of their illness in order to live out one last fantasy for a short period of time before they actually died and they'd been allowed to participate as Barbelo had accepted their exceptional circumstances and authorized them personally. They'd been required to sign some special medical release forms that Barbelo had provided to them, which completely absolved the Mindplant program from any liability, just in case they did not actually survive the vacation and return to their own body once it ended and they had then been allowed to experience a Mindplant vacation.

Such situations were rare but somehow those more unusual moments often motivated Mena and encouraged her, giving someone their dying wish was such a special gift to give someone and such special instances lifted Mena's spirits as she worked alongside such clients. Somehow such situations made the services Barbelo provided slightly more valuable and slightly more worthwhile in Mena's sight and somehow by providing such customers with a Mindplant vacation, Mena felt as if she was actually making their pending death just a fraction easier to face.

Mena quickly glanced at Quorn's profile a little more closely as she quickly inspected it, no he wasn't on death's door, was very much alive and was definitely very healthy. Quorn was absolutely nowhere near death. He wasn't an exception in that respect, just a late booking that Barbelo had squeezed in to optimize financial returns as there was a vacant personal chamber in the body preservation dormitory at the time. She quickly closed Quorn's profile and prepared to go home, relieved that finally the end of a long day had arrived as the clock struck six p.m. and she smiled. Nothing else mattered once six p.m. arrived each working day and Mena abruptly released herself from the responsibilities of work as she fled the building and prepared for her journey home. Mindplant vacations and Barbelo's vacationers could and would definitely wait until the next morning and the next working day.

Quorn's Mindplant vacation had been approved and despite Mena's concerns, the final decision was absolutely nothing to do with her at all and that was the one small liberty she could actually revel in after being denied the promotion she'd so fervently desired and lost out on to Gavin. Mena was now completely free from the heavier burden of responsibility that hung loosely around Gavin's neck as it waited for any possible impending disasters to actually occur, that might happen as a result of a management decision he'd actually made. If anything went wrong with Quorn and his Mindplant vacation, Gavin would ultimately be held accountable for that mess and not Mena, the decision to approve Quorn and his subsequent Mindplant vacation was simply not her responsibility at all and that was the one small comfort she had that she could appreciate in its glorious entirety.

CONNIE'S MINDPLANT

Connie woke up suddenly and immediately sat up as soon as she stirred from slumber, slightly confused. She quickly glanced around the bedroom as she absorbed the unfamiliar surroundings she now found herself situated inside, in complete and utter awe. Her surroundings were beautiful and elegant and the furniture inside the room a modern black and white. Rich burgundy and cream tones adorned the walls as she admired the colour coordination of the decor, which appeared to be totally immaculate.

A few minutes later she almost leapt out the bed as she glanced across at a mirror situated on the nearby dressing table and Skylar's face stared back at her, she was completely surprised by the reality of who she'd actually become. Connie had actually arrived, she was now actually on her Mindplant vacation and living, breathing and existing inside Skylar's body. She quickly climbed out of bed and then walked over towards the mirror as she glanced down at the rest of her body and admired the reflection in front of her appreciatively as she inspected every visible, intricate detail.

There were some photos of Skylar situated at the side of the bed on top of a small beside cabinet and she glanced at them briefly for a moment and then continued to look down at her new body once more. Skylar was very real. Her eyes were full of adoration and her mind completely fascinated by the transformation as everything about her exterior persona had completely changed and she was now very firmly situated inside the body of the younger, very attractive woman, whose profile she had so carefully selected. Skylar had the most amazing smile and Connie immediately felt satisfied as she glanced up at her face in the mirror and smiled at herself. Joy filled her internally as the reality struck her that the Mindplant vacation had actually worked. Mindplant could and had actually delivered on the promises written upon the glossy website.

The body of Skylar immediately somehow made Connie feel more sexy and alive as she stood in front of the mirror and posed as she admired it from every possible angle. Her pert cleavage, small waist and abundant hips offered an exterior view that was very pleasing to the eye and Connie's senses felt immediately felt invigorated as she embraced the new life and body that she now existed inside. It was a better, more fulfilling experience than buying a new dress at the store as this new body garment had transformed her whole body and her face. Now she really was Skylar a high tech, espionage consultant and vigilante who tracked down high tech criminals and solved high tech crimes. Not only was Skylar beautiful and attractive, she was also very intelligent and highly ethical too, she was the ultimate package and Connie simply couldn't have wished for anything more.

New adventures lay ahead waiting for her that this new form would offer, that she couldn't wait to actually embark upon and explore as Connie began to speculate for a moment how exactly she would find her first assignment. She hadn't actually been provided with any information throughout her consultation with Mena that specified how that would happen and she'd totally forgotten to actually ask. Connie was uncertain, but she didn't have to wait for very long.

A sudden pang of hunger somersaulted through her stomach as it crashed against the empty walls and growled angrily as Connie suddenly realized she was actually starving. She'd grab some breakfast, take a shower and then dress in something spectacular she quickly decided, before she engaged in the world of high tech espionage. Connie made her way towards the kitchen as she steered Skylar's body with ease as if it was indeed her own and entered inside, eager to explore the interior of the fridge and to her absolute delight she found some bread, a toaster and some condiments situated inside it. She quickly prepared some cereal and toast, comforted slightly by the familiarity of the food offerings inside Skylar's apartment, at least some things were the same in this very different body and world she'd woken up in. The high tech world of corporate espionage could wait she quickly determined, at least until she'd actually filled her stomach.

Once breakfast was prepared she sat down at a black, glossy table inside the kitchen and crunched on some pieces of toast as she smiled, the butter and jam sunk into the holes in the bread and tasted sweet on her tongue as the sugary remnants tickled her taste buds. She stretched out across the table and picked up a bottle of maple syrup and another slice of golden toast which she then drizzled the syrup across. Her mind felt grateful as her stomach quickly filled up, the start of her vacation hadn't been awkward at all and so far had been quite comfortable and relaxing. Just as Connie began to relax however a phone in the lounge that joined onto the kitchen, started to ring as it abruptly ended any thoughts inside her mind that there was no rush to actually go anywhere.

The noise took a few seconds to register in her mind as it wasn't a ringtone that Connie was used to hearing and there was a lack of association for a moment that the phone call might actually be for her. After a few more rings however it finally dawned upon her that she was actually supposed to answer the call and that the cellphone belonged to Skylar whose body she was now situated inside, which meant the call was actually for her. Connie smiled as she quickly stood up and then rushed over towards the small, lounge, coffee table where the cellphone was situated and picked it up. She held it in Skylar's hand for a moment as she glanced at the screen curiously and attempted to determine who the call was actually from before she attempted to answer it. An unfamiliar name appeared on the screen in front of her as a word flashed across it which simply said 'VISUAL' and she tentatively hesitated for a few seconds before she actually answered it.

"Are you ready for your first assignment?" The male voice on the other end of the phone asked politely almost immediately.

Visual's voice sounded deep and rich with a baritone tone which almost seemed to have a slightly, seductive edge as the words he spoke flooded into her ears and instantly intrigued her. Connie contemplated who Visual might actually be and what he might actually look like for a few seconds as she smiled, perhaps later on, throughout her vacation she would actually find out. Perhaps she would make that a personal mission of her own.

"Yes, well I'm almost ready." Connie replied as she smiled, she'd been caught off guard slightly by the call but could immediately sense the urgency in his voice as she responded accordingly.

"Great you have to leave in fifteen minutes." Visual confirmed.

"Sure. I'll be ready by then." Connie verified as she contemplated internally for a moment whether or not she could actually have a shower and get dressed within fifteen minutes, she'd have to rush she determined. She continued to listen to Visual silently and obediently as he imparted further instructions to her regarding the day ahead.

"I'm sending you an email with your first mission location inside it and target details." Visual clarified. "Once you arrive at the specified location, I'll send you further instructions."

"Great thanks so much." Connie replied appreciative of Visual's guidance and assistance as for now it was the only assistance and guidance she actually had.

The phone fell silent a minute later as if Visual had ended the call and Connie quickly realized that whoever Visual was, he certainly wasn't interested in exchanging pleasantries with her. Visual's conversation was clearly functional and now it had functionally ended.

She made her way quickly back out of the lounge and rushed down the nearby hallway towards the bathroom to take a shower as she prepared for her first day as a high tech vigilante and her first mission. Her interaction with Visual had excited her and so had the news of her pending mission, a mission that she would actually embark on that very same morning. Perhaps she speculated as she stepped inside the shower cubicle adorned with white marble walls, she would have a chance to actually meet Visual later that day, once her mission was complete. He'd sounded very mysterious and extremely interesting.

A romance whilst on vacation inside someone else's body wasn't a possibility that Connie was opposed to, especially when it could be one with an exciting male who had fascinated her already and filled her mind with intrigue. Exploring such romantic opportunities inside Skylar's body could be interesting, although the relationship Connie might indulge in would be purely artificial and something that may not even be desirable to continue once she actually returned to her own, real physical form. Perhaps Visual wasn't really available in that capacity at all Connie speculated, perhaps he was part of the Mindplant team or someone they actually hired just to participate in phone calls to vacationers in order to assist them in the completion of tasks or perhaps he was just a digitalized voice that may even really actually belong to a woman. A bundle of questions started to flood into her mind, all of which she realized very quickly, she actually had none of the answers to.

The water from the shower started to cascade down upon Skylar's naked flesh as Connie enjoyed the warmth, it felt fresh and delicious as she embraced it and it caressed Skylar's skin soothingly. The body she was situated inside began to tingle as she revelled in the pleasant sensation and closed her eyes for a few seconds. Perhaps when she returned from her Mindplant vacation she would actually ask Mena about Visual as her curiosity had definitely been aroused and she definitely wanted to find out more about him. She washed Skylar's skin with the beige, cloth sponge and shower cream she found on a small, white, marble shelf inside the shower cubicle as she prepared for the day ahead. Perhaps she thought, she could even ask Visual himself the next time he called if he was a real person or if they would ever actually meet. She shook her head and laughed, no such questions would definitely be awkward and perhaps they would make her look weird or perhaps he'd even interpret her curiosity as rude and impolite. Such conversations would be an embarrassment, especially with a total stranger, no it was better to wait and ask Mena instead.

Once Connie had finished inside the shower, she rushed out of the cubicle very much aware that time was actually escaping her grasp and grabbed a small towel from the nearby handrail, which she wrapped quickly around her head. She found a larger towel situated on another rail slightly below it, which she then quickly tied around her chest as it sat politely over the pert breasts she'd admired earlier that morning. They weren't her breasts, but they definitely looked good and for ten days they would be more than sufficient enough to satisfy her requirements. Connie made her way quickly back towards the bedroom and headed straight for the closet as soon as she entered inside the room. There was quite simply no more time to saunter around the apartment and admire her surroundings or Skylar's body and she knew it, her mission was on its way and she had to be ready to receive it by the time it actually arrived. She quickly pulled open the closet door and inspected the interior as she searched for suitable attire for the day ahead.

A few minutes later, after some careful consideration Connie quickly plucked out an outfit decisively that she felt would be appropriate for the day's activities as she committed herself rapidly to an outfit in order to avoid any further delays. The closet itself was huge and vast in size and actually filled up an entire wall of the large bedroom it was situated inside. Its doors were large and mirrored and slide along the floor when they were pulled open. Connie had noticed as she'd glanced inside the interior, that Skylar had an amazing, vast array of clothing which ranged from very business-like suits to sexy, sophisticated dresses that came in an assortment of colours, styles and shapes. The hangers had seemed to go on and on forever as Connie had gasped with excitement and awe when she'd first looked inside the closet, reassured entirely that she'd definitely have suitable outfits for every occasion for the next ten days whilst on her vacation. Shoes lined the floor of the closet and Connie had worked out from a quick glance, that there had to be at least sixty pairs of shoes, boots and sneakers all lined up in neat, tidy rows. Skylar was not just beautiful, exciting, ethical and intelligent, she was also a very eloquent dresser and had impeccable taste in clothing.

Connie quickly held the sharp, black, knee length dress she'd chosen, up against Skylar's body as she admired her choice, it was stylish but practical and definitely wasn't delicate, evening wear. It could be worn easily to either work or an evening function, although it did verge and lean towards being slightly more corporate but in a very sophisticated, feminine way. She quickly slipped it on as she admired Skylar's body in the large, mirrored closet doors in front of her and then turned in various directions as she inspected how it clung to Skylar's body from every angle. Skylar definitely looked elegant and sexy in a discreet, sophisticated manner and the outfit was totally perfect. She started to rummage around the floor of the closet as she searched for some shoes to wear and then picked out a pair of shoes that she really liked, which seemed to match the dress she'd chosen. The shoes fitted her feet perfectly as she slipped them on, they were pointed, black and flat with golden, embroidery patterns sewn into them, that swirled around the centre which matched the dress she'd chosen precisely and were extremely elegant. Flat shoes on this occasion were preferable Connie decided as she might need to escape very quickly and running around in high heels would be inappropriate and hence for today were totally out of the question.

She admired the pretty shoes in the mirrored closet doors playfully for a few seconds as she glanced at them actually on Skylar's feet as thoughts lingered playfully inside her mind.

MINDPLANT: TRIMORPHIA

Speculation began to swirl around inside her as she contemplated and deliberated for a moment as to whether or not Skylar was actually a real person. Was the life she now occupied actually a real person's life, had she actually paid to spend ten days inside someone else's real body? Perhaps Skylar's body was simply some kind of simulated life and an artificial existence that had been created by Barbelo and her Mindplant program to provide people like Connie with some enjoyment and entertainment for a short period of time throughout the duration of their vacations. The mental musings tugged playfully away inside her as her thoughts teased her for a moment.

She glanced down at the screen of the cellphone once more, which was situated on the bed nearby as she monitored the time and realized that the fifteen minutes she'd requested from Visual to prepare had now actually almost expired. If Skylar's body actually belonged to a real person that was perhaps paid to sacrifice her body for ten days to a stranger, where then would Skylar's mind then actually go Connie quizzed herself curiously. There were so many questions and Connie had absolutely none of the answers to any of them as she pushed the questions and thoughts to the back of her mind and glanced at the mirror once more. The issue of Skylar and whether she really existed or not was another mystery Connie quickly decided she would have to ask Mena about later, once her vacation was actually over. Skylar's appearance was definitely too stunning to waste precious moments questioning things she simply did not have the answers to and to do so would be a complete waste of her vacation time. One thing Connie was definitely sure about however as she exited the bedroom and headed back towards the lounge, absolutely no one would want to have their mind implanted into her real body and life at all, her life wasn't exotic and exciting like Skylar's was and her physicality definitely wasn't as visually appealing.

Connie began to entertain the thought of someone actually slipping inside her own body and facing her boss Hugh for a moment as she smiled, perhaps they'd put him in his place and once she returned to her own life, she'd be allocated to more enjoyable clients instead of just trouble makers. Her personal life wasn't much better than her professional life and was absolutely dry and arid, like the desert, she hadn't made any new friends since she'd moved for a work promotion over a year ago and all her family and existing friends, now all lived at least a four hour drive away which made it virtually impossible to see them throughout the working week. Her boss had insisted she should be based at headquarters instead of at a local branch and offered her a pay rise and she'd obediently cooperated. Although it had actually been over a year since she'd moved to the area she currently lived in, it still seemed as foreign to her as it did the first day she'd actually arrived. No one would want to have a vacation in her life, it was pitiful shadow of existence that simply mimicked the notion of living.

Her life hadn't always been dull and throughout her younger college years, Connie had actually enjoyed an active, vibrant social life. She'd had a large circle of friends that she'd visit bars, eateries, dance clubs and movie theatres with and she'd never thirsted or hungered for attention from the opposite sex as a sufficient number of potential suitors had approached her and propositioned her. At times she'd even indulged in romantic adventures and relationships with those she felt she was the most attracted too but moving had changed everything. Moving had not been good for her, yes she had slightly more money and was climbing the corporate ladder in some respects, but it had totally crucified her social life and her job role was mind numbingly boring. Starting again in a new place with absolutely no social contacts or friends had been difficult and the isolation had been quite soul destroying. The pigeon hole she'd been placed in at work was also totally demotivating and frustrating which had added to the overall dreariness of her life. Perhaps she contemplated quietly the ten thousand dollar salary increase simply hadn't been worth the sacrifice of actually living. Luckily for Connie however the Mindplant vacation she'd taken was not actually a mind and body exchange agreement and her body was safely tucked away inside the Body Preservation Dormitory, invisible to the whole world for ten days which meant no one else would actually be visiting her life whilst she had deserted it.

Connie quickly decided to forget about the mundane realities of her dreary life completely for the time being as she rushed back towards the lounge and quickly checked the cellphone again expectantly. For now, Connie determined she would focus solely on the fun and excitement Skylar's life offered to her as she read Visual's email and digested the instructions contained inside it, the next ten days was entirely Connie's to enjoy however she saw fit and she was totally determined that her vacation was going to be absolutely exhilarating. She simply couldn't wait to experience and savour every precious minute of Skylar's life in its entirety as she bounced down onto the sofa nearby for a moment and quickly checked that she had everything she needed.

The email that Visual had sent to Skylar's cellphone was extremely precise and the instructions contained within it very explicit as she read it a few times quietly. A small key card lay idly on the coffee table next to her and she picked it up and immediately placed it inside the small, black handbag, she'd chosen from Skylar's closet, which matched her dress. The fifteen minutes since Visual had called, had by now completely expired and Connie was now actually verging upon being late. She stood up quickly and walked back out of the lounge as she entered inside the hallway once more, which led not only towards the bedroom and bathroom, but also towards the front door and the exterior of Skylar's apartment building. She made her way quickly towards it.

When Connie arrived at the front door, she paused for a moment as she noticed a small, zebra print holdall bag situated on the floor right next to it and quickly picked it up curiously. Inside the holdall there seemed to be a few gadgets and pieces of equipment, all of which looked completely unfamiliar and very technically advanced. She swung the holdall over her shoulder decisively and then walked towards the exterior door of the apartment as she prepared to exit, it wouldn't hurt to bring it along with her she quickly decided, even if she didn't quite understand what some of the contents of the holdall actually did. There was a button situated on the wall beside the apartment front door which she quickly reached out and touched and the front door immediately swished open in front of her.

Just before Connie stepped out of Skylar's apartment into the external hallway in front of her, she quickly gave it one last glance as she prepared to depart. It was very stylish, very much like the clothing she'd found inside the closet that morning and it quickly drew her attention towards the ugliness of her own wardrobe and how drab her life had actually become. When Connie actually returned home to her real life, perhaps she decided she'd spruce up her home and her wardrobe as both urgently needed a complete makeover. Her entire life needed a spring clean and when she returned, she simply had to oppose the dreariness she'd allowed herself to wallow in and be dragged down by and actually perform one.

Skylar's apartment, she soon discovered was actually situated on the second floor and as she stepped out of the front door, it rapidly swished firmly closed behind her. She quickly walked along a relatively short hallway and then headed down the two flights of wide stairs that led towards the ground as she made her way towards the exterior door of the apartment block. Right next to the apartment building's front door, she found another button which she quickly pressed and the exterior door swung open. Connie stepped out of the door and then entered onto the street outside confidently as she plastered a huge smile across Skylar's face and prepared for the very first time to actually face the exterior Mindplant vacation world.

The street outside Skylar's apartment was unlike anything she'd ever seen before in that it was a shiny, silverish grey and almost looked as if it had been polished that very morning. The homes that surrounded her sparkled and glistened as rays from the sun bounced off the brilliant, white shiny walls that had huge slabs of glass situated inside them. An elegant, black, shiny electric car was parked right outside Skylar's home and she headed quickly towards it. There was no actual sidewalk to speak of, just a small space between the exterior front door and the car that was parked directly in front of it. Perhaps people didn't walk around whilst they were on Mindplant vacations Connie mused.

The car, according to the email that Visual had actually sent her, would take her straight to the building where she was supposed to complete her first assignment and was to be her means of transportation. The street the vehicle was situated upon was spotlessly clean and very unlike the dull, cement grey and black tones Connie was used too. Her shoes tapped gently against the ground as she walked towards the car and she stopped as soon as she arrived outside the vehicle's door. She touched the door but it seemed to be locked which prompted her to quickly search inside the zebra holdall she'd picked up from the hallway inside Skylar's apartment.

There seemed to be a star like shaped keyhole engraved into the car door and Connie quickly scrambled around inside the holdall as she attempted to find an object within it that actually matched it. A small, silver star shaped object shimmered at the base of the holdall which attracted her attention immediately and she quickly plucked it out, satisfied that it would definitely fit the car lock and open the car door. She quickly inserted it inside the star shaped hole and a few seconds later a beep emanated from inside the vehicle and the car door swung open a few seconds later. Connie quickly climbed inside the car and lowered Skylar's head as she entered to avoid bumping it on the top of the car doorframe. Unlike Connie, Skylar was definitely not petite and was actually quite tall in stature, which made entering inside the vehicle slightly more challenging.

Once inside the vehicle, the car door quickly swung closed behind her automatically as Connie glanced around the interior of the car curiously and inspected it, perhaps there were infra-red sensors situated around the door she quickly concluded. The car's interior appeared to be extremely high tech and very well equipped and although it was different in some respects to the cars she was used to, in that there was no actual driver's seat situated at the front of the vehicle and only small, leather, black bench like seats which ran along each interior wall, she quickly sat down on a padded bench seat and attempted to make herself comfortable. She quickly tried to familiarize herself with other aspects of the vehicle's interior as she glanced at a small, black, glossy table situated in the centre of the car and touched it softly. A small, black screen jutted out from the top of the small, block like table and there was some kind of control panel positioned directly next to it. A few seconds later, the control panel lit up as it illuminated in front of her and a cursor flashed upon the screen brightly as it demanded her attention.

A male voice suddenly wafted out into the air all around her as it broke the silence inside the vehicle. "Please provide the coordinates or details of your target destination." The male voice requested.

Connie quickly glanced down once more at the email in Skylar's cellphone before she replied. "Gintings Arms Inc. please." She specified politely.

"Your journey is being processed." The male voice returned a few seconds later.

A map suddenly appeared on the small screen situated inside the car in front of Connie which seemed to display the surrounding area as the car engine suddenly started and the vehicle rolled gently forward. Connie stared out of a window beside her face, totally fascinated by the new environment she was surrounded by as the vehicle moved forward. The sky was strange reddish, pink colour that somehow reminded Connie of a sunset, which seemed unusual as it was actually the middle of the morning and nowhere near evening yet. Perhaps there were some kind of weather issues in this world she quietly concluded, perhaps the red, pinkish glow was the sun and sky's natural colour throughout the day.

The car began to pick up speed as it carried her swiftly through the shiny, grey streets and whisked her further away from Skylar's apartment and closer to her required destination. The male voice inside the car that had responded to her presence had actually sounded slightly familiar to Connie as she began to speculate that perhaps it had actually been Visual's voice. Perhaps Visual was an active, permanent supervisor of some sorts who actually coordinated the actual activities that occurred throughout Mindplant vacations Connie quickly speculated. Perhaps Visual was actually watching her participation inside her Mindplant vacation right now. She quickly touched a few of Skylar's ringlets and placed each one a little more tidily around her face and then reached inside the small, black handbag for some shiny lip-gloss in order to apply it immediately. If Visual was actually watching her, Connie was determined, Skylar should look absolutely spectacular.

The vehicle continued to whiz through the city streets as Connie watched the crowds of people outside the car surge around the entrances to some buildings as she passed them. There were no individual retail shops as far as she could see that sold any kind of clothing or any other consumer household goods and there only appeared to be some huge mall like buildings that housed all the wares that humanity usually required on a daily basis. There were also large office blocks, coffee shops, restaurants and a scattering of bars that lined each street, the bars predominantly seemed to be closed, perhaps the bars opened up at night Connie quickly speculated. The people that milled around outside each of the buildings seemed real enough and were dressed in crisp suits, bright dresses and some even wore matching hats and coats.

Questions began to somersault through the passageways of Connie's mind as she watched them, were the people outside real, they couldn't possibly be, if so where did this world she was situated inside actually exist upon earth? If they were indeed simulations, they were pretty good looking simulations she quickly decided as she admired the physical perfection that faced her from every angle. She pushed her intellectual meanderings firmly from her mind as she glanced back down at the email on the cellphone screen and read the instructions inside it once more. There was absolutely no way she was going to try to stop the car simply to approach one of the passers-by and actually ask them if they were indeed real people that would be totally rude and highly inappropriate.

For some strange reason, Connie observed as she continued to journey through the streets, driven towards her destination by an invisible, anonymous driver, there actually seemed to be no children present anywhere at all and that struck her as very unusual. Perhaps simulated people didn't like to get pregnant or give birth she quickly decided, perhaps having children in the simulated world of Mindplant just wasn't actually possible.

A few minutes later, the car finally stopped at the side of a huge, white, shiny building with large windows, situated on the corner of a small, side backstreet and an adjoining main road. Connie quickly glanced down at Skylar's phone once again as she reviewed the details of her mission one final time and then prepared to exit the vehicle. Some of the instructions from the mission brief, Visual had actually provided to her didn't totally make sense just yet, but Connie had accepted as she'd avoided trying to analyse it further, once she was inside the actual building and implementing the instructions she'd been sent, the more obscure details would probably make a lot more sense.

Excitement brimmed inside Connie as it started to consume her and suddenly her nerves began to feel slightly imbalanced as she prepared to leave the car but the car door continued to remain tightly closed. She quickly glanced around the vehicle's interior slightly confused as she contemplated for a minute as to whether she'd actually forgotten anything, there was nothing to forget that she could see, no she'd definitely not forgotten anything.

Visual's voice suddenly sounded out in the quietness that surrounded her as it emanated from inside the vehicle and filled every particle of air inside it. "Target location reached." He remarked quite solemnly.

The sudden breach of silence startled Connie as she jumped in surprise as Visual's interruption had caught her slightly off guard. A few seconds later a drawer opened from inside the small table in the centre of the car that contained a small, metallic, shiny, white briefcase inside it and Connie glanced at it curiously.

"Please take your equipment case." Visual instructed.

Connie complied obediently with Visual's instruction as she leant forward and reached out towards the interior of the drawer with Skylar's hand. She gently plucked the small, white equipment case out of the drawer and as soon as she did so the car door actually swung open. Cold wisps of air immediately hit her face as soon as she stepped out of the vehicle as she attempted to shake of her nerves, which by that point seemed to have infiltrated every ounce of her being. The breeze gently whisked itself around Skylar's body as she walked, it wasn't sharp like a cold winter wind but strangely muggy somehow and almost slightly claustrophobic as it made her shiver slightly and the light, knee length black dress and light jacket she'd chosen earlier that morning, began to feel slightly inadequate.

Once outside on the street she quickly found a spot to hide, situated close to the entrance of the building that she was actually supposed to enter inside and rapidly concealed herself from passers-by. She stood just inside the nearby office block doorway silently for a few minutes as she watched the huge, glass, sparkling doorway she was actually supposed to enter inside and contemplated quietly when she should actually attempt to enter the building.

Connie was totally excited at this point as she celebrated the fact that her dream had finally come true and that now she was indeed living the exciting, exotic, exhilarating lifestyle she'd craved to for so long, albeit for only ten days. The equipment case she'd found inside the car contained another small, black case inside it that was filled with USB devices as she quickly glanced inside it curiously as she waited. The black case was much smaller than a briefcase and the rows of USB's positioned inside it were lined up almost like cigarettes inside a cigarette box. They were white and silver and as the daylight reflected and bounced off each one, they shone brightly. Skylar's black handbag now sat firmly rested upon her arm and the holdall she'd brought along from inside the apartment was slung over her shoulder as she prepared nervously to actually embark on her first mission. She was now completely and wholeheartedly ready to actually be a high tech vigilante and adopt Skylar's vocation.

MINDPLANT: TRIMORPHIA

The entrance in front of the target building cleared of people for a minute and Connie quickly decided it was time to actually make her move and enter inside. Fear surrounding what might happen when she actually entered inside the building had gripped her slightly and she had procrastinated a little as she'd continued to wait, but now she forced herself to move forward as she quickly stepped out from the hiding place she'd been positioned in and made her way towards the entrance. Each of her steps were assertively placed and she was very determined to attack her mission head on, it was indeed now or never and quite frankly it had to be now. Air filled her lungs as she began to breathe more frantically, she was extremely excited but also slightly nervous. She walked towards the entrance of the building decisively as she followed the instructions on the email she'd been provided with precisely and then entered inside.

A reception desk was situated not more than twenty metres away from the entrance of the building which was manned by a female receptionist who smiled at her as soon as she entered the huge, glass doors. The receptionist nodded politely to greet Connie as she drew a little closer and swallowed slightly nervously.

"How can I help you?" The female receptionist asked politely.

Her appearance seemed as close to physical perfection as Connie could imagine, she wore an elegant, white, knee length pencil dress and her well-manicured nails glistened with shiny pale pink and white nail polish that was somewhat reminiscent of a French manicure. The white woollen type dress she wore contrasted immaculately against her jet, black shoulder length hair and for a moment she reminded Connie somewhat off Barbelo. The perfect image she presented was very much like the polished presentation of the women from the Mindplant Centre itself and oozed perfection from every pore.

There was a large expanse situated directly behind the reception desk with security barriers, elevators and a doorway inside it and the doorway seemed to led out to some stairs. Connie knew she had say something to the receptionist in response that would encourage her to grant Connie access to the protected area that lay directly behind her as she stood and faced her silently. She took a deep breath and then crossed the remaining few steps confidently as she approached the reception desk and began to address the receptionist.

"I'm here to see Mr Wainright." Connie explained politely. "I'm Serina Dayton the technician he requested. He should be expecting me I believe." Her tone sounded confident even though Connie had absolutely no idea who Mr Wainright actually was but she followed Visual's instructions precisely as she smiled sweetly at the receptionist in front of her and spoke each word assertively to avoid betraying the actual ignorance that lay inside her.

The receptionist smiled politely as she glanced at a screen in front of her and then quickly turned back to face Skylar as she nodded. "Ah yes you're on his list as an expected visitor today." She quickly verified as she touched the screen once more and the security barriers situated directly behind her immediately opened. "Take the lift to the sixth floor." She instructed as she motioned politely towards some lifts situated nearby as she spoke. "Then once you arrive on the sixth floor, turn immediately to your right, his department is situated right at the end of that corridor."

Connie had absolutely no intention whatsoever of visiting the sixth floor or Mr Wainright but she nodded Skylar's head and smiled politely in response as she thanked her. "Thank you very much." She replied.

Once outside the elevator she touched a small panel beside it to request a lift and it arrived within seconds as the glossy, black, shiny doors swished open as soon as it slid into place. She immediately stepped inside the shiny interior which was adorned with dark coloured mirrors and the doors swished closed directly behind her.

A female voice suddenly sounded out all around her. "Which floor would you like to visit today?" The voice asked politely.

"First floor and sixth floor please." Connie replied decisively as she directed the lift to both floors in an attempt to cover her tracks. She quickly speculated that if the lift actually returned to the ground floor too quickly, the receptionist may notice and then she might become suspicious, which meant Connie had to insist the lift actually visited the sixth floor even if Connie herself and Skylar physically didn't.

The elevator immediately began to whisk Connie upwards towards the first floor as she gasped, surprised by the sheer exhilaration of the ride that lasted less than five seconds. It was extremely fast and for a few seconds it almost felt as if she was actually flying. Once she arrived at the first floor, the doors of the lift rapidly swished open as they sliced through the air with a sharp, quiet zing, almost as if they were cutting the air with a knife. She stepped out of the lift quickly and instead of heading towards the main foyer, she backtracked and headed towards a stairwell situated towards the rear of the building as she'd been instructed to by Visual.

The white marble, shiny floors that had adorned the entrance to the building and most of the hallways inside it, didn't actually extend out into the stairwell area and the flooring there seemed to compose of some other kind of glossy, grey material that Connie didn't recognize at all. She took a few steps forward delicately, worried for a moment that perhaps her shoes would create an echoing noise that might alert someone to her presence and attract undesired attention, but luckily there was no sound at all and she then continued to walk gingerly and tenderly towards the stairs nearby that led upwards.

A few minutes later, when Connie arrived on the second floor which was where her mission was actually due to be performed, she quickly exited the stairwell and entered into a hallway which led directly out to another smaller foyer. The foyer on the second floor was completely deserted as she stepped inside it and scanned her surroundings quickly as she attempted to find the control room that was supposed to be situated there, the control room was the actual location for the next part of her mission. She quickly found the entrance to the control room a few seconds later as she noticed a large, grey door situated towards the right, relatively close by and then briskly strode towards it.

The large, grey, room was silent as she entered inside it and prepared to complete the final part of her mission. True to his word, Visual had by now actually sent her some more precise instructions and even some background information regarding the target company, which meant she now had actually received three emails and not just one. The target company on this occasion was a global weapons company that had been providing guns to terrorists and her mission was to simply sabotage their systems and demobilize their operations. Such a complex task would have been virtually impossible for Connie to realize in her real life as not only did she not possess the knowledge to actually perform such a mission but she also absolutely lacked the nerve to even attempt such a brazen act of heroism.

MINDPLANT: TRIMORPHIA

Connie was a caring, considerate person, but she definitely wasn't a brave hero that challenged huge conglomerates that committed unethical acts. Inside Skylar's body and life however, Connie felt more empowered and capable of such feats and that motivated her and spurred her on as she suddenly felt encouraged that the mission ahead was actually possible and achievable.

The door of the control room swished closed behind her as Connie quickly scrutinized and inspected the room as she searched for the large server she was supposed to find as per Visual's instructions. It wasn't hard to find and a few seconds later she quickly strode towards a huge grey, shiny, oblong like object which jutted and stuck out of the floor almost as if it had been implanted and embedded there during some kind of alien invasion. She smiled as she quickly pulled a USB out of the small, white equipment case in her hands and slipped the device straight into the server port which it fitted into like a glove. Connie started to relax for a moment as relief washed over her, everything was going according to plan and she was pleased that so far her mission had been somewhat successful.

A few seconds later however, her peace was abruptly shattered as a harsh noise suddenly began to ring out all around her and she jumped with surprise. Alarms began to sound out loudly all throughout the building and Connie panicked as she froze. Skylar's cellphone beeped and she quickly glanced down at the screen as a message appeared in front of her eyes 'LEAVE THE BUILDING IMMEDIATELY. VISUAL' the message read.

Connie reached down towards the ground with Skylar's arm and quickly grabbed the small equipment case that she'd placed upon the floor, next to huge server and then rapidly rushed out of the room as she broke out into a light run. Once she arrived at the top of the staircase a few seconds later she was almost breathless as she prepared to leave the building and make her escape but above her head she suddenly heard a flurry of footsteps. She quickly glanced upwards and noticed hands on the staircase rails just a few floors above her and panic set in once more as she quickly realized the bodies those hands actually belonged to were descending rapidly towards her.

She slipped, stumbled and then quickly picked herself back up as she tackled the stairs and rushed back down towards the ground floor. From the email Visual had sent her, she knew there was an emergency exit situated at the base of the building and she quickly headed towards it. Her run was more of a stutter than a sprint as she clumsily clambered down the stairs and stopped every now and again as Skylar's feet seemed to get caught up in each other. For some reason they seemed to almost trip over themselves as they failed to cooperate quickly enough and respond to the instructions from Connie's mind as she struggled to make a rapid, seamless escape and the lack of body coordination frustrated her efforts slightly.

A few minutes later however, once she managed to arrive at the foot of the stairs, she immediately found a small hallway in front of her just as Visual had described in his email, which she knew led towards the rear of the building and towards the fire exit that would take her back out onto the street outside. She rushed down the hallway towards the fire exit door as the footsteps above her head seemed to multiply and began to echo like a herd of buffaloes stampeding. Connie's first mission was almost over.

The fire exit door, luckily for Connie opened easily as soon as she pushed it and she quickly stepped out of it and rushed back out onto the street and then immediately began to search for

Skylar's car. She quickly glanced up and down the street outside as she searched for it frantically and then spotted the vehicle just a few seconds later relatively close by. Luckily, Skylar's car was actually situated just a few metres away from her current position and she quickly made her way towards it as soon as she noticed it. Skylar's small, black handbag remained tucked firmly underneath one of her arms and the holdall still rested on her shoulder as she ran towards the car and prepared to open the door.

Once she arrived outside the vehicle she quickly began to search inside the holdall for the star shaped key like object once again, but thankfully the car door on this occasion seemed to open automatically itself when she approached it. The car door swished open in front of her and she immediately clambered inside, grateful that she didn't actually have to waste precious minutes searching for the key again as she sighed with relief. The car door shut firmly behind her a few seconds later and she quickly sat down on one of the bench like seats as the vehicle began to move away from the building. She quickly glanced back out of the car rear window as the vehicle departed to observe whether or not those who had pursued her had actually followed her out onto the street and was shocked and horrified when a few seconds later a man suddenly appeared in the middle of the road. He was equipped with a headset and in one of his hands he clearly brandished a laser gun which he angrily shook in the air as soon as he found the street outside empty.

The sight of the man and the laser gun alarmed Connie slightly as she realized how close to capture she had actually been. Fear gripped her inside and she felt slightly shaken as she winced, luckily however the distance between the two grew rapidly as the car carried her further and further away from him and back towards the safety of Skylar's apartment once more as the growing distance between them relieved her distress. The man gradually grew smaller and smaller as she leant back against the window of the car and rested as she attempted to catch her breath, it had been a very close shave indeed and she had been totally caught off guard.

Next time, Connie quietly deliberated, she would have to be a lot more careful as she had absolutely no idea what would have happened if the man pursuing her had actually caught her or even shot her with his laser gun. Perhaps that would have been the end of her vacation or she perhaps she would have suffered an injury and then had to spend the remainder of her vacation in a hospital somewhere suffering from and nursing the wounds that the laser gun had inflicted upon Skylar's body. Worries continued to gush through her mind like a bubbling, babbling stream that rushed towards a lake as she continued to pant and catch her breath, it had been a very close call indeed.

A few seconds later, the vehicle turned into another street entirely and the man completely disappeared from sight as Connie began to relax, the threat to Skylar and Connie for today was now over and she had actually fulfilled her very first mission. Some part of her felt exceptionally proud as the cellphone inside Skylar's handbag started to ring and she quickly dug through the contents of the bag to find it. She found the phone within a few seconds and then answered the call enthusiastically which she knew almost immediately had to be from Visual. The phone call quickly calmed and appeased her mind as it reminded her that somewhere within this volatile, dangerous, exciting environment she actually had some form of contact with someone that wasn't actually a threat to her, unlike the man who had just chased her out of a building with a weapon in his hand.

Visual's voice immediately greeted her. "Did you complete the mission?" He asked.

"Yes Visual their systems are totally demobilized and I've done millions of dollars' worth of damage." Connie replied proudly. "My first mission is complete.

There was a slight pause for a few seconds as quietness filled the air inside the vehicle and for a moment Connie began to actually wonder if Visual had ended the call without letting her know. He did appear to be slightly abrupt and distant whenever they communicated, therefore it was entirely possible.

Visual broke the silence a few seconds later as he verified that he was indeed still actually there. "Great that means you're ready for your next mission." He insisted. "I'll send you the details first thing tomorrow morning."

A few seconds later, the phone line went completely dead as Visual ended the call, apparently their conversation for that day was now totally over. Connie accepted his abrupt attitude without any further objections as she smiled, now she actually knew for certain Visual's voice could not possibly be a recording and that his conversations with her were actually being conducted in real time. His responses were too personal and timely to be pre-recorded, but not personal enough to verify that the two had actually struck up some kind of rapport or emotional connection as Visual's attitude towards Connie still remained completely formal and the continuity of the distant attitude he exhibited towards her, slightly surprised her. Usually, when people spoke to each other more than once, they would start to relax and perhaps even exchange some pleasantries, but Visual's tone and words had remained consistent and consistently distant. He absolutely never greeted her, he didn't bid her farewell and the start, middle and end of each call was just as abrupt as the very first conversation they'd actually had.

Connie teased herself for a moment as she contemplated that the discussions between them weren't actually conversations at all, Visual spoke, Connie listened. There was no emotion, social interaction or intimacy expressed through the words he offered to her, Visual was always completely formal and very precise. Her hopes of getting to know him more intimately or perhaps meeting him in person, seemed very remote as she contemplated whether or not she should actually try to flirt with him and see if she could push their interactions in a more romantically inclined direction. She could flirt with him and see how he responded, perhaps then he might warm up to her a little and start to open up more, then perhaps she could find out a little more about him, it was worth a try.

Visual himself, seemed completely oblivious to the curiosity and the growing interest he'd aroused inside Connie, which teased her senses each time she heard his voice and urged her to venture further down the road of romantic possibilities as her sentiments towards him gently lapped inside her heart and lifted her spirits each time he called. His attitude towards her was simply non-negotiable as he simply instructed her and then abandoned her as he left her hungry for more. Perhaps Visual was really a bald, seventy year old man that spent his entire day seated at a desk in front of a computer screen somewhere in the Mindplant Centre as he orchestrated the various vacation missions, perhaps he even had a wife and five kids, Connie mused. Connie laughed at her own imagination as she gently shook her head. Perhaps when she actually returned to the real world and her own real body, she would actually find out.

Twenty minutes later the car arrived back outside Skylar's apartment once more and stopped as Connie prepared to exit the vehicle. For some reason she now felt slightly worn out and had absolutely no desire to go anywhere else at all, except back inside Skylar's apartment. She exited the vehicle as soon as the car door swished open and steered Skylar's body gently back towards the apartment building's front door wearily as she searched in Skylar's small, black handbag for the key card to actually open it. Even though it was only just late afternoon, Connie knew that evening she would definitely not be venturing outside to explore any of the other forms of entertainment available to Mindplant vacationers as she was quite simply just too exhausted. For one night such luxuries would be something she would have to live without. Her first mission had been very energetic and extremely tiring and she now felt the full physical impact of it upon her as she simply wasn't used to rushing around buildings so energetically. Perhaps tomorrow she decided she would have slightly more energy and then she could explore the evening leisure activities on offer, once her second mission was complete.

MINDPLANT: TRIMORPHIA

She walked up the two flights of stairs and arrived back outside the front door of Skylar's apartment and then quickly opened it with the key card. The front door swished open and then closed immediately behind her as soon as she stepped inside and she walked quickly down the hallway towards the lounge. Once she arrived inside the lounge she started to relax and quickly flopped straight down onto the nearby sofa as she thought about what the next day might actually bring. Her first mission had been extremely exciting and the next day Visual had already mentioned, he would actually send her on another mission and perhaps that mission would be even more challenging, exciting and more difficult than the first she contemplated quietly. Whatever Visual had in store for her the next day intrigued her as she spread herself out lazily upon the sofa and smiled. Excitement seemed to surge through Skylar's body as it tingled and rippled almost like an electric current as Connie embraced her vacation, Skylar's body and life, now Connie was actually exciting, now Connie had actually become a high tech vigilante that could conduct missions and sabotage huge corporations and now Connie was actually living a real life.

QUORN'S MINDPLANT

The next few days flew by and four days later when Quorn actually arrived back at the Mindplant Centre for his vacation implant consultation, he was immediately shown into the waiting room again by a polite receptionist. He quickly sat down in the bland waiting room as his body brimmed with excitement and eagerness filled his core as he began to anticipate what might lie ahead when he actually ventured upon his pending vacation. The usual gadgets he carried everywhere he went accompanied him and he began to fumble around with them as he waited patiently to be seen. His phone and personal microcomputer contained several activities that Quorn would playfully engage in throughout the more boring moments of his life and he realized it would be strange for once not to actually have them beside him whilst he was on his vacation inside someone else's body as he glanced down at them and smiled. He would definitely miss them.

The table at the other end of the room, seemed to be packed full of refreshments and snacks as Quorn glanced at it quickly. He stood up and then quickly made his way over towards the table as he craved some kind of nourishment, he wasn't hungry or even thirsty but a snack wouldn't hurt and would perhaps occupy his time as he waited he speculated. Perhaps he might even see Connie again whilst he was on his vacation and that would be an amazingly wonderful experience he thought as he picked up a small packet of plain, crumbly, shortcake biscuits and then selected a cup of coffee from the nearby battered, coffee machine. Thoughts of Connie lingered inside the passageways of his mind as Quorn suddenly realized, he actually had no idea how internal interactions worked inside the Mindplant program at all. Perhaps he wouldn't even recognize Connie, even if he did actually bump into her as her mind would now be firmly situated inside someone else's body and it was completely uncertain that he would actually even know who she actually was.

Quorn wasn't easily swayed and attracted to many woman as he had a particular kind of taste, but Connie's stunning, sparkling, aqua green eyes and soft cherry lips that opened out into a wide, inviting smile had instantly caught his attention. Her dark, soft, bouncing ringlets that adorned her face seemed to compliment her petit but curvaceous figure. He'd been intrigued and now he definitely wanted to explore the interior further as the exterior had been so enticing and captivating. She'd seemed humble, polite and sweet and that had drawn him to her further as he'd begun to form an emotional connection to her and to actually wait until the end of his vacation when Connie may or may not call him would be agonizing and possibly render no results at all. Their introduction had been so fleeting and had lacked any clarity regarding a real follow up Quorn thought as he sipped on the bitter, black coffee and sat back down as he waited for the Mindplant vacation coordinator to actually arrive, Connie might not even call him at all.

His mind continued to meander playfully as he entertained the various romantic possibilities that could lie ahead with regards to a possible romance with Connie as the notion of a love affair loomed on the horizon of his thoughts and five minutes later when Mena actually arrived and entered inside the waiting room, Quorn didn't actually notice her presence until she coughed gently and interrupted his mental meanderings. Quorn quickly stood up as he paid attention to the female coordinator's arrival inside the room and glanced her somewhat apologetically.

"Quorn Penton?" Mena asked as she extended a hand towards him and smiled. "I'm Mena. I'm your Mindplant Vacation Coordinator."

Quorn nodded and quickly reciprocated her handshake politely. "Lovely to meet you." He replied as he greeted her.

"Come with me." Mena instructed enthusiastically as she walked back towards the waiting room door.

Quorn followed her a few steps behind. "Can I ask you a question Mena?"

"Sure go right ahead." Mena replied as she glanced at his face and smiled at him.

"Do you think I'll ever see Connie again?" Quorn asked curiously as Mena led him down the hallway towards her consultation room. "I mean when we're on our Mindplant vacations."

"You might." Mena replied as they walked. "You never know."

"If her mind's inside someone else's body how will I recognize her?" He asked in a slightly confused tone as he glanced at Mena's face with a puzzled expression. "It's just well I'd really like to see her again soon."

"It's hard to say if you'll cross paths again. Not many of our clients actually meet before they enter inside someone else's body for a vacation so your situation is very unusual. You might not meet each other whilst you're on your vacation at all, it all really depends on the profiles you've both selected and the scheduled activities assigned to that profile. You could be situated in very different locations and be doing entirely different things." Mena replied with an optimistic tone as she attempted to answer his question as fully as she could and reassure him, even though deep inside she was unsure that his desire to see Connie was actually even possible. "Did you manage to have a look at the profiles we sent you?" She asked politely as she attempted to steer the conversation in another direction entirely.

The truth was Mena had never actually given much thought to the possibility of clients meeting within the Mindplant vacation program itself as it was a rare eventuality that clients actually even met each other before they embarked upon their respective vacations as the coordinators usually only saw one client a day and due to time variances in appointments, it just never usually happened. Quorn and Connie's situation was not only unusual but the question Quorn had actually posed to Mena was even more unusual. Mena didn't wish to discourage Quorn or dampen his spirits as he obviously had a keen interest in Connie, but she was anxious not to encourage him too much either, when there might not actually be a mutual interest on Connie's part. False hope that would never one day be realized, broke hearts and that was something she had no desire to ignite or fuel in any capacity, she wasn't a mind reader and hence she steered carefully away from being overly enthusiastic. The heart was such a delicate, fragile component of a human being's structure and could be so easily damaged, ripped to shreds and completely destroyed and it served absolutely no purpose at all, to tease or play with someone's emotions in any capacity.

Quorn sensed her reluctance to continue the conversation in the direction he'd sent it in as he noticed she'd changed the topic and responded appropriately. He had absolutely no desire to appear weird or overly obsessive about a woman he'd only just met. "Yes I've had a look at them all and I've actually chosen one I like." He replied diplomatically. "I was just asking about Connie as I gave her my number and you know women, sometimes they'll say they'll call and then they never do. Do you think she'll actually call me?" Quorn enquired as he anxiously sought out a woman's opinion as to the prospects of a potential romance between Connie and himself.

Mena smiled. "It's impossible for me to say." She replied as she doubted her capabilities as a love advisor internally, whilst Mena could advise Quorn about his Mindplant vacation, the area of romance was totally off the cards and not something she could assist him with further. "Woman are unpredictable sometimes, at times they say they'll call just to be polite as they don't want to hurt your feelings and at other times they actually call." She replied as she smiled gently and shrugged her shoulders. "It's almost like tossing a coin in the air, you never know which side it will actually land on but at least you know you tried and threw it up in the air anyway."

The two arrived outside Mena's consultation room and she quickly invited Quorn inside enthusiastically, whilst she couldn't possibly assist him in the area of love, she could definitely assist him with his Mindplant vacation which was why he was actually there in the first place and she was eager to make a start. Quorn followed her inside the room quietly and then sat down in the seat she offered him as he glanced around the room and absorbed his surroundings.

Mena smiled as she sat down in front of her screen and then faced him. "Are ready for your Mindplant vacation?" She asked.

"I'm definitely ready." Quorn replied enthusiastically as he quickly decided that perhaps he was actually boring Mena with all the sordid details regarding his attraction to Connie and that he should try to avoid mentioning her name again. "I can't wait. I'm very excited about the profile I've chosen." He continued as he smiled.

The male profile Quorn wanted to vacation inside for the duration of his holiday had already been selected at his prior appointment, which meant that Mena would now simply be implanting his mind inside the respective body that afternoon and that disappointed her slightly. Sifting through the various profiles and helping clients make a decision about the body they wanted to occupy whilst on their Mindplant vacation was one of the responsibilities of her job, she actually enjoyed immensely. The profile of the man Quorn had chosen for his vacation had been attached to his profile as she loaded his details onto the screen in front of her and perused them. Montgomery was a slightly younger man than Quorn and also much larger framed and his main area of expertise was assassination. Quorn wanted to be a deadly assassin whilst on his vacation and Montgomery's profile had matched his requirements precisely.

"Where will my body be whilst I'm on vacation?" Quorn suddenly asked curiously, anxious to discover what would actually happen to his own physical body whilst he was actually venturing inside someone else's.

Mena smiled. "If you like I can actually show you." She offered.

Quorn nodded enthusiastically.

The two stood up and left the room as they made their way towards the Body Preservation Dormitory and Mena conversed with Quorn politely as they walked. They discussed light topics like the weather and the surrounding countryside as she attempted to avoid further deliberations surrounding Connie and her possible physical attractions to Quorn and romantic questions that Mena simply couldn't answer. When they arrived outside the Body Preservation Dormitory, Mena quickly led Quorn inside the large room as she attempted to show him where his body would be contained and maintained whilst he indulged in and participated in his vacation.

Quorn walked around the room curiously as he inspected and scrutinized the pods inside the room a little more closely. Glimmers of curiosity flickered across his eyes and danced across his black pupils like flames of fire as they teased his mind and questions leapt into his mouth. He had a few burning questions and he was absolutely desperate to present them to Mena. His questions weren't all totally polite, but they were all extremely necessary. Quorn turned to face Mena who was now situated just a few steps away from him as he stood next to a capsule and grinned slightly nervously.

He took a deep breath as he plucked up the courage that lay inside his gut and attempted to appease his inner curiosity. "How do we actually pee?'" He asked. His question felt crude and uncouth and he quickly reminded himself that Mena was actually a woman and attempted to rephrase it immediately. "Sorry urinate."

Mena immediately smiled in response, although Quorn's question was slightly unusual, she was actually well equipped to handle such queries and his enquiry didn't actually bother her in the slightest. "That's a very good question

Quorn." Mena replied as she prepared to give him a technically sound response.

"And what if we actually need to do the other thing?" Quorn continued as he interrupted her and presented her with his second question, which worried him even more than the first. His mind simply wouldn't allow him to drop the topic as curiosity pricked his thoughts further and he laughed slightly nervously as he made a mild attempt to disguise his embarrassment. Whilst the topic he'd presented to Mena was quite private and delicate in nature, his curiosity thirsted inside him and simply couldn't be quenched without an adequate response, a response which he knew only Mena could actually provide. Quorn needed answers.

Mena smiled as she attempted to respond. "Well since you're not actually eating any physical food in your daily, dietary intake but merely consuming a liquid diet, this becomes less of an issue after the first twenty four hours. The sedatives we give you on the first day of your vacation actually empty your bowels in preparation and each of the personal chambers also has a built in toiletry system that connects directly to your body that allows for any excrement or urine to be disposed of through a tube." Mena explained as she appreciated his frankness, his questions were natural and unlike many other clients she'd seen over the years, he hadn't shied away from the more difficult, trickier topics that some people often feared actually raising.

"Great." Quorn replied completely satisfied by Mena's response. He'd had some horrible visions surrounding what might actually happen if there were no toiletry provisions whilst his body was situated inside a pod and those fears had nagged and gnawed away inside his mind ever since his first appointment and somehow they'd disrupted his usual comfortable, confident stance.

A personal chamber nearby suddenly caught Quorn's attention as he quickly realized Connie's body was actually situated inside it. He smiled and drew closer to it as he inspected her face closely for a moment, she seemed to be fast asleep and there was a slight smile upon her face which glowed. Overall Connie looked relatively tranquil and peaceful and Quorn was immediately reassured as he digested her content expression, her Mindplant vacation was well underway and everything was fine, which ultimately meant in his mind things would be fine for him too whilst he was actually on his trip.

Quorn clapped his hands and then rubbed them together as he turned back to face Mena with a large grin on his face. "Right let's get started?" He urged, suddenly spurred on by the sight of Connie and anxious to participate in his vacation as soon as he possibly could.

Mena smiled. "Great come with me and we'll sort out your actual vacation straight away." She verified as she sensed Quorn's heightening excitement.

The two walked back out of the Body Preservation Dormitory and into the hallway once more as Mena led Quorn quickly back towards her consultation room, slightly relieved that he hadn't posed any more questions about Connie or about male bodily functions. Quorn was slightly more direct than most of the clientele Mena usually handled and although she could handle most of his requests, it did feel slightly awkward at times to discuss intricate, intimate bodily functions with a man.

She sped up her pace as she quietly contemplated that later that evening, she would attend her fiancée, Gideon's birthday dinner. Their favourite restaurant had been booked which was situated over an hour's drive away from their home and that meant she absolutely had to leave work and complete her tasks on time that day, in order to fully enjoy the activities they'd planned for later that evening.

Quorn sensed the sudden increase in pace and sped up also as he walked quietly alongside her. His mind was still very much preoccupied with thoughts of Connie and the possibility of perhaps actually seeing her again whilst on his vacation. Each thought teased him as they lingered inside him provocatively, stirred and shaken but not yet fully erupted or realized as they yearned and waited to spill out into reality.

Once the two arrived back inside Mena's consultation room, she quickly instructed Quorn to change as she drew a screen around him and handed him a white, clinical looking robe. She sat down in front of her screen once more and then rapidly started to process his Mindplant transfer as she waited for him to change patiently. A few seconds later Quorn's face appeared at one side of the screen as he attempted to let her know that he had actually finished changing and Mena smiled, nodded and immediately stood up. She rushed over towards the screen and then pulled it back as she prompted him to lie down on the dark, black, leather couch situated directly behind him.

"If you can just jump up on here for me, lie down and close your eyes." Mena instructed as she gently patted the therapist like couch. "That would be great and you'll be on your vacation in no time."

Quorn obediently cooperated.

Mena quickly pulled out the nearby machine and face mask from underneath the couch and then placed the mask over Quorn's mouth and nostrils as she smiled at him. She walked back over towards her desk and sat down in front of the screen again and then quickly touched it as she initiated Quorn's Mindplant vacation mind transplant. Once she'd sent Quorn on his ideal vacation, her major task for that day would then be completed and due to her plans for the evening, she felt quite relieved that on that particular day, Quorn's consultation had actually been much quicker than most.

Quorn closed his eyes as his mind and body lapsed into the realms of a deep slumber peacefully and his mind began to vacate the Mindplant consultation room as it departed from its usual vessel of residence. Thoughts of Connie pleasantly adorned his mind as he prepared hopefully to perhaps see her once again whilst actually on his Mindplant vacation.

MINDPLANT: TRIMORPHIA

A few hours later, when Quorn actually stirred from sleep, he awoke in unfamiliar surroundings as he glanced around the room he found himself inside curiously. The dark blinds that lined the windows nearby attempted to keep out any light particles that tried to enter inside them and even though it seemed to be the early hours of the morning, the room was in fact, pitch dark. The glimmers of light from the outside world were to weak and no match for the dark, solid blinds as they struggled to breach any cracks or gaps and provide an inkling of light to the interior of the bedroom and Quorn had absolutely no idea where he actually was.

A few minutes later, his eyes gradually grew accustomed to the blanket of darkness that surrounded him and he began to look around the room he was situated inside as he inspected it a little more closely. It was a simple room with black furniture, predominantly white walls and there was one light blue feature wall that faced him which broke the monotony of the white, stark blandness that surrounded him. The blue tone was more of an eggshell blue than a bright, azure blue and it glistened softly as some small particles of light from the hallway outside, seeped in, found it and clung desperately to it. The bed he lay upon was simple but elegant and composed of a black, iron frame which was adorned with white, shiny bedding.

The duvet felt warm as Quorn nestled deeper inside it and lingered for a moment, not wishing to depart from its comfort a moment sooner than was absolutely necessary. Opposing thoughts pulled away inside his mind as his internal desires conflicted, he wanted to explore this new world he'd actually woken up in, yet the warmth and comfort of his current position also widely appealed to him. The two desires clung to the hallways of his mind as they wrestled with each other and battled away inside him, until his body finally succumbed to the urge to remain in bed. He pulled the duvet further up around his neck as he proclaimed it the victor and curled up inside it, he'd get up soon, another few minutes wouldn't hurt anyone.

Curiosity continued to tease his thoughts however and a few seconds later, he quickly poked a leg out from underneath the duvet and began to inspect it more closely, it definitely wasn't his own leg and Quorn was completely surprised. He'd expected the Mindplant program to work in theory but to actually see it manifest in reality, shocked him nonetheless. The gravity of his position struck him almost like a brick falling upon as his head as he absorbed the reality that yes he now was indeed actually living inside someone else's body. The Mindplant vacations were real and so were their promises. He was really actually vacationing inside someone else's life. Quorn's mind was completely stunned, whilst he'd paid for the vacation and he'd entertained the idea, deep down inside himself he hadn't actually thought it would really be possible. Mindplant had actually pulled it off and had actually delivered what he'd paid for, this scientific organization was actually very real and their holidays actually really did happen. They could actually deliver on the promises they made and that in itself was extremely refreshing.

His discovery prompted Quorn to get up out of bed more quickly as he threw off the duvet, stood up immediately and prepared to embrace the vacation he'd actually paid for. He urgently needed to see more of this new body he was actually situated inside and when he spotted a mirror inside the small bathroom that joined onto the bedroom as he glanced through the door which was wide open, he quickly strode towards it enthusiastically. Quorn rushed inside the small bathroom anxious to see what the body he'd chosen actually looked like, now that he was actually situated inside it as he grinned excitedly.

A few seconds later as he glanced into the mirror in front of him, he immediately found the man's face that he'd seen on the Mindplant system appear within it as Montgomery's face stared back at him. He blinked and rubbed his eyes to double check it was real and then quickly stared back into the mirror once again as the man's face continued to stare back at him and mimic every movement he made. Quorn almost felt as if he'd bought a new suit and was actually trying it on for the very first time, it was like his mind had been clothed with another physical exterior by the world's most creative tailor and he was totally captivated by the experience.

"Wow this really works." Quorn muttered to himself as he admired his new temporary face and touched it gently.

He ran the tap in the sink below the mirror and a lukewarm flow of water immediately began to gush out, the water was crystal clear as he quickly scooped some drops up into his hands and splashed them over Montgomery's face enthusiastically. Once he'd refreshed himself, he'd probably feel slightly better about being awake and leaving the warmth of the duvet behind he quickly decided, a shower was definitely a good idea and Quorn needed a little time to actually adjust to his new surroundings, new body, new face and new reality.

The mirror image of Montgomery's face, the man's whose body he'd actually chosen to vacation inside, Quorn felt was definitely better looking than his own. Montgomery, unlike Quorn actually verged upon what Quorn would classify as handsome. His good looks might come in handy Quorn quickly determined and could perhaps actually provide him with some extra fun whilst he was on vacation, after all he knew he wasn't actually in a relationship with anyone in real life and that meant he could definitely have some fun with the opposite sex whilst he was there, without feeling any subsequent pangs of guilt.

Although meeting a woman and dabbling in romance hadn't been the primary objective of Quorn's vacation, it wasn't something he ruled out, though he did think it would perhaps be a little strange. Any woman he might meet, might look good and appeal to him whilst inside their Mindplant vacation body but in real life he might not actually be attracted to their real body and face at all and vice versa. The prospect fascinated him slightly but was also a little frightening at the same time, if he could actually find Connie on the other hand, that would be a romance that was a bit more certain and less risky as he knew he definitely liked her face in real life and her real body. A random beauty he might encounter that he didn't actually know, presented more difficult and complex issues and would perhaps only be good for a few days fun, but probably not for a longer lasting romantic commitment.

A thought teased Quorn's mind for a moment as he contemplated whether or not Montgomery was actually physically, well-endowed as when he'd selected his profile, there had been no way of actually knowing. He opened the pyjama bottoms he'd found himself dressed in and quickly glanced down at Montgomery's genitals. They seemed to be slightly larger than his own and hung down limply as he smiled, at least that was something he didn't need to worry about and there was nothing to be ashamed of down there. It would have been so awful if his penis had actually been much smaller or very tiny then he perhaps would have been too embarrassed to consider any kind of sexual intimacy with anyone at all.

Quorn quickly showered and then headed back towards the bedroom to dress as he prepared for his day. He had absolutely no idea what activities he was actually going to participate within that day, but he wanted to be ready for his first mission as soon as possible. How his first mission would actually start he wasn't entirely sure, but he couldn't wait for it to commence as anticipation built up eagerly inside him. Quorn didn't have to wait very long.

Once dressed Quorn quickly entered inside the kitchen and opened the fridge as he prepared to make breakfast, slightly surprised by how hungry he suddenly seemed to feel. He quickly reminded himself that this wasn't really his own body and that in real life he was probably not actually really hungry at all as he turned on the ceramic ring on top of the cooker and plucked a large frying pan from a silver shelf that sat just above it. A bottle of oil sat next to the cooker and he quickly drizzled some oil across the large, frying pan and then waited for it to heat up. Once the oil inside the pan started to sizzle he quickly threw some sausages, bacon, eggs inside it and some pancake mix that he'd prepared. The food sizzled away quietly as the aroma filled Quorn's nostrils and he smiled, it definitely smelt real enough.

A small, dining table adorned the kitchen and as soon as the food was ready and plated up, Quorn quickly sat down beside it and started to munch on the slices of bacon, sausages, pancakes and fried eggs he'd prepared. The food tasted deliciously real as Quorn savoured each mouthful and chewed on it and he had to confess the meal probably tasted even better than his own efforts would have tasted in real life at home. He swallowed each morsel of food gratefully as it massaged his taste buds as soon as each forkful actually entered inside his mouth. Every mouthful was enjoyable and he relished the flavour of the freshly cooked bacon as the fats and juices dripped down from his fork onto the plate underneath it as he ate.

The realness of Quorn's current environment prompted him to question the technicalities of the Mindplant vacation further for a moment as he quietly considered whether his vacation was actually a real bodily exchange and whether or not he was actually present inside someone's else's body or whether this was simply some kind of sleep induced simulation program? Had the Mindplant staff administered some kind of drugs into his body that created this simulation? Or had they somehow actually managed to implant the conscious mind of one person into another person's physical being? Did this body or world actually even really exist at all? The questions scurried through Quorn's mind like a torrent as they jumped and leapt over themselves and chased each other around frustratingly unanswered. Quorn quickly shook his head a few seconds later and swept the questions out of his mind as if they were dusty, dusky cobwebs.

Why should he even care about the technical realities of his Mindplant vacation he quickly decided, he wasn't responsible for the Mindplant research or the vacation itself or even there to analyse it. He was simply a customer who had paid for a vacation that he was there to enjoy, a luxury, a treat and a period of relaxation. He'd paid good money for this vacation, a lot of money and he was completely determined to enjoy it in its entirety and simply accept it for what it was. He didn't have to understand it and if the chance actually arose to see Connie again whilst he was there, that would definitely be worth the additional expenditure because Connie was definitely worth it.

The kitchen Quorn was seated inside was relatively simple with black cupboards and appliances and silver fixtures and it opened out into a large lounge which joined onto it. Both rooms were decorated in white and black, and the open plan layout provided ease of access from one room to the other. Montgomery certainly wasn't adventurous when it came to his interior decor and had stuck to a very simple colour scheme indeed Quorn quickly observed. Living on the edge wasn't something that could be seen clearly expressed inside his home he mused.

A cellphone situated somewhere nearby started to ring as Quorn ate and he paused for a moment as he glanced quickly around the two rooms curiously and searched for the source of the noise. A few seconds later, he managed to spot the cellphone situated on top of a small, round, coffee table in the centre of the lounge and he stood up quickly and rushed over towards it. He picked it up curiously and prepared to answer the call as he amused himself as to who the caller could possibly be, no one even knew about his vacation or that he was even there so it definitely could not be one of his friends or even a member of his family, that implied the phone call definitely wasn't from anyone he knew or even for him. Quorn smiled as he teased and corrected himself playfully, the phone call definitely wasn't actually for him as this wasn't his body, his cellphone or even his apartment, it was Montgomery's.

The decision to keep his Mindplant vacation a secret was one he'd made thoughtfully when he'd actually booked his trip. He'd decided his friends and family would think the whole thing was weird and would perhaps even be a little scared, they might even have perhaps urged him not to participate in it at all and hence he'd decided not to let anyone know about his plans in the run up to his actual Mindplant vacation. He'd come on this adventure very much on his own and alone as he'd wanted to experience it and try it and he was completely prepared to enjoy every single thing about it, without facing any objections or opposition from those he either knew or loved.

Quorn glanced at the cellphone screen and noticed that the word 'VISUAL' appeared across it as the phone identified the name of the actual caller. He definitely didn't know anyone called Visual, but he touched the cellphone to accept the call as curiosity urged him to respond, perhaps Montgomery knew Visual.

A man's voice greeted him immediately. "Are you ready for your first mission?" The male voice asked.

There was a pause for a moment as Quorn deliberated how strange the question seemed, there hadn't been any other exchange of words, no introduction, no greeting, just a question. He hesitated for a moment, slightly unsure about how he should actually respond. Was Visual actually someone he should speak to, listen to and trust, the question pricked his mind for a moment as a flurry of indecisiveness scampered through his thoughts. There was no real choice Quorn finally decided, who else was he supposed to speak to about his assassin missions? Absolutely no one else had called him that morning or approached the foreign apartment he'd actually woken up inside. Walking out into the streets and stopping random strangers in search of his first mission would be silly and strange and there quite simply was no one else to turn to except this strange male voice that had to be trusted, listened to and engaged further.

"Yes I'm ready." Quorn replied as he succumbed to Visual's request for participation and cooperation.

"Great I'm sending you an email with instructions regarding your first mission." Visual clarified.

"Ok." Quorn replied.

There was a short silence before Quorn actually realized that the call was over, Visual certainly wasn't a man of many words and his conversation had been direct, precise and abrupt. He quickly placed the cellphone down on top of the kitchen dining table as he sat back down and returned to eating the breakfast he'd prepared as he waited for Visual's email to arrive. The cellphone sat idly on the kitchen table beside him as he ate and glanced down at it every few seconds, eager to receive and read the email from Visual as soon as it actually arrived so that he could embark on his first mission as soon as possible. Quorn was hungry not only for food but also for excitement. Hungry for his first mission to start. Hungry to hunt down those he was to kill.

The phone beeped a few minutes later as the email from Visual arrived as promised and Quorn smiled as the phone alerted him to its presence. The last slice of bacon remained alone on the plate as he quickly stood up and picked up the cellphone to read its contents. He glanced back down at the solitary morsel of food and then quickly grabbed the remaining slice of bacon before he rushed towards the apartment front door as he prepared to embark on his first assassination experience, now it was Quorn's chance to actually fulfil his fantasies and now it was his chance to live a life he'd never actually dared to live in reality.

The email he'd been sent detailed his first target, a male involved in corporate espionage who had leaked information to a competitor, a man with a boss that now wanted him dead. He'd placed a decent sized price tag on his head and Montgomery had been hired to actually eliminate and assassinate him. Quorn quickly left the apartment building and entered inside a vehicle parked just outside the front door as per the instructions he'd been sent, Montgomery's body was larger framed than his own and that change in dimensions amused him as he crouched down to actually enter inside the car door.

Once he was seated inside the car, the door quickly swished closed behind him and a drawer in the table situated in the centre of the car immediately opened. Inside the drawer he found a laser gun and various other weapons that he'd been instructed to take long with him in order to carry out his mission effectively and he smiled. The car sped off a few seconds later as it whisked him away to the location he'd specified as per the instructions on the email Visual had sent to him and Quorn felt excited as he prepared for the mission that lay ahead.

Quorn revelled in the activities that commenced that day as he followed Jed the man he'd been instructed to kill, at a safe distance inside Montgomery's body as his target ventured outside his home and visited a nearby park for a walk. Later that morning, Jed visited some nearby offices situated just a few streets away from where he lived and Quorn continued to follow him at a safe distance as he hid behind trees, buildings and other structures and followed his target as he waited for the perfect opportunity to attack. Montgomery's body was much stronger than Quorn's and throughout the day he tested his strength playfully as he tried out his muscular frame and picked up some large boulders from the ground and carried them around. Montgomery was definitely strong.

Later that day as the dark shadows of the evening started to envelope the streets that surrounded him and night was ushered gently in, Quorn's moment finally arrived and he embraced it enthusiastically. He'd prepared for the pending execution of his target as he'd hidden behind a tree near the apartment block he'd seen the man actually exit from earlier that morning, equipped with the laser gun which he'd concealed inside the grey, casual, loose jacket he wore. The laser gun was high tech and modern and quite unlike any weapon Quorn had ever seen before and it intrigued him as he longed to fire it for the very first time. When Jed entered inside the back alleyway that led towards the entrance of his apartment block on his way home that evening, Quorn finally seized his chance as he aimed for Jed's chest and fired the laser gun straight at him. Quorn's shot hit his target hard and fast as it flew into his flesh immediately.

Jed fell to the ground immediately and cried out in pain as he grabbed his chest with his hand and blood started to seep out from the open wound that the laser ray had inflicted upon him. He rolled around on the ground in obvious agony as he attempted to stop the blood seeping out of the open wound but his efforts to actually stop the blood from gushing out were completely pointless. His hand quickly became doused in blood and the struggle for life soon ended as his body became weaker and weaker as each second passed. Jed's body finally ceased to actually move at all as he lay on the ground in a limp, lifeless heap as his life gushed out of every pore. He rasped as he waited on the doorstep of death for it to embrace him, unable to move and completely unable to retrieve himself as Quorn smiled. Jed's life was now almost officially over.

Quorn's curiosity prompted him to approach his victim, just to ensure that Jed was indeed actually on the brink of death as he quickly walked towards the back alley to inspect Jed's body. He stood silently over the damaged, wrecked pile of flesh that lay on the ground in front of him as Jed gasped and struggled to consume the last gulps of air he could inhale. Jed's hand moved slightly for a moment and then fell down the ground as he abandoned his last, fragile attempt to nurse his open, gaping, bloody wound and completely succumbed to death. His hand and chest were now completely covered in the crimson, red, liquid that had flowed out of his body and were totally lifeless. Quorn immediately felt satisfied. His mission had been achieved, his target was now definitely dead and now all that remained was Jed's corpse situated upon the cold, hard ground in front of him. The phone inside his jacket pocket started to beep as he was suddenly interrupted and he quickly fished it out as he prepared to answer the call and started to depart.

"Is the mission complete?" Visual asked him immediately.

"Yes. The target has been eliminated." Quorn replied in a regimented almost militant fashion.

"Excellent. I'll send you the details of your next target first thing tomorrow morning." Visual replied.

"Great." Quorn replied.

The phone call ended almost as abruptly as Visual's first call had and Quorn quickly made his way back towards Montgomery's vehicle which he'd parked nearby as his mind started to relax. His first mission was now completely over and the thrill of the kill had excited but exhausted him as he'd become a hunter. Jed, the corpse he'd left behind had simply been his prey and Quorn felt absolutely nothing towards him, there was no remorse, no sadness and absolutely no regrets. He'd simply killed Jed as if it was a perfectly natural thing to do and something that he did every single day.

The numbness Quorn felt inside surprised him in some respects as he began to wonder if perhaps his vacation would have an impact upon his real life and mind-set as he walked towards Montgomery's car. He'd orchestrated an actual murder and that thought frightened him slightly as he wondered if perhaps he would start to perceive death and violence as some kind of norm. He quickly shook his head, perhaps he'd just been numb as he felt Jed wasn't actually a real person and just part of some simulated activity in some kind of artificial environment. Was Jed a real person or had he actually killed a body that perhaps simply housed another vacationer's mind,

MINDPLANT: TRIMORPHIA

Quorn couldn't be totally sure as images of the human form he'd just slaughtered, occupied his thoughts and ran through his mind.

Once he arrived outside the car, the door immediately swung open and he quickly entered inside as he prepared to return to Montgomery's apartment, for that day his assassination missions were over and now he could enjoy himself and totally relax. The car carried him rapidly towards his destination as questions continued to plague his mind and he became slightly intrigued by the various possibilities and elaborate, intricate complex details surrounding his actual victim. His entanglement with his own Mindplant vacation provoked further thoughts inside him as more questions flooded into his mind and began to confuse him slightly. Could death be the way an actual vacationer exited from their vacation? Would Jed now be situated back inside his own body and perhaps wake up? Or was he just someone that existed within the Mindplant vacation world purely to enable Quorn to fulfil his objectives and desires to be an assassin? The possible answers to his many questions eluded him as he quickly realized, he had absolutely none of the answers and deliberating them further was a complete waste of energy and time. He was simply there to enjoy a vacation, not to dissect every inch of his participation within it, guilt had no place there and concerns about who his victims really were, simply weren't his to carry or worry about.

The next few days were extremely hectic for Quorn as he continued to be set missions and participated in them enthusiastically. He murdered a few more men, participated in some high speed car chases and even on one occasion actually had a physical fistfight. The act of killing became increasing thrilling as he embraced each day with more and more enthusiasm and each execution he carried out seemed to provide a greater adrenaline rush inside him than the previous one as the thrill of the kill heightened and he began to feel more alive.

His evenings were spent visiting some bars he'd found in the heart of the city, which bustled with attractive females and he began to participate enthusiastically in some sexually intimate experiences inside the bar toilets, Montgomery's car and even inside his apartment. The strangers he met, he simply enjoyed as he welcomed the comfort and luxury the companionship of each woman provided to him, without actually asking them any further questions or making any further demands for commitments from them. He exchanged no promises with them and indulged eagerly in no strings attached physical intimacy as he savoured his ability to satisfy each one with Montgomery's abundant bodily proportions. Afterwards, once they were both sexually satisfied, the two would then simply separate and go their respective ways with absolutely no frustration or negative feelings expressed. He didn't express any and neither did any of the women he actually encountered.

The sexual enjoyment he experienced was enhanced further by some of the bars in the centre of the city, which provided not only alcohol in abundance but also a drink that once consumed provided the drinker with an actual sexual experience. The drink known as an 'Erotic Shot' seemed to provoke some kind of hallucination that flooded into a person's mind and simulated a sexual experience which invoked the senses and provided sensations inside their body as if they were actually engaged in an actual, physical sexual act. It was extremely intoxicating and had to be consumed in a private cubicle inside the bars in which it was served. Quorn wished the drink existed in reality as it would in his opinion, solve a huge amount of problems for sexually frustrated men that often had difficulty finding a partner to enjoy and spend their lonely nights with.

Quorn quickly became engulfed in a world of lust and death as his desires consumed him and he almost started to forget who he actually really was. He'd embarked upon more than just a vacation, Mindplant had in a matter of days, completely changed who he actually was. The lifestyle Montgomery lived had become almost normal to Quorn as he soaked himself in the power he enjoyed as a result, he was absolutely tantalised, fascinated and captivated by its lure which seemed to drug him every day as he enjoyed his addiction to it wholeheartedly. His desires gripped his body and ran through every drop of blood in his veins as he revelled in the power he now held inside the palm of his hands. He could now control life or death and that power lured and enticed him as he embraced it eagerly and Visual continued to send him killing missions every single day.

Visual's distant attitude towards Quorn and his remoteness didn't actually bother Quorn at all and he completely ignored it, not even once did he try and engage Visual in a deeper conversation as he simply accepted his instructions each day and delivered the dead bodies. Quorn didn't even try to understand who Visual actually was, he simply didn't care, he just accepted Visual's anonymity and the missions he sent him at face value as he murdered the targets Visual instructed him to kill each day and in some respects it was almost as if Quorn had simply become a mechanical creature no longer governed by human emotions and moral reasoning that controlled his actions. A killing machine that savoured and devoured each death like a lion that pounced upon its prey and swallowed it whole as he relished the missions he performed each day more and more and yearned for the next to actually present itself. Just as Quorn started to become comfortable with the daily slaughtering's he performed and the regular sexual meanderings with strangers however, he suddenly hit a brick wall. A dilemma suddenly presented itself to him and it was one he simply could not just walk away from.

The day started off pretty much the same as usual in that Quorn ate breakfast, showered, dressed and then waited for a call from Visual. The call came as expected by mid-morning and his instructions were emailed to him as per Visual's normal routine and he made his way towards the car parked outside as he prepared for the attack upon his next target and prepped himself mentally. Once inside the vehicle, he inserted the target's coordinates into the control panel and then the vehicle moved off as it made its way towards the target's home. Throughout the journey he glanced at the email Visual had sent him as he inspected the details of his target further and prepared to identify them. The photo of his target as usual was attached to the email and as he opened it in order to review the person he was actually supposed to slaughter, his mouth suddenly dropped wide open in complete and utter shock. He rubbed his eyes with disbelief as he glanced down at the photo completely stunned and bewildered, Quorn's next target was actually a woman. Today was definitely different.

The email and photo inside Montgomery's cellphone, caught him totally off guard as he swallowed slightly nervously, perhaps Visual had made a mistake he quickly concluded. The two men had never spoken more than a few words to each other and a struggle quickly began to erupt inside Quorn as he became slightly disturbed and realized that he was actually slightly fearful to question Visual's commands. He was completely torn apart by the conflict within him that this new mission actually presented as the thoughts inside him began to spiral through his mind in a confused state.   Quorn started to panic as a tightness gripped his throat as he had absolutely no desire to kill a woman at all. Quietness surrounded him as the vehicle carried him steadily towards the target's home as he contemplated quickly what he should actually do next.   His throat became parched and dry and began to grate with each inhalation as he gasped for air, hardly able to breathe or swallow. It was like a nightmare there was no escape from. The car suddenly stopped as it entered inside a quiet side street and Quorn shook his head as he began to question himself further, could he Quorn actually go through with this mission? Could Quorn actually kill a woman?

All of a sudden the compassion and emotions that had eluded him all week and the remnants of his humanity that still remained inside him, exploded as they filled his body and his stomach sank like a heavy weight to the ground. His heart became strapped down tightly by a rope of guilt that seemed to twist itself around his lungs and ribcage and tie him securely to the floor as it gripped and paralyzed his body. The car by now had arrived at its destination and had actually stopped moving but for a few minutes he was simply unable to exit as paralysis seemed to grip him tightly by the throat.

The building where his intended victim lived, sat quietly in front of him almost as if it was waiting for him to make a final decision as he glanced at it. Suddenly he noticed the woman in question, that he'd actually been sent to kill, step out of the main entrance as he froze in shock as reality hit him even harder in the face, she was definitely real and she was definitely a real woman. Killing men had seemed like child's play, but killing a woman was an entirely different eventuality altogether and not something Quorn was sure, he could participate in. Women were soft and gentle and Quorn as a man felt he was supposed to protect them, care for them and nurture them, not kill and murder them. Deep down inside he knew he wasn't prepared for this at all and he wasn't sure he could actually orchestrate this murder and mission as he glanced at her face fearfully. Perhaps he'd go to hell if he killed a woman he quickly speculated as in Quorn's mind such an act was a complete taboo and a total, utter monstrosity.

He quickly glanced down at Montgomery's cellphone once more as he considered the possibility of sending Visual an email response before he actually went any further, perhaps he could clarify first that this was indeed the correct mission and that this woman was indeed the correct target. A voice suddenly sounded out inside the vehicle all around him as Quorn almost jumped in surprise as it interrupted his thoughts.

"The target is leaving the building." Visual's voice verified as it echoed throughout the interior of the car and urged him to leave.

Quorn was immediately shaken out of his thoughts as the words vibrated through the car and clung to each particle of air inside the vehicle as he almost choked. He felt completely paralyzed. Perhaps questioning Visual further he quickly determined would irritate him as his words clearly clarified that the woman on the street in front of him was indeed his intended target for that day. Quorn's lack of cooperation would perhaps be deemed as silly and meaningless after all Quorn was the one who had actually asked to be an assassin and there had been absolutely no agreement that his targets would only ever be men. His pangs of conscience due to the gender of his target may seem a little obscure to Visual and even perhaps slightly childish.

He stepped out of the car and emailed Visual quickly as he followed the woman reluctantly, it wouldn't hurt to clarify that she was indeed the intended target and he really needed to be sure.

Her name was Skylar and unlike his previous targets suddenly her name seemed to matter, it was pretty just like her and Quorn had noticed already, she was indeed a very beautiful woman. Luckily for Quorn, Skylar seemed to be occupied in her own thoughts and tasks as she walked at a steady pace in front of him and didn't seem to notice Montgomery's presence at all. He followed her at a safe distance quietly as he kept well out of sight and hid behind buildings and cars strewn across the roadside.

A few minutes later, the attractive woman entered inside a nearby park as she headed towards a large building situated at the other end and Quorn continued to follow her. He hid behind trees that lined the walkway as he attempted to remain not so close that she would actually spot him but close enough to her so that she would still be in sight as if she was too far away Quorn knew he would lose sight of her completely. The park itself smelt crisp and fresh as the dew rested on top of the leaves and green, lush, bed of grass that covered the interior. The soil gave off a clean, earthy scent and Quorn could feel a slight dampness in the air as he walked. The rain that had fallen the previous night had caressed the ground and left the grass and pathways moist and damp as they shimmered and glistened, almost as if they'd yearned for the rainfall's visit and appreciated it immensely.

Quorn waited eagerly for Visual's email response as deep down inside he hoped that it would absolve him from the mission and clarify that yes the mission was indeed a huge mistake, then perhaps he mused he could perhaps actually get to know Skylar instead of trying to assassinate her and maybe even take her for a coffee. His wait seemed to last forever, even though in reality only five or ten minutes had actually passed by before the email response from Visual actually arrived.

Skylar walked down the park path towards Quorn as he hid behind a tree which seemed to be an adequate hiding place as she appeared to be completely oblivious to his presence. She had by now completed her visit to the building nearby and was actually returning to the apartment block she lived in as he watched her quietly. Fear suddenly gripped him and the air began to evaporate around him as his chest tightened and she drew closer, she was even prettier in person than her photo was. He began to feel slightly claustrophobic as reluctance began to suffocate him and wrap itself tightly around his neck almost like a noose. For the first time since he'd actually arrived inside Montgomery's body, he was actually shocked by something that he was required to do and struggling to actually deliver.

His emotions had completely shifted in one morning from the indifference he'd basked in throughout the first five days of his vacation and now become a deep, solid, passionate wave of fear. Would God forgive him if he actually killed a woman? A giver of life and a mother of nature. His conscience was pricked as he contemplated further that to orchestrate such a murder in any capacity, would be an action that perhaps haunt him for the rest of his entire life. The email response from Visual as Quorn read it, unfortunately verified that he had not made a mistake as Visual confirmed the mission to him once more and Quorn read his response with sadness. Yes indeed Skylar was a woman and he yes indeed he was actually supposed to kill her. He shook his head sadly as he contemplated quietly that perhaps saying no was actually an option, which then prompted him to ask himself whether or not he really had a choice. What would actually happen if he refused to comply with his mission, the question swirled around the passageways of his mind as he stood completely still behind the tree and considered it quietly for a moment. Up until this point in time, he'd just slaughtered his targets and simply hadn't cared but now suddenly he needed to ask this question and be provided with an actual answer.

Time was running out and Quorn knew Skylar would soon be in close physical proximity to him and then he would definitely have to make a choice. He stepped back a little further behind the tree to avoid being spotted as he quickly prepared another email to send to Visual, this time he would ask if he could actually be assigned to another target and perhaps be allocated another mission perhaps that would be a diplomatic way out of the tricky dilemma he now faced.

Skylar approached the tree Montgomery was hidden behind quietly as she walked towards the park exit on the path nearby, suddenly however she turned her face towards him and noticed his presence. She glanced at him at him curiously for a moment as she noticed there was something slightly familiar about him and then started to walk towards him. He glanced up quickly again a few seconds later and to Quorn's utter surprise, he suddenly found Skylar right in front of Montgomery's face.

The whole world seemed to stand still for a moment and freeze as Quorn quickly realized, Montgomery's frame was actually much larger than his and that he hadn't quite hidden his body sufficiently from sight. Skylar had actually spotted him from the nearby pathway. It was too late now to send an email to anyone as Skylar was right in front of his face and there was quite simply no way, he could possibly avoid her. For a few seconds there was complete silence as Skylar glanced at him curiously and inspected his face and then suddenly her eyes shone with a glimmer of recognition as she smiled at him.

"I know you. You're Quorn the guy I met at Mindplant. You're on a Mindplant vacation just like me." She remarked as she looked him up and down inquisitively and then smiled as she gave off a light, lilted laugh. "You gave me your business card the day I actually went on my vacation, inside the Mindplant Centre waiting room." She insisted as she nodded at him with certainty.

Quorn gasped with shock as reality sank into his thoughts like a boulder being tossed into a deep, lake of water, the woman actually situated right in front of him was Connie, the woman he'd been so attracted to and admired from the very first moment they'd met at the Mindplant Centre.

The situation was becoming more horrifying by the second.

"Yes that's right. How on earth did you recognize me?" Quorn asked her curiously, totally stunned by her perceptiveness as he mustered up some courage inside him and finally managed to offer a response.

"That small scar you have on your chin, it's still there." Connie replied as she smiled at him.

"Really. I hadn't noticed." Quorn replied slightly confused by the fact that he hadn't actually noticed that the small scar on his chin had actually remained intact, despite entering inside Montgomery's physical form. He quickly attempted to normalize the situation and regain control of his emotions as he pushed some words out of his mouth almost by force. "Would you like to go for a coffee?" He offered politely, anxious to disguise and mask the internal turmoil that currently swirled around inside his gut.

By her reiteration of past events. that no other woman except Connie could possibly have known, Quorn knew straight away the woman situated directly in front of him was definitely Connie and that sudden realization horrified him. His mission had suddenly become horrifically complicated as her identity hit his mind like a brick, not only was his target a woman and a beautiful woman but she was actually a woman he liked in real life. It was completely horrifying as this certainly wasn't the manner in which Quorn had hoped to meet Connie again, inside or outside of his vacation

"Sure that would be great." Connie replied enthusiastically as she nodded at him and accepted his invitation. "I just have to drop this piece equipment at home first." She remarked as she held up a small package that was situated inside one of her hands.

Random thoughts ran riot throughout Quorn's mind as if they were monkeys that swung from tree to tree in the depths a forest. The next logical question Connie would be sure to ask him would be, why had he actually been hiding behind a tree near Skylar's home. He quickly attempted to manoeuvre the conversation as far away from the park as he could and focus Connie's attention upon something else as he smiled at her.

"So how's your vacation been so far?" Quorn asked politely as he began to contemplate internally for a moment how strange it was to call the apartments they occupied whilst on their Mindplant vacations home. The buildings they resided in weren't actually their homes at all, they belonged to the bodies they'd taken a vacation inside. They were borrowed homes not their actual real homes.

The two started to saunter gently towards the entrance of the park as they talked about the various things they'd encountered since they'd actually entered inside their Mindplant vacations as the mood lightened and Quorn sighed internally with relief. He'd managed to buy himself some time and postpone the awkward questions that Connie might ask him and avoid making a decision as to whether or not he would actually treat Skylar like a real assassination target for the time being. His relief however was short lived as they neared the park exit and Connie separated from him momentarily and the distraction that their conversation provided ceased to engage his thoughts.

Once Connie actually left his side, Quorn began to pace the park gates as he waited for her to return as fear began to claw around inside his mind and the pertinent issue of whether he was actually going to assassinate Skylar presented itself at the forefront of his mind once more until it became completely overbearing. The thoughts gnawed away inside him with each step he took as fear welled up inside him until he almost choked. The problems he now faced were unsurmountable and an obstruction of reluctance blocked his throat as the final revelations gripped his airwaves and he struggled to breathe. The worry inside him escalated as each second passed and plunged itself deep into his stomach like a sack of potatoes as pain gripped his body. He almost doubled over and quickly stretched Montgomery's hand out towards one of the gates nearby to steady himself as he digested the horrific truth and reality that he was now actually faced with, Connie was actually Quorn's target and he was actually expected to kill her that very same day.

MIND OVER MATTER

The agony for Quorn was short-lived as Connie reappeared five minutes later and the two Mindplant vacationers sauntered gently over towards a nearby coffee shop as they discussed the Mindplant vacations they'd enjoyed and the various different experiences they'd encountered since they'd actually woken up inside their respective vacations and bodily hosts. They entered inside the small, intimate venue situated just on the edge of the park and sipped on frothy, creamy lattes as Quorn related some of the more fun details about the various experiences he'd had in some of the bars he'd visited whilst on his Mindplant vacation and Connie listened to him quietly. Quorn seemed to deeply admire some of the peculiarities and intricacies of the world he'd embraced and appeared to be almost hypnotized by the many wonders he'd discovered inside it as she listened to him speak.

Once the two had spent almost two hours discussing their Mindplant vacations, Quorn invited Connie back to Montgomery's apartment and she accepted his invitation enthusiastically. The two sat in Montgomery's lounge on the large, black leather sofa as the afternoon disappeared and the evening was gently ushered in and hungrily tucked into a pizza they had bought on their way. They glanced at each other a little curiously as they discussed and admired the somewhat more youthful, attractive, alien bodies that their minds now occupied as the early evening approached and made jokes about the new bodies they'd actually chosen for their vacations. The evening was young as it danced outside the windows and lingered playfully against the slates of glass, it mockingly wisped and wrapped its strands around every inch of the building outside as it clung to the air with a dusky light and waited for the night to chase it away and substitute it with a blanket of darkness as the two inside Montgomery's apartment continued to engage in a deep discussion seemingly oblivious to the time of day, which no longer seemed to matter.

"What's your overall opinion of the Mindplant vacations?" Quorn asked Connie politely as he suddenly noticed that he'd talked a lot and she hadn't had a chance to actually say much at all.

"It's been." Connie paused for a moment before she continued. "It's been, fun." She glanced into Montgomery's eyes with a slightly anxious expression for a few seconds as she paused. "Quorn I think I'm trapped here. I was supposed to leave my vacation today and I haven't." She continued nervously. "What if we're stuck here for the rest of our lives?"

Quorn-Montgomery stared at her for a moment completely stunned by her response before he nodded thoughtfully, her comments definitely made sense as he'd actually arrived after she had and by now technically she should have actually left her vacation and returned to her own body. He hadn't considered for a moment that there might be anything actually wrong with the Mindplant vacations or imagined that anything could actually go wrong as from his point of view everything up until that very morning had been absolutely perfect. Now however Connie was clearly letting him know, that yes something indeed had gone wrong and that something was very far from perfect. Uncertainty gripped him inside as he paused for a moment slightly unsure how to actually respond as the possible negative eventuality of being stuck inside the Mindplant vacation forever suddenly struck him. His airways tightened as his thoughts caused him to panic and became almost like a rope that sought to choke him as he contemplated further the real implications of what Connie had just said.

She started to cry and broke down in front of him as Quorn-Montgomery quickly drew nearer and he quickly tried to console her. He quickly placed his hand gently on her shoulder in an attempt to comfort her, lost for words and completely confused by her remarks. A few more minutes passed by as Quorn struggled to find the words inside himself that could possibly alleviate her obvious distress as he attempted to be brave and tackle the issue head on.

"Hey Connie don't panic." Quorn finally blurted out as he tried his best to sound confident. "I'm here, we'll figure this out. You're a high tech vigilante right? We'll find a way to hack into the system or something and find a way out." He quickly reassured her. Although Quorn's tone sounded enthusiastic, deep inside he was situated very far away from the location of certainty as his doubts betrayed him and his voice wavered slightly.

Connie-Skylar nodded.

Luckily for Quorn, Connie was completely oblivious to his inner turmoil and believed his reassurances even though shadows of doubt clouded his mind and thoughts as he spoke each word. Quorn was situated a complete world away from the confident image he'd attempted to present but he smiled boldly in an attempt to sustain it.

"Perhaps getting ourselves out of the Mindplant vacation is our final mission." Connie suggested as she attempted to appease her own mind. Quorn was right she wasn't a boring, client liaison officer right now, she was a high tech espionage vigilante and that thought struck her mind like a dart as it pierced her doubts and disabled them momentarily. She was sharp, capable and well equipped and with Skylar's assistance she could handle this situation and actually find a solution. "Your right, we'll find a way out."

"Right." Quorn agreed as he accepted her analysis, his agreement was only surface deep however as he was totally unsure that he could actually deliver such a solution for her or even for himself.

Reality began to disturb him as worries accumulated inside him and although Connie's confidence in his reassurances indicated that a deeper level of trust had somehow developed between them which transcended the familiarity of strangers, he was completely unsure what might actually happen next. The bond that existed between them both now also presented a variety of problems to him as he accepted that he would not be able to fulfil his mission and he might not be able to actually resolve her problems either. He didn't want to disappoint her belief and trust in him but the problems were mounting and he didn't actually have any of the answers. Quorn felt totally frustrated and exasperated by the situation and it felt almost as if he was trying to thread a tiny needle with a huge, thick chunk of rope.

"I tell you what, let's wait until my vacation is over and if the situation is not resolved by then we'll start looking for other solutions and try to find a way to get out of here." Quorn remarked decisively as he touched her hand gently.

"Is it ok if I stay with you in the meantime?" Connie asked. "I really don't want to be on my own and I really don't want to go back to Skylar's apartment."

"Sure." Quorn replied. "You can stay here as long as you want, you can sleep in the bed, I'll sleep on the couch."

"That won't be necessary. I really don't mind. You can sleep in the bed too." Connie insisted as she smiled at his politeness, it was rare that a man would be so conscientious and so considerate and his chivalrous attitude danced through her thoughts as she acknowledged in her mind that usually most men would have totally take advantage of the situation and wouldn't have hesitated to jump straight into the bed right alongside her and make the most of her vulnerability. Quorn was different she quickly determined, Quorn was a gentleman.

"I really think its best I sleep on the couch." Quorn insisted again, deep inside he knew he wanted Connie with every part of his being but he was adamant to stick to his values. He didn't want to take advantage of her obvious fragile, emotional state and he could sense that she was scared and seeking some kind of comfort from his presence. Whilst Quorn would usually be flattered that a woman trusted him so much, right now he was actually more worried about his own motives and ability to resist a woman physically, he knew he was so deeply attracted too. Quorn definitely wanted Connie to give herself to him but not like this, he wanted her to be sure, confident and certain, not scared, worried and pushed into his arms through fear.

"I don't want to be alone right now." Connie continued as she invited him again, slightly unsure as to whether Quorn was rejecting her or the body she was now situated inside. Skylar was the image of physical perfection, her face was stunning and her body very visually attractive so his rejection seemed slightly illogical.

Quorn-Montgomery held her hand for a moment as he gazed into her eyes intensely, anxious to explain himself to her but not wishing to actually voice the words that occupied his mind. "You won't be alone. I'm here." Quorn insisted. "If we spend the night together in the same bed, I want it to be because you want to, not because you're scared to be alone. Believe me I can't actually believe I'm saying this myself as there's nothing I would love more. You're a beautiful woman both as Connie and as Skylar but it wouldn't be right, not like this."

"I understand." Connie reassured him as she accepted his position and the honourable attitude he displayed towards her.

He quickly stood up, held her hand and then led her towards the bedroom and she followed him quietly. Once inside the room, he quickly grabbed some blankets from a cupboard and smiled as he turned back to face her.

"I'll be in the lounge if you need me." Quorn reassured her.

"Thanks Quorn." Connie replied as she smiled. She quickly removed her shoes, climbed inside the duvet and then nestled against its warmth.

Quorn-Montgomery nodded as he touched his chin gently and felt the small scar that he'd had since childhood on his face. Connie was smart and very observant and he'd been totally surprised that she'd even recognised him, he certainly hadn't recognized her. He walked back towards the lounge and then switched off Montgomery's cellphone as he attempted to avoid any calls from Visual. For now, he quickly decided there would be no missions and no more assassinations, at least not until Connie's situation had been fully resolved. Inwardly Quorn felt very much at peace with himself as he stood by the sofa and prepared a makeshift bed quietly, now not only had he actually managed to actually find Connie, he'd even managed to have more than a two minute conversation with her and that was in his mind, the most positive outcome of his entire vacation.

He lay down quietly upon the sofa and covered himself with the blankets he'd found, it wasn't as comfortable as Montgomery's bed but it was definitely the right thing to do in the circumstances he was in. Tomorrow would perhaps bring solutions and if not Quorn was very determined they would actually find some for themselves. Sleep began to embrace him as he gently drifted off peacefully, comfortable in Connie's presence and reassured by her companionship, for the first night since Quorn had actually arrived in his Mindplant vacation, he would actually be spending an entire night in the same house as a woman and it was extremely appropriate in Quorn's mind, that the woman in question was actually Connie.

The next morning when it arrived, felt pretty much the same as the day before as Quorn-Montgomery stood by the window of the lounge and glanced out onto the street as he began to consider what the two should actually do next. The leaves rustled on the trees outside as the wind teased them, wrapped itself around them, twirled them around and then tugged at them until they released their grip from the branches they were attached to, they were then whisked high up into the sky as they spiralled through the air, liberated and free, never to return to the brownish wooden branches they had left behind. Today for Quorn would be the day of enlightment, today Quorn was actually due to leave his Mindplant vacation and return to his own body and by the end of that day if he hadn't, the two would definitely actually know whether they were both truly stuck in their Mindplant vacations or not. If it transpired that they both were, that would then allow Quorn to actually start tackling the problem head on and attempt to get them out somehow. He speculated for a moment what might happen if he actually returned to his body and Connie didn't, she might be left behind stuck in Skylar's life form forever. Montgomery's body shivered with fear as Quorn quietly considered the prospect of actually leaving Connie behind trapped and alone, it was a more scary thought than them both actually being stuck in Mindplant together.

Connie-Skylar broke his thoughts and concentration a few seconds later as she entered inside the lounge and smiled at him. She walked over towards the window and stood next to him as she greeted him politely.

"Good morning." Connie remarked.

"Good morning." Quorn replied as he greeted her enthusiastically. "Did you sleep well?"

Connie-Skylar nodded enthusiastically.

"Hungry?" He asked.

Connie-Skylar nodded again and flashed him a grin.

"Great I make a smashing breakfast." Quorn insisted.

Quorn-Montgomery quickly made his way towards the kitchen nearby and started to prepare some breakfast for them both and Connie-Skylar followed him a few seconds later. She stood by the kitchen dining table and watched him as he plucked some mushrooms, bacon, tomatoes, an onion and some eggs out of the nearby fridge and started to prepare an omelette.

"I'll fix us some food." Quorn insisted.

"Anything I can do to help?" Connie asked politely.

"Sure you can cut up some mushrooms if you like." He suggested.

Connie-Skylar nodded as he handed her a pack of mushrooms which she immediately opened and then started to wash gently in the sink as he quickly sliced some onions and tomatoes and then cut up some slices of bacon. He whisked the eggs inside a bowl as the frying pan spat gently on top of the ring and the oil started to heat up inside it.

"I definitely miss my kitchen." Connie suddenly remarked quite solemnly.   "I miss my latte machine."

"Well perhaps we'll get our real bodies back today."   Quorn replied enthusiastically.   "Then you'll have your kitchen back."

"What happens if we don't, or what happens if you do and I don't?"   Connie asked anxiously. "Then I'd be left here all alone and stuck."

There was an empty silence for a few minutes as Quorn contemplated how to actually respond to her question. Connie had hit a nerve and he was completely unsure what to say in order to reassure her. She'd voiced the unspoken question that had plagued his thoughts and tormented his mind earlier that morning, a question that had weighed his body down almost as if it was poison; a question with an answer that seemed to elude his mind much like an unfaithful husband avoids a questioning, nagging, suspicious wife.

He took a deep breath and then attempted to break the silence as he offered a response. "It's very unlikely that, that would actually happen but if it does I'll get help." He promised. "I'll find out why you're stuck in here and try to help get you out."

"Do you really think you'll be able to do that?" Connie asked as she faced him, uncertainty and disbelief clouded over her eyes for a moment as doubts crawled through her veins and skin.

Quorn sensed her fears immediately, she was extremely worried that he'd perhaps leave and she'd be stuck in her Mindplant vacation alone, forgotten by the world and stranded indefinitely. "Sure it's probably just a mistake or a system problem." He explained in a reassuring manner. "We'll both be back inside our real bodies very soon."

The omelette sizzled away in the frying pan in front of them both as she nodded and accepted Quorn's reassurances. She wasn't entirely convinced by his words but right at that moment in time, she had no choice but to actually accept them. Hope and trust had to satisfy her and fulfil her and hope had to live inside her, the hope that she would be able to leave soon and the hope that she would actually be able return to her own physical body, being frustrated, worried and speculating over things she could not determine or control right now wouldn't help her or anyone else and Connie knew it.

MINDPLANT: TRIMORPHIA

The morning for Barbelo was busy as the Mindplant Centre buzzed with activity as the staff arrived at work and then busily started to perform their various work duties. She had several funding requests to finish up that day and she took a quick break as she quickly collected a coffee from the staff kitchen and then made her way back towards her office anxious to drink it whilst it was still hot. On her way out of the kitchen as she rushed back out into the hallway, she almost bumped into Gavin as he approached her from the other direction and she immediately turned and faced him apologetically. Unusually, Gavin had a slightly confused expression on his face which seemed taut with worry and tension as he glanced into her eyes and for a moment and Barbelo was quickly reminded of a scared rabbit caught in a trap as she quickly absorbed his distress.

"Barbelo there's a problem." Gavin started to explain slightly anxiously. "Some clients haven't returned from their vacations and seem to be stuck in the Mindplant program."

Barbelo nodded as she indicated that she was actually aware of the situation. "I know. They're trapped in the system due to the adaptations that I did last month." She explained as she glanced at Gavin's face and attempted to appease him by not only acknowledging the problem but also taking responsibility for it. "Sometimes Gavin the more experimental side of my research can have some unforeseen complexities. I'm rectifying things at the moment."

Gavin was slightly relieved by Barbelo's admission as he was aware of her additional experimental work and although he had no idea exactly how experimental she actually was, he trusted her implicitly. "We'll have to be careful no one leaks this." He continued in a hushed tone. "The government funding's are due for renewal this month and we don't want them to be alerted to the experimental nature of some of your research."

Barbelo nodded.

The two stood in the hallway as Gavin continued to talk and elaborate further as Barbelo nodded her head at regular intervals, although her face seemed completely focused upon his words, her mind totally wasn't. Thoughts scurried around inside her head chaotically as her focus slipped away as she quickly became distracted and a few minutes later she switched off to his conversation entirely. There was absolutely nothing Gavin could actually tell her about funding processes and government institutions as she'd romanced their representatives for years. His conversation in her mind was unnecessary and pointless but she smiled and nodded reassuringly anyway as if it actually wasn't. The coffee cup Barbelo gripped inside one of her hands began to feel lukewarm as she took a sip of its contents and then smiled, her coffee was definitely getting colder and Gavin showed no signs of stopping or slowing, she had to go.

Barbelo interrupted Gavin in mid-flow and rushed to end the conversation as politely as she could. "Gavin I trust you to take care of the funding and monitoring returns." She reassured him. "I'll attend the funding meetings as I usually do and I'll sort out the system problems." She clarified politely.

Gavin nodded obediently as he glanced around the hallway quickly for a moment, just to reassure himself that they were still actually alone as the last thing they both needed right now was prying ears that they hadn't noticed.

"I'll prepare a briefing for the staff that work with the vacation clients and explain the situation to them as they may have realized that something unusual has happened and I'd like to reassure them that everything is under control." Barbelo explained. "The less people that actually know there is a problem however the better."

Gavin nodded in response. "I'll organize a meeting with the relevant team so that you can brief everyone." He insisted. "I'll advise them also that this is a very confidential situation."

"Thank you Gavin for your assistance." Barbelo remarked as she touched his arm gently to indicate her appreciation, reassured by his loyalty to her and his faithfulness. Throughout her trials, Gavin would indeed stand by her and she'd definitely made the right choice when she'd employed and promoted him and he'd proven that to her every single day through his steadfast loyalty and devotion to his work. "I'll email you a list of who should attend as soon as I get back to my office and we'll hold the briefing this afternoon."

Gavin nodded.

The two parted and headed off in different directions as Gavin smiled, comforted by the huge responsibility he'd been given. The briefing Barbelo wanted to hold was a very urgent task and had to be arranged before complicated questions were raised and she had clearly displayed her trust in him as she'd asked him to assist her in its organisation and that encouraged him immensely. He rushed back towards his office as he prided himself on Barbelo's faith in him, not only had she promoted and entrusted him but she'd also confided in him and their conversation reinforced his faith not only in her but also in himself.

Later that afternoon as the scheduled time for the briefing approached, Gavin stood at the top of the small board room with the ten employees he'd invited along, seated in front of him as they faced him expectantly and waited for Barbelo to arrive. Such group briefings rarely ever happened and the meeting was unusual in the sense that usually Barbelo would only hold one to one daily meetings with staff on their own. The fact the ten employees had all been gathered together inside one room added a sense of mystery to the occasion as they glanced at each other's faces a little curiously and speculated internally as to why they were actually there.

Jenson, one of the male Body Preservation Dormitory Medical Advisors, turned to face Mena as they waited and presented her with a question as curiosity danced through his mind. "What do you think Barbelo wants tell us?" He whispered.

Mena shrugged, she was completely oblivious as to the nature of the briefing. "Your guess is as good as mine. I've been kept in the dark just as much as you have." She replied quietly. Mena glanced at the ground for a few seconds and paused before she quickly turned back to face him and provided him with a morsel of speculation to chew on. "Some of the clients haven't returned from their Mindplant vacations when they were supposed to." She whispered quietly as she leant towards him. "Perhaps it's about that."

Jenson nodded. "Really since when?" He enquired. His voice was tinged with nervousness as he probed Mena a little further for more information.

"Some were supposed to return last week and two more were due to return this week." Mena replied anxiously. "It's a little worrying."

The two continued to whisper to each other as they discussed the various bodies that had not returned yet from their respective vacations as Gavin stood at the top of the room blissfully unaware regarding the topic of their discussion. Gavin glanced down quickly at his wristwatch nervously as he waited patiently for Barbelo to arrive, she was now two minutes late and the employees inside the room were becoming slightly restless.

Outside the small boardroom in the hallway, Barbelo stood alone for a moment as she prepared herself for the briefing that was about to take place, slightly nervously. The buzz of conversation that emanated from inside the room could clearly be heard as she listened silently for a few seconds. She inhaled and took a deep breath and then straightened the black, pencil dress that wrapped itself around her body and flattered her tall, slim build as it clung to her curves and accentuated her frame. Now she actually had to face the Mindplant Centre employees that were waiting inside the boardroom expectantly for her address, now she had to deliver some kind of answers and now she actually had to provide them with some reassurances there was an actual solution to the problems she had induced. Barbelo took a deep breath and then stepped bravely inside the room as she prepared to face her staff.

The boardroom fell immediately silent as Barbelo entered the room and smiled at Gavin reassuringly, the twenty chairs inside it were aligned in a circle that sat in a regimented arc as she walked towards the front of the room but only ten chairs were actually occupied. She stopped at the top of the room and then immediately turned to face the occupied chairs and the ten employees who had been chosen to attend.

Barbelo coughed gently as nerves caught the inside of her throat and although the cough itself was actually quite pretentious and wasn't a real cough as such, it was enough to distract her audience for a moment as she prepared her thoughts and readied herself to address them. She stood up tall and then began to deliver her address confidently even though inside herself, she actually felt extremely nervous.

"I've called you all here today as we have a slight problem on our hands." Barbelo announced. "There are a few clients that appear to be stuck inside the Mindplant program who have not yet returned to their physical bodies when they were supposed to. I'm working to rectify this at the moment with several of our engineers and we hope to have things sorted out in a few days' time."

The boardroom was as quiet and still as a morgue as Barbelo paused for a moment and sipped on a glass of water that Gavin had kindly prepared for her before she'd actually entered inside the room. Everyone inside the boardroom continued to listen and wait as they clung onto her every word and movement as they watched her intently. Each sip she drank seemed to create a loud gulp as she pushed each mouthful of water down inside her body and swallowed it. She quickly glanced around the room for a few seconds as she quietly contemplated whether anyone else could actually hear the sounds of her swallowing each mouthful and then inhaled deeply as she prepared to continue her address.

"Some of our funding is due for renewal over the next couple of weeks, therefore we cannot possibly have any leaks about this crisis." Barbelo insisted. "We are doing all we possibly can to resolve the situation and hope to have things straightened out very soon." Her words flooded out into the room in a gush and were met by a deadly, awkward silence.

The implications of her words did not need to be explained as everyone present immediately understood the possible ramifications as a wave of uncertainty quietly washed over them. Everyone inside the room had a vested interest in actually complying with her request and ensuring that leaks did not occur as that would result in funding rejections and jobs would be lost. The occupants of the board meeting room knew as employees they would ultimately be casualties of any such rejections and being that their roles were quite unique, everyone was aware it would probably be a while before they managed to find suitable employment somewhere else. Barbelo despite her faults was actually a great employer in that she paid them well and even though they were tied to very strict confidentiality agreements, she prided herself on providing each one with a good standard of living and excellent work conditions. Barbelo's request made absolute sense to her, to Mindplant's survival and to everyone else seated inside the boardroom as she finished her address and prepared for any questions anyone might ask.

"Does anyone have any questions?" Barbelo asked as she prepared to finish her briefing.

Mena glanced around the room a little nervously for a few seconds, slightly unsure whether or not she should actually ask her question before she finally raised her hand. "Will we be able to get the clients back into their bodies soon? Or will they be trapped for a while?" She asked as worry started to collate inside her and tie itself around her ribs and lungs in a knot.

Barbelo understood Mena's concerns as she accepted her question humbly, she had simply asked the question Barbelo knew was on everyone's minds and behind their lips. She glanced around the room as empty faces stared back at her expectantly and waited for her response. Everyone wanted answers, reassurances and clarification and she knew it.

"Definitely it's just a glitch, a temporary setback. Nothing we can't fix." Barbelo finally replied after a slight pause. She smiled convincingly but her hesitation betrayed her and relayed the reality of her own uncertainty as the room continued to remain totally silent. Her audience now seemed reluctant as she sought the room of confused faces for support. "Things will be back to normal very soon." She insisted as she nodded reassuringly.

A few employees finally broke the stagnation of stillness as a minute or two later they started to nod their heads and accept her response and Barbelo smiled. The nods of acceptance began to increase as if they were contagious as they spread out across the room and relief washed over her body, somehow her reassurances seemed to have been accepted and somehow she'd managed to convince the majority present inside the boardroom, that she did indeed have the situation somewhat under control.

"Everyone can go back to work now." Barbelo insisted as she released the occupants of the boardroom and allowed them to return to their duties.

She stood at the top of the room and watched quietly as all the employees departed, deep down inside herself she knew there was still a small remnant amongst them that were still very unsure, unsure that Barbelo could really resolve the situation, unsure that the clients would actually be returned to their bodies and unsure that the funders wouldn't find out the truth and ultimately pull their funding. The doubters however she knew wouldn't be convinced through further discussion, they would only be convinced when the client's minds had actually been returned to their physical forms. Controlling potential leaks was paramount in her mind as investors and financiers Barbelo knew would be a lot more sceptical than her audience of employees had been, they did not rely on her financially and it would take more than just a few flippant remarks to actually convince them.

Gavin hung back as the boardroom emptied and then when the last employee had left, he walked over towards Barbelo and smiled at her to encourage her politely. She nodded at him appreciatively, Gavin had been a tower of strength and a steadfast pillar of support as usual and he'd protected her vision loyally throughout the years. Barbelo had given him an opportunity and a job, when so many other companies had denied him that chance and his commitment to her and the problems that had arisen was unfaltering.

Barbelo smiled at him. "You can go back to work now too Gavin." She clarified as she released him. "Thank you very much for your assistance."

Gavin nodded obediently and then left the room quietly as he made his way back towards his office. The hallway was quiet as he entered inside it and started to walk towards the rear of the building, occupied by his thoughts. Suddenly Mena stepped out of the kitchen situated at the midpoint of the hallway in front of him and blocked his way as she smiled at him, she'd waited for him until he'd actually vacated the boardroom and as she approached him, she gently tugged his arm. Mena had a few pressing questions that she felt it would be better placed to ask Gavin instead of Barbelo and she'd waited for an opportunity to present them to him when he was actually alone.

"What do you think will happen now?" Mena asked quietly as they started to walk down the remainder of the hallway together.

Gavin glanced at her face for a few seconds before he offered a response, he could tell from the tone of her voice, she was slightly worried about the missing vacationers and deep down inside so was he. "Don't worry Barbelo will fix things! She'll get them back out of there. It'll be fine. I have every confidence in Barbelo's abilities." He replied as he sought to reassure her and himself.

Mena nodded. "How's Chivonne?" She asked quickly as she sought to change the topic of conversation and focus on something a bit lighter, she could sense the tension in Gavin's voice and could tell he was just as worried as she was. "Soon you'll be a daddy." She teased playfully.

"She's great. I know I will." Gavin replied. "I can't wait."

"It'll be great fun, you'll get to play with toys without looking silly or childish." Mena teased as they walked. "The nappies can be a bit off-putting though. Especially the stinky ones."

Gavin laughed.

The two arrived outside Mena's consultation room and parted as they smiled at each other, Mena entered inside the room as she contemplated quietly that perhaps Barbelo had made the right choice when she'd promoted Gavin. Perhaps by giving him more responsibility at work she'd actually prepared him for more responsibility at home. Perhaps she could forgive them both and hope that one day she would be promoted into another more senior role. She sat down by her desk as she prepared for the tasks she had to perform that day and sighed, Barbelo's briefing had interrupted her usual routine and schedule and now she had to catch up.

Gavin continued to make his way briskly towards his office which was actually situated at the other side of the building as he walked down the next hallway alone. Regardless of Barbelo's briefing and any Mindplant vacation problems, he still intended to leave work on time that day as he'd promised to take Chivonne for dinner and there was absolutely no way he was going to let her down. He smiled as he thought about Chivonne, whom he'd been married to now for two years. The two had been college sweethearts and had waited for years before they'd actually married and started trying to have a family, once Gavin had found secure employment they'd engaged and then subsequently married a year later and then once he'd been promoted, they'd decided to start a family and Gavin had finally impregnated the woman he adored.

The door that led into Gavin's office was closed as he approached it and he touched the infrared, panel lock with his security card as soon as he arrived outside and it swished open a few seconds later. Once inside the room, Gavin glanced at the large pile of funding returns that waited for him on top of his desk and the new client applications that needed to be checked and authorized, some of which had to be completed that day before he actually left work that evening, it was going to be a long afternoon and he knew it. He shook his head as if he were shaking away any worries he had, like bits of unwanted dust that had fallen and accumulated upon his clothing which he'd decided were totally unnecessary and had absolutely no home there. Gavin had to focus on his own work tasks now entirely and not Barbelo's system problems, which he knew would definitely not be resolved today as he definitely had a lot to do.

He sat down behind his desk as he reassured himself inwardly that Barbelo was a strong, determined, capable, competent woman and she'd proven time and time again she could handle whatever happened at Mindplant as she took problems in her stride and handled them, Barbelo would resolve the situation as she always did and everything would be fine and so to would Mindplant. The scientific research organisation that Barbelo had formed meant a lot to Gavin as it had actually birthed more than just Barbelo's vision since its inception, it had also provided him with the financial stability he needed to potentially give birth and life to his first offspring. It was more than just a job or an organisation to both Barbelo and Gavin and they had a very deep connection to Mindplant as their loyalty and affection towards the scientific technology that had transformed their lives, ran more deeply inside their veins than blood itself. Gavin started to tackle the paperwork on top of his desk as he lifted up the first funding return and began to read it as he sighed, his working day was far from over.

The day and morning had left Connie and Quorn filled with dismay as their minds continued to remain firmly situated inside the bodies of Skylar and Montgomery as no answers presented themselves and neither of them returned to their physical, biological selves. The two discussed their plan of action for the day ahead as they glumly accepted the reality, their situation was not actually going to correct itself and it seemed as the hours passed by, Barbelo was not actually going to correct it either.

"I can pick up some pieces of equipment that might help us from Skylar's apartment." Connie suggested. "Some of the equipment I utilized on my missions might help us infiltrate the Mindplant system and find a way out."

Quorn agreed.

The two exited Montgomery's apartment and made their way quickly towards Skylar's apartment as they accepted the answers they needed to escape their Mindplant vacations for now lay completely outside their grasp. They avoided the main streets as they walked and stuck to the emptier backstreets that were quiet and deserted. Quorn had been totally adamant that whilst they were unsure about what was actually going on, they should totally avoid congested, populated areas. He'd kept Montgomery's cellphone switched off and advised Connie earlier that morning to do the same with Skylar's and she'd obediently complied with his request. The two continued to make light conversation as they walked and it wasn't long before they neared Skylar's apartment.

"The first thing I'm going to do when I get back inside my own body is go shopping." Connie remarked. "What about you?"

"I think I might spend the first weekend in bed." Quorn replied. "All this rushing around performing missions has been quite hectic and hanging out in bars every evening, it's almost been as tiring as having two full time jobs and I'm not as young as I used to be."

"Have you noticed there's no kids anywhere?" Connie asked Quorn curiously. "Kind of strange right?"

"Yeah perhaps they leave them at home." Quorn suggested.

"Or perhaps they don't have any." Connie ventured. "A world with no kids, they must save a fortune on diapers."

"And they probably have a lot less arguments." Quorn insisted.

They both laughed.

Their walk had lasted approximately twenty minutes and they were thankful a few minutes later as they turned a corner and finally entered into the road where Skylar's apartment was actually situated. The main entrance stood patiently waiting for them as they walked eagerly towards it but as they approached it Quorn-Montgomery suddenly stopped and paused thoughtfully for a moment. He pulled Connie-Skylar to one side as he forced her to walk slightly behind him cautiously as although the entrance nearby appeared to be quiet, he didn't want to take any risks and felt it was possible that the building was perhaps being watched.

The two cautiously made their way inside the building as Quorn-Montgomery took the lead and walked slightly in front as he scanned the hallway in front of them. Once they arrived at the foot of the wide staircase that led to the second floor where Skylar's apartment was actually situated, they walked quietly up it as they scanned the area all around them for any potential threats but could see none. When they arrived on the second floor, they found the front door of Skylar's apartment slightly ajar as they approached it and they both froze. The hallway was quiet and there was no sound to be heard, but Quorn-Montgomery opened his jacket and quietly removed a laser gun that he'd hidden inside it as he turned to face Connie-Skylar and quickly put his finger on his lips and motioned to her to be completely silent. She nodded in response and then the two continued to walk quietly towards the apartment door and then made their way inside the apartment extremely quietly.

Quorn-Montgomery quickly scanned each of the rooms inside the apartment as he searched for intruders cautiously, most of the rooms he entered into appeared to have been ransacked and trashed. Skylar's apartment looked as if it had been burgled, someone had been there recently and it certainly hadn't been Connie or Skylar. The two stood quietly for a moment inside the bedroom as they absorbed the destruction that surrounded them, unsure what to actually do next as they both shook their heads in dismay.

Quorn finally decided on a plan of action after a few minutes of quiet internal deliberation. "Get some clothes quickly and any equipment you can find." He insisted. "We can't stay here a minute longer than we absolutely have too." Inside himself he wasn't entirely sure what they should both do next but one thing he did know for certain, they had to leave Skylar's apartment as soon as possible. They had to leave and they had to leave now.

Connie-Skylar glanced quietly around the room as she absorbed the mess completely frozen to the spot and numb with fear. Quorn-Montgomery looked at her and then walked over towards her and gently touched her arm as he urged her to move. His gesture was enough to awaken her out of her paralysis as she nodded and then started to pick her way back through the mess. She walked towards the closet nearby as she stepped gingerly over objects scattered across the ground.

"Why would anyone do this?" Connie asked curiously. "I mean what would this actually achieve?"

"I'm not sure and until we are sure, we definitely shouldn't come back here." Quorn replied.

Connie-Skylar nodded as she picked up a holdall bag from the floor near her foot and started to briskly pack some items inside it. She rammed in as much as she could as she contemplated the mess inside Skylar's apartment further and who could have possibly been there whilst she'd been absent. Perhaps the intruder was someone she'd sabotaged whilst on one of her missions she quietly contemplated. Whoever they were they'd certainly made a mess.

"Be quick." Quorn urged. "We don't have long and I'm not sure how safe it is for us to actually be here at all."

Connie-Skylar nodded and started to rush as he left the room and walked back towards the lounge. When Quorn-Montgomery entered inside the lounge, he immediately noticed Skylar's equipment cases, a laptop and a few other devices strewn and scattered across the floor and he quickly picked them up as he attempted to salvage them from the wreckage. He started to fumble around with the devices and take them to pieces as Connie-Skylar entered inside the room and stood by the door as she watched him quietly for a few minutes.

"What are you doing Quorn?" Connie asked curiously.

"Checking for and removing any tracking devices." Quorn explained. "We need to be sure that they won't be able to track us when we leave here."

Connie-Skylar nodded in understanding as Quorn-Montgomery continued to strip the devices as she waited patiently nearby. Five minutes later, once he was satisfied that his task was complete, they prepared to actually leave the apartment as Quorn-Montgomery held Skylar's small, white equipment case in his hands.

Connie-Skylar smiled at him. "You managed to find my equipment case?" She asked as she touched it affectionately for a moment. The small case was more than just an equipment case to Connie as it held various memories from the missions she'd been assigned to perform throughout the duration of her Mindplant vacation inside it.

Quorn-Montgomery nodded. "I did. Somewhere under all the rubble." He replied. "It might come in handy."

Connie-Skylar nodded in agreement as she glanced down at the equipment case once more, this time however with a slightly more cynical stare. Whilst she'd enjoyed the various missions she'd performed at the time they'd actually happened, the realization that she was now trapped inside Skylar's body had since tarnished her memories and her smile had slowly faded and been quickly replaced by a frown. When each experience had originally occurred they had been clean and pure, now however that was no longer true, now each memory was tainted, now each memory was dirty, clouded, jaded and impure as they'd been struck by the lightning of despair and frustration that her trapped status denoted, her present suffering now completely redefined and altered her past enjoyment as history was written before her very eyes.

Once they were both satisfied that they had retrieved anything that could possibly help them from inside Skylar's apartment, the two exited the lounge and prepared to vacate the apartment building as they walked towards the apartment front door. They stepped out of the front door of Skylar's apartment quietly as they entered inside the external hallway outside and then suddenly froze as they both heard a noise from the staircase below them. Quorn-Montgomery quickly, gently grabbed Connie-Skylar's arm and pulled her back inside the front door of Skylar's apartment protectively, anxious to determine what the source of the noise was before they actually proceeded any further. He rapidly pulled the laser gun back out of his jacket pocket and held it up firmly in his hands, poised and ready as he put his finger on his lips to indicate that Connie should be completely silent. She nodded in response.

The two stood absolutely still inside the internal hallway that led to the front door of Skylar's apartment about ten steps away from the entrance as they waited and watched in complete silence. A few seconds later a man dressed in a dark, grey suit pushed open the front door and stepped inside as they both held their breath. The man was armed with a laser gun that he held tightly inside his fist and he certainly wasn't a potential friend, he'd come to the apartment to kill Skylar.

The silence that gripped the air as it clung to each particle was almost deafening as Quorn-Montgomery reacted almost immediately, he quickly raised his laser gun and fired it directly at the man's chest. He left no room for questions, deliberations or disputes as the ray from the laser gun hit the man at full force and he faltered and stumbled. A few seconds later he grabbed the wound the laser gun had inflicted desperately and then collapsed onto the ground in front of them in a heap. Connie gasped with surprise and fear as she observed the scene in front of her, completely frozen to the spot.

There was no time for further hesitation however as Quorn quickly decided they had to leave the apartment immediately and quickly grabbed Connie-Skylar's arm. He pulled her rapidly towards the front door and they walked back outside into the external hallway as they both panted anxiously. He paused for a second as they both stood outside the door of the apartment rooted to the ground deep in thought as he quickly contemplated what they should actually do next. A thought suddenly hit him like a shard of ice as it pierced his chest as he quickly realized, if there was a man inside the building there would probably be more men situated outside the building, waiting for them to exit or for that man to return.

He turned back to face Connie-Skylar once more and pulled her towards him silently as he led her back towards the apartment and they entered inside it. In some ways Quorn felt his Mindplant vacation had actually prepared and equipped him for that moment as he'd handled the assassination of the strange man that had hunted them with ease. Connie certainly wasn't used to murdering people and the taking of life and she definitely wasn't a physically aggressive person, which had meant that he'd had to step up and handle the physicalities that presented themselves to them as he'd protected her. He led her quickly back towards the bedroom and they both entered inside, he rushed over towards a window and opened it quickly as Connie-Skylar glanced at his face curiously for a moment, unsure and uncertain about the window being a suitable exit. Quorn-Montgomery rushed back over towards the bedroom door and then quickly shut it behind them as he pushed a chair up against it to secure it. Connie watched him silently, slightly confused by his actions as he turned back to face her once more.

"There'll be more of them outside." Quorn explained. "It's safer to leave this way."

"How will we get down from this floor though?" Connie asked as a worried expression crossed Skylar's face and Connie quietly considered the distance from the window to the ground below it.

Quorn-Montgomery smiled as he started to strip sheets from the bed nearby and quickly knot them together. He tied one end of the sheet rope to the bed post and then continued to tie multiple sheets together to make the rope as strong as he possibly could.

"I've thought of that. This bedroom window is the only other way down, we can avoid the front of the building this way. You'll go first and then I'll follow you." Quorn explained.

Connie-Skylar nodded and then quickly rushed towards a nearby cupboard inside the bedroom and started to dig out more sheets and blankets to assist him. It wasn't an elegant means of departure but it would definitely get them out of the building safely and hence she had to cooperate fully.

Once the sheet rope was ready Quorn-Montgomery swung it out of the window and nodded towards Connie-Skylar as he indicated that she should climb out first and start to make her way towards the ground. Her hands trembled a little with nerves as she attempted to comply with his plan but somehow she managed to hold onto the rope tightly and clambered out of the window as she started her descent. She glanced quickly down at the ground for a moment and paused as nerves gripped her flesh as she quickly realized the distance between her and the ground was vast. It wasn't going to be an easy escape and she knew it, she shook her head and then decisively started to slide further down the sheet rope as she attempted to reach the ground as quickly as she could. The sooner she slid down the sheet rope, the sooner the dangerous, risky escape would be over and she was anxious to get off the sheet rope and back onto solid, concrete ground as quickly as she possibly could. There was quite simply no choice as she knew the men searching the apartment might kill them both if they actually found them there, which meant the sheet rope for now was her best chance of survival.

The ground luckily for her was by now only a floor down and that reassured her slightly as she became more confident. The sheet rope itself didn't actually quite reach the ground, but there was a pile of garbage bags below her that she felt could break her fall as she slid down the remaining part of the sheet rope and then dropped of it and safely landed on top of them. Once on the ground she glanced quickly back up at Quorn-Montgomery once more as he leant out the window, she could see his face clearly as he watched her and she smiled and nodded at him. He nodded back at her in response and as soon as he observed that she was safely on the ground, he proceeded to climb out of the window himself as he quickly followed her. Connie-Skylar waited and watched as she stretched her arms upwards and held the bottom of the sheet rope steady in order to assist him as much as she possibly could.

Once Quorn-Montgomery reached a safe distance from the ground, he quickly released the rope and dropped down the remaining distance to the shiny, grey street below him. He landed nearby on his backside and smiled slightly as Connie-Skylar quickly stretched out a hand towards him and helped pull him to his feet. He accepted her gesture of assistance graciously as he held her hand and she pulled him up gently, although they both knew deep down inside he didn't really actually need her help at all.

"I had to let you go first as I wasn't sure how long the sheets would hold. I didn't know how strong they were." Quorn explained as he rubbed his backside that had been slightly damaged by his fall. "I weigh a lot more than you do." He teased playfully.

"Where should we go now Quorn?" Connie asked him, slightly unsure about what exactly they should actually do next.

They both glanced around the back alleyway slightly nervously for a few seconds as they searched for any threats that might be lurking, unnoticed nearby, luckily however the street was completely empty and silent.

"I'm not sure but we definitely can't come back here." Quorn replied assertively as he took her arm and started to guide her towards the alleyway entrance.

The two walked quietly and cautiously down the remainder of the back alley as they headed off in the opposite direction from the street, where the apartment block entrance was actually situated. Once they arrived on the main street at the end, they headed off in a completely different direction as they avoided both Skylar and Montgomery's apartments and the areas they were situated inside completely. They roamed around from one back street to the next aimlessly for what seemed like hours as they deliberated over where they should actually go next and what they should actually do.

The streets started to darken as night approached and indicated clearly to them both that it was about to enter. They both knew as darkness started to wrap it's arms around them, they had to find somewhere safe to actually spend the night and they had to find somewhere to do so relatively quickly. Luckily about thirty blocks away, on the outskirts of the city, the two finally found an abandoned underground train station which appeared to be quite isolated. There were stairs that led underground and as they approached the entrance cautiously, they noticed it seemed peaceful and quiet. Derelict, rundown buildings surrounded it which appeared to be abandoned and they discussed it as they contemplated spending the night under the ground.

"We can hide in here until the morning." Quorn suggested.

Connie-Skylar nodded. "Sure it looks safe enough." She agreed.

They entered inside the depths of the earth carefully, unsure of what might actually be lurking in the darkness below them waiting to attack as Quorn-Montgomery gently held onto Connie-Skylar's arm and led her down the dark stairs that lay before them, quietly and cautiously. Not a word was exchanged between them as they walked.

When they arrived at the bottom of the stairs, they peered out into the pitch, black darkness in front of them curiously but couldn't see anything at all. The two stood completely still for a few minutes as they stared out into the black expanse that sat still, stagnant and expectant in front of them as it waited to devour, embrace and engulf them. Finally after a few minutes pause, which seemed like almost an eternity to them both, Quorn-Montgomery stepped bravely out into the darkness as he prepared to enter inside the underground depths. Connie-Skylar took a step forward as she started to follow him but just as she stepped forward into the darkness however, four people also stepped out towards them. The two froze with fear and shock as they contemplated internally who the four strangers might actually be as their bodies became firmly rooted to the ground.

The faces of the four strangers could not be seen clearly due to the darkness that surrounded them and that anonymity frustrated Quorn-Montgomery immediately. Two of the strangers stretched their arms out towards them, grabbed them both around the neck and Connie-Skylar gasped with fear as a gun was quickly held to her head and she froze. The people were still not clearly visible to either of them and simply looked like dark shadows within the darkness that surrounded them. Connie and Quorn were totally unsure what to do for a moment as they considered quietly whether or not they should try to fight them back or struggle. It wasn't actually apparent yet whether the four strangers who had captured them were even actually human, never mind whether they were actually friends or foes. A few seconds later however their question was answered.

"Don't move." A rough male voice suddenly instructed from the depths of darkness.

Quorn-Montgomery sighed in despair as he realized they'd been captured and there was nothing at all he could actually do about it. He resigned himself to the prospect that their flame of hope, regarding their pending escape plan and safe haven for the night, had now been truly extinguished. The underground station that he'd hoped would provide a sanctuary and mask them both from the threats outside, they'd now found actually presented them with another threat instead of the safety they'd sought there. His mind abandoned the false expectations he'd held when they'd entered inside the structure as he prepared to face a new, unknown threat head on. If these four strangers were anything like the man he'd encountered inside Skylar's apartment, death for them both was imminent and he knew it. He'd been caught off guard and now Quorn knew he would have to find a way to overpower the four enemies in front of him, if that was what it transpired they actually were. Quorn was outnumbered but it wasn't impossible.

"Who are you?" A female voice asked a few seconds later, a little more softly. Her words infiltrated their ears kindly as they drifted out through the darkness towards them and provided a glimmer of hope. "Why did you come down here?" She enquired politely.

"We're trapped in our Mindplant vacations." Quorn explained rapidly as he attempted to establish whether the four strangers were actually potential allies or enemies as quickly as possible. "Someone tried to kill us and we were just seeking refuge down here for the night or until we can find a way to escape."

The rough male voice sounded out again from the darkness as it interrupted him and began to probe him further, almost as if it was interrogating him. "How do we know you're telling the truth? How do we know you're not lying?" The male voice questioned as it demanded further explanations.

Connie immediately jumped on the opportunity to provide the male voice with some kind of reassurance as she noticed that unlike his first remarks, his tone now sounded slightly softer. "Why would we lie?" Connie asked quickly as she interjected in a soft, almost pleading manner.

The four people that lurked in the shadows of darkness whispered quietly amongst themselves for a few minutes before one of them, a male, finally stepped forward out into the small rays of light that drizzled down from the stairway entrance above their heads. The remaining three strangers, two men and a woman followed his lead a minute later and as they stood together in the small circle of light, they smiled. The guns were immediately removed from their heads and the arms that had been tightly gripped around their necks, rapidly released them. Connie-Skylar and Quorn-Montgomery glanced at their faces and bodies, which they could now see very clearly, slightly nervously as they waited for them to clarify their position.

"Welcome to our world." The gruff male voice remarked in a much softer tone. "I'm Concept, that's Matter, she's Spiral and that's Weaver." He explained as he pointed to each one of the three people situated beside him.

Concept, the owner of the rough voice that had challenged them initially, seemed to be quite handsome in a rugged kind of way and somewhere in his mid-thirties and Connie immediately admired his physicality as she digested his presence. The other two men Weaver and Matter and Spiral, the only female amongst the group stretched out their hands towards the two in a friendly manner as Concept introduced them.

Connie sighed inwardly with relief as she reciprocated their friendly gesture. "I'm Connie and that's Quorn, those are our real names." Connie replied as she embraced their offer of friendship and shook their hands eagerly. "Are those your real names?" She asked curiously.

"Not really, they're kind of nicknames we assigned to ourselves based on the tasks we perform each day. Like you we're also trapped. We all went on our Mindplant vacations around the same time and then found each other within them." Concept explained. "All except Spiral who we found a bit later."

Connie-Skylar smiled as a wave of calmness washed over her body and she relaxed, luckily the four people they'd found were just like them and weren't a threat to them at all and she quickly accepted Concept's explanation at face value. She turned to face Quorn-Montgomery who by this time had also started to shake hands with the four strangers and smiled at him. His handshake seemed slightly more cautious and a little more reluctant than her own had been and Connie immediately sensed, he was still slightly suspicious and unsure regarding their identity and the validity of their story.

She nodded at him as she encouraged him to embrace the strangers situated in front of them, whether they were actually friends or foes was not something they could determine that night and Connie knew that deep down inside. They both had very few choices right now and their only real option for that night was to surrender and accept them and trust what they'd said. They had to trust that these four strangers were potential allies and they also had to trust that they would not actually physically harm them as going back outside to the surface right now was simply not a viable option. Tomorrow would provide opportunities for them both to establish and clarify the reality of the situation and who the strangers actually were more fully, tonight however, they both simply had to accept the offer of friendship at face value as it accompanied the accommodation they both needed and that was something neither of them could actually change. They'd entered into the four stranger's hideout and hence they were the guests and Connie accepted her position humbly as she had absolutely no desire to go back out on the streets that night and hunt for another possible sanctuary.

Quorn-Montgomery glanced at her face and then nodded in agreement as he accepted the mandatory requirements of their current position. His eyes had by now grown accustomed to the darkness as he noticed the dusty, train station platform spread out in front of them. The accommodation they'd found, whilst not luxurious would provide them both with some much needed rest and he succumbed to the fatigue inside him as he attempted to relax. He smiled at the group of four that surrounded him as he attempted to embrace them a little more enthusiastically, not wishing to worry Connie further. Deep down he knew it was absolutely unreasonable to keep dragging her around the streets in the darkness unnecessarily and he had no desire whatsoever to actually do so. They had found a place of safety and had been welcomed into it by its occupants, who had accepted their presence and need for shelter. The effects of fatigue on both their bodies, due to the hours they'd spent wandering around the streets earlier that day had begun to take their toll, not only their bodies but also their minds even before they'd actually entered inside the underground station and Quorn knew he had absolutely no reasonable choice or viable alternative right now to offer.   Right now acceptance, trust and the underground station was indeed for that night, their only viable option and it would be selfish of him to actually even attempt to oppose that.

TRAPPED

The two groups followed Concept as he led them down the dark underground platform nearby and started to accept each other as they began to make light conversation. They entered inside the depths of the underground station as they walked along the dusty, grey concrete ground for a few minutes before they arrived at the end of the platform and a narrow passageway which was situated at the bottom. They quickly formed a single, file line and began to follow Concept down the narrow passageway as Spiral, Matter and Weaver positioned themselves at the rear and walked delicately along it. Concept led the way and began to discuss the various provisions they'd managed to make since they group had actually initially arrived less than a week ago.

"We've built a kind of sanctuary down here." Concept explained as he led everyone inside the interior of the dark tunnel. "We've been quite safe at night, but the missions to the surface to secure enough food to eat consistent meals every day, can be a little bit rough at times."

Weaver lit a torch as they walked which generated just enough light to allow them to see where they were actually going. Everyone followed Concept quietly as he guided them into depths of the dark underground hideaway and towards the end of the long, narrow passageway where a door was situated. It was far from elegant and dusty and grimy as oil glistened on the walls around them but it was safe. They arrived outside the door, a few minutes later and Concept quickly pushed it open for everyone and then stepped back as he allowed them to enter inside. Once they'd entered the door, they immediately found another much smaller passageway inside it which actually had a junction situated at the bottom. The passageway that led to the left, led directly into a large room and the passageway that led to the right, led off into the darkness in a completely different direction and neither Connie nor Quorn could see where it actually ended from their current position.

"We've built a kind of base down here to help us survive." Concept explained as he led everyone through the open, rectangular doorway on the left and into the large room beyond it.

"How long have you actually been down here?" Connie asked curiously, slightly surprised as she glanced around the large room and noticed that it seemed relatively well equipped and quite well organized.

"Not long. Almost a week." Concept clarified as he walked towards a small generator positioned on the floor nearby and switched it on.

Some lights inside the room immediately lit up but even with the lights on, the room still seemed somewhat dim. The computers and equipment that lined the room walls became clearly visible as Connie and Quorn quickly observed that everything inside the room actually looked quite old fashioned and somewhat obsolete.

"We had to scavenge whatever we could find and this old equipment we found, although it looks useless is actually less likely to be traceable and that means it's harder to track." Concept explained.

"What do you in here exactly with all this equipment?" Connie asked curiously, slightly in awe of how well coordinated Concept's efforts seemed to be. She touched a screen situated nearby delicately and some dust floated off her hands as it fell to the ground and she winced slightly.

Spiral smiled as she watched. "It's not the cleanest of hideouts, but right now cleaning is the last priority. Escape, food and hiding is much more important." She clarified.

"Do you have a plan to actually try and get out of here?" Quorn probed a little more impatiently, less interested in the equipment and much more interested in any possible escape plan that the group may have formulated.

Concept walked towards him and sat down on top of crate nearby as he faced him. "Quorn if we manage to actually escape from our Mindplant vacations, who's to say we'll ever find a way back to our real bodies? I mean if we're trapped in here on purpose, it could be highly unlikely that we ever will." Concept insisted.

"He's right Quorn. We don't know what their objectives actually are yet. We don't know why we're actually trapped inside here." Connie observed. "What if that man had killed us at Skylar's apartment, where would we actually be right now, would we be physically dead? Or would it just be these bodies that we are living inside that would be dead?"

Concept nodded in agreement. "There are so many questions that we just don't have answers to right now." He explained.

Connie-Skylar nodded as she found a vacant crate situated next to Concept and quickly parked herself on top of it.

"The answer to our questions can only be answered by one person." Matter insisted as he drew closer and sat down on a crate next to them both.

Concept nodded as he picked up a remote from a shelf nearby and touched a switch on it, suddenly a screen that filled one wall of the room lit up and a grid appeared in front of them. He started to zoom in on buildings and houses within the grid as everyone watched him quietly.

"We're currently searching for the man who can provide us with some answers to our questions at the moment and we've managed to narrow down his location to one of four squares on the grid map." He explained as he stood up and pointed to four squares on the grid in front of them. "He usually moves within these four blocks and changes his hideout every few days, which means it's hard to pin point his exact location at any given moment in time." Concept continued.

"Who are you looking for?" Connie asked curiously as intrigue began to fill her interior. "Who is he?"

"We're looking for Maverick." Concept explained. "Maverick understands the Mindplant system as he helped design and create it. That's why he's actually trapped inside here. He was one of the initial volunteers that entered into the unofficial program at its inception, before it was actually even open to the public."

Spiral nodded in agreement as she listened. "Maverick knows Mindplant's weaknesses and its loopholes." She insisted. "Maverick knows him." Spiral continued in a whisper as she placed her hand across her mouth.

Connie-Skylar and Quorn-Montgomery glanced at her curiously for a moment as they digested her comments, she'd aroused their curiosity and created a sense of heightened mystery deep inside their minds, that provoked and lurked in their thoughts as it scurried around chaotically around like a whirlpool, debating the possibility and existence of unknown entities, who may or may not ever be found. They hadn't even known Maverick existed and now there was also another presence that Spiral had referred to that possibly also held the keys to their potential escape.

"Him? Who do you mean by him?" Quorn asked after a short pause as he sought to clarify the presence of the second entity she had referred to, that was now present hidden somewhere in the depths of the conspiracy they had found themselves completely engulfed by.

"Visual." Spiral explained. "Visual is the embodiment of the Mindplant program itself. He runs it, he controls it and he orchestrates most of what happens inside it. The Mindplant program is his life, his breath, his very existence. Visual is the Mindplant program."

"You're talking about a program almost as if it's an actual person." Connie remarked as she laughed slightly nervously, somewhat disturbed by the fact that the voice she'd once thought of as attractive was actually really a program that was now actually holding them captive.

"He is a person, well kind off a person I guess, which means the Mindplant program itself is therefore a kind of person too in some respects." Concept explained. "In some ways the program is a living, growing organism that evolves, just as Visual evolves. The two are intertwined, inseparable and absolutely dependent on each other as they coexist."

A man's face suddenly appeared on the screen in front of them as Concept touched the remote again and the grid disappeared. The screen filled with a large, somewhat pixelated face which composed of predominantly black, white and grey tones.

"Meet Visual." Concept announced. "He carries out the daily maintenance within the Mindplant environment. He makes you believe the illusions inside it are real and he is our opponent. If Visual or his Exterminators catch you, you die."

"Visual is not our friend." Spiral confirmed as she glanced up at the screen and screwed her face up at the image in front of them. "And neither are the Exterminators he created."

The room fell silent as everyone faced the screen and absorbed Visual's appearance quietly, Connie-Skylar stood up and walked over towards the screen as she remembered how she'd initially speculated over Visual's human identity at the beginning of her vacation. Visual definitely wasn't human by any stretch of the imagination and her initial interest and attraction to his voice immediately began to wear off rapidly as she touched the screen gently and shivered slightly. Now Connie's question had finally been answered.

Quorn-Montgomery stood up and followed her and then stood next to her as he glanced at the screen directly in front of him and put a face to the voice that had sent him his assassination missions each day. "How strange." Quorn remarked. "He actually sounded quite human to me."

"Is he actually real?" Connie ventured, completely surprised by Visual's computerized form.

Concept laughed. "In some respects I guess he is and in some, I guess he isn't. He's a scientific, computerized Mindplant control program that was originally designed and created by Barbelo and Maverick. He exhibits some behavioural manifestations that may indicate he may actually utilize and exercise some grains of free will and he seems to evolve somewhat from day to day, but essentially he's almost completely controlled by Barbelo's commands and the Mindplant program boundaries that he functions within."

"Everything you experienced whilst on your vacation, everything you did, everywhere you went, everyone you interacted with was an illusion, an illusion created by Visual. He creates and controls every illusion you've actually experienced within the program itself." Matter explained to them. "The only places Visual doesn't seem to bother about much are situated inside the Unoccupied Zone, outside the heart of the city. That's where we are right now and the only real person he does not actually control, aside from the human vacationers within Mindplant, is Maverick."

Weaver smiled as he sat down in front of the screen and attempted to elaborate regarding the issue of Visual a little further. "What did you actually do whilst you were on your vacation?" He asked Connie and Quorn politely.

"I was a high tech vigilante." Connie replied.

"I was a deadly assassin." Quorn explained.

Weaver smiled at them both and nodded. "Right it's only logical that this is a simulated existence and world, think about it for a moment if you actually killed someone whilst on your vacation and the people inside this world were actually real, you'd be killing a real person and they would die. The body that contained the other vacationer would then be dead and the mind that belongs to the body would no longer be able to return to it, which means every part of this world actually has to be an illusion." Weaver explained.

The two nodded in agreement as they accepted his explanation, what he said had to be true as there was quite simply no other logical explanation. They embraced the slight disappointment they felt inside quietly. The Mindplant vacations were not actually real in some respects and although the essence of their minds was no longer actually present inside their own bodies, they had definitely not been implanted into real human vessels but merely into some kind of simulation of human existence.

"Visual creates illusions and then more illusions around those illusions and you interact with them. It's like an onion with layers and layers that only become visible as you strip each layer away. The deeper layers of illusion that you cannot see are necessary to control how you interact with everyone around you, they determine what events occur inside the simulated environment whilst you are actually on your vacation and what you actually do whilst you participate in your vacation experience." Matter explained. "Mindplant is a highly complex, simulated environment."

"Are the bodies our minds are actually residing inside right now real? I mean do they actually belong to real people?" Connie asked slightly confused by the fact that Skylar's body seemed so real and so human.

"We don't actually know who the simulated bodies actually belong too and we haven't worked out how that part of the system actually works yet." Spiral explained as she attempted to offer an answer. "We think the bodies may belong to dead people and that their identities, DNA and personal attributes were incorporated and simulated somehow from morgue files, but we're not totally sure."

"If there is no actual physical exchange of consciousness into a real live human being's body that exists, not even on a temporary basis, how does this actually work?" Quorn asked. "How do our minds exist outside of our bodies?"

"It's just the mission simulations and lifestyles of the bodies you are within that are fake. Computer generated illusions by Visual." Matter insisted. "Your consciousness, your thoughts and your mind were actually really transferred into the profiles of the simulated dead bodies that exist somehow within the Mindplant system. Your mind right now is not actually present inside your own body and whilst you are on your vacation inside Mindplant. Your mind has to actually be transferred back into your body before you can leave. It's quite a complex blend and marriage they've created between reality and illusion that combines some aspects of both, those strands are then weaved carefully together to form the overall Mindplant environment."

"We don't fully understand it ourselves yet." Concept explained as he shook his head. "We don't actually have all the answers but we're hoping Maverick does."

"Can we actually get out of here?" Quorn urged, anxious to focus on the most important issue at hand.

"How did you even find out about Maverick?" Connie enquired as she pondered over his existence further for a moment.

"Until we track down Maverick, we're not actually sure that we can get out of here ourselves. We just don't have all the answers I'm afraid Quorn." Concept explained as he stood up and paced the room thoughtfully. "We discovered his existence when we infiltrated some old system files that existed about the Unoccupied Zone, files that were no longer utilized, buried and forgotten about. Files hidden within a fragment of one of the systems we found. We then started to search for him, but they're searching for him too apparently as although he created the system with Barbelo, something happened between them that wasn't positive and he then became stuck inside it. We don't know why or how but we do know they're hunting him down, just as they're hunting us down."

"But if he's stuck inside Mindplant too, how can he possibly help us?" Quorn enquired as he glanced at Concept's face in complete bewilderment as he deliberated the obvious contradiction internally, that a man who was trapped in Mindplant as they were would possibly be able to free them or anyone else.

"Quorn, he's the only hope we have." Concept explained quietly as he drew closer to him and laid his arm gently upon his. "If Maverick can't get us out, no one else can."

The room fell silent as everyone listened to Concept speak and accepted the reality that all their hopes rested on one man, one man that could not be found and one man that like them was being hunted down by Visual and the Exterminators.

"What happens if we die? What happens if they kill us?" Quorn asked. "Do we return to our own bodies or enter inside another body in the Mindplant system?"

Concept shook his head. "We're not actually sure yet, no one was willing to die in order to find out. It wouldn't help anyone else really as those left behind would never actually know what happened to them once they'd died." He insisted. "Finding Maverick is our only solution."

Everyone in the room nodded in agreement as they accepted Concept's wisdom and the final conclusion of the discussion. The search for Maverick would continue the next day and hopefully one day soon, they would actually find him and be able return to their own bodies. Tomorrow would bring fresh hope and a fresh chance of salvation as they embraced the reality that the day was indeed over and no further attempts to find Maverick that day could actually be made.

The remainder of the night the group spent inside the underground station as they relaxed and bunked down in the iron frame bunk beds situated in the small rooms at the bottom of the passageway that led off to the right hand side of the junction. The surroundings were very basic and a far cry from the lavish apartments that Quorn and Connie had enjoyed whilst on their respective Mindplant vacations and they missed the comforts they'd enjoyed. They adapted however graciously, appreciative and thankful just to have a safe place for the night where they could actually rest their heads. Grateful to be sheltered from the unknown threats that might lie lurking outside in the shadows of the night and grateful that they were not completely alone.

When the next morning arrived everyone woke up relatively early as Concept visited each small room and gently shook each bed occupant inside the small, iron bunk bed frames. One by one they stirred as he encouraged and urged them to get up and prepare for the day ahead. Breakfast had already been prepared and Concept knew some makeshift showers would perhaps have to be taken, before the day's mission and plans were actually implemented and conducted.

"Rise and shine people. We have a lot to do today." Concept teased as he visited the final small bedroom and tapped gently on the iron frames of the bunk beds inside it.

The two bed occupants that lay on top of the bunk beds situated inside the room, Spiral and Weaver both started to stir from the depths of the peaceful sleep they'd managed to find the previous night and then climbed slowly out of the bunk beds still half asleep. One by one they landed on the ground and stretched their bodies out as they forced themselves to wake up and prepared to participate in the day ahead. There were early morning duties and tasks that had to be carried out that Concept had prepared for them as he demanded their attention immediately.

"We have a full day ahead of us people." Concept explained as he stood in the passageway outside the small bedrooms and addressed all the occupants inside the various small rooms in front of him. "We need to get moving."

The small rooms had no actual doors to open or close, just black, rectangular door frames and a gaping rectangular hole. Concept stood and watched everyone prepare as he waited for them patiently to join him as he planned the day ahead internally. Spiral was the first to depart as she bounced out into the passageway enthusiastically and stood beside him.

"What's the plan for today Concept?" Spiral asked politely as she grinned at him.

"We'll split into two groups, Quorn you'll come with us and we'll spend the day searching for Maverick. Spiral, Connie and Weaver you'll go out on the food scavenger hunt." Concept replied briskly.

Matter nodded obediently as he quickly dressed up and then fished a tiny, black comb out of his back trouser pocket, which he utilized to fix his hair in a tidy, attentive manner. Concept led his respective group down the hallway as soon as they were ready to depart and they left the food scavenger hunt group, Spiral, Weaver and Connie alone. The three hung back a little as they prepared themselves for their day in a slightly more leisurely fashion and indulged in some make shift showers, they then gathered inside the control room and nibbled on some crusts of bread and drank mugs of warmish milk as they attempted to fill the gap inside their stomachs.

"Is everyone ready?" Spiral finally asked as she stood up and smiled as she urged them to depart from the control room which they were now seated inside. "We should really get moving."

"What is the food scavenger hunt exactly?" Connie asked curiously as she drew closer to Spiral and the two stood beside the control room door.

"We go out and search for food and things that we might be able to use." Spiral explained.

"What happens if you don't find any food?" Connie enquired, vaguely aware that their hunt might not actually be successful and that they may return hungry and without any edible items with which to satisfy their empty stomachs.

"Sometimes we catch rats, mice and other vermin in the underground tunnels nearby or fish in the river." Spiral explained. "Whatever we catch, we then cook on the fire stand further down the underground railway passage. It's not elegant but it fills the gap. It's rare that we actually ever go totally hungry."

Connie grimaced as the thought of eating vermin suddenly struck and appalled her. "Sounds gross." She replied.

Spiral smiled as she held Connie's arm gently and led her out of the control room towards the exit as Weaver stood up and followed them quietly. He stopped off on his way at a large wall cupboard situated in the passageway outside the control room door to collect some laser guns and once he had enough guns for all of them he closed the cupboard door and followed them outside towards the platform that led back up to the surface and exterior Mindplant world.

"We can't always find good food." Spiral explained to Connie as she walked briskly down the train station platform. "Sometimes we have to resort to other solutions."

The two women arrived at the foot of the stairs that led up towards the street and then paused as they waited for Weaver to catch up with them. He arrived a few seconds later and then handed them both small, silver laser guns that he took out of the pockets inside his jacket and smiled.

"Do we really need these?" Connie asked slightly concerned by the thought that she actually needed to carry a weapon and totally reluctant to actually do so.

Weaver smiled gently as he absorbed the worried expression on her face. "We always carry them, just in case." He explained as he attempted to appease and reassure her. "They're more of a precaution than a necessity."

The laser guns themselves were so small that they fitted neatly inside their jacket pockets, which meant they could be easily concealed from anyone who may glance at them and it immediately reassured Connie that they were not noticeable. The three once armed continued towards the surface quietly as they made their way up the stairs that led outside to the street and prepared to face the simulated Mindplant world. The streets outside the train station were deserted and empty as they exited and Connie was slightly confused by the absence of people as she glanced around the surface of the simulated Mindplant street.

"Where are all the people? I mean when we arrived here last night it was late and it was quiet, but now its early morning and there's still no one around." Connie asked Spiral and Weaver curiously.

"This part of the city is on the outskirts, it's always quite deserted and abandoned. It's known as the Unoccupied Zone." Weaver explained. "No one actually usually ventures this far away from the main city centre. You're lucky you actually found us here really. No one else has."

Connie, Spiral and Weaver started to walk towards one end of the street as they picked their way through the debris and rocks scattered and strewn all over the abandoned road. When they arrived at the end of the road, they then quickly turned into another road which was also empty and similar in nature in terms of its deserted and depilated state. The run down state of the area made it quite apparent to Connie at this point that Visual didn't actually bother to maintain the unoccupied areas of the city and simply ignored them.

This part of the city was called the 'Unoccupied Zone' for a reason, not only was it unoccupied but it was also run down and unkempt. The streets looked untidy and some of the buildings lay in ruins, desperately in need of repair. The three continued to walk for approximately another fifteen minutes through the quiet streets, until they finally arrived at an area that bustled with life. They stood quietly on the corner of the street as they concealed themselves slightly inside the entrance of a building on the edge of the more vibrant area and watched the simulated people walk around the square nearby as they conducted their affairs.

"Are they real people or illusions?" Connie asked as she pondered further as to their existence for a moment.

"Some might be real, majority are definitely not I guess. A few might be vacationers like us perhaps." Weaver replied.

"How do you know who is who?" Connie enquired immediately as she answered his response with another question, somewhat confused as she observed the people nearby curiously.

"We don't, so we just ignore everyone." Spiral explained as she shrugged her shoulders. "We just act like we're program simulations too, that way we don't get caught or attract unnecessary attention."

"All the program simulations are controlled by Visual, he keeps them functioning so that the

MINDPLANT: TRIMORPHIA

Mindplant program world works and seems real. From what we've worked out, the people generated by Visual mainly perform the same routine tasks every day, except when they actually engage and interact on Mindplant vacationer's missions or activities. When they actually interact on vacationer's missions, they then deviate from their usual patterns and tasks as they follow an alternative program route to fulfil the objectives of the Mindplant vacationer's mission. They have to deviate this way in order to provide a full, interactive experience to each vacationer inside the program." Weaver explained.

"How do you act like a program simulation?" Connie asked curiously, slightly puzzled by the explanation that Spiral had offered her.

"Once we walk out in the streets in the Occupied Zone, amongst people and program simulations, we speak less, absolutely never speak to anyone else besides ourselves and one of us usually follows slightly behind whoever is leading." Weaver explained.

"And whatever you do, don't ever hesitate." Spiral insisted with a very serious expression on her face. "If you hesitate you stand out and then people will notice you. Being noticed is a very bad thing. You have to blend in if you want to survive."

Weaver waited for a few seconds and then stepped out into the street nearby quietly. Spiral watched him as she waited for around thirty seconds and then gently took Connie's arm and led her out onto the street alongside her as she followed him. The two women followed Weaver down the street at a slight distance as they walked past some office blocks, coffee shops, restaurants and a park situated in the centre of the square nearby. Some office workers were seated outside the coffee shops sprinkled around the square as they drank cups of coffee and engaged in discussions and they appeared totally normal to Connie as she passed them. They looked just like real people situated on any inner city street in the real world and there was no actual indication at all, that they or their surroundings were not real.

"They all look so real." Connie whispered to Spiral as they walked further down the busy, bustling street.

"The illusions are fabrications of fragmented data, designed to appease the soul and entice the flesh, even in the real world we're always surrounded by illusions. Mindplant is not really that different when you actually think about it. People's misrepresentations, false advertising and false media projections, Visual just created a fake world that's not so very different from our own." Spiral explained. "The only real difference is that in this world our desires are fulfilled vicariously, through simulations and other vessels that represent our physical existence which ultimately means we don't have to carry the burden or suffer the consequences of our actions."

"True." Connie replied as she reflected further on Spiral's explanation and the wisdom it contained for a few minutes internally.

The two women continued to follow Weaver as they walked through a few more streets until he finally he led them into a quiet backstreet alleyway. Unlike the bustle of the surrounding area they'd just passed through, it was empty, deserted and quiet. Situated halfway down one side of the alleyway was a solitary dumpster which stood right outside the back door of a café, Weaver quickly headed towards another dumpster situated on the other side of the alleyway slightly further down as he quickly hid behind it and then watched and waited quietly. Connie and Spiral joined him less than a minute later and smiled at him, relieved that they had all arrived safely and without any unplanned interruptions to their journey as they prepared to wait for the food they needed.

"It's not a glamorous, gourmet menu, but it sure beats rats and cockroaches." Spiral whispered to Connie as they crouched behind the dumpster.

The three watched the backdoor of the café nearby intensely as they focused their attention upon their hunger in eager anticipation. Hunger had by now started to flood into their stomachs as their bodies growled gently and expressed the need for food. The café whilst it only offered what could be rescued and salvaged from dumpster, still offered the best solution available to them even if it was in the form of sloppy leftovers. It definitely wasn't elegant, but it was food and their hungry bodies demanded that they should wait patiently for their hopes and appetites to be fulfilled as the hours quietly started to slip by.

On the other side of the city, Quorn-Montgomery, Concept and Matter arrived outside the old, abandoned museum that they'd identified as a possible location for Maverick that day and entered inside. They pushed open the huge, iron, black doors and entered into a large room which contained a few pieces of dusty furniture and a couple of battered statues as they ventured further into the dusty, unkempt building and pursued their effort to find Maverick. The building itself now only seemed to house dusty, disused statues, torn, damaged paintings, redundant equipment and broken windows and was clearly very run down and totally abandoned. Broken glass lay scattered all over the stone floor around them and as they made their way up some wide stairs situated at the far end of the room, they soon found themselves inside a huge, exhibition room. The broken shards of glass crunched below their feet as they entered inside the exhibition room which they found empty asides from some pieces of broken equipment and several battered statues that were strewn across it

A corner at the far end of the room had a ceiling that jutted out over part of the room which attracted their attention immediately and they rushed over towards it. On the ground underneath the small ceiling that jutted out over their heads as they drew closer they could clearly see the remnants of a fire. The three began to examine the area more closely enthusiastically, relieved that there was indeed some signs of life. The pile of ash lay dormant on the ground black, grey and extinguished as Matter knelt down beside it and picked some ashes up in his hand. He let some ashes slowly trickle back down to the ground through his fingers and then shook his head as he glanced back up at Concept's face for a moment.

Matter sighed. "The ashes are still a little warm." He explained in a frustrated tone. "We've just missed him again. He's gone again."

Concept nodded as he listened to Weaver and accepted their defeat. He sought to appease Matter as he placed a hand gently on his arm, the search for Maverick was frustrating for them all and every time they thought they had almost found him, he'd already gone by the time they actually arrived at the location they'd identified on the system. Maverick was very elusive and seemed to be always one step ahead of them and whilst that frustrated them, deep down Concept knew Maverick had to be in order to actually survive. He was being hunted down every day just like they were, though the hunt for Maverick he imagined was slightly more aggressive than the hunt for the missing vacationers. Whilst it was positive that Maverick was one step ahead of Visual's trackers, that added to the difficulty of actually finding him however and also to the possibility of the group finding a possible escape.

"We'll try and locate him again once we get back to our hideout. We're definitely getting closer." Concept insisted. "We better get out of here, if we managed to get this close to his most recent location that means the Exterminators probably won't be far behind us." He continued as he glanced around the room anxiously.

Matter nodded in agreement as he quickly stood up.

Both men were frustrated and the expression upon their faces said everything as they glanced around the large, warehouse like room and surveyed the deserted interior as they shook their heads.

"The ashes from the fire were still warm, that means he was here not long ago." Concept remarked as he patted Matter gently on the back. "That means we'll find him soon." He encouraged.

"Yeah I guess. Perhaps we just need to get up earlier and start our search a little earlier each day." Matter suggested.

Matter was responsible for most of the main tracking work regarding Maverick's possible location and that meant the responsibility for missing Maverick fell more heavily upon his shoulders and hence his disappointment was more severe. Missing Maverick again Matter immediately interpreted as a personal failure on his part and the glum expression on his face clearly expressed his inner sentiments.

"You're doing the best you can Matter." Concept politely reassured him. "Maverick is a very difficult target to track."

Matter nodded in response quietly.

The three men started to make their way back towards the top of the stairs as they accepted and surrendered to defeat. Quorn followed Matter and Concept a step or two behind quietly as he contemplated how close they had actually come to finding Maverick, the elusive being that they were searching for and desperately needed to meet and how close they had come to perhaps escaping the Mindplant vacation, their quest was indeed extremely frustrating.

A sudden noise inside the large exhibition suddenly distracted the three men and they stopped walking immediately. Concept and Matter rapidly scanned the large room for the source as they stood firmly rooted to the spot. They glanced at a corner of the room and quickly noticed two shapes start to form from a pile of sawdust situated upon the floor and Concept quickly stretched out towards Quorn-Montgomery and grabbed his arm, he then dragged him behind a nearby statue like object that was quite large in size as Matter followed them both in silence.

MINDPLANT: TRIMORPHIA

The two piles of sawdust on the floor started to increase in size until they were the size and shape of two large men and Concept motioned to the other two men next to him to be completely silent, they both complied with his request immediately. Various pieces of redundant equipment and statue like objects were scattered all around the room and luckily the statue Concept had actually chosen was large enough to shield them from view as the two Exterminators fully formed and their presence officially arrived inside the large exhibition room.

"Who are they?" Quorn whispered curiously into Concept's ear as he watched the two men fully form in front of his eyes, amazed and stunned by their sudden appearance.

"They are Exterminators. Exterminators can form anywhere within the Mindplant vacation world, out of any material object that has matter." Concept explained in a whisper as he replied. "If they find Maverick or us they'll kill us." He verified.

The three men continued to observe the Exterminator's manifestation occur silently as the two shapes nearby developed faces, right before their eyes. The two Exterminators were positioned between the three men and the entrance to the large exhibition room, which meant for the time being the three men were actually stuck right where they were as they crouched behind the statue they'd hidden behind silently and waited. Once the Exterminators had fully materialized, they walked briskly through the large interior of the room towards the corner where the ashes from Maverick's fire were situated and inspected them quietly for a few minutes. The Exterminators, Riotous and Chaos glanced at each other and shook their heads as they accepted that they too had actually missed Maverick.

"Maverick is gone." Riotous remarked as he kicked the ashes somewhat aggressively, irritated and perplexed at their failure. "We've missed him again."

Chaos drew closer to him and nodded in agreement. "We'll find him next time and when we do we'll finish him." He insisted somewhat more calmly. "He can't elude our grasp forever."

"Visual said, Maverick's using a masking system to evade our probes and now there are actually ten Randoms inside the Mindplant system. If they all actually find each other and they find Maverick to, we could have an astronomical problem on our hands." Riotous continued.

"We'll track them all down soon." Chaos replied. "It's just a matter of time now. If they'd died when they were supposed to, whilst on their Mindplant vacations then we wouldn't even have to clean up this mess in the first place."

"Visual's losing his touch." Riotous remarked.

"Barbelo did some system adjustments to the Mindplant program. That's why all these Randoms are lose inside Mindplant in the first place. That's why we were instructed to find them and kill them, to try and get them out. Visual's just cleaning up Barbelo's mess like we are." Chaos insisted.

Concept quickly took a laser gun out of his jacket and indicated silently towards Quorn and Matter to do the same as they continued to crouch behind the statue and they both complied immediately. The three men then sat completely still and hardly dared to draw a breath or move an inch as they continued to observe the Exterminators nearby quietly. Fear clung to every particle of air around them as it taunted them and filled their bodies and their stillness reflected the stillness of the damaged, battered statues that surrounded them as they froze.

The three men watched in total silence as Riotous and Chaos began to walk back down the large warehouse like room, towards the nearby exit as they gave up their search for Maverick for the day. Much like them, the two Exterminators seemed frustrated by their search which had borne no actual results as Maverick had managed to avoid them and slipped through their grasp. The two Exterminators paused for a moment beside a statue close to where the three men were hidden as they continued to deliberate over Maverick's absence further.

"The number of Randoms in the Mindplant system seems to be increasing every day. We really need to get this situation under control and very quickly, before they actually find Maverick." Riotous observed as knots of frustration tinged his voice with each word he spoke.

"If they actually find Maverick, they might even find a way out and escape from whatever Barbelo has planned for them, then she'll be really angry and she might even delete us." Chaos solemnly analysed.

"Don't worry we'll find them all soon, they can't hide forever." Riotus reassured him as he slapped his back gently.

Chaos and Riotous glanced around the abandoned, exhibition room quickly once more and then prepared to leave. There was nothing to stay there for and they shook their heads in frustration as they concluded their search, their search for Maverick that day was over and he'd beaten them again. The two Exterminators walked towards a wall next to the entrance of the room as they prepared to depart.

"Let's go back to base and see if Aggress, Strangler and Grim have had any luck locating any Randoms." Chaos suggested.

Riotous nodded.

The two Exterminators started to walk briskly towards the blank wall nearby and a few seconds later they simply seemed to melt into it as they abruptly disappeared. A flurry of sawdust immediately fell to the ground and formed two distinct piles as they vanished and their life forms disappeared just as suddenly as they'd arrived as each grain dropped down to the floor once more lifeless and redundant. Quorn, Matter and Concept watched their departure from behind the statue in silence as the two Exterminators completely disappeared right before their very eyes.

Matter stood up, stretched out his body and started to move out from behind the large statue they had hidden behind. "That was close." He remarked.

Quorn followed him quietly.

"That was too close." Concept insisted as he analysed how close they had actually come to being captured. He shook his head, the three men had definitely come closer to finding Maverick, but they had also come closer to possible capture and death at the hands of the Exterminators. He had no desire to be exposed to the Exterminators in such close physical proximity ever again as he accepted that they'd had a very narrow escape on that particular occasion. "Way too close." He muttered.

"What are Randoms?" Quorn asked curiously as he replayed the conversation he'd overheard the Exterminators having for a moment and speculated further as to who they were actually referring too.

"We are Randoms!" Concept explained as he patted him gently on the back and smiled. "You are a Random. I'm a Random. Everyone that goes missing inside the Mindplant system and that doesn't return after their vacation when they should do, are classified as a Randoms. It simply means that we now exist within the Mindplant world in a random status and that we might randomly appear anywhere and at any time. Randoms do not participate in the scheduled organised activities, events and situations that are simulated, generated and programmed by Visual, hence our existence within Mindplant is now Random and we are Randoms."

"I guess that kind of makes sense." Quorn remarked somewhat bemused by the nickname he'd been given and by the explanation that Concept had provided.

Matter walked back over towards the pile of ashes once more and shook his head with frustration. "So close to capture and we still didn't find Maverick." He stated in a somewhat mournful tone. "It's so sad and so frustrating."

"Let's get out of here." Concept urged as he walked over towards him and patted his back gently. "We don't know when the Exterminators might actually come back."

"I'm not scared even if they do come back." Matter insisted bravely. "They're just made out of whatever they form from. They're not really a huge threat to us."

"They're not called Exterminators for nothing." Concept remarked. "They probably change form when they're in attack mode and solidify into more deadly beings. I wouldn't like to risk it and actually try to find out. Plus they can always use weapons and they don't even need to be close to us or made of anything special to do that."

"What do you think Barbelo's plan is, if she actually catches us?" Quorn asked curiously. "Or if the Exterminators manage to kill us?"

"I'm not really sure." Concept replied. "But she's definitely up to something, even her own programs mentioned that she'd performed some strange adaptations to the Mindplant system. It could be dangerous."

The three men made their way quietly back towards the wide stairs as they departed from the large exhibition room within the abandoned museum and headed back towards the exterior door that led to the street. Their mood was slightly subdued as they walked as they all knew the search for Maverick would have to start again as soon as they returned to their hideout and Matter in particular knew he would actually have to spend that evening analysing each point within the four boxes in the grid pedantically. It had been so frustrating to be so close to actually finding Maverick and yet so far away and the despondent mood that engulfed the three men, rested firmly on their shoulders as they took each step somewhat glumly.

On the other side of the city, Connie, Spiral and Weaver continued to watch the back door of the café as their wait became excruciatingly painful. Lunchtime had arrived and departed and as they continued to wait and the afternoon passed by extremely slowly, they'd begun to become increasingly frustrated. There hadn't been a single movement at the back door of the café and no signs of food at all. The evening finally started to draw in as it crunched down on top of their shoulders and a duskiness settled into the air that surrounded them as it drove the daylight firmly into hiding and nestled comfortably into the environment as the day departed and the evening prepared for night to fall.

Weaver shook his head totally discouraged by the hours that had passed and the lack of food discarded by the café they'd selected earlier that morning. By now the food venue should have thrown away something he concluded. Perhaps, he mused it was time to give up the wait, call it a day and find another solution as the café they'd found that day was just not participating with their dietary requirements. There were no Exterminators anywhere around to guard it as there sometimes were at venues that offered food solutions and he had hoped that they'd have been able to actually secure food there quite easily. The three had waited hours however and even through two meal sittings and still the café staff had not actually disposed of any waste food at all.

Weaver glanced at Spiral and Connie quietly, they looked just as fed up and bored as he was. Just as he was about to stand up, pull the plug and abandon the wait however, the back door of the café finally opened and a man walked out with a large bucket in his hands. He sighed with relief as the man emptied the contents of the large bucket into the nearby dumpster and then walked back inside the doorway he'd exited from just a moment before. A few minutes passed by as Weaver waited patiently just to ensure the man wasn't actually going to return before he leapt out from behind the dumpster they were hidden behind and made his way quickly over towards the other dumpster situated next to the back door of the café.

Spiral smiled as she turned to face Connie. "At least we'll eat well today." She insisted. "Sometimes Exterminators guard the food venues and we can't get access to any food. When they guard our usual food sources we then have to spend more hours searching for a new source. It can be very problematic and very time consuming."

"What or who exactly are Exterminators?" Connie asked curiously.

"Visual's killers, they look for us inside the Mindplant program and can appear anywhere at any given moment in time." She explained. "That's why we have to find Maverick as soon as we can, he knows the truth and I think he'll know how we can escape."

The two women continued to watch Weaver quietly as he opened his rucksack and pulled out a large, plastic container from inside it. He quickly started to pluck out some slabs of meat and potatoes from inside the dumpster that the man from the café had dumped inside it just a few minutes beforehand as they watched him. The container was quickly filled up as he scooped each item he wanted out of the dumpster and deftly placed them inside the plastic container situated in his hands. Once he was satisfied that the container was full, he quickly placed it back inside the rucksack once more and then made his back towards Spiral and Connie and nodded at them.

"Let's go." Weaver urged.

Spiral nodded and stood up quickly as she held onto Connie-Skylar's arm and guided her towards the exit of the alleyway they'd just spent most of the day hidden inside. Weaver organized his rucksack as he shut it and then swung it over his shoulder and then quickly followed them. When they arrived at the edge of the alleyway, the two women paused as they waited for Weaver to catch up with them, he arrived beside them just a few seconds later and then nodded at them both as he walked back out onto the nearby street that lay directly in front of them. The two women waited for just under thirty seconds as they hid from the sight of passers-by behind the wall of a building, anxious not to be spotted by anyone on the main, city street nearby, before they stepped out onto the busy, city street and quickly followed him.

The three started to weave their way through the passers-by as they made their way back through the bustling, city streets and headed towards the underground railway station once more and the sanctuary where they knew, they would be safe. Thirty minutes later when they finally arrived at the top of the road where their hideaway was actually situated, Weaver quickly checked the street was clear before they actually entered inside the underground structure, to ensure it was safe to proceed. The underground station was a closely guarded secret and so far the group had managed to remain there completely undetected, but each time they actually ventured outside onto the city streets of the Mindplant world and entered into the Occupied Zone, they all knew they ran the risk of being sighted or followed back there.

A few minutes later Weaver led the two women towards the underground station entrance as he quickly reassured them that everything was fine and that they had not actually been followed back from the city. The three entered back inside the underground station satisfied and happy that their mission had been successful as they looked forward with eager anticipation to consuming the food that Weaver carried safely inside his rucksack. Their bodies were exhausted and worn out by the long day they'd had and the painful wait they'd endured for the morsels of food they'd finally actually managed to retrieve.

Rats scurried across the floor in front of Connie-Skylar and Spiral as they made their way back down the underground station platform and headed towards the safety of the control room once more. Weaver followed them a few steps behind as he reflected quietly on the food hunt that day and why it had actually taken so long to yield the results they required. He'd have to look for another food source for the next day's hunt he quickly decided, that source wasn't adequate, they'd been out in the street for an entire day, which had exposed them to the risk of being discovered by Exterminators for a longer period of time than was absolutely necessary.

Connie winced and suddenly yelped in shock as a rat darted out in front of her and almost touched Skylar's foot. "Yuck." She yelled as a horrified expression immediately crossed Skylar's face.

Spiral giggled and held her arm as she attempted to comfort Connie. "You get used to them after a while." She insisted. "They look worse than they really are."

"They look awful and they bite people." Connie insisted.

"Only if you taste good." Weaver teased.

Rats were not like mice, they were less intimidated by the presence of human beings and Connie knew they would even actually attack people as they were braver than mice and were best avoided whenever possible. She quickly veered away from the path of the rat and walked along one side of the platform as close to the wall as possible as she attempted to avoid further encounters.

"Do you think the others will be back soon?" Connie asked Spiral curiously as she yearned internally for the presence of Concept and Quorn once more. She'd missed them both throughout that day and now she was eager to see them.

Spiral nodded reassuringly in response. "They'll be back soon." She replied as she smiled and nodded. "They have to be, we have an agreement that when the night arrives and darkness falls, everyone in the group has to return to the underground station as when night comes, most of the simulated people in the Mindplant program actually disappear. That means our presence is more noticeable due to their absence and if we're actually still out on the streets that puts us in grave danger because Exterminators patrol the streets of the city at night."

The three entered back inside the main control room a few minutes later as Weaver walked quietly at the rear consumed by his thoughts. Once inside the large, control room, Weaver opened his rucksack and quickly plucked out the large, full, food container and then handed it to Spiral before he sat down in front of the system and switched it on. The grid map appeared on the screen in front of him as he started to search and inspect every inch of it, absorbed by his task of finding an alternative food source for the next day.

"Right time to sort out some food. I'm completely famished." Spiral remarked. "What are you looking for Weaver?"

"I need to look for an alternative food source for tomorrow." He explained as the two women watched him quietly. "That one just took too long to provide any results. It's way too risky to go back there again."

Spiral nodded. "I think you're right. Do you want to come with me Connie, I'll be sorting out the food in the kitchen or do you want to stay with Weaver?" She asked politely as she prepared to depart.

"I'll stay with Weaver if you don't mind." Connie replied. "I just want to wait here for the others and make sure they're alright."

"Cool I'll be in the kitchen." Spiral replied as she nodded. "If you need me for anything, it's just past the bedrooms we slept in last night and the bathroom."

Connie nodded.

Spiral left the room a few seconds later as Weaver continued to focus on the grid in front of him thoughtfully. He touched the screen in front of him and it split into ten smaller screens and then zoomed in on some streets and roads as he started to search the city. His eyes skimmed over each focus point as he navigated his way around each street quickly and searched each one rapidly as Connie sat on top of a nearby crate and watched him quietly.

"What are you looking for? What do you need to see?" Connie finally ventured after a few minutes of silence. She'd been slightly unsure about voicing her question, fearful that she might actually distract Weaver from his task which seemed to demand intense concentration from him, however she'd managed to pluck up the courage to interrupt him as the urge to break the silence between them overwhelmed her and curiosity defeated her uncertainty.

"A few things really." Weaver explained politely as he turned to face her and paused for a moment. "There are camera's situated in each street throughout the heart of the city. They monitor the key vantage points within the grid, these vantage points we've identified as the city's main activity centres. We don't have coverage of the whole city however and their capacity is limited." He continued. "I'm looking for possible food sources that are not too close to areas that are heavy with activity throughout the day. The less people that are around, the better as it means we'll be less at risk from being spotted. I'm also doing a spot check on Maverick, just in case I can see any of his tracks at the same time."

"How come you know all about this stuff?" Connie asked curiously as she appreciated his knowledge and expertise regarding the city surveillance systems further for a moment.

"Well whilst I was on my Mindplant vacation, I was actually a high tech security specialist which meant I actually had access to some camera systems and equipment and I even managed to bring some of the equipment along with me when we arrived here. It was really helpful as that allowed us to tap into most of the city and the camera surveillance systems almost immediately." Weaver explained.

"That was a huge help." Connie replied politely.

Weaver nodded in agreement as he smiled, slightly flattered by her remark. "It definitely comes in handy sometimes." He replied.

After twenty minutes or so Connie grew bored as she stood up and exited the room. She made her way down the dark passageway that led towards the small bedrooms where she'd spent the previous night as she attempted to occupy herself in something she could actually contribute too. Once inside the small bedroom that housed the tiny, iron bunk beds she quickly located Skylar's white, equipment case and returned to the control room once more with it tucked tightly under one of her arms.

She entered back inside the control room and sat down next to Weaver on an empty crate as she placed the equipment case upon her lap and then opened it. "I managed to bring this along with me." Connie explained as she began to pick out pieces of equipment and devices from inside it.

"What is it?" Weaver asked curiously as he attempted to peer inside the interior of the equipment case and inspect some of the devices situated inside it. "What do those do?" He asked.

"Skylar whose simulated body I'm actually living inside right now is actually a high tech vigilante, this is her equipment case and these are her tools." Connie explained as she opened up the case more widely to reveal the tools inside and then placed it upon an empty, grey, crate nearby.

Weaver smiled as he glanced inside the white, equipment case curiously and then began to pick up, examine and inspect each item it contained. Connie began to explain to him what each item situated inside the case actually did as he rummaged through the contents eagerly and they engaged in a deep discussion about how each item could possibly be utilized to assist the group in the search for Maverick or in the search for a possible escape route and the other daily tasks they had to perform in order to survive as thirty minutes quickly flew by. Connie attempted to distract herself from thoughts regarding the safety of Concept, Quorn and Matter as she fully participated in the conversation and the worries soon fled from her mind as she welcomed not only the much needed distraction but also embraced the possible contributions she could offer to the group that might actually assist them with their escape, from not only Mindplant but also from Barbelo's plans for them.

CROSSING PATHS

The control room was quiet as Spiral sauntered inside and balanced a tray carefully on her arm which was filled with bowls of piping hot, steaming food. She walked towards Connie and Weaver and then placed the tray down on the top of a vacant crate next to them both and then picked up a bowl of hot food for herself. Steam rose from each bowl as she sat down on a nearby crate and started to devour the contents of her bowl hungrily.

Spiral glanced up and paused for a moment. "Help yourselves." She encouraged as she smiled at Connie and Weaver. "Today's offerings and menu isn't that bad." Her expression suddenly changed as a worried frown crossed it. "Aren't the others back yet? It's getting very late." She asked.

Nigh-time was fast approaching and Spiral knew that Exterminators lurked on the streets at night, hungrily searching for any vacationers they could find that had deviated from their vacations and escaped the fate that Barbelo had intended for them. They hunted them fearlessly as they sought them out upon the emptier streets that night-time adorned itself with and absolutely no one wanted to be captured. It was an undesirable position to be in and nagging worries scurried through her mind as her concerns grew deeper and deeper as each moment passed. They were the hunted and the prey and the Exterminators were the relentless hunters.

Weaver shook his head. "No they're not back yet." He confirmed as he picked up a bowl from the tray nearby and some cutlery and then eagerly spooned mouthfuls of food into his mouth. He nodded a few seconds later as he glanced at Spiral's face. "You've done a great job Spiral, it's definitely very edible. No one would actually know that it came out of a dumpster."

Spiral smiled. "I try my best to please even with garbage."

Connie-Skylar giggled.

A few minutes later Matter, Concept and Quorn-Montgomery finally arrived back as they entered inside the control room and immediately greeted everyone. The three men smiled at the sight of the tin, silver bowls filled to the brim with food as they sat down on some vacant crates scattered around the control room.

"Something smells semi decent." Concept remarked. "Good, I'm starving."

"I'm so glad you guys are back." Spiral exclaimed excitedly as she leapt up to her feet and prepared to serve food to the hungry men that had just returned. "I'll sort out some bowls of food for you three guys now, just give me a few minutes."

Concept, Matter and Quorn-Montgomery nodded weakly, physically exhausted from their escapade that day, which had not only taken them to the other side of the city as they'd hunted for Maverick but afterwards also on a salvage hunt for equipment parts. They were extremely grateful to finally return to the sanctuary the underground station provided with a few pieces of equipment in hand that could help them in their search and they welcomed Spiral's attentiveness as her warmth embraced them.

"I'll help you." Matter volunteered as he quickly stood up. "I'm not scared of the kitchen like some of these guys are. I'm a modern man."

Concept smiled.

The two left the room as Matter followed Spiral towards the makeshift kitchen situated at the other end of the passageway and they began to discuss the events of their day. Spiral delicately balanced her bowl of food in her hand and continued to eat it hungrily as they disappeared into the dusty, dark passageways to collect the remaining food that Spiral had saved for the other group's return.

The four that remained inside the control room started to discuss their day as they sat on the scattered crates around the room. Connie longed to ask the two men that had returned about Maverick but held her tongue for a moment as she attempted to be patient and give them some time to gather their strength. Weaver continued to shovel spoonful's of food into his mouth as he glanced up at them and urged them to discuss the results of their mission that day, he was slightly less patient than Connie.

"I guess you guys didn't find Maverick then." Weaver quickly observed as he interrupted the silence and stated the obvious.

Concept shook his head. "We didn't. He'd gone by the time we'd arrived." He explained. "We'll have to try again tomorrow."

Weaver nodded in understanding. "He sure is slippery."

"Why can't you find him? Why does he keep moving around?" Connie asked curiously.

"He has to avoid the Exterminators." Concept explained. "They're trying to find him and exterminate him as he knows the truth about the Mindplant program."

A few minutes later, Matter and Spiral both returned with bowls of piping hot food in their hands as they entered inside the control room and passed them out to Concept and Quorn-Montgomery. The two men smiled as they accepted the bowls of food appreciatively and then started to eat hungrily. Matter sat down on top of a vacant crate next to Concept and started to eat his own bowl of food as he listened to Weaver discuss his day.

"Connie gave me some helpful equipment and she actually knows how to use it." Weaver explained in-between the mouthfuls of food. "She's got a system interrogator device and that could help us find Maverick or maybe even a way out of here." He continued.

Concept thought about his suggestion for a few seconds before he offered a response. "Sure we can use tools like that but not here. That would have to be done somewhere else, perhaps on the other side of the city. We need to make the most of the equipment but also avoid Visual tracking the intrusion. If we utilized that kind of device here, it would led them straight to our hiding place." Concept explained. "We just can't take that kind of risk."

Weaver nodded in agreement as he accepted Concept's thoughtful response. "Who'll go to the other side of the city with Connie then?" He prompted as he demanded an immediate plan of action.

Concept glanced up at his face thoughtfully for a moment before he responded. "Matter, Quorn and I will escort Connie tomorrow. Weaver you can go out with Spiral on the usual food scavenging hunt. Quorn's assassination skills might come in handy and Matter your matter manipulation skills may be needed also." Concept insisted.

Everyone inside the control room nodded in agreement.

When the next morning arrived it stole in through the darkness of the previous night and tore it to shreds as it burst into the day and the occupants of the underground hideaway started to stir. The iron bunk beds that held them firmly inside as they'd slept peacefully within the small compact bedrooms, had given everyone in the hideaway a peaceful night's rest, despite the flimsy mattresses and as soon as they rose, they prepared enthusiastically for the day ahead. The group had slept well after midnight the previous night as they'd stayed up to formulate their plans for the next day and as a result they'd woken up slightly later than usual that morning.

The underground hideaway was filled with excitement as all its occupants, showered and dressed as they prepared for the day ahead. Connie was the last to enter the shower in the makeshift bathroom and as she stood underneath the hosepipe, the sparse drops of water dripped gently down upon Skylar's body as she rubbed her skin gently with a bar of soap. The water bubbled and spurted out of the small, thin hose, which protruded from a small, tap like object which hung down from the wall nearby. The straggly hose which had been strapped to the wall with a piece of rope was far from elegant and it was very basic in that the flimsy provision and had no real substance to it, but it was just about sufficient enough to shower with. The water was icy cold as it hit Skylar's skin and she shivered. Despite the cold temperature of the water however, Connie still managed to embrace the delicious freshness it provided somewhat as the drops ran down over

Skylar's skin and sparkled. It certainly wasn't luxury, but she did feel refreshed afterwards.

The underground station hideaway itself was powered by old fashioned power generators that provided just enough energy for a few basic necessities but heating of water or the air inside it, was just a luxury the generators couldn't quite stretch too. The generators barely provided enough lighting and power to operate the grid system and hot water had been deemed a non-essential requirement by Concept who had prioritised finding and tracking Maverick above access to hot showers. Heating enough water to bathe with each day was just an impossible realization and everyone had accepted and grown accustomed to the cold showers they had to take each morning graciously, including Quorn and Connie.

"We can't plug into any energy sources used by the main Mindplant system or it will send signals which can be tracked." Matter had explained to Connie and Quorn the morning after they'd arrived. "I've managed to find a way to manipulate the old generators I found here when we discovered the hideaway, so we do have access to some basic power provisions, but it's definitely not going to be what your accustomed too and you won't be able to have any hot showers at all."

The two had understood the difficulties the group faced and had accepted the situation graciously, they like everyone else in the group had very little choice and they certainly could not return to either Skylar or Montgomery's apartment, not if they wanted to stay alive and certainly not just to take a hot shower.

Cooking for mealtimes was usually conducted on two small, electric rings inside the small kitchen and the rings were also utilized to prepare water for hot drinks and to clean utensils. Sometimes food was also cooked by natural fire in one of the underground tunnels nearby, especially when it came to vermin or fish, in order to ensure that such morsels of food were crispy and cooked well enough to eat. Rats, Spiral had worked out were much easier to consume when their skin was fried to a crisp as the crunchiness seemed to somehow distract from what they actually were and make them slightly easier to swallow. Absolutely no one wanted to assume the laborious task of trying to heat small pans full of water to actually clean their bodies with and the lack of power and time constraints quite simply did not permit such luxuries anyway. Finding Maverick and food were tasks that Concept had insisted the group should prioritize and hence that meant, warm water showers were totally out of the question.

A small, strip cloth hung down from a hook on the wall nearby and as Connie finished showering, she stretched Skylar's hand out towards it, it wasn't quite a towel but it was adequate enough to dry her body with. She quickly dried herself off and then dressed up, rapidly aware that she was actually the last person to get up that morning and that the group she was supposed to go out into the city with that day, would now actually be waiting for her.

When Connie-Skylar entered inside the main control room everyone immediately turned to face her as her mission group for that day quickly stood up and prepared to leave. Connie had definitely delayed their departure and even though no one actually expressed it directly to her, she could tell.

"Ready when you are." Connie said as she smiled slightly apologetically at Concept, who by now she'd actually started to take quite a shine too.

Concept nodded as he picked up a laser gun and waist holster from the top of a nearby crate and then walked over towards her. He tied the laser gun firmly around Connie's waist as he quickly armed her and then concealed the weapon with the bottom of her top. The moment between them was filled with sexual tension as he touched her waist for a moment longer that was actually necessary and glanced into her eyes. She inhaled deeply as he stood extremely close to her and his breath brushed against her face, it was fast, heavy, deliciously warm and filled with masculine energy as it gently caressed her cheek.

"Just in case you need it." Concept explained as he justified the presence of the laser gun.

Connie-Skylar smiled in response and nodded in understanding whilst inside herself, she toyed with the sudden urge to return his comment and flirt with him for a second but restrained herself from actually doing so. The words 'I don't know about the gun but I definitely need you right now' quickly ran through her mind as she teased herself playfully. She analysed Concept and her attraction towards him further for a moment as she stood quietly next to him, Concept was rugged, charming and handsome in a way that Quorn wasn't, much closer to Connie in terms of age and his presence simply oozed and exuded masculinity from every pore. He wasn't her usual type but something inside her deeply attracted her towards him, something that she quite simply couldn't begin to explain, not even to herself. Deep down she was attracted to him in a way that Quorn could never compete with and since Quorn and Connie had never actually agreed to engage each other in a romantic capacity, she felt free to explore her attraction to Concept more fully, if indeed the opportunity actually presented itself. For now however, Connie held her tongue as she accepted it wasn't exactly the appropriate time to explore such attractions more fully as there were definitely more pressing issues that had to be faced and resolved first. Romantic possibilities that such attractions created, had to for now remain completely abandoned, neglected and alone as Connie continued to focus on the more pertinent problems the group all faced together. Her attraction to Concept would definitely have to wait, but it was definitely something when she actually returned to her real body, she was more than willing to explore and investigate very thoroughly.

The control room fell silent as it emptied and the first group departed as Spiral and Weaver watched everyone leave and bade them farewell solemnly. The worries that clung to each of their minds were unspoken as they both accepted that the difficult mission the other group aimed to achieve that day significantly increased their exposure to danger.

Concept paused just outside the control room door for a moment and glanced quickly back at Spiral and Weaver before he continued his journey towards the surface and smiled. "Will you guys be ok?" He asked, slightly worried that the two might feel slightly abandoned as he took the rest of the group on a mission that was situated much further away than usual.

Spiral nodded reassuringly back at him as if to indicate that everything was perfectly fine, though deep down inside she felt extremely worried and uncomfortable about their mission, but she knew it was definitely a necessary one. "We'll be fine. Just make sure you guys actually come back in one piece." She insisted as she smiled warmly at him.

"Should we try to look for Maverick after we finish our food hunt?" Weaver enquired.

"Definitely and we'll try and look for him too whilst we're out." Concept replied as he nodded in agreement, appreciative of Weaver's suggestion. He turned to face Matter who was situated right next to him. "Let's go." Concept insisted as he brandished a laser gun in his hands. "The later we leave, the later we'll return." He remarked.

The four disappeared completely from the passageway outside the control room as they quickly made their way towards the surface and left Weaver and Spiral to prepare for their food scavenger hunt. The two made their usual preparations quietly as they reflected internally about how alone they would actually be for the remainder of that day. They both knew it was highly unlikely the other group would return until very late that evening and that meant they would both spend longer than usual without their protection and companionship.

The underground platform was silent as the four walked briskly along it as Connie contemplated curiously for a moment whether Concept and Matter could possibly be Mindplant program simulations themselves. Perhaps she speculated, all four they'd encountered inside the underground station were part of the vacation simulation and perhaps this was the final mission. It was a strange notion but it wasn't beyond the scope of possibilities after all Barbelo had created this obscure world and perhaps this was the final adventure inside it. She played devil's advocate for a moment and decided to interrogate Concept delicately as her thoughts and doubts teased her mind and simply refused to depart.

MINDPLANT: TRIMORPHIA

The three men in her group had actually walked along the full length of the train station platform slightly ahead of her and by now had actually reached the base of the stairs that led up towards the surface. Quorn-Montgomery and Matter had actually already started to make their way up towards the street that lay directly above their heads, but Concept had waited at the foot of the stairs as he'd hung back for a moment. He smiled at Connie-Skylar warmly as she approached him.

"You guys aren't an extra adventure inside the Mindplant program are you?" Connie teased Concept gently as she flashed a playful grin at him. "I mean you're definitely real people trapped here like we are right?" She queried as she approached the first step.

Concept smiled at the question she'd raised as he turned to face her. "Connie I would never lie to you. I'm as real as you are. I'm really trapped inside here too just like you are." He replied as he touched her hand gently for a moment and stared into her eyes intensely. "I don't blame you for asking me though. In Mindplant it's hard to know what's real and what isn't."

Connie began to speculate what Concept might actually look like in real life as they hung back at the foot of the stairs together for a few seconds more. The two other men by this time had actually disappeared from sight as they'd walked out onto the street above their heads, which meant they were truly alone and had a moment together they could explore in any way they wished to.

Connie quickly grabbed the chance to present another question to Concept that she was desperate to know the answer to as she smiled at him. "What do you look like in real life Concept?" She ventured curiously as she attempted to ascertain whether her attraction to Concept could actually be sustained in the real world when they did indeed actually return to it. Her current attraction towards him, she was very much aware was currently reliant and based on a superficial and artificial image, that may or may not transcend as expected when he actually returned to his real physical body and himself.

Concept nodded and smiled as he immediately sought to reassure her. "I'm around the same age and I kind of look a bit similar. I selected a profile that closely resembled my own in terms of physical appearance when I came on this vacation. I didn't want to deviate too far from my physical self as tempting as it was to actually do so." He insisted. "Although the missions and lifestyle I participated within whilst on my vacation are vastly different from my real life. How about you?"

"Well in real life I'm actually about five years older than I am here. I think that's about the only huge difference, though Skylar is definitely prettier than I am and quite a bit taller. My eyes are really green, not brown and my hair is really black not brown." Connie explained honestly and humbly.

Concept nodded and smiled. "We better get moving." He replied as he gently took her arm and led her up the stairs. "Those guys will be waiting for us."

The two walked out of the underground station entrance and found Quorn-Montgomery and Matter waiting for them right beside it. Neither of the two men, asked them what they'd been doing or why the two had been delayed as they avoided prying into their private discussion and instead focused upon the task ahead.

"Where do we go from here Concept?" Quorn enquired quietly as it suddenly dawned on him, whatever romantic interest he held in Connie had now slowly slipped out of his grasp and it was unlikely that it would ever be realized. Quorn knew, he'd allowed Concept the space too swoop in and now Concept held Connie's heart firmly in his hands. He accepted his position solemnly as he glanced at Concept's face and ignored the romantic invasion and his loss in the battle to win Connie's heart.

"We have to go this way." Concept explained as he pointed towards one end of the road and nodded. "We probably need to find some kind of transportation too."

The group started to walk briskly through the quiet, deserted streets of the Unoccupied Zone as they scanned the each one for some possible means of transportation. Once they'd walked about ten blocks, they suddenly found a solitary car parked in one of the streets and Concept quickly pounced on it. The group of four quickly gathered around him as he approached the car door and plucked a tool out of his rucksack. He slipped the metal object inside the gap between the door and the body of the vehicle and it immediately slid open. Once the vehicle interior was accessible, he quickly motioned towards the rest of the group to get inside.

"Connie, can you override the vehicle's controls." Concept ventured as he entered inside the car.

Connie nodded and removed a device from her equipment case that she'd brought along with her. "I can try."

"It'll be much quicker this way. It'll save us about three hours walking time." Concept explained as he glanced quickly around at the rest of the group and attempted to justify his actions.

Quorn-Montgomery and Matter nodded in agreement as Connie-Skylar started working on the car's internal system. After just a few minutes however, she stopped and paused as she glanced at Concept thoughtfully with a slightly, confused expression on her face.

"Concept if I actually do this, they'll be able to track the car's movements immediately. It might be too risky." Connie suggested.

Concept glanced at her for a moment and then nodded in agreement. "You're totally right this would put us in danger. Ok we'll find another way to get there." He replied decisively. "Forget the car."

The group quickly climbed back out of the vehicle and abandoned it as Concept led them back out onto the street once more. The chilly air hit their faces as they walked and caused them to shiver as their flesh was exposed to the harsh impact of the temperature that surrounded them.

It was a far cry from the warmth of the luxury apartments they'd basked inside whilst on their Mindplant vacations and the warmth they'd felt inside the car for a moment had reminded them of that luxury. They faced the breezy air that whisked around the Unoccupied Zone as it teasingly reminded them of what they were currently lacking with each step they took. The underground station barely provided any warmth and was very drafty and although it wasn't as cold as the streets, it definitely wasn't anywhere near the warmth they'd grown accustomed too throughout the period of their initial participation in their respective Mindplant vacations. The four continued to walk quietly down the streets for a few more blocks until they suddenly found an overground train station and Concept smiled as they approached it.

He urged the group to enter inside enthusiastically as they drew closer to the entrance. "We can get to the other side of the city more quickly this way." Concept insisted as he enthusiastically leapt up the stairs.

The three members of the group agreed with him and continued to follow his lead as they rushed up the stairs and a few minutes later, found themselves on a glossy, silver platform that was completely empty. A shiny, silver train stopped beside the platform a few seconds later and the four quickly entered inside one of the carriages. There were a few people scattered around the interior of the carriage, some of whom were actually seated on silver, bench like seats as the group glanced at them slightly curiously. The passengers inside the carriage however, neither stirred nor turned to face them as they entered, either totally oblivious or completely disinterested in their presence. There was not even the slightest inkling or remotest suggestion that anyone's curiosity had been pricked as the carriage occupants simply continued to stare directly in front of them and didn't even flinch.

A surge of light suddenly zapped out of nowhere and engulfed the train as it shot out of the platform and departed abruptly. Inside the carriage, a man sat with his face hidden from view as he held a book sized, grey gadget up in front of him, upon which he seemed to be reading some kind of document, a middle aged woman was also seated nearby on one of the bench like seats as she fumbled around with some shopping bags situated on the bench next to her and carefully guarded her purchases. An elderly man sat directly opposite Concept and Connie-Skylar, who had both chosen to actually sit down on a bench seat next to each other, he hadn't even blinked as they'd approached the bench and sat down and he seemed to be quite engrossed by his own thoughts as he simply stared into the distance silently.

Quorn-Montgomery and Matter had opted to stand by one of the train carriage doors, slightly reluctant to make themselves too comfortable, just in case they actually had to make an abrupt departure from the train. They both carried very serious expressions upon their face as they stood in complete silence and stared directly in front of them as the train sped rapidly towards its next destination. Their regimented stance reminded Connie somewhat of soldiers as she glanced at them for a moment, both men looked prepared for any unexpected eventuality or inkling of danger that might present itself as they guarded themselves, the entrance to the train and those in the group situated inside the carriage alongside them.

"Do you think any of the people are real?" Connie whispered to Concept curiously as she turned to face him. "Do you think any of them are vacationers like us?"

"Most of them definitely not." Concept replied as he shook his head gently. "But perhaps he could be." He continued playfully as he nodded his head towards a teenager nearby.

The young man he pointed out, stood situated next to one of the carriage doors and even though he wore some small, silver, ear insert headphones, the music he played was so loud, everyone inside the carriage could actually hear the beats emanate from his ears as some noise escaped into the carriage around them. He tapped the ground with his foot enthusiastically in time with the beat as some small remnants of the melody wafted through the air and teased their ears.

"It's nice to be so young isn't it? No responsibilities, no worries and no cares." Connie whispered in Concept's ear as she glanced at the teenager.

"Remember he's not really, real." Concept whispered back as he smiled at her.

A few seconds later, the train rapidly swished into the next platform and the group's destination station and as soon as the doors of the carriage opened, the four quickly rushed outside. They stepped out onto the platform and then walked briskly down towards the exit as they arrived on the other side of the city within record time. They'd arrived much sooner than they'd originally anticipated as the actual train journey itself had only taken a few minutes, which was a total relief to them all as a potential three hour walk around the exterior of the Occupied Zone hadn't exactly been a joy they'd been looking forward too and would have been quite tedious and laborious for everyone.

The four prepared for their next task enthusiastically as they headed towards the exit as the train shot out of the platform next to them, rapidly consumed by another swish of light that engulfed it. They paused for a moment on the platform as they turned and watched it disappear.

"How's that for speedy travel?" Concept joked. "Sure beats walking."

"Our world is so far behind." Quorn quietly observed.

"A few faster trains, lots of fake people." Connie observed. "Our world's not so bad. Would you really want to live in a real world created and run by Barbelo?"

"Definitely not." Concept replied.

Everyone laughed.

Once the four arrived at the top of the stairs that led back down towards the street, they made their way towards the ground in silence as they contemplated the task ahead of them thoughtfully. Everyone knew it was going to be extremely tricky as they considered the gravity of what they had to actually do next as entering inside a facility that was actually part of the Mindplant Vacation program itself was a huge risk and they all completely understood that.

For Connie, the mission she faced weighed more heavily upon her mind as her role lingered in her thoughts. Connie knew that everyone in the group present and absent was totally reliant upon her to perform the tasks that lay ahead successfully. She had to deliver and there simply was no room for any mistakes or any possible failure. The entire trip to the other side of town had been due to the skills she'd garnered throughout her vacation and the tools she'd gained access to from Skylar's body, apartment and occupation and now she simply could not afford to fail or let everyone down and she understood that implicitly.

The vacationer's disappearance and their avoidance of the Exterminators meanwhile, had not gone unnoticed by Barbelo who was becoming increasingly frustrated as each day passed by. She called an urgent meeting inside her office with

Gavin to express her concerns as she attempted to find a solution to problems that had been caused as a result.

"They've all gone missing inside the program." Barbelo explained when Gavin arrived. "They've totally disappeared. They're not in the apartments we designated to the bodies their minds were implanted into and they've not shown up anywhere else."

Gavin glanced at her face for a moment as he stood inside her office quietly and contemplated how to respond thoughtfully. It wasn't often Barbelo called him for an urgent meeting this way and he could sense her distress. "Can't Visual help you find them?" He asked curiously.

Barbelo's tone was tense and exasperated as she replied. "Visual has to maintain the program for the other clients on vacation. He's already sent out five Exterminators to hunt for them, but they haven't been able to track them down yet."

"Exterminators?" Gavin asked as he looked at her with an anxious and confused expression. "What are Exterminators?"

"Oh they just help to exterminate people and bring them back into their real bodies. They end the vacation sequence through the termination of the simulated life that a vacationer's mind is situated inside, whenever there's a problem." Barbelo quickly explained as she shook her head and attempted to justify her approach as if it was a perfectly normal part of the Mindplant vacation process in this type of situation. "It's nothing to worry about. I am however very worried about Maverick, if they find Maverick that might complicate things even further."

"Who's Maverick?" Gavin asked curiously as it slowly dawned upon him there were a lot of things about the Mindplant vacations he was actually unaware off.

Barbelo looked at him sharply for a moment as she suddenly realized that she'd blurted out Maverick's name and that Gavin actually had no idea who Maverick actually was. Now she had placed herself in a predicament and now she had to actually explain who Maverick was and why the vacationers meeting him might be a problem. She scanned her mind for a suitable explanation rapidly as the tension mounted within her, whatever explanation she found and furnished Gavin with, she knew it couldn't be the actual truth.

"Oh he's just someone I worked with on the program before I started this vacation centre."

Barbelo replied as she attempted to dismiss his query as quickly as possible.

"Why would they find him inside the Mindplant program and why would that complicate things?" Gavin continued as he probed Barbelo further, her answer raised more questions in his mind than it satisfied.

"He was one of the first people to enter inside the Mindplant program." Barbelo gushed as she began to pace the room slightly nervously, desperate to end a conversation that she accidentally led in a direction she did not actually want it to go in.

The room fell silent as Gavin quietly considered Barbelo's response carefully, inside he felt completely bewildered and confused by her answers and now he was even more alarmed than ever. Her replies made absolutely no sense whatsoever and the implications of each one began to worry him very deeply, he'd visited the body preservation dormitory almost every working day and he was fully aware, there was actually no long term resident situated inside it that could possibly be Maverick. The deeper implications of Maverick's absence from the Body Preservation Dormitory meant, if he was actually situated inside the Mindplant program he'd been there for years without his physical body actually being preserved. Gavin began to speculate internally how Maverick could actually exist within Mindplant for so long as he glanced at Barbelo suspiciously.

"Gavin continue working on the project bids for the funders." Barbelo urged as she sensed the worry and concern she'd created inside him with her unguarded remarks and slack responses to his questions. "Things will be back to normal soon." She reassured him as she casually dismissed him, whatever problems she now faced, she quickly accepted Gavin couldn't possibly help her to alleviate or resolve as he simply didn't have the scientific knowledge required to assist her in any capacity and to involve him further would perhaps create more problems than it would actually solve.

The tension between the two eased slightly as Gavin nodded and walked towards the door, grateful to have a reason to leave Barbelo's presence as he embraced her dismissal immediately, without further discussion. Once he'd departed and Barbelo was left alone, she stood by the large window situated at one side of her office and glanced out of it thoughtfully as she contemplated the situation further, totally absorbed by her thoughts. Things were getting worse, not better and now she also had to worry about the doubts she'd triggered inside Gavin's mind and his curiosity regarding Maverick's identity and situation. Barbelo sighed, she had inadvertently ignited those doubts within Gavin and triggered a snowball of thoughts that could run down the hill of contemplations until they became a huge avalanche of fear. What she'd started inside Gavin's mind was now totally irreversible.

The bland, beige hallway outside was quiet as Gavin made his way back towards his office as fires of dissatisfaction stoked his thoughts and disturbed his mind. He quietly contemplated the possibility as he walked that perhaps Barbelo was not the innocent person he'd always assumed she was and that perhaps there were some darker, shadier secrets prevalent below the surface of the Mindplant program that he was unaware off. Perhaps the pure perceptions he'd once held about Barbelo's motives were a total lie. He'd always considered Barbelo to be a sincere, accountable, transparent person, yet now he was suspicious and uncertain. Her attitude towards him had been dismissive and uncooperative and for the first time had made him feel slightly uncomfortable to even be in her presence. The mention of Maverick and the presence of the Exterminators within the Mindplant program had alarmed him and that alarm dug deeper inside him as each moment passed by.

Once he arrived back inside his office, Gavin sat down behind his desk, totally consumed by his thoughts which raged through the passageways of his mind like wildfire and the spacious setting of his surroundings, on this occasion for once, failed to appease him as he shook his head. The slightly more expensive, nicer furniture and considerably more lavish décor that adorned the walls was far superior to the dull beige that eclipsed most areas within the Mindplant centre but even the sharp, grey, black and red tones that beautified his surroundings, right now failed to provide even the smallest grain of comfort to him.

Positive thoughts fled from his mind as the dirty secrets surrounding the Mindplant program he'd started to unravel, chased them quickly away. What he'd once felt pride in, was now tainted and overshadowed by the darkness of what he'd started to discover, dark hidden truths whose depths and true nature were still very much unclear and uncertain.

The cellphone lying on Gavin's desk nearby suddenly started to ring as it interrupted and distracted him. Gavin glanced at it quickly for a second and then smiled with relief as the caller's face flashed on the screen in front of him. It was Chivonne, his wife and her call eased his mind slightly for a moment as he answered his phone and quickly greeted her. Everything Gavin did in life, everything he was and everything he aspired to become was for her. She was the cornerstone of his world and his existence, Chivonne was his lifeline as when they'd actually met back in college he'd almost given up on relationships in total despair after suffering a few heartbreaks and she'd completely revived him and his belief in love. He appreciated her sincerity, her tenderness and her devoted loyalty.

"What time will you be home tonight sweetie?" Chivonne asked cheerfully as her voice greeted him enthusiastically.

"About eight." Gavin replied. "I have to stop off on my way home at the Central Library."

"Oh ok I'll put your dinner in the oven and keep it warm." Chivonne insisted. "Is everything at work ok?" She asked slightly surprised by the unusual detour from his usual journey home.

Gavin contemplated his response carefully before he answered. He definitely didn't want to worry Chivonne as he was very conscious with regards to her physical condition, she was actually five months pregnant and the last thing he wanted to do was cause her any distress whilst she was carrying his child. He decided for the moment it was actually wiser to keep his concerns regarding Barbelo to himself, at least until he was completely sure that he understood what was really going on, which at the moment, he knew he totally didn't.

"Everything's fine." Gavin finally returned after a short pause. "I just have to conduct a little bit of research about something that's come up at work."

Chivonne satisfied by his response, reassured him cheerfully. "Great I'll see you when you get home. I'm making your favourite, peppered steak, baby potatoes, mushroom and cream sauce and buttered corn on the cob." She continued.

Gavin smiled as warmth filled him inside and his mind relaxed slightly. "You're such a darling." He teased playfully.

"And I'll give you an extra slab of peppered steak just for that." Chivonne teased.

"I'll see you soon sweetheart." He insisted.

"Can't wait." Chivonne reassured him.

When their conversation ended, Gavin placed his cellphone back down on his desk and then glanced at the screen in front of him, there were still three hours left before he would actually leave work that day and for the first time since he'd actually started working there, he was actually looking forward to leaving. Today, everything had changed for him and he no longer felt the comfort and warmth that his work environment had once provided, now home time became a much more welcome prospect than ever before and one he fervently looked forward to.

Inside the Mindplant environment, evening approached as the daylight started to grow faint and dimmed and the four in the group that had trekked to the other side of the city earlier that day, sat quietly behind some bushes situated just outside the high tech centre they'd identified as being the correct venue for the elaborate Mindplant system infiltration they'd planned. The grey stone structure had a large, glass entrance situated at the front of it, which was manned by workers and virtually impossible to enter without being spotted. Some of the unwanted occupants inside the building, guarded the doors, which had meant the four had, had to wait for them to leave for the day before they could initiate the next step in their plan.

They hid quietly inside the grounds of the building as they watched the entrance quietly and waited patiently, their wait had been exceedingly long and excruciatingly painful as the hours had passed by very slowly, but Concept knew this was the only building they could possibly utilize in this manner and that meant, they simply had no other choice. The building itself, housed the most powerful, technologically advanced equipment in the city and if there was any way at all into the back passageways and inner workings of the Mindplant program, Concept knew it could only be found inside the walls of the building situated directly in front of them.

"Everyone's leaving now." Matter observed as he suddenly sat up and pointed towards the entrance nearby attentively.

The other three members of Concept's group immediately sat up attentively and turned to face the building's entrance as they peered through the leaves of bushes they were situated directly behind enthusiastically as smiles of relief began to appear upon their faces. They watched quietly as two men exited the glass doors and headed towards their cars which were parked in the parking lot situated at the front of the building on the right hand side. Four other men and women followed the two men outside a few minutes later and politely bid farewell to each other as they also abandoned their work stations for the day. Once the six bodies had actually entered inside their respective vehicles and the cars had vacated the parking lot, Concept quickly rose to his feet as the last of the cars disappeared into the distance.

"We have to go inside right now." Concept insisted as he urged the rest of the group to accompany him. "We don't have very long. It's going to start getting dark very soon."

"Do you think there's still anyone else inside the building? Like a night guard or something?" Matter asked curiously.

"If there is, we'll have to take care of them." Concept insisted. "We really don't have the time to wait any longer or any other choice."

Matter, Quorn-Montgomery and Connie-Skylar nodded as they stood up and prepared themselves for the actual mission they'd waited all day to actually perform. It was now or never and they were all very determined, it quite simply had to be now.

FINDING MAVERICK

The group made their way towards the back of the building as they avoided the temptation to attempt to enter inside through the main, front entrance which they knew was more likely to be guarded by cameras. The rear of the building would provide a much more discreet means of entry and offer a slightly less obvious breach. Connie-Skylar, Quorn-Montgomery, Concept and Matter walked around the rows of bushes that lined the neatly cut emerald green, grass gardens which adorned the exterior of the building as they discussed the mission ahead quietly. The fresh scent of the recently cut grass prompted a smile to appear on Connie-Skylar's face as she reminisced for a moment internally about home, soon perhaps she would be back inside her own body and soon perhaps she would actually be back inside her own home, it was a looming possibility which nestled gently upon the horizon of maybe and was dependent on the success of the mission ahead.

Everything inside the Occupied Zone was perfectly maintained and perfectly manicured and even the blades of grass Connie quickly observed as she walked through the grounds, seemed to be cut precisely to a particular height and were extremely even. The bushes that surrounded the top of the grounds seemed almost like the collar of a dress as they sat firmly at the top of the lawn and their dark, brown stems contrasted perfectly against the lush green tones of the leaves they bore. If Connie wasn't situated inside Mindplant and if she wasn't a trapped vacationer, she would have almost enjoyed the brief walk through the immaculate grounds that surrounded her.

The rear of the building was totally deserted as the four walked towards it and searched for an entry point, luckily there were no other buildings in close proximity, which meant their mission would be free from prying eyes and it would be easier to actually achieve their goals. They quickly found a door with a small, glass window and Concept picked up a rock from the ground as he approached it. He wrapped his sleeve around the rock and then used it to smash the window of the door quickly, it was a messy and crude way to gain access the building but it was the quickest way and absolutely necessary. Time was running out and finding a more diplomatic means of entry was a luxury the four simply could not afford to expend, the reality was they did not have the time to indulge in pleasantries and Concept knew it, darkness would soon embrace their surroundings and they had to return to the safety of their hideout before that actually happened.

Once Concept had dug out some of the remaining sharp, shards of glass from the broken window, he quickly slipped his hand down inside the space and then stretched downwards further as he searched with his hand for the release switch inside the building. Luckily he found the switch was reachable as it was positioned right beside the back door and as soon as he touched it, the door sprung open. The four entered inside the building quietly as Concept led the group down a nearby passageway which brought them straight into a large, dimly lit room.

"According to the building blueprints I found, this is the room we need." Concept quickly explained. "If we have any chance of finding any answers or any way out of here, it has to be inside this room." Concept verified.

Connie-Skylar nodded as she started to inspect the equipment inside the room and attempted to establish what she exactly she needed to do to actually access its functionalities. She quickly found a huge terminal in front of a large screen that filled one of the walls and sat down in front of it as she opened her equipment case up and immediately connected some devices to it. The screen lit up instantly as the rest of the group surrounded her and watched in total silence.

Concept sighed with relief as he stood absolutely still at the rear of the group and watched Connie quietly, even if their mission that day did not provide a way to rescue them and return them back to their physical bodies, they might perhaps be able to utilize the system to find out something more about Maverick that would assist them further somehow. Connie had managed to actually get inside the system and now there simply had to be something inside it that she could find which could assist them further. He was absolutely determined his group would not return to the underground station that day empty handed after their long wait outside the building. Their long wait would not be for nothing, they had to return with some kind of results and be gifted with some kind of reward or their sacrifice and extra effort, just wouldn't make any sense at all.

Meanwhile on the other side of the city, the food scavenger hunt wasn't faring as well, Weaver and Spiral had visited a few of their usual, regular sources and even some new ones, but today for some reason they'd found every source heavily guarded by program simulations in the form of people and they'd even spotted some Exterminators. It had been a totally frustrating day as they'd known there was no way they could actually risk being spotted attempting to retrieve food from the dumpsters near the guarded venues or risk actually being caught by Exterminators as they discussed their alternative plans of action and tried to identify another possible food source.

Before the two had left the underground train station earlier that morning, they'd even tried to conduct a search for Maverick and used the usual tracking systems to determine his last known location. Their intention was to complete both tasks in one outing, if that was even remotely possible and if indeed his last known location was situated near any of the food source spots they were going to visit that day. The tracking system they used relied heavily upon images and indents from twenty four hours beforehand and that meant even when they managed to spot Maverick or traces of him, they were always at least a day behind his actual physical movements. The only positive aspect surrounding this delay was that the tracking system they used was the same system the Exterminators utilized and hence everyone was subjected to and restricted by the same time lags.

Concept had managed to find a real time mapping system, Tracking Real-time Activity Map (TRAM) but it only focused on certain parts of the city, most of which were in the Occupied Zone, which meant it was completely useless when it came to the issue of trying to track down Maverick. The Unoccupied Zone, which had been totally abandoned by the program simulations had very few tracking facilities, which had enabled the underground station to remain a safe hideaway but restricted their success when it came to actually locating Maverick.

The actual entrance to the structure that housed their hideaway was completely hidden from the view of any cameras at all by another building that sat right next to it, which actually directly covered the front entrance and obstructed the view from the streets that surrounded it. That obstruction and several other large buildings situated nearby, had meant the Tracking Activity Monitoring System (TAMS) the monitoring system which covered most of the city, struggled to capture any motion beside the entrance to their hideaway or even in the nearby surrounding streets.

Unfortunately that day however, Maverick's last location was not situated near any of the food source spots the two had planned to visit, which meant their possible contribution towards the search for Maverick had been completely abandoned but as their food hunt bore no results, the two started to become increasingly frustrated. They walked down a quiet back street as they started to discuss the possibility that perhaps for today, vermin from the railway tunnels was the only food option available.

Weaver suddenly stopped in mid conversation as he grabbed Spiral's arm and gently pulled her into a doorway nearby and then rapidly placed his finger upon his lips as he motioned towards her to remain completely silent. Spiral complied obediently, aware that something was definitely wrong and that, that something could be, extremely dangerous. He peeked out of the crack between the door and the doorframe a few seconds later and then turned back to face her with a very worried expression.

"There's Exterminators in the street outside." Weaver explained in a whisper.

Spiral quickly stepped forward, glanced through the crack in the doorway and noticed that his observation was indeed correct as she immediately spotted two Exterminators, Strangler and Aggress on the other side of the road they were situated in. They were positioned a few buildings further down from where the two were situated and luckily for them both, hadn't actually noticed them at all. The two Exterminators were unfortunately however not alone and a third man was with them, but it wasn't a friendly gathering. Strangler had his arm firmly wrapped around the man's neck in a tight lock as Aggress stood next to him and watched. Spiral's body began to tremble with fear as she quietly observed them both and their powerless victim.

"Do you think he's one of us?" Spiral whispered as she turned back to face Weaver. "Do you think he's stuck here like we are?"

"No doubt about it at all. He definitely is." Weaver replied. "It's the only logical explanation. Why else would they capture him?"

MINDPLANT: TRIMORPHIA

The man's body was dropped down to the ground a few minutes later as Strangler released him, it was limp, motionless and lifeless as it flopped towards the ground and landed rapidly in a heap. Weaver pulled Spiral gently further back inside the doorway as he urged her to conceal herself from view more adequately and then quickly pulled the door almost shut behind her. The tiny gap he left between the door and the doorframe allowed him just enough space to peek out into the street as he watched the Exterminators outside on the street in total silence. He began to feel slightly fearful as worries scurried through his thoughts and body almost as if they were tiny electric shocks, he was alone now with Spiral and he was totally unsure that he could defend them both sufficiently against two actual Exterminators, if they did indeed actually notice their presence. Weaver was scared.

The two Exterminators picked up the man's lifeless body and then started to carry it towards a nearby alleyway. They walked by the doorway of the building that Weaver and Spiral were actually hidden inside, oblivious to the presence of the trapped vacationers inside it, completely consumed by their task as Spiral and Weaver held their breath and watched them. The vacationers dared not even breathe just in case they were overheard and once twenty seconds had passed by and Weaver was sure that the Exterminators had actually gone a safe distance away from the building, he gently tugged at Spiral's arm as he indicated it was time to depart.

"Let's follow them." Weaver suggested bravely. "Let's find out where they're going and see what they actually do with the man's body."

Spiral hesitated for a moment, slightly unsure that his suggestion was actually a good idea before she offered a response. "Do you really think we should?" She asked quietly. "What if they catch us too? They could kill us both."

Weaver paused thoughtfully for a moment as he considered their position, whilst he was nervous and extremely scared, he simply couldn't resist the urge to actually follow them. He'd always wondered what actually happened to people once the Exterminators caught them and killed them and today the opportunity to find out, had actually presented itself. He weighed up their options quickly inside his mind as he considered various alternatives before he offered a response.

"Perhaps you should continue with the food hunt or return to the underground station and I can follow them alone." He suggested diplomatically after a few seconds pause as he attempted to find a compromise and viable option that would suit them both.

"What if they catch me?" Spiral enquired slightly nervously as she expressed her reluctance to actually be left alone.

"Your right you have to stay with me." Weaver insisted as he accepted that although the proposition he'd made was an attractive one, it wasn't a wise one as it would place Spiral in an extremely vulnerable position if he actually abandoned her and left her to wander the Mindplant streets alone.

They both knew there were definitely more than two Exterminators inside the Mindplant program and Weaver had only seen two outside, which meant there were definitely others situated somewhere else. Concept had clearly instructed everyone that no one should ever venture outside onto the surface alone and if Weaver left Spiral alone now, he knew he would be acting in direct opposition to Concept's precise instructions and guidance. For a moment Weaver felt paralyzed with uncertainty and completely unsure what to actually do as a rare opportunity had presented itself and it was one he knew he might not actually ever get again. Time was definitely not on his side as he struggled to arrive at a decision, he had to go now if he was going to follow the Exterminators at all and Spiral would just simply have to come along with him.

"Don't you want to know what might happen to us if we actually get caught?" Weaver urged as he attempted to convince Spiral that they should definitely follow the Exterminators and overcome their fear together. "This is our chance to find out exactly what they would actually do to us." He continued as he succumbed fully to his curiosity which had been pricked and was now creating a ripple of nagging desires inside his mind to follow the Exterminators quickly before it was too late. "I need to know. I need answers."

Spiral glanced at Weaver with nervousness in her eyes as she began to nod her head slowly in acceptance. Weaver quickly glanced out of the doorway once more and then panicked as he noticed the Exterminators had now exited the street they were situated upon and had actually disappeared from sight completely. The opportunity would be lost if they didn't move right now and there was quite simply no more time to entertain uncertainty or fear, he grabbed Spiral's arm gently, opened the building door and then steered her towards it. There was no more time to deliberate, Spiral's fear or even his own could not overrule the desire Weaver held inside himself to determine and discover the truth, they had to go now.

The two walked down the road briskly as Weaver accepted that he too was scared, he refused however to be intimidated by his own emotions as he allowed his curiosity to govern his steps. A minute or two later, the two entered into an alleyway and they suddenly caught sight of the two Exterminators once more as they continued to carry the limp male body in their arms as they walked. There was a dumpster situated at the bottom of the short road, which was completely deserted due to the fact that it was situated just outside the Occupied Zone and the Exterminators quickly dumped the lifeless body inside it. Weaver and Spiral quickly hid behind another dumpster as they watched the two Exterminators quietly, their mouths and tongues completely silenced by fear.

A few minutes later, the two Exterminators walked past the dumpster they were hidden behind and Weaver and Spiral crouched closer towards the ground to avoid being discovered or spotted. Luckily for them both, the two Exterminators were deeply engrossed and engaged in their conversation and seemed completely oblivious to their presence as they passed by the other side of the large, rectangular, garbage bin and didn't even so much as glance at it or them. The two waited for a few minutes until the Exterminators had actually left the alleyway completely and then rushed over towards the other dumpster. They quickly peered inside as they began to inspect the man's body that lay silently amongst the pile of garbage it contained. Fear stole their words and nervousness froze their tongues as the two glanced at the stranger's face in complete and utter silence. He was very real.

Spiral stepped back and started to cough as her stomach started to wrench and turn over inside her body. The sight of the lifeless body inside the dumpster actually made her want to physically vomit as her eyes accepted the reality that the dumpster contained. Weaver drew closer to her and stroked her back gently as she continued to cough.

"Do you think he's actually dead?" Spiral asked in almost a whisper, scared that she might be overheard by invisible spectators or a pair of unnoticed ears.

"We'll find out in a minute." Weaver replied as he stepped closer to the dumpster once more, leant forward over the side and prepared to touch the discarded man's body that lay within it. He stretched his arm downwards and touched the corpse and as he felt the coldness of the man's skin against his hand, he shivered. "He's definitely dead." He confirmed.

The news broke Spiral's heart and she started to cry as she collapsed in a heap upon the ground, unable to cope with the fact that she had actually seen a man be murdered. A man that was now actually dead and who so easily could have been one of them, if only they had actually arrived in the street just a few minutes before they actually had. Weaver placed his arm gently around her shoulders as he crouched beside her and attempted to comfort her.

"If they find us they'll kill us too." Spiral insisted through her sobs.

Weaver nodded in response as he accepted the reality she presented to him, there was nothing he could actually say at this moment in time to reassure or comfort her as the trauma they'd both witnessed had quite simply overwhelmed her and completely destabilized him. He held her arm and then started to guide her back towards the entrance of the street as he reminded himself, they still had to actually had to find food to eat that day and a dead body that neither of them could actually save would not feed hungry mouths. They had to resume their scavenger food hunt.

The two walked in silence almost like wounded soldiers, numbed by the shock of what they'd seen and scarred by the visions of death that filled their minds as they stumbled back down the alleyway and headed back towards the street from which they'd come from. Potential death lurked around every corner waiting for them with each step they took as they realized now each step had to be tread much more carefully. When they arrived back at the entrance to the main street, they paused for a moment as they contemplated which direction they should continue their food search in.

"Don't worry they won't find us. We'll be fine." Weaver insisted as he attempted to reassure Spiral. "Now we have to try and find some food." He urged as he quickly tried to normalize the situation and stabilize them both emotionally by drawing their attention back to the most important task of the day, a task that they had not yet completed.

Spiral nodded as she wiped the tears from her eyes and prepared herself once more to face the busy city streets nearby as she pulled herself together. "Yes you're right. We have to find food now." She mumbled.

MINDPLANT: TRIMORPHIA

The two walked slowly back towards the Occupied Zone as they started their search for food once more and resumed their scavenger hunt, Weaver was slightly relieved as they walked that Spiral hadn't broken down completely as he wouldn't have known what to do if she had. Somehow she'd managed to retain control of her emotions in the face of horror and her bravery encouraged him. The usual rucksack Weaver always carried alongside him whenever he ventured outside on food scavenger hunts, still sat firmly on his shoulder empty and he was determined to fill it with some kind of food and get them both back to the safety of the underground station before darkness engulfed the streets. He was very much aware now, the night was indeed coming and the day had almost completely run out and Weaver knew it simply wasn't wise to be out on the streets of Mindplant when the darkness of night actually arrived.

The evening had flown by for Concept's group as they prepared to leave the building that they'd actually broken into just an hour before. They'd extracted most of the data they could find that they felt they needed and Concept had begun to grow increasingly concerned as each moment passed and the night started to draw in.

"We have to leave right now, they could notice the system breach at any time and it's getting late now." Concept insisted with urgency in his voice as he pushed everyone to conclude the mission and actually depart.

Concept put his foot down and urged everyone to leave as although it was tempting to continue, he knew they simply couldn't afford to. The longer the group actually remained inside the building, the more likely it was that they would actually be caught as each second increased their exposure to the risk of capture, either inside the building or on the return journey back to their underground station hideaway. The level of risk was increasing and escalating as each minute and second passed by and everyone inside the room knew it.

The other three members of the mission group, Connie-Skylar, Matter and Quorn-Montgomery nodded in agreement and then quickly packed up Skylar's equipment case and headed towards the door. Darkness had started to envelope the Mindplant world outside the windows and they could see the night had almost arrived as they scrambled to exit the building as quickly as possible. The exterior of the building was quiet as Concept ushered the group out of the concrete, grey construction and then closed the back door firmly shut behind them.

"We can't come back here ever again." Concept remarked as they walked briskly through the grounds situated at the back of the building. "Once they notice the broken window tomorrow morning, they'll know we've been here and they'll be watching the building more carefully in future, just in case we return."

Everyone nodded in agreement.

"Do you think the data we've collected will provide the answers we need?" Matter asked curiously.

"If it doesn't at least we'll be slightly more informed about what's actually really going on." Concept insisted. "If it does, then perhaps we can find Maverick straight away and we'll have the answers we need directly from him. Either way we can't really lose. It was a risk worth taking."

"True." Matter agreed.

"How do you feel about being a Mindplant criminal and actually orchestrating the burglary of a building?" Connie teased Concept playfully as they walked next to each other.

"I rather enjoyed it actually." Concept returned as he smiled. "There's no one I'd rather commit acts of rebellion with than you guys. You were the perfect criminal companions."

Everyone laughed.

The four soon arrived back outside the train station once more and quickly made their way up the stairs that led towards the platform, anxious to return to the safety of the underground sanctuary as soon as they possibly could. Once they arrived on the platform, they found it quiet and empty as they waited for the train to arrive that would actually carry them back to the safety and the other side of the city once more. The group were relatively happy and satisfied with what they'd achieved that day and hopeful that they'd managed to actually retrieve something that might be helpful as they smiled at each other warmly. Their mood was light and their hopes were high as excitement embraced them and high expectations lifted their spirits as they contemplated what information and data they may have possibly managed to salvage that evening. A real escape plan and the answers they sought were now perhaps just within their grasp.

An hour later, the group finally arrived back at the underground station where they found Weaver and Spiral already seated inside the control room, the four were happy but exhausted as they entered inside the room and flopped down onto vacant crates beside them. Everyone amongst the group of four was hungry and Concept tried to ascertain how successful the food scavenger hunt had been that day as hunger pangs rumbled through his stomach.

"Did you manage to find some food?" Concept asked eagerly almost as soon as he entered inside the room. "We're starving, it's been a long day."

Spiral nodded. "I'll go get you guys some food right now." She replied as she quickly stood up and headed towards the makeshift kitchen.

"You'll never guess what happened to us today." Weaver started to gush as he glanced at Concept and Matter, anxious to relate the details of his day to them both as soon as he possibly could.

"What happened?" Matter asked enthusiastically as he encouraged him to elaborate further.

"We saw two Exterminators murder a man." Weaver explained. "A man just like us." He continued as a very serious expression crossed his face.

Concept, Matter, Quorn-Montgomery and Connie-Skylar sat and listened to Weaver, intrigued and captivated by his discussion as they hung onto his every word and he described exactly what he'd seen to them. He related every specific, intricate detail that came into his mind as he continued to speak until five minutes later Spiral interrupted him as she arrived back inside the control room with a tray filled full of bowls of food.

"Do you think they'll kill us too if they catch us?" Connie asked as she absorbed the details that Weaver had divulged to them, like a sponge soaking up drops of water as her mind immediately became completely saturated with fear.

Weaver nodded adamantly. "They definitely will."

"Weaver's right." Quorn verified. "I never actually told you this Connie but I was actually supposed to kill you that day we met on our vacations." He explained as he nodded in agreement. "Skylar whose body your mind is inside, she was actually my target."

Connie glanced at his face for a moment as confusion laced her eyes and hurt and shock needled her inner sentiments. "Really?"

"When I realized who you actually were I just couldn't do it." Quorn continued.

"Seriously?" Connie asked. "That was your mission. They instructed you to actually kill me?"

"Yes but I totally couldn't go through with it." Quorn replied as he immediately attempted to reassure her.

"Do you think when we die inside the program, we actually die in real life?" Connie asked curiously as she glanced at Weaver and Concept faces anxiously and searched their eyes for answers.

Weaver hesitated for a moment as he glanced back at her completely unsure how to respond to the question she'd raised, before he finally blurted out a response and attempted to address her question honestly. "I'm not totally sure."

Concept remained completely silent.

The reality was, neither man knew the answer to her question and hence they were both quite reluctant to actually offer one. They had no real idea what would actually happen to them if they died inside the Mindplant program and even less notion regarding what impact and implications their death would have on their real physical bodies and real lives.

"What about you guys, how was your day? Did you manage to obtain any useful data?" Weaver suddenly asked as he attempted to steer the conversation towards something slightly more positive and lighter.

Concept nodded as he replied. "We did. Connie managed to extract a lot of data and information, so hopefully we brought back something useful."

"We managed to access some files but some were encrypted with a code that even I couldn't break, not even with Skylar's equipment." Connie explained. "We got everything we possibly could."

Spiral began to hand out bowls of food to everyone inside the room and cutlery as everyone's focus suddenly turned towards the lacking's of the evening meal that was currently on offer.

"No meat today?" Matter asked as he cast his eyes rapidly over the slim pickings of the day that filled the bowl inside his hand and observed slightly glumly that there was no meat, fish and poultry situated inside it.

Spiral shook her head. "I'm afraid not. Today it's just pasta, tomato sauce and salad. That's all we could find. Sorry."

Matter accepted her apology humbly as he started to eagerly consume the food inside the bowl. "Can't expect to eat meat every day, not when you're in our position." He reassured her cheerfully, very much aware that the lack of meat and poultry wasn't actually Spiral's fault.

Spiral held her spoon inside her hand above her bowl, poised for a minute as she glanced down at the ground sadly, her heart weighed down by grief as it sank slowly towards the floor. "I wonder who he actually was in real life, the man we saw die today." She remarked solemnly. "If only he'd crossed our paths sooner, an hour or two earlier perhaps then we could have saved his life or helped him somehow."

Weaver was touched by her remark as he empathized with her sorrow and he quickly stood up, made his way across the room towards her and then placed his arm gently upon her shoulders. "There's nothing more we could have done." He reassured her. "He'd already been caught by the Exterminators when we arrived."

"Do you think there are more people like us?" Connie asked curiously. "Vacationers trapped inside the Mindplant program."

"I'm sure there are. I'm not sure how we can find them though as there's absolutely no way to identify them and track them down." Concept remarked. "We were just very lucky to find each other the way we did, when we actually did."

"Our focus for now has to be on finding Maverick and actually finding a way out." Matter interjected as he shook his head. "Saving other people who may or may not even exist and who may or may not be trapped in here, would be like chasing illusions. We're not even sure there are others and even if there are, we have no idea how to actually find them. For now we have to try and focus on the things we are sure about and the things we do know."

Concept and Weaver nodded in agreement.

"He's right." Concept affirmed. "We can't risk spending our time looking for people that might not even be in danger."

The group tucked into their meal as they left the discussions regarding the dilemma's they faced firmly behind them, at least for that evening. They were anxious to explore the data and information Concept's group had returned with and that spurred them on as they quickly consumed their meal and then crowded around the screen to examine the information that had been gathered earlier that day. The data the group had managed to retrieve revealed some hidden things to them about Mindplant that surprised them all as they stared at the screen in front of them.

"Barbelo's done this before." Concept observed. "Her first program was implemented ten years ago, ten people died and her research was abandoned, though not by choice, through fear of discovery. The research program she created back then was known as Brain Break and she was known as Lucille Vanquis." He explained.

"How come they let her form Mindplant?" Weaver asked curiously.

"No one actually found out about the deaths until a year later. After the experiments went wrong, she simply abandoned the project and building that she'd acquired the one year lease for, changed her name, moved to another country and then reinvented herself but continued with her work." Connie explained. "Mindplant was the actual manifestation of her second attempt to realize her research."

"How does Maverick fit into all of this?" Weaver asked.

"He was her associate but not actively involved in the first project, he was more or less in the background. When she embarked upon her second attempt, he actually joined her and they created and formed Mindplant together." Connie explained.

Matter shuddered as he listened as he sat on a crate nearby. "This is starting to sound very creepy."

"There's more." Connie continued. "The government is now actually funding some of Barbelo's research and there is absolutely no way the government would fund such a program if they knew about Barbelo's past operations, the human deaths and her experimentation.

"Do you think she'll kill us all, like she did to those other people at Brain Break?" Spiral asked fearfully.

The group inside the room glanced at each other for a few seconds as they absorbed the reality that Barbelo was actually capable of murdering everyone inside the room without so much as even a pinprick of remorse. The prospect of Barbelo's murderous tendencies and capabilities terrified them and the fact that Barbelo had actually killed people before and suffered absolutely no ramifications or consequences at all, completely turned their stomachs over as the vomit of fear weighed down heavily inside their bodies like a solid brick.

The group turned their attention back towards the data extraction and worked late into the night as they attempted to distract themselves from the prospect of death and Barbelo's murderous tendencies. They sat around the screen and analysed each piece of information they'd managed to retrieve and when the early hours of the morning drew in, Weaver and Spiral were the first to succumb to tiredness as they finally called it a night and buckled to fatigue. The two departed from the control room and left everyone else still fighting the urge to sleep which heavily conflicted with their desire to continue their search for answers as they sauntered towards the iron bunk beds that waited to embrace their tired bodies.

A couple of hours later, Concept finally stood up and insisted that everyone else should also call it a night and rest as he realized how late it actually was and how tired everyone was becoming. Depriving themselves of rest he knew would not change anything or be helpful and might even increase the risk of capture the next day, due to resulting drowsy and tired reactions.

"We have to try to find Maverick again tomorrow." Concept urged. "We have to be fresh and rest properly just in case we cross paths with the Exterminators again."

Connie-Skylar, Matter and Quorn nodded in agreement and then started to make their way quietly towards the small dormitory like rooms that contained the small, iron, bunk beds they usually slept on as Concept walked behind them quietly. He reflected upon their evening as he walked, they'd been somewhat satisfied by the information they'd uncovered and their perceptions of Barbelo and Mindplant as a result had now changed as they'd begun to have an increased understanding and awareness regarding their current situation. Sleep wouldn't come easily that night due to the startling revelations that had been uncovered but now at least everyone in the group now knew, they weren't the first victims to fall for Barbelo's scientifically elaborate, mind boggling, brain implant schemes and they probably wouldn't be the last. Concept was grateful as he climbed up onto the top bunk above Matter's body and lay down, that at least the group had the comfort of each other's presence and the safety of the sanctuary they were situated inside, it wasn't much compared to what they had in the real world but for now, it simply had to be enough.

When the next morning arrived, everyone inside the underground hideout woke up bright and early and quickly prepared for the day ahead. They all dressed up and showered and then gathered inside the control room as they prepared for the day's tasks that lay before them. Although they hadn't managed to find anything out the day before that would assist them in their search for Maverick, they had definitely managed to ascertain more information about the Mindplant program itself and Barbelo's cruelty towards those she experimented upon and the truth had horrified them.

Concept began to instruct the group as they stood quietly in front of him. "We'll split into two groups." He explained as he handed out small laser guns to everyone inside the room. "Connie, you'll come with Matter and I and Quorn you'll go with Weaver and Spiral."

Everyone nodded in agreement as they quickly concealed the laser guns inside their jacket pockets and then moved closer to those in their respective groupings, they then waited for further instructions from Concept. Today was the first day that Quorn and Connie would actually be going out onto the surface in separate groups and that for a second made them both feel slightly nervous.

"Will you be ok?" Quorn asked Connie quietly.

The two stood next to each other for a moment as they paused before joining their separate groups and smiled at each other. It was a big step for them both and required a huge degree of trust as they contemplated their separation internally for a moment.

"Sure." Connie replied even though she felt slightly nervous inside. "I'll be fine."

The two separated as they made their way across the room towards their respective groups which were situated on either side of the control room and then waited for Concept to clarify the plan of action for the day ahead. The air inside the control room was taut with excitement and tension which grew rapidly as each second passed by. Concept paced the room and then paused by the large screen on the wall as he started to impart instructions to the two groups situated in front of him.

"Your group Weaver will search these two buildings in these squares on the grid and we'll focus on these two buildings in the other two squares." He explained as he pointed towards the grid map on the large screen in front of them.

Weaver nodded in agreement.

"Is everyone ready?" Concept asked as he glanced quickly around the room.

Everyone inside the room smiled and nodded in response.

Spiral raised her hand for a moment and Concept nodded as he encouraged her to proceed with her question. "What should we do if we cross paths with any Exterminators?" She asked curiously as she began to speculate what might actually really occur, once they left the safety of their hideout once more.

The question lingered in the air as it hung for a moment unanswered as Concept glanced into her eyes thoughtfully and contemplated how to respond. It was only natural he quickly reminded himself, that Spiral would feel fearful after what she'd witnessed the previous day, but this was also the main reason that Quorn had actually been assigned to her group. Spiral wasn't very physically tough as her frame was quite slender and graceful and Weaver wasn't confident with weapons whereas Quorn was. Quorn would take that killer shot, whereas Weaver might freeze and panic.

Concept smiled as he attempted to reassure her. "Avoid them if you can and if you can't avoid them, use the laser guns immediately and shoot to kill." He instructed. "It's either them or us and no one should take the threat they pose lightly. If you do not kill them, they will kill you." He insisted. "Quorn will be with you and he's very handy with a gun. I trust him to help you both."

Concept felt reassured as he scanned the two groups in front of him, he would definitely kill if he had to and he would protect Connie, Matter could take care of himself. He'd definitely made the right decision by splitting everyone into these two groups as it was more likely in these groupings, they would actually return to the sanctuary later that evening, safe and alive.

The control room emptied a few minutes later as the two groups made their way up towards the surface and entered onto the street outside quietly. They hardly spoke a word to each other as they walked, their minds fully focused on the tasks ahead and the potential threat of a collision at some point throughout that day with the Exterminators as now they fully understood that such an encounter could have deadly consequences and that forced them to take the possibility of running into one a lot more seriously.

The two groups parted once they arrived on the surface as they headed off in their respective directions and Concept led his group towards the first location, they'd identified as a possible hideout for Maverick that day. Weaver led his group down the road in the opposite direction as they also joined in the search for Maverick and left the usual food scavenger hunt until later that afternoon.

Both groups hardly spoke a word to each other as they focused intensely on the road ahead of them and scanned every inch of it for Exterminators.

After approximately an hour of walking, Concept's group finally arrived at the first abandoned building they'd identified as a target location which was situated in the Unoccupied Zone and entered inside. Maverick usually stuck to the outskirts of the city and seemed to avoid the Occupied Zone as much as he possibly could and that avoidance worked out in their favour as it meant most of their efforts to track him down also kept them firmly outside of the Occupied Zone and reduced the risk of them being spotted or noticed by a simulated passer-by. Being outside the Occupied Zone more frequently also reduced their exposure to any Exterminators who might be patrolling the inner city areas as they searched for Maverick or them.

The hallway was completely silent as they entered inside the building and the broken glass that was scattered across the hallway, crunched below their feet as they walked. They delicately picked their way through the broken shards of glass as they attempted to avoid drawing any attention towards themselves or making any more noise than was absolutely necessary. Suddenly as they reached the midpoint of the hallway, Connie-Skylar stopped abruptly and froze as she heard a noise from somewhere above her head. Her hesitation was immediately noticed by Concept who quickly drew closer to her.

"What's wrong?" Concept asked quietly as he scanned the hallway in front of them and searched for signs of any third party presence.

"I feel like someone's here and I heard something up there, right above us." Connie explained.

Concept gently touched her arm as he attempted to reassure her. "I know what you mean. I can feel it too." He verified.

The three continued to walk cautiously further inside the building until they arrived in a large room situated at the far end of the hallway. It was almost empty and bare but there were stairs inside it that lead upwards towards the next floor situated in one corner of the room.

"Let's go look upstairs." Concept whispered as he started to walk towards the stairs at the other end of the room. "It might be Maverick you heard."

The two other members of the group nodded in agreement as they began to follow him towards the staircase. Silence accompanied them and wrapped its arms around them as they placed their feet on each step with care, not daring to speak so much as a word, just in case their hushed tones would be overheard and delicately avoiding any shards of glass or stones strewn across their path. If someone else was indeed inside the building alongside them, the three had no idea yet whether that entity was actually a friend or a foe and until they were certain, they were anxious to attract as little attention to themselves and their presence as possible.

The three members of Weaver's group arrived outside the first building they were supposed to inspect not long after as they too actively participated in the hunt for Maverick that morning. The first building they'd targeted was an old, abandoned bakery that stood quietly in front of them as the three approached the entrance and then quickly made their way inside. The bakery had been identified as a potential hideout for Maverick earlier that morning and they were all extremely hopeful that it would yield results as they stepped into the dusty shop situated at the front of the building quietly. The hunt for Maverick that morning had begun even earlier than usual as everyone had followed Matter's advice based on some of his last searches and the two groups had even skipped consumption of the usual tea and bread they normally enjoyed each morning for breakfast.

The three made their way through the dusty shop front which was filled with empty bread shelves and headed towards the back of the shop where the actual bread factory itself was situated. They held their laser guns at the ready, prepared for any Exterminators that they may find lurking in the passageways as they ventured deeper inside the building and explored its interior. The eerie silence of the vacant premises blanketed their ears and almost deafened them as they walked.

At one end of the shopfront they found a passageway that led out into a long hallway which had at least twenty doors on the left hand side, each of which led to smaller, store rooms and there was also a huge set off doors situated halfway down the hallway on right hand side. The first small, store room they entered inside actually had a broken window in one corner of the room and Weaver rushed across the room towards it as soon as he noticed it, filled with excitement.

"He's either here or he was here." Weaver gushed. "Let's split up and search the rest of the rooms. Spiral you start from the other end of the hallway and check the small, store rooms and work your way back towards me and Quorn you can check out the larger, factory room on the right hand side of the hallway."

The two nodded in agreement as they accepted Weaver's instructions and then quickly made their way towards the relevant sections of the hallway as per his allocation in order to begin their search. Once they reached their respective starting points, they quickly made their way inside the rooms as they conducted their search quietly and methodically, conscious of the fact that Maverick may not be the only presence situated inside the bakery and anxious to avoid attracting negative attention from any Exterminators that may also be lurking nearby.

The large set of doors that led into the huge, main factory area were slightly stiff as Quorn-Montgomery pushed them and then stepped inside the large open space. Inside the factory room, redundant bakery equipment was scattered across the concrete ground, idle as dust gathered upon each item and caked the tops with a white, greyish, and icing like layer. The layer of dust seemed to dress each of the obsolete machines almost like a coat and he could tell immediately, the bakery hadn't been operational for a very long time as the air inside the room was extremely musty. The gentle embrace from the scent of warm, freshly baked bread that the factory had once been so accustomed to had been completely consumed and replaced by the mouldiness that accompanied its stagnation and it was slightly harder to breathe as a result. He started to creep around the room quietly as he tried to avoid bumping into any machines or equipment that lay in his path and tiptoed around each one. Quorn knew the factory room was huge and that his search was definitely going to take him a while as he resigned himself humbly to the laborious task that lay ahead.

On the other side of the city meanwhile, Concept's group continued their exploration of the abandoned sculpture gallery as they stepped out on the first floor and found a large set of doors directly in front of them. Concept stepped forward boldly and pushed the large doors open firmly and then the three made their way cautiously inside. Once inside the room, the three quickly glanced around and found it occupied by dusty statues and various art exhibits, some of which were large in size.

The exhibition room itself had a very high ceiling that arched above their heads and from the first glance it appeared as if the room was empty and void of human occupants but due to the size of the large statues situated inside the room however, Concept knew it was actually impossible to tell that it actually really was. He quickly signalled towards the other two members of the group and indicated that they should spread out and search in various directions and then proceeded to start searching a section of the room himself. The three spread out and began to scour the huge exhibition room quietly as they searched for any possible signs of life.

Inside the room, unknown to Concept and his search party however, two Exterminators, Extinct and Chaos lay in wait as they hide behind two statues quietly and watched them. They had also chosen the building just as Concept had as a search location for Maverick that morning and had entered inside the building before Concept's group had actually arrived. When the Random's (Connie, Concept and Matter) had entered inside the building and main exhibition room, the two Exterminators had adjusted their expectations accordingly as they'd accepted that whilst they hadn't found Maverick yet, there was now a possibility that they could capture some Randoms instead. Capturing Random's was almost as delicious and just as satisfying to them as the possibility of capturing Maverick as both targets had evaded capture and frustrated them and both targets actually still needed to be caught.

The three searched the room quietly and quickly lost sight of each other as they became engrossed in their task. They crept around the various pieces of artwork and statues that obstructed their view as they searched the room which was very large. All three knew they had to actually search every inch of the interior, which is why they split up in an attempt to do so more quickly as someone had made the noise that Connie had heard and that someone could possibly be Maverick.

The area that Connie had been instructed to search seemed empty as she navigated Skylar's body around it cautiously and thoroughly. She stopped for a moment beside a large, animal statue, distracted slightly as she inspected it a little more closely. On one side of the huge, magnificent beast, she noticed that the animal seemed to have some grooves and a large, deep gash which looked very realistic and she admired the craftsmanship further as she absorbed every intimate detail appreciatively. A spear protruded out from the deep wound, which was twisted into the Terracotta that almost gave the statue the appearance that the animal had been struck by the spear just minutes beforehand on that very same day. The statue towered above her head as she contemplated what kind of animal it might be for a moment, she was uncertain as it certainly didn't look like any kind of creature that Connie had ever seen before but the effort that had gone into the statue's creation captivated her for a moment as she admired the complexity of every intricate detail situated directly in front of her. Her appreciation however was exceedingly short-lived.

A few seconds later Connie-Skylar suddenly jumped in shock and gasped as she was grabbed aggressively around the neck from behind. She could feel a gun being held against her head as her throat tightened and her breath faltered. Her body was gripped with fear and quickly became paralyzed as she struggled to breathe and almost choked. Horror struck her as she rapidly realized there was nothing she could actually do now to escape her captives grip and that struggling and fighting against them, was not even a viable option.

The Exterminator, Extinct whose arms were wrapped tightly around her neck, that was actually responsible for her capture, locked his arm around her neck even more tightly as Matter suddenly ventured out from behind the nearby statue they were actually situated behind and slowly approached them. Extinct stared at Matter in an extremely threatening and intimidating manner as soon as Matter made an attempt to actually draw closer.

"You take another step and she dies." Extinct barked.

The Exterminator's threat sank rapidly into Matter's mind as he nodded his head silently and immediately accepted defeat. He quickly took a step back anxious not to provoke Extinct any further in order to avoid any further damage being inflicted upon Connie. Matter instinctively knew there was absolutely nothing else he could possibly do as the Exterminator had Connie tightly in his grip and he could technically actually kill Connie before Matter even reached him to challenge him physically. He quickly contemplated for a moment that perhaps he should fire his laser gun at him, but concluded that too would be impossible. Extinct cleverly held Connie in front of him as he facilitated her as a type of shield and his body was barely even visible at all, which meant he would be extremely difficult to aim for. There was no certainty that even if Matter aimed carefully, he wouldn't actually hit Connie instead and if he actually did try to fire, it was more likely, especially if the Exterminator moved to avoid the laser ray, that Matter would end up hitting Connie and he knew it. The reality was Matter wasn't very confident regarding his precision with a laser gun and definitely wasn't prepared to take the risk as the thought of possibly injuring Connie was just a risk to great to take.

The standoff between Extinct and Matter was soon interrupted as a few seconds later Chaos, the other Exterminator approached Extinct from the other side of the statue and smiled at him with satisfaction. Finally, Extinct had managed to catch a live Random and although their search for Maverick had been fruitless, they would not return to Barbelo empty handed that day. Capturing a Random wasn't quite the same as catching Maverick but it was still an adequate catch and made their day somewhat more worthwhile nonetheless as they hadn't actually expected to find any Randoms inside the building that morning at all.

"Should we try to capture the rest of them?" Extinct asked Chaos quietly.

Chaos who by now was situated right next to him, gently shook his head. "No let's just take this one for now." He replied. "We'll get the others later."

Extinct nodded in agreement and then pulled Connie-Skylar towards a wall situated just a few meters away from the statue as he prepared to depart and Chaos followed him. The two Exterminators walked straight into the wall with Connie-Skylar and melted straight into it right before Matter's eyes as he watched, powerless to stop them. They disappeared rapidly as the wall seemed to consume them and two piles of small rocks then dropped down onto the floor directly underneath the spot of the wall, which they'd entered. Matter shook his head in frustration.

Matter quickly glanced around helplessly in horror and then walked over towards the two piles of small rocks situated at the foot of the wall, he picked a few rocks up and then threw each one back down towards the floor in a frustrated fit of rage. His body now felt completely numb and his mind had been utterly traumatized by his own inability to intervene as the shock of Connie's capture hit him and he touched the wall directly in front of him. He could feel nothing however, only the wall's solid, cold form as his mind absorbed the reality, the Exterminators were definitely not coming back anytime soon and neither too was Connie. Paralysis set in as his feet became firmly rooted to the floor almost like a tree that had spread its roots deep down into the depths of the ground he stood upon.

Concept suddenly interrupted Matter's state of shock as he walked around one side of the statue nearby and arrived on the scene. Matter couldn't speak at all but simply looked at Concept and shook his head in disbelief as Concept approached him. Concept nudged Matter gently as he sensed that something had indeed gone profoundly wrong and tried to provoke him to speak.

"What's going on?" Concept asked curiously as he quickly absorbed Matters' shocked appearance. "What's happened?" He glanced around quickly for a moment and then pressed Matter for information again as he turned back to face him. "Where's Connie? Have you seen her? Did she come this way?"

The events that had just transpired inside the exhibition room had totally shocked Matter and for a few seconds, he was completely unable to respond as he contemplated how exactly he could actually explain the events that had just occurred to Concept. His body was still frozen and stiff as the cold, frosty icicles of shock and disbelief engulfed him. The silence and stillness within him however was broken by Concept a few seconds later as Concept gently shook his shoulder and demanded an answer from him. Matter was abruptly shaken out of his thoughts as he shuddered and quickly came back to his senses.

"The Exterminators took her." Matter explained quietly as he began to relate the details of Connie's capture sheepishly to Concept. "There was nothing I could do. They held a gun to her head and then they disappeared straight into that wall." He continued as he pointed towards the wall nearby that the Exterminators had utilized as an exit, just a few minutes beforehand, ashamed as he accepted his failure to protect her.

The silence that greeted his words was understandable as Concept stood completely still for a moment and simply stared at the empty wall in front of him.

"They just disappeared, straight into the wall." Matter stuttered as he pointed towards the solid, still wall directly in front of him.

The offending wall stood quietly in front of them both as Concept glanced at Matter's face, looked back at the wall and then looked back at Matter once more. Concept began to rub his head with frustration and despair as the horrific reality they both now faced struck him like an arrow straight in the heart.

"How will we explain this to Quorn?" Matter pleaded in an almost whimpering voice as he squeezed out each word. "He'll be devastated. He trusted us to protect her, to look after her and I've failed."

"We've failed." Concept replied as he acknowledged his own contribution towards the horrifying situation. "I've failed."

Concept was completely traumatised, the very woman he'd wanted by his side to protect, that he'd felt drawn to and attracted to, the very woman he'd wanted to walk beside and get to know once they arrived back inside their own real biological bodies and their real lives, he'd actually lost. Concept had taken Connie from Quorn's capable, protective arms and she'd been captured whilst in his. Explaining that reality to Quorn was going to rip his heart to shreds as he mournfully accepted the loss of the woman he yearned to hold more closely. His throat grated as it suddenly became dry and parched like the desert sands and he struggled to breathe.

"I just pray to God the others have found Maverick." Concept remarked solemnly as he shook his head, disgusted by his own negligence. "It's even more crucial now than before."

The two men despondently prolonged leaving the building for as long as possible as they walked aimlessly around the huge, empty room silently for at least another thirty minutes. Part of Concept hoped as they walked that Matter had been mistaken and that Connie would suddenly reappear from behind one of the statues nearby and smile at them but his hopes were never realized. Connie had gone and Concept simply had to accept it. He was reluctant to actually leave the building without Connie, but he knew deep down inside himself as he paced the room, she would never return.

A sudden wave of inadequacy washed over Concept for a moment as he almost drowned in the depths of his internal sorrows, he was the leader of the group and Connie had been with him when she'd actually been captured. Perhaps he should resign he quietly contemplated as he began to doubt his leadership capabilities, her disappearance was mind numbingly traumatic and his absolution was not forthcoming as his conscience remained disturbed. He simply couldn't forgive his error in judgment easily, failure was such a bitter pill to swallow and Concept was a very proud man.

The emotional distress the two men felt started to consume them as they walked despondently back towards the door that led to the stairs and exit. They did not even mumble a word to each other as they left the building in complete and utter silence as there was absolutely nothing either of them could say at that moment in time that would ease the discomfort they felt inside, reduce the pain or diminish the horror of what had actually transpired within the abandoned art gallery. Their search for Maverick for that day was definitely over.

Meanwhile on the other side of the city, Quorn completely oblivious to the fact that Connie had actually been captured, continued to search the large factory room he been assigned too. Montgomery's body allowed Quorn to present a more formidable, physical threat to anyone that approached him as it was significantly larger framed than Quorn's actual real body was and that factor comforted him slightly as he searched the large factory room quite boldly. He held the laser gun confidently in his hand as he crept around each machine, wall and corner silently and attempted to search every nook and cranny of the factory room thoroughly.

His search seemed fruitless however as he found nothing but redundant equipment and vermin that scurried away into dark corners and holes as soon as he neared them. Some sacks of grain lay upon the concrete floor with holes in them that gave any visitors present a clear indication that vermin were now the main residents of the abandoned bakery, which they'd clearly squatted inside and claimed as their own. The rats that occupied the building had gnawed away at each one in the search for food to survive and grain had spilled out onto the floor and surrounded each sack as a result, however the vermin seemed totally unapologetic regarding the mess they'd made.

"Nothing here but rats and grain." Quorn muttered quietly as he walked back towards the entrance of the room, slightly dismayed that his search had not actually rendered any results. "Rats and grain, rats and grain, that's all there is."

There was absolutely nothing of interest to Quorn inside the large, factory room and as he headed back towards the door, he shook Montgomery's head gently in frustration. Suddenly however as he approached the door, someone grabbed him aggressively from behind and gripped him tightly around the neck and he froze immediately.

"Don't move an inch." A deep, husky voice threatened.

A gun was quickly held firmly to the back of Quorn-Montgomery's head and he stood completely still as he partially surrendered to his capture. He quickly analysed his options internally and considered for a moment that perhaps he could utilize Montgomery's large frame which he now controlled to overpower his captor. Uncertainty filled his mind as he contemplated that perhaps he'd actually been caught by an Exterminator and he began to weigh up his options. There was no actual way of knowing who the man was that walked slightly behind him as they pushed a gun into his back and forced him towards the centre of the factory like space. Quorn almost buckled as he walked, slightly stunned that he'd actually been caught so easily and that he'd been so unprepared as each step he was forced to take denoted his failure.

The other two members of the group, Weaver and Spiral were completely oblivious to Quorn's predicament as they finished up their inspection of the small, back, store rooms and reached the mid-point and then paused for a moment as they discussed their next plan of action briefly amongst themselves. The twenty small, store rooms along the left hand side of hallway had by now been completely searched but Spiral had discovered a few more situated right at the very bottom of the hallway in another passageway altogether that actually led off from the main one they had already searched.

"Let's continue searching." Weaver urged. "We might still find Maverick." He encouraged.

"Maybe we should check on Quorn first. I haven't seen him for a while now." Spiral insisted as she avoided acknowledging her frustration regarding their lack of results as if it was an unwanted advance from an undesirable suitor. "Make sure he's ok."

"Ok." Weaver agreed.

The two walked towards the large, factory room doors situated on the right hand side of the hallway as they considered the results of their search slightly glumly, they'd been engrossed in their task for most of the morning and for some of the afternoon but as time had slipped out of their grasp quietly, they both knew if they didn't actually find Maverick soon, they'd have to abandon the search altogether. They still had to conduct the food scavenger hunt they'd been assigned to perform that day and failing to return to the underground station without either food or Maverick was simply a disappointment neither of them could face carrying.

Inside the large, factory room, the deep, male voice that had forced Quorn-Montgomery towards the large machine situated in the middle of the room, began to interrogate him further at gunpoint.

"Why are you looking for me and what do you want?" The deep, gruff voice demanded.

"You know I was looking for you?" Quorn asked totally caught off guard by the question posed. "You're Maverick?"

"Yes now what do you want from me?" Maverick asked as he continued to speak in a gruff manner.

The question posed, shocked but also comforted Quorn somewhat as he realized that his captor was indeed, definitely Maverick. That realization however also presented another problem as he considered more thoughtfully that Maverick might also possibly be a threat to him and to the rest of the group. Quorn was totally unsure what to actually do next or say as he'd never actually considered for a second that Maverick might also actually be a threat to them at all. The group had been so busy trying to actually find Maverick and had anticipated his participation in their plans automatically, it just hadn't even crossed any of their minds for a moment that Maverick might also be their enemy.

Silence occupied the air as it hung over their heads and Quorn's mind went completely blank. His tongue became twisted and tied to his empty thoughts and he was quite simply lost for words and unable to respond. He struggled as he searched his mind chaotically and explored possible responses he could offer when he actually did manage to find the nerve to speak at all. Quorn had been thrown off balance completely.

The group had focused so much attention upon actually finding Maverick, they'd actually neglected to plan what might and could happen when they actually did. Perhaps some part of them had accepted that they never really would, perhaps some small part of them had doubted entirely, that a real moment of interaction between themselves and Maverick would ever really actually occur. Now however, that eventuality and moment had occurred and now Quorn was faced with the frightening prospect that not only had he found the elusive Maverick but that Maverick might perhaps actually want to kill them all too.

ESCAPE ROUTES

The seconds passed by as Maverick gripped Quorn-Montgomery more tightly around the neck and he gasped for air. The laser gun continued to be dug deeper into the back of his head as Maverick became more impatient as each second passed. Quorn had to offer him a response that would satisfy his questions completely and he had to do it very soon. He dug deep inside himself as he mustered up a grain of courage and quickly decided that honesty was indeed the best policy as he attempted to confront the fears he felt, head on.

"We're trapped inside the Mindplant program. We were looking for you to help us find a way out." Quorn quickly stammered as he tried to explain the group's situation, the words seemed to tumble out of his mouth as he shook with fear.

"How do you know who I am?" Maverick asked him suspiciously. "How do I know you are not working with Barbelo?"

"Concept told me about you. He's trapped too. I'm not sure how he found out about you." Quorn explained very nervously. "I think he found some old files on some pieces of old equipment and your details were inside them."

Maverick immediately released him from his grip and then stepped back as he inspected him curiously. He absorbed every inch of his frame and stature as he studied him for a few minutes in total silence. His appearance wasn't like an Exterminator's Maverick quickly concluded as he inspected every intricate, visible detail, from the fine lines on his face that detailed his maturity and age, to the small scar on his chin and the larger built shoulders that Montgomery's body carried around everywhere. Exterminators were usually perfectly refined with no fine lines and no visible scars as they quite simply absolutely never scarred, not even when they were injured as their bodies weren't human and weren't made of the same tissues that the human frame composed off.

"Well you're definitely not an Exterminator." Maverick observed as he smiled at him. His smile was slightly crooked and slanted upwards towards his eye on one side of his face as he relaxed and began to express himself slightly more playfully. "If you were, we'd have probably have had a fight to our deaths by now."

The human identity of Quorn appeased Maverick slightly as he relaxed and leant against a redundant machine nearby, no longer threatened by his presence.

"We need to find a way out of Mindplant." Quorn remarked in an almost pleading voice. "And you are our only chance to do that. You are our only hope. We need you to help us." He insisted as he presented his request to Maverick and the purpose behind their search.

Up until that point in time, Maverick had remained a complete enigma to the whole group that searched for him fervently and Quorn gently savoured the first opportunity he actually had to see the man he'd heard so much about in person as he glanced at his mature, slightly weather beaten face and the deep grooves that decorated and adorned his forehead. His face carried the signs that he'd borne many years of duress, stress and pressure clearly upon it and that to Quorn was totally understandable, he could relate to how being trapped inside the Mindplant system could drain and stress someone. He'd been stressed by his own situation and unlike Maverick, he hadn't even been there for years.

Maverick drew closer to him and smiled. "Don't worry, I'll help you guys if I can." He replied reassuringly as he slapped him gently on the back.

Silence filled the room once more as Quorn glanced quickly down at Maverick's hands for a moment and realized there was actually no laser gun present. He was surprised and slightly confused by its absence.

He inspected Maverick's face curiously as he speculated further as to where the weapon might have actually gone. "Where's your laser gun?" Quorn enquired softly as curiosity pinged his mind and forced him to verbalize his thoughts.

Maverick sat down on a small, empty platform that belonged to one of the derelict machines beside him and smiled. "There is no gun." He replied as he laughed gently. "Guns are pointless, if the Exterminators actually manage to catch up with you, that means it's usually too late for guns. I don't always carry one around with me."

A noise distracted them both as Weaver and Spiral entered inside the large, factory room and walked towards them. The two men turned around and stared at them as they approached cautiously, slightly unsure as to who the stranger was they now found Quorn engaged in a deep discussion with.

"Are these your friends?" Maverick asked politely.

Quorn-Montgomery nodded.

Maverick stood up politely as he prepared to be introduced and immediately stretched out a hand towards Spiral.

"Maverick, meet Spiral and Weaver, they're trapped here just like I am." Quorn explained. "Spiral and Weaver meet Maverick." He continued as he smiled.

Spiral and Weaver relaxed slightly as soon as they heard Maverick's name being mentioned and smiled politely as they reciprocated his gesture and shook his hand. The pleasantries and introductions were over a few seconds later as Maverick glanced quickly around the room and suddenly remembered that the Exterminators could actually enter inside the building at any time and capture them all.

"We should leave here. If you managed to find me that means the Exterminators will probably be here soon too." Maverick explained.

The three nodded in agreement as they prepared to leave the bakery with Maverick in tow, satisfied, comforted and appeased by the fact that they'd finally succeeded in their mission and finally managed to actually find him. The three were filled with fresh hope as they walked towards the exit beside Maverick that a resolution to their problems and a possible escape from the Mindplant program was now within their grasp as they smiled at each other enthusiastically.

"We should take you to meet the others." Quorn insisted. "Concept's been looking for you longer than I have. He knows more about the Mindplant system than I do and he'll be so relieved, we've actually found you."

Maverick nodded in agreement as he expressed a willingness to comply with his request. "Sure can't do any harm I guess. I just have to grab my rucksack from the one of the store rooms. I left it there when I heard you guys enter the building. I thought you might be Exterminators."

The four wandered out of the bakery onto the street five minutes later as they prepared to head towards the underground sanctuary, it was completely isolated and totally empty as they parted from the dusty, old, abandoned building and talked amongst themselves excitedly. The three were filled with excitement as they conversed with Maverick as they walked, extremely appreciative of his presence. Their sincerity touched Maverick deep within who for some reason, started to trust them as he accepted the full extent of their dilemma and the problems they faced. The vacationers it appeared, from what they had said were also unwilling hostages captured inside Barbelo's Mindplant program just like he was. Their dream vacations had become an immeasurable nightmare with depths of horror they could not even begin to fathom or completely understand. Barbelo had hoodwinked them with her pretentions of innocence, baffled them with her intellect and scientific expertise and they had been inadequately equipped to handle the results. He felt a duty towards them, a duty to assist them and a duty to give them something that perhaps it was too late to actually achieve for himself. There was still a chance for them, a small glimmer of hope that their minds could actually still be returned to their bodies intact, even if Maverick's own couldn't.

Since Maverick had been trapped, throughout the years, he'd actually helped a few trapped vacationers, not many usually managed to actually find him at all however as he lived a completely, isolated existence and had shut himself off entirely from the Mindplant vacationer's world. He avoided the simulated people created by Visual and the Exterminators as much as he possibly could and spent virtually all of his time in the Unoccupied Zone. Maverick glanced at the faces of the trapped vacationers as he walked quietly beside them as they headed down the street outside the bakery, he'd help them if he could he decided, he owed them that much as he had created this world alongside Barbelo and he had contributed to the monster she had become. In some ways, Maverick felt partially responsible for their traumatic experiences inside Mindplant as he resigned himself to accept the reality that he had actually enabled Barbelo to achieve what she had and the mess that ensued as a result was also his to clean up.

Maverick and Quorn-Montgomery walked slightly ahead of Weaver and Spiral as they headed briskly back towards the safety of the underground hideaway and the two men engaged in a slightly deeper discussion as they walked.

"Can I ask, if it's not to personal a question. What actually happened between you and Barbelo?" Quorn enquired curiously. "I mean how did you actually end up stuck inside here?"

Maverick shrugged his shoulders and laughed. "You know women Quorn one minute they love you, the next minute they absolutely hate your guts." He explained. "She had different agenda's and I'm not sure marriage or a life partner was ever really one of them. Somehow I got in the way of her personal ambitions. I found out too many things, things that she absolutely didn't want me or anyone else to know."

"She is a very attractive woman. I can see why you were interested in her." Quorn replied.

"Attractive but poisonous." Maverick replied. "Full of venom. One bite and your dead. Don't let that charming smile deceive you. Barbelo would kill you as soon as glance at you if she felt you posed a threat to her work."

"Not the kind of woman you'd take home to meet your mother then?" Quorn teased playfully.

"She's the kind of woman that would give your mother a premature heart attack." Maverick insisted as he smiled.

Quorn instantly took a liking to Maverick as he observed that he still managed to retain a positive outlook towards the world and the people within it, even after enduring so much suffering at the hands of Barbelo. He wondered how he would have coped if a woman had done a similar thing to him, he probably wouldn't have, what Barbelo had done to Maverick was simply beyond imaginable and a horror filled nightmare.

The underground hideaway was quiet as Concept and Matter returned and found the control room empty. The two men sat inside the room in total silence as they grappled with the knowledge of what had happened earlier that day internally. Concept continued to shake his head in disbelief as he regurgitated his actions and contemplated how he could have possibly avoided Connie's capture. She had been a victim of his carelessness and as much as wanted it to change that, there was no amount of thinking that would actually bring her back.

"We have to be more careful in future." Concept suddenly remarked as he broke the silence. "Connie just wasn't sufficiently equipped to deal with any Exterminators." He observed mournfully as his head hung low and despair dripped from his tongue with every word he uttered.

Matter nodded his head solemnly in agreement. "I wish I could have done something more. I just froze." Matter blurted as he started to explain himself. "I didn't know what to do. I didn't want Connie to get hurt."

"It's really not your fault. It was too late for you to do anything really, by the time you'd arrived they'd already captured her. I blame myself for not keeping her by my side in the first place." Concept reassured him. "It was a tricky situation, there was nothing more you could have done."

"But still if it was you Concept, you would have tackled them and shot them. You would have probably rescued her and Connie would still be here right now." Matter insisted as he began to question his own lacking. Sentiments of inadequacy quickly filled him inside as he spoke each word sadly. "I feel so ashamed."

"It really wasn't your fault. Please don't blame yourself." Concept insisted. "It was mine, I shouldn't have left her alone. If it was Spiral it would have perhaps been different. She's been exposed to the Exterminators and she would have known how to avoid them and protect herself, Connie just wasn't prepared." He insisted as he accepted he'd made a huge error of judgement when he'd allowed Connie to roam around the large exhibition room on her own in such a potentially dangerous situation.

Matter shook his head as he continued to scold himself. "If you'd been the one to find them, things would have been different. I just know it." He insisted his voice laced with sorrow and regret.

"I'll explain what happened to Quorn." Concept volunteered as he assumed responsibility for breaking the bad news.

Matter nodded his head in acceptance.

The burden of guilt rested heavily upon both their shoulders as it seemed to weigh their bodies down towards the floor almost as if their hearts, minds and thoughts had become too heavy for their bodies to carry as both men accepted defeat and simply could not be appeased. They would never be able to agree on the issue of responsibility and both Matter and Concept knew to carry on deliberating the matter was extremely pointless, it was quite simply a rhetorical debate that would never allow for a final conclusion to be reached as both men accepted their mutual failure and sank into the murky depths of their guilt ridden silence. Connie, was gone and that was something that could not be reversed, no matter how much they actually discussed it.

The city streets above the surface were unusually quiet as the group of four that remained outside made their way back towards the underground hideaway as quickly as they could. They had to cross a few roads inside the Occupied

Zone in order to reach the underground hideaway more quickly and as they did so they noticed that the roads for once were almost empty as they walked. Maverick related the story of how he ended up trapped inside the Mindplant simulated world to the three in Weaver's group as they travelled through the city by foot, it wasn't pretty and it further clarified how devious and calculated Barbelo really was to each of the vacationers as they listened.

The four entered into the Unoccupied Zone as evening started to set in and continued to walk at a slightly slower, more relaxed pace as they all knew there were less threats present on the streets that surrounded them. Suddenly Spiral remembered that there was no food for the day and that the day was almost over, the four would be returning to base empty handed and their stomachs would definitely be hungry.

"Should we try to find some food?" Spiral suddenly asked Weaver.

Weaver shook his head. "We should definitely return with Maverick first and then perhaps we can come back outside, or perhaps just for today we can make do with barbecued rats."

Spiral smiled. "Crispy rats it is then."

Maverick suddenly paused, rather abruptly and stood completely still as he listened carefully to the street around him, the other three stopped and looked at him as they scanned the street and searched for the source of his alarm. There was nothing unusual that they could see however and they were slightly confused by his hesitation.

"What is it?" Spiral asked Maverick curiously.

"Do you hear that?" Maverick replied as he urged her to listen.

A slight buzzing sound started to come from one end of the street and Maverick quickly grabbed Spiral's arm and gently pulled her inside the doorway of a nearby building. The other two men followed them both silently, completely oblivious as to why they had to hide inside the doorway of a building and totally baffled by Maverick's behaviour.

"We have to hide quickly." Maverick urged as he pushed the door of the building open, hard and fast.

The motive behind Maverick's sudden rush soon became apparent as the buzzing noise grew louder and Maverick quickly closed the door behind them. He rushed them down a short hallway and then entered into a room on the right hand side, the room appeared to have once been a lounge, now however it was completely abandoned, disused, dusty and torn apart. The four stood by the grubby dirty window as they peered out onto the street nearby and watched quietly.

"We're really lucky that we're inside the Unoccupied Zone, if they'd come a few streets earlier, we'd have had it." Maverick explained in a low tone.

"Who or what are they?" Spiral asked curiously as she glanced at his face slightly confused.

"They're Watchers." Maverick explained as he pointed out towards the street through the dirty window situated directly in front of him. "Visual's spies. Whatever they see they transmit back to Visual immediately and if they see you, Exterminators will immediately appear."

Two small diamond like objects the size of a football, floated around in the street outside the window just a few buildings further down as Spiral watched them quietly. Maverick quickly pulled everyone away from the window and urged them to hide behind the wall next to it, just out of sight as the Watchers came closer. The four held their breath, scared to be heard as they waited for about thirty seconds for the Watchers to pass the building they were hidden inside. The Watchers continued to move along the street as they scanned every inch of the ground around them and once they had moved further up the street and were a reasonable distance away, Maverick quickly turned to face Spiral, Weaver and Quorn-Montgomery and urged them to leave.

"We have to go now or they might come back." Maverick insisted as he took Spiral's arm gently once more and led her back towards the hallway, the other two men followed him silently.

"Can they actually hurt us?" Spiral asked curiously.

"They can yes. They're equipped with some laser guns and they can fire them at targets specified by Visual." Maverick explained as he pulled open the front door that led back out onto the street and urged Spiral to depart quickly as he nodded at her. "They can be quite dangerous."

The four rushed back out onto the street and then headed quickly in the opposite direction as they took a detour. The Watchers had added another two blocks onto their journey as they attempted to utilize another route back to their sanctuary in order to avoid any kind of confrontation with them. Weaver led the way confidently as he walked at a slightly more brisk pace and rushed everyone along, the day was almost over and he knew the darkness of night would soon spread out over the city and engulf them.

Inside the control room Concept and Matter continued to sit with glum expressions on their faces as they waited for the other group to return. The reassurances they had attempted to provide to each other had not even remotely penetrated their emotions and neither of them could be consoled as they sat and waited quietly.

Just as darkness started to descend on the streets, the other group returned as Maverick, Quorn-Montgomery, Weaver and Spiral arrived back at the underground station and rushed inside, anxious to get off the streets as quickly as possible. The four stepped down onto the platform of the train station as Maverick glanced at his surroundings curiously.

"Great place to hide out." Maverick observed as he appreciated their ingenuity, for vacationers they'd done exceptionally well in managing to find a place that kept them off the streets and reduced their risk of capture.

"We've been hiding out down here ever since we found out we were trapped." Weaver explained as they arrived outside the door that led into the back passageways. He pulled the door open and held it politely open for Maverick as he nodded at him and urged him to enter inside. "We've created a kind of base in the underground station control area just through this door."

Maverick smiled as he stepped inside the doorway and immediately found himself inside a smaller, narrower, darker passageway. "They've never found you?"

"Not yet." Spiral replied as she smiled at Maverick, who for some reason she had developed quite a fondness for. She'd started to bond with him quite quickly as in her opinion, he was a highly likeable character. He was quiet and thoughtful, much like she was and she could sense that somehow she could actually trust him. Although she rarely felt comfortable around strangers, Maverick somehow had managed to put her at ease very quickly and had an aura about him that she sensed was very sincere. "We've done our best to avoid capture and to avoid leading anyone else down here." She explained.

Maverick nodded as he listened to Spiral as he walked. "It's quite dark down here. I can see why not many people would come down here." He quickly observed.

Spiral smiled. "I know it's been really good for us so far. Absolutely no one comes to this part of the city at all."

Glimmers of light suddenly emanated from the passageway in front of them as it wove around in an arch. The control room doorway sat directly in front of them as rays of light shone out from inside it and Maverick sighed with relief. For a moment, he'd been worried that there was actually nothing down there but a dark, dismal hideaway with no facilities inside it at all that he could actually utilize to assist them, the light from the control room however provided him with an ounce of hope that perhaps there was something more down there than just dark, musty underground tunnels and a bunch of rats.

The four stood quietly outside the entrance to the control room for a few seconds as they prepared to enter inside. Spiral looked a little worried as she contemplated that they had actually returned to the hideaway without any food that day but Weaver stepped confidently forward as he led the four inside the control room with an enthusiastic grin on his face. Today his group had something more than food, something far more superior and something with far greater substance, today his group had actually brought back Maverick.

Weaver strode into the room and stood proudly in the centre as he presented Maverick to Concept and Matter. "Guess what you guys, we've found Maverick." He gushed as he announced Maverick's presence to them both, his eyes were bright with excitement.

The despondent look on the faces that greeted him immediately created confusion in Weaver's mind as thoughts swirled around inside him like a whirlpool and he stopped abruptly in mid flow. He glanced quietly at the two men's bodies which were slumped down in their chairs as he absorbed the tension inside the room and paused. Something had gone very wrong.

"What's wrong?" Weaver asked as he immediately drew closer to Concept. "What's going on? What's happened?"

His question remained cast down on the floor unanswered as it was met with a stony silence and he sensed a reluctance from either man to respond. He glanced around the room anxiously for a moment as he attempted to work out what had happened for himself and a few seconds later it hit him like a slap in the face, Connie wasn't actually there.

"Where's Connie?" Weaver asked slightly nervously.

Concept stood up, took a deep breath and then faced him as he broke the news to Weaver and the other members of his group, sadly. "We've lost Connie." He explained in a very solemn tone. "The Exterminators took her and there was nothing we could do about it. They had a gun pointed at her head."

Shock and despair ran riot throughout the control room as the news hit the minds of those who had just returned, Quorn-Montgomery immediately collapsed onto a nearby vacant crate, defeated as he held his face in his hands and started to grieve. Weaver rubbed his head in bewilderment and Spiral began to cry as she fully digested Concept's words. All three had been totally caught off guard and this was the very last thing they'd expected to hear. Suddenly the achievement of finding Maverick and their moment of joy completely evaporated as the happiness they'd felt just moments before totally abandoned them.

Maverick stood quietly at one side of the room as he accepted that, right now, his arrival was not the most important thing. He had absolutely no desire whatsoever to intrude on an obvious moment of grief that had been inflicted upon the occupants of the control room as pain spread out amongst everyone inside the room, in front of his very eyes.

"How?" Spiral demanded in total disbelief and shock as she stared at Concept sharply. "How did this happen?"

"The Exterminators were lying in wait inside the building and we had no idea when we entered inside. We spread out and searched the interior main exhibition room as we usually do and by the time I reached the part of the room she'd been searching it was too late, they'd already caught her and gone. There was nothing I could do." Concept pleaded as he glanced into her eyes nervously and sought for some remnants of forgiveness.

Spiral shook her head as she rejected Concept's negligence. Forgiveness couldn't come yet, not for Concept and not from her. Silence filled the air between them as it cut through the atmosphere like a knife as Spiral shook her head and walked over towards Quorn. She attempted to comfort him as she placed her arm around his shoulders and ignored Concept completely.

"I'm so sorry. I'm so very sorry." Spiral insisted in a very gentle, soft tone as she attempted to pacify him.

Weaver suddenly remembered that Maverick was present and attempted to offer him an explanation for the dismal, shocked mood inside the room. "Connie's one of us. She was trapped here too." He quickly explained. "The Exterminators caught her today whilst she was out with Concept, they were searching for you."

Maverick nodded in understanding. "Don't worry, if she's still inside the program, I'll help you find her. We'll get her out too." He reassured him.

Weaver nodded appreciatively.

The victory of finding Maverick was lost as the tremendous loss of Connie detracted from it and negated its impact, the day held bitter sweet results as the group sat quietly inside the control room that night and mourned. Maverick spent most of the evening beside Weaver as they sat down on crates in front of the system and he attempted to show him the information the group had managed to actually collate and the various systems they currently had access too. No one mentioned or raised the issue of food at all that night and it was almost as if as everyone's appetites had fled from their thoughts and abandoned them completely as food became a forgotten priority which simply no longer seemed to matter.

The night was restless for Connie as she lay paralyzed in the darkness she'd been placed in, deep within the depths of ground. She'd lost consciousness when the Exterminator had actually grabbed her and when she'd reopened her eyes, she'd found herself totally weak and completely surrounded by darkness. Skylar's body that her mind was still situated inside was completely limp and she simply couldn't move any part of it through sheer exhaustion. She screamed inside as her frustration grew but her screams remained silent and could not be verbalized as tiredness defeated her and dragged her into the pits of sleep once more. Her eyes began to close and she contemplated her fate as the night darkness swept over the graveyard above her and consumed it. There would be no answers today and she had no way of knowing what tomorrow might bring she softly concluded as she slipped into a deep sleep and surrendered to fatigue.

That night as the group rested inside the underground station, Concept tossed and turned as sleep evaded him and his mind was haunted by images of losing Connie. He simply couldn't rest peacefully nor could he fully accept her disappearance. The pain had pierced his heart as the arrow of failure had struck him and remained lodged firmly inside him. The efforts from Spiral to console Quorn had been like a drop in the ocean, pointless and irrelevant and they had not even begun to penetrate the surface of the pain that Concept knew Quorn felt inside. Concept now had a new companion as sorrow accompanied him and engulfed his heart as he grieved and tossed and turned on the iron framed bunk bed upon which he lay.

A few hours later, when Concept somehow managed to actually drift off into some kind of sleep, even in a dreamlike state peace could not be found as nightmares troubled and disturbed him. He woke up in a sweat several times and simply couldn't find any of the usual solace that sleep usually provided to him. It was a painful night and when the morning hours were gently ushered in, Concept was grateful to be able to get up and occupy his mind with other activities as he arose a couple of hours before everyone else and analysed the grid quietly alone inside the control room.

When everyone else in the underground hideaway woke up, they joined him as they congregated inside the main control room and started to organize themselves for the day ahead. There was some debate over the tasks that should be carried out that day as the group contemplated what they should actually do next amongst themselves. Connie's disappearance and abduction greatly contributed to the indecision that was prevalent amongst them all.

"We need to find a way out of here." Spiral quietly observed. "But we also need to find Connie."

Maverick stood up as he shook his head. "It's probably a little bit more complicated than that now." He remarked as he contemplated internally the various complexities of their current situation.

"Are you still actually alive Maverick in the outside world I mean?" Spiral asked him curiously as she sat down on a crate close to him. "Are we still alive?"

"You're still alive, but my situations slightly more complex." Maverick replied as he smiled. "Connie's may be slightly more complex too now, but I'll have to check."

Concept strode across the room towards them both and sat down beside them on a vacant crate as Maverick plucked a device out of his pocket and showed it to Spiral. A holographic display emanated from the circular shaped gadget as he opened it up and everyone inside the room gathered round to watch as the Body Preservation Dormitory suddenly appeared in front of them within the Mindplant Centre. Their eyes filled with surprise and intrigue as he zoomed in more closely on each of the bodies situated inside the personal chambers that appeared in front of them. The appearance of their bodies as Maverick zoomed in on each one, provided an instant reassurance to everyone inside the room that they were indeed still actually alive as they identified themselves inside some of the personal chambers. Each of their bodies were encapsulated peacefully inside the transparent pods they'd been placed inside at the beginning of their vacations and Maverick carefully scanned each one as he inspected them quite closely, just to verify that everyone present was indeed still alive and accounted for.

"You are all still alive. Very much so. How long you remain that way however, is uncertain. I have no idea what Barbelo intends to do next and what her intentions are towards you." Maverick explained. "Not everyone who has a run in with Barbelo and her experiments actually survives." Maverick continued as he glanced up at Concept's face. "We have to leave here now, we can't stay here any longer. My presence in the Mindplant program leaves magnetic traces wherever I go, which materialize in the form of tracks. These tracks can't be traced for at least twenty four hours, which is why the Exterminators and Visual are always a step behind me and I've managed to avoid capture. I installed a time lag in their tracking programs that they can't override." Maverick smiled as he continued. "You vacationers don't leave such tracks, which is why they probably haven't found this place yet as they're totally reliant on visual sightings. The various surveillance programs they use to monitor the Unoccupied Zone are extremely inadequate and sparse but now I'm here though, that changes everything. Now you're with me, they will hunt you more vigorously in much the same way they hunt me and be able to pick up the magnetic traces I leave behind everywhere I go."

"At least Connie's body is still there too." Quorn observed quietly. "So that means she's still alive somewhere."

Concept nodded as he rose to his feet and then glanced around the room at the rest of the group. "Clear out our equipment and we'll take what we can. We can travel down the railway tunnels and find other hiding places in other parts of the city. We'll have to keep moving around every day." He instructed.

His instructions were accepted and obeyed immediately as the rest of the group prepared to leave without any further debate. They quickly packed up some equipment and necessities into rucksacks as they quietly prepared to leave the sanctuary that had almost become like a home. Concept and Maverick continued to engage in a deep discussion as they assessed possible areas in the city that were relatively isolated and abandoned, that could be utilized as adequate hiding places and viewed them upon the grid map on the large screen in front of them. One thing started to worry Concept internally however, there was one huge drawback to Maverick's presence, Connie would no longer be able to find the group if she did actually manage to escape from Barbelo's grip.

The morning for Connie remained dark as she woke up and found that darkness still surrounded her and there wasn't even so much as a glimmer of light to be found. To her relief, she was still breathing and very much alive, although she had no idea whereabouts in the Mindplant program she was actually situated. She stretched her arm up into the darkness and her hands touched a smooth, wooden ceiling situated directly above her head, which seemed to be in very close physical proximity to her body. Panic quickly engulfed her as she attempted to push the ceiling upwards in an attempt to free herself but failed to achieve anything. Her efforts were futile as she struggled for a while inside the wooden container she was trapped inside and then finally gave up as she accepted the reality of her situation. Connie had been buried very much alive.

"Some vacation this turned out to be." Connie remarked as she considered the irony of her circumstances further for a moment. "Sometimes boring is not a bad thing. Perhaps someone will find out where I am and then come and rescue me." She mused as she listened for a moment to the earth above her and searched for a sound or some kind of indication that someone was actually present on the surface of the earth above her head. "Perhaps Concept or Quorn will come and get me out." Silence greeted her however as thoughts of defeat continued to echo around inside her mind and she accepted the horrible truth, no one was coming and no one who would actually rescue her even knew where she actually was.

MINDPLANT: TRIMORPHIA

The time passed by quietly as the minutes turned into an hour and Connie lay inside the wooden box extremely still, movement consumed air and she had absolutely no desire to suffocate before someone had the chance to actually find and rescue her. She attempted to limit the depth of each breath she took and make each one as short as possible in order to consume less air as she attempted to prolong her life. Connie had absolutely no idea how long she would actually be buried inside there and that meant she had to try and conserve the air supply inside the wooden box for as long as she possibly could.

Back at the underground railway station, the group evacuated the hideaway as Concept mournfully led them out into the underground passageways at the end of the platform. A mist of sadness seemed to float around them as they walked and an aura of worry began to follow each of them as they left the sanctuary of their hideaway behind and headed out into the darkness quietly. Concept totally understood everyone's mood and their concerns as he led them down the tunnels quietly as he too had worries on his mind and nagging thoughts that plagued him.

A thought gnawed away inside his mind that bothered him, much like the rats that scurried through the underground tunnels gnawed on a piece of rope they found, if Connie managed to escape the underground station would be the first place she would come to look for them but they would no longer be there. It had been a safe haven to them, a sanctuary and a refuge from the horrors of the Exterminators and the other risks that lurked on the surface above their heads but now it would be completely empty and abandoned even by them. Concept sighed inwardly as he accepted the situation, there was simply nothing he could do now to avoid the move. The group had finally managed to track Maverick down and moving from the underground hideaway was the price they now had to pay in order to have a chance to escape. He knew individually, he would definitely have to try to find another way to rescue Connie no matter what it took as losing her was not a price he was prepared to pay and that was something that was in his mind absolutely non-negotiable.

The group walked and walked for what seemed like miles and miles further down the dark, twisted underground tunnels, their bodies laden with rucksacks and large bags as they searched for the station Maverick and Concept had agreed upon as a suitable resting place for the coming night. They'd had to leave some items behind in their last hideaway as it had simply been impractical to carry them for any kind of distance. The rucksacks they carried on their backs were filled to the brim and they'd even strapped bits and pieces to parts of their bodies with pieces of rope which slowed down their pace slightly as they walked through the dark, dusty tunnels.

Maverick and Concept led the way as the rest of the group followed them a few steps behind, rats wove in and out of the pathways and train tracks all around them as they scurried along busily and attended to their affairs. The rat's presence didn't bother anyone within the group as by now they'd grown accustomed to them and they knew that the rail tracks that surrounded the underground station were their home and that the rats had actually been there when the human vacationers had arrived. They'd never attacked anyone and usually moved out of the way as soon as human feet approached them and hence they were not regarded as problematic.

Concept engaged Maverick in a deep discussion as they walked. "How long have you actually been inside the Mindplant program?" He asked politely.

"About five years now." Maverick replied.

"You never tried to leave?" Concept asked as he glanced at him with shock and horror written all over his face. "But you know the system. You know its weaknesses, you helped design it."

"It's not that simple Concept." Maverick returned. "My body's frozen and only Barbelo, myself and one other person actually know where it is. She's the only one at the moment that can actually free me as my mind is stuck inside here, which definitely won't happen as I know too much. If that decision is left in Barbelo's hands, she'll keep me here for eternity." Maverick explained. "She can't actually kill me as there is the tricky issue of the detonator, which may go off if she does and then she might die too." He continued. "I installed it inside my body right before I entered inside the Mindplant program, just in case."

Concept smiled. "Smart move."

"When you're dealing with a woman as calculated as Barbelo you have to watch your back and ensure you're protected." Maverick insisted. "She'll do anything to protect her work and no man or any other human being comes before that. When I met her, I was naive and totally underestimated her. She's dangerously devious."

Concept nodded in understanding as he listened to Maverick speak, he could relate to his words as he'd actually met Barbelo very briefly when he'd passed her in the hallway, the day he'd attended his vacation consultation. She'd paused to converse with him for a moment and he'd noticed she seemed to be a very strong willed person from their brief interaction, though he'd had no idea how deeply the aspirations and ruthlessness inside her actually ran through her veins.

"Where's your body right now?" Concept asked curiously.

Silence hung over their heads for a moment as Maverick quickly glanced behind him to ensure that no one else could overhear their conversation. The other members of the group lagged slightly behind them, distracted and occupied by their own discussions which relieved Maverick slightly as their lack of attention to the intimate dialogue being exchanged between the two men meant that their discussion was relatively private.

"My body is situated inside a cryptic bank somewhere within the grounds of the Mindplant Centre. Barbelo can't move me as if she does the whole cavern it's situated inside will explode and the Mindplant Centre will be totally destroyed." He replied. "I can also detonate the explosives at any time from within the program itself which is why they're hunting me down so aggressively. Barbelo knows all about the explosives and if they kill me inside here, I'm no longer a threat to her or her world. I'm in a difficult predicament however as if I simply destroy the Mindplant Centre, I'll also destroy myself which means I'll then die here too."

Concept contemplated Barbelo's Mindplant Centre, her research and Maverick further as he attempted to understand Barbelo's motives. "What exactly is her agenda?" He asked. "I just don't get it."

Maverick laughed. "Barbelo's agenda has no real definition. Everything Barbelo does is an experiment. She wants to explore the boundaries of science and push them as far as she can. She doesn't care about the ramifications, or the casualties." Maverick explained. He paused for a second and stared into Concept's eyes intensely. "Your life means nothing to her. To Barbelo you're simply a means of securing funding and your existence and participation within her program puts your status on par with that off a lab rat."

MINDPLANT: TRIMORPHIA

Concept was perplexed as he quizzed himself internally for a few minutes as to why he'd actually been drawn into participating in that kind of vacation experiment in the first place. He was shocked and surprised that Barbelo was able to orchestrate her experiments without proper regulatory constraints or controls and he was stunned that no one actually controlled the direction of her work besides herself, even though she relied on government funding. It relieved Concept that no one else from the group was listening to his conversation with Maverick as the truths he explained Concept felt would simply escalate in the levels of panic they felt inside them, it was bad enough that Connie was missing without adding even further to that worry and alarm.

Meanwhile inside the Mindplant Centre, Barbelo sat in her office as she analysed the results of the Exterminators and shook her head in frustration. So far the Exterminators had only managed to capture four Randoms out of the ten that were actually present inside the Mindplant system and they were no closer to catching the elusive Maverick at all and the reality regarding their lack of achievement irritated her immensely. Maverick had successfully evaded capture and his presence inside Mindplant had tormented and haunted Barbelo every day for the past five years, Barbelo shook her head with frustration as she stood up and began to pace the room.

Maverick was like a flea that Barbelo couldn't shake off, he was extremely elusive and had managed to avoid capture many times and she'd finally adapted and learnt to live with the constant provocation and with him. The weight of his existence and the threat he posed to her, she'd carried upon her shoulders each day as she'd ignored him as much as she possibly could but recently due to her additional experiments and the increased number of Randoms inside Mindplant, Maverick was becoming harder to ignore. The looming funding deadlines coupled with the missing vacationers had created overwhelming anxiety and pressure inside Barbelo's mind and now Maverick had actually met the vacationers inside Mindplant, she feared she would lose control of the situation entirely. He was the one person that could free them and they were the only people that could also possibly free him.

Lunchtime arrived and Barbelo made her way down towards the secret subterranean basement she'd created for herself which comprised off three rooms. The employees she hired, that worked inside the Mindplant Centre actually had no idea that this part of the building even existed at all and Barbelo would often seek solitude within it, whenever she felt a need to. The basement served a few purposes in that it was where she actually performed her experimental 'death experiences' which was why no one else knew of its existence and it was also where she actually lived.

Once inside the main basement control room, she sat down in front of the large, wafer thin screen that lined one wall and glanced around the room thoughtfully. On one side of the room was an underground tunnel which led directly out of the basement control room, the central room of the three, straight into a cave situated inside the mountain directly at the rear of the Mindplant Centre building. Inside the mountain cave, the frozen body of Maverick had been kept in a refrigerated state for years, ever since she'd trapped him inside Mindplant and Barbelo absolutely never, ever ventured inside it as she feared that if she entered inside the cave, she might experience feelings of remorse and regret and if she actually glanced at Maverick's face again it might stir up the fondness she once held for him and she might even feel the urge to rescue him herself. She had absolutely no desire to rescue Maverick at all and hence she avoided the risk of invoking those sentiments within her, like the plague.

At one point in time, Barbelo had actually harboured some feelings of fondness towards Maverick but she'd placed those firmly on ice alongside Maverick's body, when she'd buried him alive deep inside the mountainside. She'd crucified any emotions that were tied to him and created a mountain of resistance towards him inside her heart, much like the mountain he had been actually buried alive inside. The two had actually met when she was a research student, throughout her younger years, over ten years ago when she'd attended a science convention. Maverick had charmed her and she had accepted his advances in total adoration. She'd recognized him immediately from some of the science journals she'd read as he'd been an upcoming expert in the field that she'd held an interest in. He'd made a beeline for one of the vacant seats that surrounded her as she'd sat in the convention room and waited for the expert speaker to attend and deliver his talk and she'd accepted his presence and interest in her almost immediately. His flattering advances had pleased her and although he was almost five years older than Barbelo, his approach had been refreshing as most of the other scientists and attendees in the auditorium were at least fifteen to twenty years older than they both were.

Maverick had pearly, white teeth that flashed beneath his dark, cherry plush lips as he'd smiled at her. His dark, jet black hair was short and well maintained, all of which had added to his impressive stature. He wasn't a slim man but reasonably well built which his height masked a little as he was actually quite tall in stature and that gave him a somewhat slimmer appearance. They'd both attended the convention to listen to one particular speaker that specialized in an area of science Barbelo was intrigued by and it had fascinated Barbelo at the time, that someone else relatively close to her own age range was as deeply interested in the topic as she was. That common interest had sparked and created an instant connection and an understanding between them which transcended the mutual physical interest they both seemed to have in each other and bonded them somehow in a mysterious manner almost instantly as she'd embraced him and accepted his presence in her life.

The lecture itself had been centered around 'Magnetism and Human Interactions' and the scruffy looking professor had eventually shuffled up to the podium and delivered his lecture, when he'd finally arrived as the two had sat next to each other and listened to him speak intently. For Barbelo the lecture itself had been heavenly as she'd absorbed every word and analysed how she could actually incorporate his teachings into her own research. The scientist himself, Barbelo had known rarely made public appearances and hence it had been an opportunity that was unlikely to ever actually happen again. She'd savoured every moment as she'd sat with a Dictaphone in her hands and captured every word he'd spoken enthusiastically. A lot of his work and findings had then assisted her as she'd built upon them and explored them in her own research as she developed Brain Break and the Mindplant Centre from them.

Once the initial meeting between Barbelo and Maverick had taken place, they'd kept in touch through phone calls and emails but they didn't actually meet again in person for another two years. The reason for the lengthy gap had simply arisen due to variances in the physical locations of their respective research placements at the time as they had both been situated two thousand miles apart and were based at two completely different research institutions. Barbelo and Maverick had both known at the time their research placements were like gold dust and not something they could easily sacrifice for a romantic interest that may only result in a fling and that may or may not work out in the longer term.

Once their respective research placements had ended, they'd met up once more and decided to team up on the work required for the initial Mindplant program which they'd decided to call Brain Break. They'd still been unable however to unite properly in order to focus on their work as they'd moved around the country for a while and tried to find ways and means to finance the work they wished to actually perform. Barbelo had eventually become frustrated and grown impatient and unknown to Maverick she had started to engage in her own research for the program without him and even initiated some live testing. She'd performed some Mind transplants and unfortunately some participants involved in the experimentation had actually died throughout that process

Maverick, when he'd discovered what she'd done, had then quickly helped her to change her identity, reinvent herself and start again. He had stood by her and had believed in her innocence as he'd helped to save her from the catastrophe she'd invoked. Throughout Barbelo's trials, Maverick had been there for her one hundred percent as he'd organized plastic surgery for her in Switzerland with a surgeon he knew and even flown her out to actually receive it.

The surgeon who had performed the cosmetic surgery had died within a year in suspicious circumstances, but Maverick had continued to support Barbelo throughout the many trials that occurred and continually believed in her innocence. Eventually however Maverick had begun to realize that he was too deeply involved and implicated in the situation himself and that Barbelo had possibly been responsible for at least ten deaths, perhaps even eleven and that he'd helped her clean up the mess without any questions at all. Maverick had simply believed in her sincerity and he'd accepted her errors as if they were honest, genuine mistakes.

At one point in time, he'd actually hoped to marry Barbelo and he'd felt it was his duty to protect her and help her cope with the mistakes she'd made. Brain Break had been shut down, buried and forgotten as they'd distanced themselves from the disaster as he'd covered up any connection Barbelo had once had to it. Maverick luckily for him, hadn't actually been connected to any part of the operation itself in terms of the documentation as Barbelo had handled and managed all the official documents which meant he wasn't officially tied to Brain Break at all in any legal capacity. Despite his lack of legal connections to Brain Break however, Maverick's heart had been deeply intertwined and entangled in Barbelo's existence and his emotions had committed him to a deeper contract between them both, one deeper than any legal document could possibly have formed.

The two had fled to another country, found another laboratory and started again as they'd rebuilt Brain Break from scratch and called it Mindplant. The new research centre had been built very discreetly and aside from the government funders and those who were specifically selected to participate in the program, not many people knew much about what actually happened inside the walls of the building as they'd retained a low profile and avoided exposure to publicity. The loyalty and support Maverick had shown Barbelo had been accepted gracefully and utilized to strengthen her, though deep down within her soul, she'd always known the truth, the deaths at the first research centre had been her fault as she had made mistakes and she'd gone just a few steps too far as she'd experimented a little bit more than she should have done. Barbelo had adapted the Brain Break program a little too much and take a few more risks than she should have and had completely ignored the safety regulations she'd known she was supposed to adhere too as she'd overridden them as if they were simply irrelevant obstructions. She'd simply thrown the safety guidelines aside into a trash bag of undesirable considerations that had lain in a heap somewhere in the back passageways of her mind like a pile of garbage that waited patiently to be taken to the dump.

Luckily Barbelo had managed to avoid an international hunt by authorities, who'd simply attributed the deaths to some kind of cult suicide. They hadn't even actually discovered the dead bodies until a year after the deaths occurred, which meant by the time they'd found the remains there was very little left to see except bones. The participants in the Brain Break program had been sworn to secrecy by Barbelo and they had all adhered completely to that request. They had all been homeless vagrants that were paid extremely well for their participation in the Brain Break program, who'd been easy targets for Barbelo. She'd known that such people usually had very few relatives that would actually care about their welfare and absolutely no work commitments to attend to, which meant their absence from life and the world, would not be missed or noticed if anything actually went wrong.

Their bodies had lain rotting in a small, hut like building situated a ten minute drive away from her laboratory for twelve months, untouched, undiscovered and undisturbed as she'd fled with Maverick and absolutely no one had known. In those days her name had actually been Lucille Vanquis and she'd simply shed her name alongside the remnants inside her memory of the dead carcasses she'd left behind. She'd closed the door of remembrance on the shadows that lurked within the dark passages of her mind that enveloped and contained her memories of Brain Break and the deadly program she'd actually created.

The new Mindplant centre had been established close to a small town that was relatively quiet and most vacationers who actually attended the program either flew in or drove for a few hours to actually attend, due to the remote location.   Maverick had assisted Barbelo and helped her to rebuild a new research centre and had even contributed technically to her work. Not long after doing so however it had become apparent to him, that Barbelo was not as sincere as Maverick had first imagined her to be and it soon became evident that some of the mistakes she'd made and the risks she'd taken, had actually been taken intentionally and were indeed intentional errors.

Once Barbelo had noticed that Maverick had become suspicious and that his attitude towards her had changed, she had then trapped Maverick inside the Mindplant program as she'd handled the threat he posed to her work and ultimately her existence. He was the only person who could link her to the previous scientific disaster she'd invoked and Maverick had then regretfully discovered that the woman he'd actually saved, did not actually possess a sincere bone in her body and that the tragic accidents that had occurred had not been accidental at all.

Barbelo fixated her attention upon the screen in front of her as it flickered for a moment and then filled as two Exterminators appeared in front of her. She'd summoned them as soon as she'd entered inside the basement room and now they'd actually arrived. Usually when she summoned them, she'd have to wait for a few minutes before they appeared as they terminated any tasks they were engaged in and then attended to her call, hence the slight delay in their response was expected. Chaos and Extinct greeted her politely with a nod as they appeared on the large screen in front of her and Barbelo nodded back in response.

"We have a problem gentlemen." Barbelo explained gruffly. "A huge problem."

The two Exterminators, Chaos and Extinct stared back at her as they stood completely still and didn't flinch at all as they focused intensely on every word she spoke as she sat directly in front of them. Barbelo was their master, their God and their creator and the attention they paid to her every word reflected their dependency upon her. The Exterminators existed purely to fulfil Barbelo's every instruction and that was indeed their only purpose for being and they all knew and respected that chain of command.

"Some of the Randoms have found Maverick." Barbelo explained in an angry tone as she stood up and started pacing around the dark, grey, stone, basement room.

Extinct and Chaos looked at each other for a moment as they contemplated how that could even be remotely possible, they had tracked Maverick for years and never once actually found him, yet a group of inexperienced vacationers loose in the system had managed to actually find him first. The notion that a few Random vacationers had managed to do in a week what they had failed to achieve in years, confused them as they quietly glanced at each other and absorbed Barbelo's revelation.

"When exactly did this happen?" Extinct asked as he turned to face Barbelo once more.

"I think it happened yesterday and now it seems, Maverick's formed some kind of alliance with them. He's assisting them to avoid capture and it seems he may even perhaps be trying to help them to escape from the Mindplant program itself." Barbelo remarked, her voice sounded agitated, annoyed and irritated as she continued to pace the room angrily. "If we can't find them and kill them inside the program, we can't actually get them out of it."

The two Exterminators looked extremely uncomfortable as they listened to Barbelo rant and humbly accepted their failure.

"If we find them, we'll kill them on sight." Chaos replied a few seconds later as he attempted to appease her.

MINDPLANT: TRIMORPHIA

"How will that even be possible? You've only found four out of the ten Randoms so far Chaos and Maverick's evaded your grasp entirely for almost five years now. When exactly will you find them?" Barbelo scorned as she challenged them. She glanced at their faces sharply, her eyes laced with malice as her tongue dripped with words of criticism and sarcasm that clearly expressed her obvious dissatisfaction with them both.

A union and alliance between Maverick and Randoms inside the Mindplant program was a nightmare that Barbelo simply had no desire to endure. Maverick was a huge threat to her, a threat that could tear down her world in a second, if he actually managed to find a way back into the real world and the Randoms could help him do exactly that. The Randoms, she'd intended to perform Memory Overwrite operations on before she pulled their minds back inside their real bodies through death terminations, instead of the usual prescribed sleep awakening program in order to eliminate any threat they actually posed, however if they found Maverick and he helped them leave Mindplant another way, the system adaptations she'd performed would be wasted, her opportunity lost and they would then also pose a threat to Mindplant's very existence and to her.

If Maverick actually helped them to escape, the system adaptations she had implemented so carefully, for her own purposes and her own enjoyment, would be totally wasted and even worse, the vacationers would actually remember all off their experiences inside the program, once they returned to their actual bodies. It was a total nightmare and a nightmare Barbelo quite simply had no desire to cope with at all. She'd planned to experience their deaths through her own mind implantation and Maverick's alliance now threatened to sabotage her efforts to explore a totally new area of human, scientific advancement.

"You need to find them and kill them immediately." Barbelo barked as she stood up. "I have to overwrite their memories. They cannot escape with their memories of their experiences intact that would put everything I've worked so hard to achieve in jeopardy."

The Memory Overwrite process itself was a little dangerous but it was another of Barbelo's creations and she'd managed to utilize it successfully on a number of previous occasions. She'd designed a probe and program that could interrogate human memories and overwrite the details she didn't want Mindplant participants to remember. The process itself could result in brain damage and sometimes even physical death, but since any negative effects of a Memory Overwrite didn't manifest immediately and only impacted on individuals after a significant lapse in time, Barbelo knew any subsequent damage suffered as a result of a Memory Overwrite would never be connected to her or Mindplant. Those risks were reduced further in that usually the negative side effects only affected two or three people out of every ten and Barbelo had absolutely no qualms about taking those kind of risks in order to hide the secrets she needed to conceal.

Usually Barbelo only ever attempted to perform Mindplant adaptations with one or two vacation participants at any given time, from any given group of vacationers, this time however she'd exceeded her usual limits and actually applied the adaptations to ten of the Mindplant participants at the same time. The Mindplant program modifications had been fine, until the allocated vacationers they'd been applied to, had actually gone missing. Once her experimental digression and the Memory Overwrite process was complete, she had actually fully intended to return all ten of the vacationers to their real bodies but the vacationers she'd targeted for her experimental purposes on this occasion, had unfortunately all disappeared within the program before she could do so, once their return from their vacations back to their bodies had been delayed and that had complicated the situation drastically.

"Death is the only way out for them now. If they don't die inside the program, they could be trapped inside it forever. Maverick is so simplistic, he has no idea, he's actually obstructing their return by hiding them, not assisting them." Barbelo explained. "There's also a danger that Maverick may decide to move them around and place their minds inside different bodies and if that happens, they'll be even harder to track down. He has the capability to do that." She verified.

The two Exterminators, Chaos and Extinct listened silently as she briefed them further, regarding her concerns and the immediate course of action she expected them to take, unable to respond due to the shame of their failure.

"Visual will help you capture them." Barbelo continued. "I'll instruct him to put the Mindplant program on automatic programming for a day or two and then he'll be able to assist you properly as you hunt for the missing vacationers. I need them to die, their memories to be overwritten and their minds to be placed back in their bodies before someone raises the alarm and time is running out."

Chaos and Extinct nodded obediently in response and then waited patiently for further instructions from Barbelo as she touched a control pad in her hand and summoned Visual. The frustration and anger Barbelo felt inside, had mounted up inside her like a dam filled with water and now it felt almost as if it would burst, overflow and gush out of her pores at any second. The presence of Chaos and Extinct as they stood on the screen in front of her, did nothing to appease or reassure her and provided Barbelo with absolutely no comfort at all, inside her mind Barbelo knew right now she needed competence and rapid results to extinguish an escalating crisis, both of which she felt only Visual could actually provide.

CONSEQUENTIAL DILEMMAS

The afternoon sauntered slowly by as Gavin sat inside his office and fidgeted nervously as he glanced at the time on the screen in front of him. He yearned for the seconds, minutes and hours to pass by faster as he longed to leave work for the day and return to his home. His recent discussions with Barbelo had changed his attitude towards work somewhat and now he longed for each moment he spent at the Mindplant Centre to pass by as quickly as possible. Barbelo's experimentation was becoming riskier and more complex and that made him extremely nervous as things were rapidly unravelling into a mess and he had absolutely no desire whatsoever to be caught up in the cross fire when Barbelo's transgressions were finally exposed. He'd participated in it, Gavin had actually authorized the vacations for the participants that were now stuck and trapped inside the Mindplant program and that meant now he was actually implicated.

The phone on Gavin's desk started to ring and he glanced down at the screen quickly, although he already knew who would actually be calling him. He liked to see Chivonne's name, face and smile, appear on the screen of his cellphone and he smiled as picked up his phone and glanced at it. Chivonne, his innocent, sweet wife had absolutely no idea regarding the difficult dilemmas he now faced and was implicated in and as the tentacles of complexity and foul play wrapped themselves tightly around his neck, they attempted to strangle him. She had no idea what impact Barbelo's work and her deviation into the darker areas of science could possibly have upon their lives and Gavin had absolutely no desire to impart that information to her.

He decided to avoid her call, through fear that his voice would betray him and that she would sense the anxiety building up inside him immediately. He was on edge and right now and Gavin would not be able to disguise that, especially not to Chivonne. His wife knew every part of him and she'd sense he was upset and she'd sense whatever had upset him was serious. Gavin allowed the phone to ring for a few seconds longer until it finally stopped and then quickly sent her a text message.

'In a meeting sweetie. I'll call you later. Love you xxx.'

He smiled for a second, comforted in the knowledge that no matter what went wrong at work and with Barbelo, Chivonne would always be there for him. She'd never betray or hide any dark, devastating secrets from him and he'd definitely made the best choice possible when he'd chosen her as a life partner and she'd accepted him wholly and exclusively. Their union was the one thing in his life that he was eternally grateful for, especially throughout the more trying moments. Unlike his professional relationship with Barbelo, who's only real loyalty and dedication was to her company and the objectives of her research, Chivonne was his army and ally in the battle of life. Barbelo he knew differed in that she could terminate his employment at any given moment in time if he challenged her or if he attempted to address any problems in a way she did not like, Chivonne on the other hand would face any problems beside him and so far had absolutely never dumped or deserted him.

Chivonne sent him a text back a few seconds later as the beep on his phone interrupted his thoughts and he smiled as he opened it and then read it.

'Great I'll speak to you later. Love n hugs. Chi x.'

Gavin smiled, Chi was the nickname he'd given her whilst they were dating. He'd wanted to call her something that no one else did and he'd found that shortened version of her name appealing. She usually called him Gavin but in their more intimate moments, she would often call him 'Chim' which made him smile. When he'd asked her one day what it meant, she'd explained to him that it simply meant 'my breath' and he'd smiled.

"You're my breath of fresh air." She'd elaborated. "The one that helps me cope and live after all the drama of life is done with me. You give me the hope that beauty can still exist amongst the despair and pain that life sometimes throws at us."

Chivonne's love fitted Gavin's heart like a glove and he knew there was quite simply no other woman in the world for him beside her and somehow miraculously his love fitted her heart too. For the first time ever in a relationship Gavin was actually content, happy and satisfied, which for him was a very unusual situation in comparison to some of his past romantic experiences which had quite frankly been total disasters.

The day for Connie became more and more distressing as the air in the underground coffin she was still trapped inside, started to run out. She began to gasp and inhale more deeply in an attempt to fill her lungs but Skylar's body had become very weak as she lay perfectly still and tried to avoid movements of any kind. In an attempt to conserve the air for as long as possible, she held her breath as often as she could for as long as she possibly could and then swallowed gulps of air in short, quick spurts. Connie was completely traumatized by her predicament. There had been no noise at all from the ground above her head since she'd woken up that morning and she still had absolutely no idea where she was, what was going on or what was actually going to happen to her.

She'd hoped and prayed that either Concept, Matter, Weaver, Spiral or Quorn would find her on time, before she took her last breath and before she succumbed and surrendered to the death that lingered all around her as it waited to grab her life, seal her fate and led her into the dark abyss of nonexistence. Uncertainty clouded over her mind and the mist of doubt spread out amongst her thoughts as if it was a foggy morning as she waited for a rescue she was unsure would ever actually happen. If and when her rescue ever actually did arrive, it slowly dawned upon her that she may not even still be alive to actually receive it.

There were things Connie had not yet done with her life and regrets now lay dormant in her mind, she hadn't had a child, she hadn't never actually been married and she began to wonder for a moment if perhaps these joys would now remain eternally absent and never actually grace her life with their presence. The negative image of those eventualities stirred inside her as she was prompted to try and make another attempt to actually escape, she quickly stored the ugly deliberations firmly on a shelf at the back of her mind once more and committed to making one more escape attempt. Precious air would be consumed but she simply couldn't suppress the urge to actually try once more, she simply had to try. She quickly kicked the top of the wooden coffin as hard as she could and screamed out loudly at the top of her voice and then a few seconds later lay back once more completely still as she fell totally silent and simply listened. The only thing that greeted her was silence as her call for help remained unanswered and she succumbed to defeat.

Her foot throbbed as she broke down and wept tears of frustration which flooded from her eyes and drenched Skylar's face. Connie started to accept the desperate nature of her situation as the devastating reality gripped her, this would perhaps really be the end of her life and she perhaps would really die in this senseless, obscure manner without any dignity and without a valid reason. Despair overwhelmed her body as the rational thoughts fled from her mind and the negative emotions gripped her limbs like an iron clamp. She sighed as she resigned herself to the fact that, she no longer had a choice but to simply accept her pending death.

The position she had been placed in by Barbelo was unfathomable and absolutely horrifying, there were things she wanted to say to people in her life that for the first time she was unsure she would ever get a chance to; lingering words, thoughts, explanations, unresolved complex misunderstandings and various other intricate emotional explorations which she now realized may never actually ever occur at all. Death hovered all around her as it wrapped itself around every air particle inside the wooden coffin she'd been buried inside and almost suffocated her. Death waited to invade, devour and ravage Connie's mind and Skylar's body as it prepared to drag her to an unknown, foreign destination, one she knew she would never actually return from. Once death took her and wrapped its claws around her, Connie feared that she would, never live again, never feel again and never exist again, it would enter inside her body, claim her as its own and never release its grip. Hope abandoned her and chance disappeared as they left her completely isolated and alone with only fear and despair as her companions in the prelude to death.

"Some vacation this turned out to be." Connie muttered woefully as she started to sob. "Vacation of death."

Her heart began to chill with fear as it quickly became frozen like a large lump of ice inside her ribcage and she accepted that death was the most probable outcome for her now and had the highest probability of actually occurring. She closed her eyes and remained as still as she could as Skylar's body succumbed to the loss of energy and weakness that had invaded it, due to the restricted access to air and nourishment. No rescue would come now and her fight for life was definitely over.

The afternoon drew to a close as Barbelo made her final preparations regarding Connie's Memory Overwrite. She'd spent most of her day in the basement and amended all the necessary details as she'd overwritten every single event that had occurred since the day Connie had been scheduled to actually leave her vacation and return once more to her body and stored all the amended memories in a Memory Replacement File. When the evening entered the day, Barbelo made her way quietly towards the Body Preservation Dormitory and prepared for the final adjustments she had to make before she returned Connie to her real life. The Memory Overwrite had been essential as Barbelo could not risk retrieving Connie's mind from the Mindplant program and implanting it back into her own body in the condition it was currently in. Her memory would in its current state would divulge the true nature of Barbelo's work and Connie would then perhaps sabotage the Mindplant program itself and Barbelo's life.

Scandals were not something that Barbelo could afford to face right now, scandals cost funding and she had to operations to sustain that needed to be lubricated by sufficient financial resources, resources that she had made an effort to secure. She had salaries to pay, program costs to meet and a relatively, luxurious lifestyle she was accustomed to financially maintaining. A few memories inside Connie's mind, Barbelo was determined were not going to be threat to all that she had built and hence she'd had no other choice but to prepare a Memory Replacement File in order to overwrite them.

The Body Preservation Dormitory was quiet as Barbelo stepped inside the large room and smiled. Neither Gavin nor Mena were around and that was a relief, she'd assigned them both to extra work tasks that day intentionally in order to keep them busy and as far away from the Body Preservation Dormitory as possible. Their absence meant there would be no prying eyes and no awkward questions from either of them, questions that Barbelo had absolutely no desire to answer as she performed Connie's Memory Overwrite, Mind Extraction and Mind Replant.

Behind the front desk at the top of the room, Clovis the medical guard on duty sat almost like a statue as he watched the screen in front of him intently and monitored the bodies and vital signs of the vacationers in the personal chambers in front of him. His presence didn't actually bother Barbelo in the slightest as he was a quiet, reserved man in his late forties and his medical training was very basic, which meant he would not actually notice anything suspicious or question her actions in any capacity as Clovis had a very limited understanding of the human anatomy and even less of an understanding, regarding the intricate scientific complexities of the Mindplant system itself.

Barbelo glanced at his face and smiled. "You can go for a break now Clovis." She instructed.

Clovis glanced up at her face quizzically, slightly unsure as he hesitated for a few seconds before he actually attempted to respond. "I was actually going to take my break a little later today. I'm not due for a break yet."

Barbelo stared at him sharply. "You can take your break now Clovis." She reiterated in a slightly firmer tone which instantly denoted and clarified to him, he was actually being instructed not asked to participate. "You can have an hour not thirty minutes today." She continued with a slightly softer tone as she smiled at him innocently.

Clovis glanced at her face curiously for a moment and then stood up as he prepared to leave the room. He was a peaceful man by nature and that dictated his compliance with Barbelo's commands without any further debate. A power struggle with Barbelo was quite simply something Clovis had absolutely no desire to participate in, not today or at any other point in time in the future and he quickly vacated the room and left Barbelo alone as he made his way down the hallway outside and headed towards a nearby coffee machine.

Barbelo waited for a couple of minutes and then sat down behind the desk he'd vacated as she quickly touched the screen in front of her. She keyed in some commands and a few seconds later Visual appeared in the middle of the screen in front of her.

"Is Connie ready to die?" Barbelo asked abruptly. Her voice echoed throughout the room as her words bounced off the stone walls that surrounded her, each one as cold and indifferent as they were.

"Yes. Chaos buried her as you instructed. Alive." Visual replied.

Barbelo nodded and then quickly touched the screen in front of her once more as she started to load the Memory Overwrite sequence. "I'll perform the memory overwrite and then we can cut off her air supply." Barbelo explained.

Visual nodded.

"Have the Exterminators managed to track down Maverick yet or any of the others?" Barbelo asked impatiently, her voice riddled with discontent.

Visual shook his head.

"Maverick is really starting to get on my nerves. If he continues to be a problem, I'll have to find a way to put him out of his misery forever." She barked angrily.

Visual nodded.

"Maverick's body is still at my disposal, a fact that he seems to persistently ignore. He fails to give that tiny detail the respect and observance it deserves. Somehow he's under the impression that I'll never terminate his life. He's mistaken. I have no such loyalties or emotional attachments to him anymore." Barbelo ranted as she vented her frustration and anger. "What once existed in my heart, disintegrated and evaporated with the passage of time and eroded with each incidence of sabotage he orchestrated. He's now a traitor and a very dangerous traitor."

Visual listened quietly as Barbelo's anger heightened as he accepted his failure and then tried to calm her down. "We'll find him." He reassured her. "It's just a matter of time now. We're closing in on them and pinpointing their location as we speak. He's running out of places to hide."

Barbelo nodded as she listened. "Make sure you do Visual, Maverick could cause the downfall of us all." She remarked. "Leaving him to run around like a loose cannon is no longer an option. Up until now his antics inside the Mindplant program have been mildly entertaining, now however he's becoming a problem. A very serious problem."

A few seconds later Visual disappeared as Barbelo touched the screen in front of her to end the communication paging program and then quickly stood up, she made her way over towards the personal chamber nearby that housed Connie's body and observed her body functions silently for a few minutes. Connie breathed in and out peacefully as she slept. Barbelo walked round to one side of the pod and opened up a discreet panel in the wall next to it and a small screen with a menu directly appeared in front of her. The control panel connected directly to the Mindplant system and was hidden underneath a flap that only opened when she touched it and no one except Barbelo even knew it was there. Each personal chamber had a hidden control panel screen situated in the walls beside them, invisible to unsuspecting eyes that had no notion they even existed as Barbelo absolutely never accessed them when anyone else was in the Body Preservation Dormitory besides herself. Barbelo quickly keyed in some commands.

"Initializing Memory Overwrite and Replacement Process Sequence in ten seconds." Visual suddenly remarked as his voice echoed out into the quiet dormitory around her, each word he spoke caused a slight vibration in the air.

The small screen in front of Barbelo went blank for a few minutes before another menu appeared and she quickly touched the 'PROCEED' command, the screen then displayed a small, digital sand hourglass in the centre and the sands inside it immediately started to trickle from the top of the hour glass towards the bottom. She closed the panel flap back down over the small screen and then returned to the monitoring desk nearby and quickly sat down. Barbelo knew in her mind that she'd arrived at the point of no return now as she prepared for Connie's return and the questions she might face. In less than an hours' time, Connie's memory would be totally overwritten and the prescribed changes that she'd programmed into the system earlier that day, whilst in the basement would actually take effect. It had taken Barbelo several hours to prepare the Memory Overwrite and she'd spent most of the afternoon isolated and alone as she'd attended solely to that task.

Barbelo was not prepared to sacrifice Mindplant for Connie and her work took precedence over all those she deemed to be participants in servitude to the scientific accomplishment, evolution and achievement Mindplant was designed and created to realize. She was a pioneer, an orchestrator and an implementer of their contribution to the future and in her mind, their actual consent to her experimental meanderings was neither needed nor required. It was a subversive, hidden cost and one that was not factored into the glossy brochure, website descriptive or organized structure that was presented to the outside world, vacationers or the government financiers. Barbelo did however have one small regret.

Although Barbelo cared little for Connie or anyone else that attended the Mindplant program and those she selected to participate in her death experiments, she did care about the body she would now lose inside the Mindplant system itself. Her experimentation with death came at a price and when Barbelo slaughtered Skylar's body inside the Mindplant program, she knew it would never actually be retrievable ever again. Once a body was actually killed inside the program through the Accidental Death sequence it could never be utilized again to house another person's mind inside it. Connie's mind would return to her own physical body later that day but Barbelo in that process would also actually lose access to Skylar's body and persona forever. Barbelo relaxed for a moment as she waited for the Memory Overwrite to be performed and contemplated her achievements as she attempted to console herself.

The Mindplant vacations were an amazing experience and although her work had strayed far from the ethics and morals she'd been taught at the various scientific institutions she'd attended throughout the years as she'd pushed them politely to one side, her justification had always been that science should not be confined by human standards established by minds she felt were inferior to her own. Her work now had as a result, strayed far from the path of acceptability and she'd simply insisted to herself that these morals and ethics were not her own and refused to allow her work to be confined by them. Barbelo in her mind was simply utilizing humanity to fulfil scientific advancement and explore depths of human thought that had never fully been examined before. Several institutions and regulatory bodies had attempted to curb her desires and hamper her development and achievements in the past when she'd worked under their stewardship as they had constrained her activities with rules about human life and detailed boundaries but she'd waited patiently for her moment of freedom and when it had arrived, she'd pushed straight through the prescribed guidelines and simply done whatever she saw fit to.

Barbelo felt satisfied as she sifted through Connie's memories on the screen in front of her as the Memory Overwrite was performed, that she'd replaced and overwritten all the necessary moments that needed to be disguised. There would be no harmful memory re-enactments and no ramifications as Connie would not remember any of the Randoms she had hidden out with inside the Mindplant program at all when she actually woke up later that day. All their interactions inside the Mindplant program would have been totally replaced and would no longer exist.

She waited patiently for the memory overwrite process to finish as she thought further for a moment about Gavin who she knew could potentially become a problem to her, if he actually managed to piece together all the bits of information she had accidentally revealed to him. His marital status coupled with his wife's pregnancy worked in her favour as it dictated a greater reliance and need for job security and financial stability, all of which made Gavin slightly more vulnerable and much more likely to actually compromise his ethics. Gavin would at least in the short term, have to turn a blind eye to any doubts he had and Barbelo knew it.

The screen in front of Barbelo suddenly beeped as the Memory Overwrite process ended and she sighed sadly as she glanced at Skylar's image on the screen in front of her. She quickly replayed some moments of Skylar's existence within the Mindplant program itself and watched them as she reminisced and mourned for a moment. Inside she was semi regretful that now Skylar's life would actually be terminated as Skylar was amongst one of her favourites from the thousands of Mindplant profiles and she'd always been a very popular choice amongst Mindplant vacationers, ever since Mindplant's inception.

An external sigh escaped her body as Barbelo shut down the viewing program and then prepared to leave the Body Preservation Dormitory as she stood up. She walked towards the door silently as Clovis returned and nodded at him politely as she left the room. Clovis nodded back at her in response as he acknowledged her, but neither uttered a word to each other which was not unusual, Barbelo wasn't the type of boss to mince her words playfully around and they rarely ever held a discussion unless there was a task to be performed and that would usually be communicated at a more formal briefing inside her actual office.

Five minutes later, Barbelo arrived back inside her underground basement control room as she prepared for the moment she longed to experience, the moment she had made all the system adaptations for in the first place and the moment she actually lived for. Her moment had finally arrived, the moment that she'd pulled ten vacationers out of the usual Sleep Awakening sequence to actually indulge in, now the Accidental Death sequence would be activated and the termination of a life would occur inside

Mindplant itself and she would experience it, in its glorious fullness.

Barbelo sat down in front of the main screen inside the central room in the basement and watched it closely as Skylar's body appeared in front of her. The coffin Connie's mind lay inside within Skylar's body was quiet and not a sound could be heard as Barbelo quietly spectated and waited. Evening and darkness finally drew in as Barbelo prepared for gleefully for what she knew lay ahead. Connie's death.

The group who had travelled throughout the depths of the underground tunnels had arrived at their new hideout earlier that day and had made themselves as comfortable as they could. Late in the afternoon, they'd hunted for Connie and food as they'd split up into two groups and ventured outside. Their search for Connie had been entirely unsuccessful and Concept had returned with Maverick and Matter not only empty handed but also worn out. Luckily, Spiral and Weaver who'd ventured outside to perform a food scavenger hunt had managed to salvage some food, but the pickings were thin and barely sufficient enough to make a proper meal with. The mood within the hideout that evening was slightly despondent as they accepted their defeat and inability to actually find or rescue Connie.

Quorn hadn't left the new underground sanctuary at all that day and had remained inside the new hideaway as he'd dealt with the devastating shock of Connie's disappearance. Both he and Concept had decided it was for the best as venturing outside when he was in such a distracted, emotionally turbulent state of trauma wasn't advisable, especially when there would be Watchers and Exterminators lurking on the surface nearby.

Weaver and Spiral had arrived back at the hideaway first that evening and then Concept's group had returned shortly afterwards. Quorn-Montgomery had glanced up at the doorway of the control room he'd been seated inside expectantly as the three men entered inside the room, his eyes filled with hope as he'd searched for Connie in their midst. The three men had simply shaken their heads as they'd entered the control room doorway and then sat down on vacant crates solemnly next to him.

"We can always go back out tomorrow and try to look for her again." Matter suggested.

Maverick shook his head sadly in response. "It's pointless now, we won't find Connie alive."

He explained as he faced everyone inside the room and presented the reality to them. "Whatever Barbelo intended to do with Connie, she'll have done it by now."

Concept nodded in agreement as he surrendered to Maverick's observations. "He's right. She'll be gone now."

Quorn-Montgomery stood up and kicked an empty crate nearby in frustration as he vented and Concept quickly walked over towards him as he attempted to calm him down. He touched his arm gently for a moment in complete understanding regarding the frustration he felt.

"Quorn we can't help Connie anymore from here. Not like this. We have to get out of here and back into our own bodies, that's the only way we can help her now." Concept insisted softly. "I promise you, I'll do everything I can to find her and make sure she's fine." He turned to face Maverick as he pressed him for more urgency regarding their actual departure from Mindplant and attempted to appease both Quorn and himself. "How do we actually get out of here Maverick?" He asked. "We really need to leave as soon as possible before Barbelo and Visual actually catch us all. If that happens, then we'll be no use to Connie or even to ourselves."

Maverick nodded in agreement. "There are two ways out of here." He explained. "You can be caught by Barbelo and she can implant your mind back inside your body, if she really actually intends too at all or you can return through another procedure known as a Mindjolt."

"What's a Mindjolt?" Spiral asked curiously.

"More importantly what are the risks of a Mindjolt?" Weaver enquired even more curiously.

Maverick smiled and nodded as he prepared to address their questions. "Gather round and I'll explain each option to you more thoroughly." He insisted. "Then you can each make an informed choice."

Everyone in the room immediately drew closer as they sat down on top of the crates positioned around him and stared at him as their eyes demanded answers. Maverick nodded enthusiastically as he prepared to provide them with more complete explanations, he'd aroused their curiosity and ignited sparks of hope inside them and now he knew he had to explain the various complications both options would actually present in reality. The possibility that there was actually another way to leave the Mindplant vacations and return to their own bodies asides from the death that lurked on the surface above their heads, provided everyone in the room with fresh hope and motivated them as they listened intently to Maverick's every breath and waited quietly for further clarification.

The control room they were gathered inside was similar in shape and size to the one inside their last underground hideaway but slightly smaller and not as well equipped. There were some pieces of disused equipment situated inside it but they were dusty and in need of repair. Maverick and Concept had concluded upon their arrival earlier that day that even though the facilities were sparse, the notion of mobilizing them to make the control room more useful was totally pointless due to the fact they had to move to a new hideout every twenty four hours and as a result they'd simply accepted the meagre facilities and coped with them as best they could.

Maverick glanced at their expectant faces and then started to speak. "If I perform a Mindjolt, there is a risk you could actually return to the wrong body." He explained. "That's why I was slightly reluctant to suggest it. Now though since Connie is missing, I think it's an option, we should definitely explore."

Concept, Weaver and Matter all glanced at each other slightly uneasily for a moment as they contemplated the implications of his comments further.

"What happens if we return to the wrong body?" Concept asked curiously as he attempted to understand the dangers and risks they were about to be exposed to more fully.

"Well you would actually be trapped inside that body for the rest of your life." Maverick explained. "There are no second chances. If the Mindjolt process goes wrong, it stays wrong. The results of a Mindjolt can never be fixed or changed. It's a bit hit and miss I'm afraid."

"How is that possible?" Matter asked. "I thought this whole program was illusionary and that we're not really inside it at all."

Maverick smiled. "It's illusionary in some aspects, but the separation of your body, consciousness and mind isn't. That definitely happened. Your mind, thoughts and relative states of consciousness are definitely not inside your actual body right now. That part is very real." He insisted. "Barbelo extracted them and now they only exist within the Mindplant system within the body profile she placed them inside."

Weaver stood up and started to pace the room thoughtfully as he considered Maverick's revelations more deeply for a moment. "What actually happens if we allow ourselves to get caught and Barbelo puts our minds back inside our own bodies?" He asked curiously as he examined the alternative choice available to them.

Maverick shook his head. "I'm not totally sure. If she intends to bring you back alive, she'll probably perform a Memory Overwrite on each of you, which will overwrite your memories so that you can't remember anything about your vacation that is damaging to her." Maverick explained. "You'll all then have to die inside the program to actually return as she's hardwired the exit procedure so that no one can return from their Mindplant vacation right now without dying first that's part of the experimentation with death that she's dabbling in."

Spiral glanced at Maverick thoughtfully for a moment as she contemplated the options he'd presented them with and shivered as she attempted to respond. "Why would she do that?" Spiral asked slightly confused by Barbelo's experimentation. "Why would she want us to actually die whilst on our Mindplant vacations?"

"Now that's another question entirely." Maverick replied as he smiled. "Barbelo seems to have strange fixation for death. She wants to experience it and live it. Somehow she enjoys it.

When you die here, she's found a way to implant her mind into the same body profile in order to experience the death you suffer alongside you."

"What a weird chick." Weaver grunted. "Not someone you'd want to go on a date with. I mean seriously I got low standards and can date most women but that's just way too weird, even for me."

Maverick smiled.

"What are the implications of a Memory Overwrite?" Matter enquired, vaguely aware that there must be some kind of risks and consequences attached to the procedure in order for Maverick to bring it to their attention as he had.

"It can be quite dangerous, you can suffer brain damage, brain anomalies and sometimes even death." Maverick explained. "Neither situation is ideal and each choice carries its own set of risks." He paused and glanced at each of their faces as he contemplated the difficult choice that lay ahead of them before he continued. "At the end of the day, it will really come down to your personal preferences. Each of you will have to make the choice and decision for yourselves."

Concept, Weaver, Matter and Spiral nodded as they listened.

"What about you? How do you get out of here?" Spiral asked as she stood up, walked towards him and then knelt down beside the crate he was seated upon. A worried expression crossed her face as she contemplated the possibility further that perhaps everyone would leave and Maverick would still be trapped there, fighting and avoiding the grasp of the Exterminators into eternity.

Maverick smiled appreciatively as he accepted her concern regarding his own welfare, it wasn't often that a Mindplant vacationer actually extended such compassion towards him and he felt extremely touched as a result. "If even one person participates in a Mindjolt, I can give them a Mindfile that they will deliver to someone back in the real world, who can actually help me restore my mind back to my physical body." Maverick explained softly. "This is my situation however and your decision must not be based on my problems but rather on your own risk preferences." He emphasized.

"How come your still here? How come no one's helped you get out yet?" Quorn asked Maverick curiously.

Maverick laughed softly. "Not many people find me. Most who are trapped inside Mindplant usually get caught by the Exterminators. Most leave through the death experiments that Barbelo performs.   Those who are not trapped, she reimplants their mind through a Sleep Awakening program.   Only a few trapped vacationers have actually ever found me and like you, they each had to make their own choice.   I'm not here to make your decisions for you, only you can do that." Maverick explained.

Everyone glanced at each other for a moment in silence as they each contemplated what they should actually do internally and weighed up the options they'd been presented with.   It was an extremely hard choice and neither solution seemed to fully resolve their situation, in that both solutions bore risks that were difficult to carry and would perhaps cost them something significant in the future.

"I suggest we all find somewhere to rest in the back rooms and sleep on it.   Tomorrow when we wake up, we can make our final decisions and choice."   Concept suggested.   "It's getting late and our minds are not fresh right now."

Although   Concept   suggested   further deliberation to the other members of the group, the decision in Concept's mind for himself was already made, however he wanted to give everyone else a little more time to consider the solutions that was best suited to them.   It was imperative to him that everyone made a totally independent choice and that each of them had the space to actually do so. The control emptied as the members of the group prepared to retire for the night until only Concept and Maverick remained and the two men glanced at each other and smiled.

"I've already made my decision." Concept informed him decisively. "I'll be going back to my body via your Mindjolt." He smiled. "I'm very sure. I need to remember everything that happened to me, to all of us. I need to remember Connie and I have to try and help you get out."

Maverick nodded appreciatively and smiled. "She means a lot to you right?" He asked.

Concept nodded.

"Thanks Concept. No one's ever tried to return that way before. In as much as people are often dissatisfied with their lives, the possibility of actually landing inside someone else body and being stuck there permanently doesn't appeal much to many people." Maverick explained.

Concept nodded in understanding. "I'm prepared to take that risk."

"Thanks." Maverick replied.

Concept stood up and gently patted him on the back. "I have to sleep now. Gather my strength for tomorrow."

Maverick nodded and stood up.

The two men made their way out of the control room and headed into the back passageway as they continued to discuss their plans for the next day. They sauntered slowly towards the small back rooms inside the underground station that housed some small, black, iron bunks beds almost identical in size and shape to the ones they'd slept in whilst they'd occupied their first underground hideaway. Concept managed to find a vacant bunk bed in one of the small rooms and climbed into it carefully, anxious to avoid disturbing Weaver who was fast asleep in the bunk bed below. He stared up at the dark, black ceiling directly above his head and thought further about his decision to return through Maverick's Mindjolt option as he contemplated quietly whether or not he had actually made the right choice.

Neither of the options was particularly appealing but he couldn't let go of the memories he'd built with Connie and if he didn't return that way, Maverick would perhaps be stuck in Barbelo's Mindplant hell forever. His conscience felt appeased and at ease as he reassured himself, he was definitely doing the right thing. Maverick had assisted them and saved their lives and now Concept wanted to extend and reciprocate that act of heroism back towards him. It was absolutely essential that someone actually returned to the real world with real memories of what had really happened to the group whilst they'd been trapped inside their Mindplant vacation. Concept as the leader of the group knew that riskier responsibility ultimately fell upon his shoulders and that therefore he had to be the one to return via the more dangerous method. He'd failed to protect Connie but hopefully by making this choice and returning to his body this way, he could ultimately make that wrong, right once more. The other option of leaving Barbelo's way, through her death experiments didn't appeal to him at all and he had absolutely no desire to participate in Barbelo's experiments further. Barbelo methods were distasteful and indigestible to Concept who now found her and her scientific experiments totally repulsive.

Someone had to destroy Barbelo's Mindplant program, someone had to attempt to end the abuse she was inflicting upon unsuspecting vacationers and someone had to remember exactly what had happened to everyone throughout their vacations. Concept accepted that Barbelo would never be stopped or challenged unless Maverick's mind was returned to his body and an actual vacationer returned with their memory intact and leaving with Maverick was the only possible way he could actually hope to achieve that. Concept closed his eyes and allowed sleep to embrace him as he comforted himself with the thought that he was definitely doing the right thing and the only possible thing he could do as he accepted he had to sleep, tomorrow he knew would be a very long day.

The night surrounded the Mindplant Centre as Barbelo worked away quietly in the peacefulness of her basement and waited for the moment of Connie's death to arrive. The building was completely silent and only the night watchman and a medical guard actually remained on the premises as the majority of the employees had vacated the building earlier that evening to attend to their own affairs. This was the moment within the Mindplant vacations Barbelo savoured and the reason why she'd made all the system adaptations she actually had and this was actually the whole purpose of her work. She touched the screen in front of her and started to cut off the air supply inside the coffin that Connie lay in as the trickle of air that had continued to flow inside it, immediately started to reduce and Barbelo stared at Skylar's body on the screen in front of her.

The impact of the reduction in air was immediately noticeable as Connie began to gasp for breath, she coughed and spluttered as Skylar's body began to convulse. Barbelo shook her head slightly regretfully. If Connie had simply been killed as she was supposed to be by Montgomery, Barbelo knew this situation would have actually been much easier for her as she would not have had to perform such an intricate Memory Overwrite sequence and would have only have had to overwrite her actual death departure. The experience of death she craved would have already occurred and Connie's mind would have already been implanted back inside her body days ago, Connie would then have returned to her everyday life, oblivious to the reality of Barbelo's experiments and the further complications that could now arise as a result, would have been avoided entirely.

One of the basement rooms had a personal chamber situated inside it, which was completely empty and Barbelo quickly stood up and made her way towards it. She climbed inside it and lay down quietly. Her personal chamber was slightly different from the ones situated inside the Body Preservation Dormitory in that it wasn't enclosed and when she lay inside it there was no lid to cover the top of her body. A mask lay at the head and she quickly placed it over her face and then inhaled the sleeping gases as she began to lose consciousness.

A few minutes later Barbelo woke up and found herself actually inside the coffin within Skylar's body. Her mind had been implanted inside Skylar's body along with Connie's mind, just as she'd planned and Connie was totally unaware of her presence. The process she'd implemented which she referred to as Dual Convergence actually allowed two minds to inhibit the same physical form at the same time. This procedure was another one of her creations and was slightly more complex than the usual vacation Mind Implants that were usually performed for Mindplant vacationers.

The Dual Convergence Mind Implant method could take one of three forms and Barbelo had set three parameters for its functionality. The three forms were Mutual Participation, Dominating Participation and Confidential Subjugation, which allowed various degrees of flexibility and the dominance of by one mind by the other within the body both minds been implanted into and were housed inside. According to the respective parameters of Mutual and Confidential Subjugation, dominance by one mind over the other could be actually implemented without or without the other person's actual knowledge. Mutual Participation simply meant that both minds were aware of each other's presence and participated in decision making together. It was a highly complex, technical form of Mind Implantation that had taken Barbelo years to develop, but it was the hidden jewel in the crown of her research work.

For the purpose of Barbelo's death experiment with Connie, in this instance, Barbelo had chosen to be the dominating mind within the parameters of Confidential Subjugation. The implications of that choice meant that Barbelo could feel, understand and experience every thought and feeling that Connie endured and could actually control them also if she so wished too, but that Connie continued to be the main recipient of Skylar's suffering. During the entire process, Connie would remain totally unaware of Barbelo's presence, being that Connie's mind was the subordinate one, although Barbelo could actually divulge her presence to Connie if she so chose to, through

Thought and Expressed Communication methods, both of which allowed thoughts to travel from one mind to the other through telepathic impulses. For the purposes of Barbelo's death experiments however, she had absolutely no desire to communicate with the victim's mind at all and hence she'd ignored these functionalities entirely.

Barbelo glanced quickly around the coffin as she lay inside the darkness happily, the moment she'd waited for with eager anticipation had finally arrived. She was motivated, excited and stimulated as she waited to savour the death experience she longed to participate in and the air flow inside the coffin reduced further. Connie continued to cough and splutter as she gasped for breath and even pushed Skylar's hands against the sides of the wooden box as Skylar's body continued to fight for life and her throat tightened. She was totally oblivious to Barbelo's presence and to the fact that her mind was now actually sharing Skylar's body with Barbelo's mind. Her mind started to slip out of consciousness as Skylar's eyes closed and she choked as her throat grappled and fought for the last remaining drops of air inside the coffin of death.

The moment Barbelo had longed for galloped in quickly as she revelled in the events inside the coffin and actively spectated. The emotions inside Connie's mind of fear and panic, delighted Barbelo as she embraced every ounce of death that was on offer, Connie was completely traumatized, whilst Barbelo was engulfed in total ecstasy and impatient as she waited for the deadly climax to arrive. The fight for life continued as Connie fought internally for air and Skylar's body continued to convulse and surge as she made her way reluctantly towards death. Barbelo was ecstatic as Skylar's body became limp and still and Connie finally succumbed to death. The last drop of air had now been consumed and the fight for life was ultimately over as Skylar's body lay completely still inside the coffin, numb and lifeless. Barbelo relished the experience she'd yearned and felt a tremendous sense of satisfaction as she accepted that Skylar's death had now actually been realized.

A few minutes later, Barbelo smiled as she woke back up inside her personal chamber and removed the mask from her face that had provided sedation to her body and then quickly climbed out. She smoothed down her dress and then made her way back upstairs towards the ground floor and headed back towards the Body Preservation Dormitory at a brisk pace. Barbelo still had one final task left to complete that day, she had to reintroduce Connie back to her own body, her real life and the real world.

Once Barbelo arrived inside the Body Preservation Dormitory, she immediately dismissed Felix, one of the night medical guards who was seated behind the monitoring desk inside the room. He smiled and nodded politely at Barbelo to acknowledge her presence as she quickly addressed him.

"You can go for an extra thirty minute break tonight Felix. Come back in exactly half an hour." Barbelo instructed him as she flashed a smile at him. "Don't worry I'm here."

The medical night guard smiled and nodded appreciatively as he stood up and abandoned the desk he was seated behind gratefully. He made his way quickly towards the door and then left the room in complete silence, as he accepted her dismissal willing and did not question Barbelo further. Night shifts were long and lonely and the short breaks the night guards were allowed to take, often provided staff with a welcome opportunity to stretch their legs as they visited the various coffee, snack tables and food machines dotted around the building. Felix hummed happily to himself as he walked off down the hallway in search of snacks and refreshments and left Barbelo alone inside the dormitory with the bodies of the sedated vacationers.

Once Felix had been gone for about twenty seconds, Barbelo quickly initiated the Memory Overwrite Sequence once more as she quickly overwrote the last few death scenes that Connie had endured and experienced throughout the final moments of Skylar's life. She removed and replaced the final memories which required amendment from Connie's mind and then initiated a simple Sleep Awakening sequence. The simple awakening sequence Barbelo knew would ensure that when Connie did actually wake up, she would only remember that Skylar had fallen asleep and that she'd reawakened as Connie.

The Memory Overwrite Sequence was completed in approximately ten minutes and once it was finished, Barbelo stood up and took a deep breath as she prepared to bring Connie's body back to life. She walked towards the personal chamber Connie's body was situated inside and prepared to wake her up as she smoothed down the sides of her dress, satisfied that Connie would soon back in the real world and would have absolutely no idea what Barbelo had actually done to her. Connie's body lay inside the transparent pod completely still, silent and motionless as Barbelo approached it and tilted the personal chamber into a horizontal position. She opened the lid and then switched off the monitoring support functions that regulated the human life situated inside the personal chamber and pumped in sedatory gasses at regular intervals.

Connie woke up a few seconds later and then sat up. She glanced at Barbelo's face and smiled. "I'm back." Connie remarked happily, blissfully unaware of what she'd actually been through.

Barbelo smiled and nodded enthusiastically. "Yes you were on vacation slightly longer than you'd planned and we'd originally anticipated. We gave you the option to extend your vacation for six more days and you actually choose to do so." Barbelo explained. "You must have been enjoying yourself."

"How long have I been actually been away?" Connie asked surprised.

"Sixteen days." Barbelo replied. "However you did indicate you would be willing to participate in a special, promotional extension to your vacation if the opportunity arose when you first completed your vacation preferences so there was no additional cost."

Connie was surprised as she smiled. "Really. Oh lord. I must have been having a lot of fun." Connie remarked. "Yeah, I did have twenty days holiday booked at work so it's not really a problem in that respect, I saved my holidays for the entire year."

Barbelo smiled. "I'm glad you enjoyed it. We do try to make our vacations as enjoyable and pleasant as possible." She replied. "It's our primary objective." She stretched out a hand towards Connie and assisted her to climb out of the personal chamber as she smiled. "I can drop you back at your hotel if you like." She offered. "I took the liberty of you booking you in for a couple of additional nights when you extended your vacation."

Connie nodded enthusiastically as she clambered out of the personal chamber and glanced around the room at the bodies that surrounded her. She noticed Quorn's body was still inside a personal chamber nearby and thought that it was strange for a moment as his vacation should have been shorter than hers and technically he should have returned to his own life and body by now. Perhaps Quorn had chosen to extend his vacation too, she quickly concluded.

A few minutes later the two women left the room as Barbelo held onto Connie's arm gently and led her out into the nearby hallway, relieved that Connie had simply accepted her explanations at face value and hadn't asked any awkward questions. Connie was still dressed in the soft, white, clinical wrap robe that she'd been dressed in when she'd entered inside the Body Preservation Dormitory which was customary attire for clients when they were placed inside personal chambers throughout the duration of their vacations, which meant she had to change. Barbelo quickly escorted Connie towards a changing room situated in a hallway nearby as she engaged her in light conversation and prepared her for her departure.

"You'll find your clothes and belongings in the first locker inside that room." Barbelo explained as she pointed towards a locker close to the door. "Once you've changed, I'll drive you into town. It's very late now and I'm actually going in that direction myself." She offered.

Connie nodded appreciatively and then entered inside the changing room, she'd actually initially attended her appointment in a taxi as she'd felt slightly unsure about leaving her car in the parking lot they offered for so long unattended.

The city she actually lived in was situated around a five hour drive away and she'd left her own car parked in parking lot outside the hotel that she'd stayed in the night before she'd gone on her Mindplant vacation as she'd felt it would be a little more secure there. She'd paid a small fee for doing so and the hotel had accommodated her request willingly, she'd probably have to give them a bit more money as the extension to her vacation had been unexpected she quietly deliberated as she started to dress.

Once dressed, Connie prepared to leave the changing room as she picked up her car keys and handbag that lay inside the same locker she'd found her clothes inside. She quickly glanced inside her handbag and found the small business card that Quorn had handed to her, situated inside one of the small pockets, she smiled when she noticed it as she remembered their meeting. Images of Skylar and the various missions she'd performed, occupied her mind as she basked in the experience and vacation she'd just enjoyed as the two women walked quietly towards the entrance of the Mindplant Centre building. The experience had been absolutely amazing for Connie and something she would possibly never actually do ever again, but she'd really enjoyed it.

MINDPLANT: TRIMORPHIA

Once Connie returned home she decided, she would definitely give Quorn a call, even though as far as she could remember, they hadn't actually met again whilst on their vacations as Quorn had hoped they might. Quorn was definitely someone she could develop a friendship with in the future she decided, he was polite, considerate and respectful. She had actually made a friend and that was something positive to take away from her Mindplant vacation experience to accompany her holiday memories. The thought of returning to her real life encouraged her as she decided that whilst the Mindplant vacation had been unique, exciting, thrilling and exhilarating, being amongst familiar faces and the environment she was accustomed to, was something she now eagerly yearned for once more. The Mindplant vacation itself had been artificial and nothing real or lasting would ever evolve from her interactions inside it. There were no physical souvenirs to return home with which she could look at to remind her of her trip, just a few memories inside the shelves of her mind that could never be actually shown, given to or admired by anyone else.

The hallway was quiet as Barbelo led Connie briskly towards the front exit, relieved that Connie was displaying absolutely no signs of trauma at all.

There seemed to be no actual recollection in Connie's mind of the actual death she'd experienced or of the traumatic hours she'd actually spent buried alive, that she'd endured. She seemed happy, relaxed and satisfied that she'd enjoyed her Mindplant vacation and was totally oblivious to the reality of what she'd actually experienced.

An hour later as the two women arrived outside the hotel in the centre of the small nearby town, Barbelo smiled pleasantly at Connie as she pulled up in front of the entrance. The car door beside Connie immediately popped open as Barbelo touched the control panel inside the car and Connie quickly prepared to get out. She glanced back at Barbelo appreciatively for a moment before she departed.

"Thank you so much for such an amazing experience." Connie remarked as she smiled.

"It was my pleasure." Barbelo replied as she smiled in response.

Connie climbed out of the car and then shut the door quickly behind her as she left Barbelo alone inside the car with only Visual as company. She walked briskly towards the entrance of the hotel as Barbelo quickly commanded Visual to drive her back to the Mindplant Centre and the car started to roll forward gently as Visual assumed control of the vehicle. Connie disappeared into the hotel entrance as Barbelo departed and she smiled with satisfaction, the secrets of her Mindplant program had been retained and Connie was definitely none the wiser regarding her participation in the death experiment Barbelo had invoked, her day had been a tremendous success.

Barbelo reflected further upon the Mindplant Vacation deaths quietly as Visual drove her back towards the Mindplant Centre. The deaths within Mindplant Vacations were unlike the deaths that had actually occurred in real life when she'd implemented the Brain Break experiments, in that vacationers could actually could return to their life's and bodies totally intact afterwards, completely oblivious to what they had been involved in or exposed to, once their vacations were over. That thought comforted Barbelo as it meant she could continue to enjoy the death experiences she yearned for indefinitely. The real life deaths of the past that had occurred throughout Barbelo's experiments at Brain Break had meant absolutely nothing to her, but they did attract undesirable attention towards her work and hence it was preferable her work was actually implemented without actual, immediate physical bodily harm for the purposes of longevity. Real physical, immediate deaths of human beings caused problems and in the longer term Barbelo knew Brain Break had quite frankly been unsustainable.

Shortly afterwards, Barbelo arrived back inside the Mindplant Centre as she headed towards one of her basement rooms and prepared to rest for the night. She always slept inside the building and never actually left the premises at night as she had no external residence that she went home to each day. The basement within the Mindplant Centre was essentially her home and the third, large basement room actually contained a bed, a closet, a sofa and a small kitchenette inside it, which was where she actually spent most of her leisure time.

Barbelo lay down quietly on the wide, king-size bed as she closed her eyes and smiled peacefully, through the Mindplant vacations she'd finally found a way to achieve a sustainable method of public participation in her death experimentation, that still allowed her the ability to enjoy and indulge in the death experiences she actually wished to explore. Perhaps tomorrow she mused, the Exterminators would catch more Randoms and perhaps tomorrow she'd have another opportunity to enjoy more of the death experiences that sustained her zest for life and motivated her.

Mindplant and the death experiences Barbelo enjoyed within the confines of her experimentation and research were in their entirety, what Barbelo actually lived for and without either of those, she knew her life would simply crumble into an undesirable monotony of dreariness and become a semi existence which actually served no purpose at all. Barbelo and Mindplant were co-dependents in that she needed Mindplant as much as Mindplant's survival depended upon her and it was a marriage of complete and utter convenience, coexistence and co-dependency. She slipped into a deeper slumber as she comforted herself in the knowledge that for another day, she'd managed to successfully to sustain Mindplant's survival and her own. Tomorrow would perhaps bring an opportunity to enjoy a more complex death scenario, especially if multiple Randoms were actually captured and Barbelo wanted to be completely refreshed and totally ready to indulge in the increased ecstasy such experiences would provide.

TOMORROW OR YESTERDAY

The next morning arrived promptly as it rushed in almost too early for Concept, Maverick, Spiral, Weaver, Matter and Quorn, who woke up still slightly tired but excited about the day ahead. The day ahead held the prospect firmly by the hand that they had finally found a way to leave their state of limbo, trapped in the simulated Mindplant vacation they'd once been so eager to visit as the group gathered around Concept inside the main control room and discussed their various options and choices amongst themselves. Weaver and Spiral's selection was quite obvious to Concept before they even mentioned it and he intuitively knew what they would pick, before they even voiced their selection. The two had opted to leave

Barbelo's way and expressed their decisions slightly apologetically to Maverick.

. "I'm so sorry." Weaver insisted as he glanced at Maverick, pricked by a sudden awareness that Maverick might feel slightly disappointed by his choice.

Maverick shook his head immediately in response as he reassured him that it wasn't a problem and that everything was perfectly fine. "Don't be sorry. It's your life. It's your decision." He replied. "We can't all be the same and make the same choices in life."

Weaver nodded cheerfully as he accepted Maverick's attempt to encourage him.

Quorn and Concept had both indicated that they would return Maverick's way and that left only Matter to render a decision, who still remained slightly unsure and couldn't commit to either of the options on offer. Quorn was adamant that he only had one possible choice and that for him there was actually no real choice at all.

"I have to go back your way Maverick." Quorn insisted. "It's the only way I can make sure Connie is ok. I have to remember everything that happened."

Both Maverick and Concept nodded in understanding as deep down they empathized with the reason for his choice and immediately accepted it without any further questions or discussion. If Quorn returned to his body Barbelo's way, it was highly likely that he wouldn't even remember who Connie was at all, never mind that he had actually spent significant periods of time with her and that loss of precious memories was a cost Quorn simply wasn't prepared to pay.

The most risk averse members of the group Spiral and Weaver, had been allocated to the food scavenger hunts for precisely that very reason. Those activities were deemed less risky than searching for Maverick and hence had been their main contribution to the group's survival. Neither of them were the type to take obvious risks and even though they could stand up for and protect themselves somewhat, Concept had been able to almost predict which choice they would actually make even before they actually expressed their decisions to him, Matter on the other hand was slightly more unpredictable and less decisive, which meant Concept was still a little unsure regarding which way he would finally decide to return to his body.

Maverick was deeply relieved and grateful that finally two volunteers would actually take the plunge and leave the system through the Mindjolt which he would perform for them. The two men, Concept and Quorn could possibly free him from his stifling, stagnant existence and return him to his own body once more and that refreshed him as he longed to be back inside the vessel that usually contained his mind. The body that had carried his consciousness for so many years, had provided him with shelter from the harsh realities of the external world and been his hiding place which he'd dwelt within whilst walking upon the face of the earth. He relished the thought of breathing in real air once more through his own physical lungs and looked forward to ending Barbelo's reign passionately. Inside his own body and human form, he felt that he could actually ensure the Mindplant technology and research was destroyed forever and that provided him with an ounce of hope.

"No more Erotic shots for you two lads." Concept teased as he slapped Weaver and Quorn on the back. "Once we're back in the world of the living such delicacies will be well and truly over."

Weaver and Quorn smiled.

Maverick grinned. "Yeah I created those. A perk of the job, I dabbled in a bit in sexual satisfaction for lonely hearts."

"If those drinks existed on Earth, there be a lot less lonely men around." Quorn added. "You're a total genius Maverick."

"What are Erotic Shots?" Connie asked curiously as they weren't something she'd discovered or explored throughout her vacation. She glanced at Spiral who shrugged and looked almost as confused as she was.

"You don't want to know." Concept replied as he shook his head. "Believe me, you just don't."

The group prepared to move on once more in order to avoid detection as they started to gather up their rucksacks and the bits of equipment they'd brought along with them. They had to find another underground station to hide in as the plan to return to their own bodies would not actually be initiated until later that day, which meant in the meantime they still had to avoid the Exterminators that everyone knew would still be tracking them.

"I want you all to go back, but I want it to be on our terms." Concept insisted as he glanced around the room at the rest of the group as they prepared to leave. "If the Exterminators find us before we leave in the manner in which we've planned, they'll take that choice out of our hands. This way we control how and we control when, we actually return to our own bodies."

MINDPLANT: TRIMORPHIA

Everyone agreed.

The walk to the next hideaway took a few hours as Matter continued to deliberate his decision quietly as the group walked alongside him and uncertainty taunted him. Everyone else in the group had already made their choices and they discussed them excitedly as they walked, eager to finally be escaping the scientific program that had ensnared them. Matter envied their assertiveness somewhat for a moment as he listened to their discussions, so often he felt frozen when he was put on the spot and his paralysis surrounding his choice reminded him of the day the Exterminator's had shown up and actually taken Connie. The indecision he felt at critical moments in time was his one weakness in that he would often spend so long deciding what the right thing to do was and how to do it, he'd often miss the window of opportunity to do anything at all. Matter smiled as he vowed to work on himself when he returned to his own body, he'd still not married yet, largely due to his procrastination and indecisiveness and the years were passing by, soon he knew he would be a bachelor who had past their best before date and he would remain on the dusty shelves of single life expired, out of date and mouldy. Procrastination and indecisiveness were engrained in his being and issues he'd struggled with for years.

There was one final alternative choice, that both Maverick and Concept hadn't mentioned and Matter considered it as he walked, he could actually stay inside Mindplant on his own but that final option was even more risky than the first two and completely unappealing as it would mean he would be avoiding and confronting Exterminators by himself. The third option was totally out of the question.

The underground tunnels were dark, musty and rat infested as they continued to make their way towards the next location and Concept and Maverick edged slightly ahead of the group as they took the lead and walked alongside each other quietly. Concept had a very personal question he wanted to present to Maverick and he took the opportunity to pose it as the other members of the group trailed behind them both.

"Do you think Connie will remember me?" Concept asked Maverick inquisitively as they walked.

"Definitely not." Maverick replied honestly. "Barbelo will have overwritten her memories by now and she won't remember you, me or anyone else she hid with or anything about the time she spent trapped inside the Mindplant program."

Concept nodded his head in understanding. "Such a waste. We shared a couple of intimate moments." He said sadly.

"Look on the bright side." Maverick added as he smiled. "If you actually meet Connie again in real life and you don't actually fancy her as much as you thought you might, you can totally avoid a relationship and dating entirely."

Concept smirked slightly. "I guess."

"You have to see each other when your minds are actually inside your real physical bodies before you make real romantic commitments to each other. It's totally essential." Maverick insisted.

Concept nodded as he accepted his sensible approach and the reality that the moments he'd shared with Connie would now be totally non-existent to her and that only he would carry the remainder of the feelings, he had started to develop towards her. It wasn't ideal but at that point in time, there was very little Concept could actually do about it.

When the group finally arrived at the next underground station, they immediately made themselves at home and settled in as they sat inside the control room and discussed how the rest of the day would proceed. They started to plan in more detail how exactly Weaver and Spiral would find the Exterminators and surrender to them and Matter was finally placed on the spot as Concept demanded a final decision from him.

"How are you returning Matter?" Concept urged. "You have to make a decision now."

The rest of the group suddenly turned to face him as they waited expectantly for an answer.

Matter rapidly tried to untie the knot of deliberations that had grown within the passageways of his mind as he faced the two options he'd been presented with. "I'll go with Weaver and Spiral." He finally blurted out slightly meekly as if he was somehow a little ashamed of taking what he felt was the softer option.

Concept nodded as he accepted Matter's choice and slapped him gently on the back. Deep down some part of Concept had actually suspected that Matter would eventually opt to return that way, but he'd given him space to decide and not pressed him or pressured him for a commitment until he absolutely had to. Matter was the most thoughtful and reflective person amongst the group and Concept knew it, he tended to weigh up decisions in his mind and contemplate each possible outcome very carefully, logically and methodically, before he actually committed to a course of action. Concept on the other hand was much more impulsive and decisive and that was why it had been easy for him to make his decision almost immediately. The two men were very different in nature and in some respects and complete opposites but it was one of the things about his character that Concept had grown to respect and appreciate, whilst they'd been trapped together inside the Mindplant program.

"Are you three ready to leave?" Maverick asked as he glanced at Weaver, Spiral and Matter and prompted them to prepare for the journey ahead.

They nodded in agreement and then stood up quickly.

Spiral hugged Quorn gently as she prepared to depart. "Look after yourself." She insisted as she glanced into his eyes with genuine, heartfelt sincerity.

Quorn nodded. "Be careful." He advised.

Spiral smiled. "I'll be going back with Weaver and Matter. I'll be totally fine." She quickly reassured him.

Concept and Maverick prepared to escort those who'd chosen to depart via Barbelo's route to the surface as they walked towards the control room door quietly. The three that were leaving Mindplant, Quorn noticed had huge smiles upon their faces as they walked towards the door and it seemed almost as if their attitudes had been completely transformed as they'd shed the burden of imprisonment they'd carried, trapped inside the hellish vacation program Barbelo had created almost instantly as their journey of liberation began. A wave of assertiveness seemed to have infiltrated every pore of their being and it was as if they had been invigorated and energized by brush strokes of enthusiasm and hope and as if bright colours of happiness had actually been painted onto their hearts by an artist of optimism. The change in mood inside the room, was contagious as enthusiasm and hope touched Quorn inside and started to drag him out of the mournful state he'd so comfortably wallowed and existed in ever since Connie's capture. Quorn smiled as he thought about Connie once more, encouraged that he might possibly see her again soon as he started to plan some of the things he would actually discuss with her, if indeed that opportunity actually presented itself to him as the five departing members of the group quickly vacated the control room and left Quorn alone with his thoughts.

When the five arrived on the surface, they paused outside the entrance to the underground station as Maverick pulled out a scanning device and began to search the nearby area for Exterminators. Once he'd identified some nearby tracks, the group quickly headed off in the direction of the Exterminators as Spiral walked alongside Maverick quietly. She had a few questions she wanted to ask Maverick about her method of departure and she knew she only had a short time to present them to him as once she was in the grip of the Exterminators, Maverick would definitely no longer be present. She inhaled deeply and then posed her questions as she attempted to overcome her fears, the truth wasn't always pretty or even nice but she had to know the reality in its totality.

"Will the Memory Overwrite sequence damage our brains immediately?" She asked curiously, slightly worried by the deeper implications of the choice she'd actually made.

Maverick glanced at her face thoughtfully for a few seconds as the question hung in the air awkwardly between them, before he responded. "Not necessarily." He finally replied softly. "Often any brain damage suffered occurs progressively and sometimes it can actually take up to a year for the full effects of the Memory Overwrite procedure to be rendered upon a human body. The damage of the sequence has to reach a place of equilibrium in order to fully manifest and it takes a little bit of time for that to actually happen." He shook his head as he smiled hopefully at Spiral and then attempted to reassure her. "Some people are never even affected at all."

Spiral nodded in understanding.

"That's probably why they've never actually managed to track any brain damage back to the Mindplant program itself up until now." Maverick continued. "The time lag, disguises the connection and correlation between the two, making it very hard to prove."

Spiral understood the implications of his remarks and her choice as Maverick conveyed them clearly to her. If Spiral actually suffered any kind of brain damage as a result of the Memory Overwrite Barbelo had performed in the future, Barbelo would absolutely never be held responsible, nor would any damage to Spiral's health ever be traced back to the Mindplant program at a later date. Maverick had made it absolutely clear, Barbelo would never be blamed for anything at all.

Concept caught up with them and overheard Maverick's comments. "I'm more worried as to whether she will actually let them return at all." He observed as he interrupted them.

Maverick turned to face him and smiled. "She can't let them all physically die. It would be too suspicious. She's reliant on government funding right now and is still accountable to them, which means she can't let everyone die like she did last time." He explained. "If she could, she'd probably would have just killed you all by now. She can perhaps afford to let one person die in real life and that wouldn't be too much of a problem for her as she'd simply attribute it to underlying health problems she knew nothing about prior to their participation in the program. Barbelo can't kill everyone though, not this time."

Concept was relieved by Maverick's reassurances as he relaxed in the knowledge that at least most of the three would make it out alive. "Good these guys need to survive and make it out alive."

The three continued to walk along the road quietly as Matter and Weaver sped up and then joined them, Concept's mind lingered on thoughts of the brain damage any of the three might suffer as a result of Barbelo's experiments as he walked. They could be robbed of their faculties at any given moment in time at some point in the future and there was very little he could actually do about it, the whole situation was complex and there really had been no easy decision to make. The consequential effects of each choice was totally unpredictable and could vary from person to person, Barbelo was not only devious but inexplicably cruel.

Maverick sensed his concern as he hung back for a moment and walked alongside him. "Look when I get back inside my real body, I can make a serum for them, which will negate and neutralize any possible effects of the Memory Overwrite Process." Maverick insisted. "However if Barbelo actually decides to kill any one of them during the Mindplant transfer process, there's nothing I can actually do about that."

Fresh hope sank into Concept's mind as he listened to Maverick and nodded, the situation was far from ideal but it was a possible solution and he immediately felt slightly comforted by Maverick's offer. The possibility of a serum to negate the effects of the Memory Overwrite process was promising.

The group of five, hid in doorways and the hallways of buildings along the way as they walked towards the Exterminators and scanned the streets, determined to avoid being noticed by any program simulated passer-by's or Watchers, until they actually wanted to be. Once they'd walked around ten blocks or so as Maverick had anticipated and predicted, they suddenly caught sight of Chaos and Extinct as the two Exterminators exited a building and walked out onto the street that the five had actually entered. The group quickly slipped inside a doorway and hid in the hallway of a building nearby as they watched them quietly.

Spiral turned to face everyone as she prepared to say her goodbyes to Maverick and Concept. "I guess this is it." She remarked slightly sadly as she hugged each of the men gently. "I'll see you back in the real world soon." She smiled and nodded. "If everything goes according to plan, which I'm sure it will."

The two men smiled at her and nodded in agreement, Concept felt slightly comforted by the fact that Spiral was not actually going out into the lion's den alone and that she would return to the real world and face Barbelo, accompanied by Weaver and Matter.

"You just have to let the Exterminators catch you now." Maverick instructed gently as he smiled at Spiral. "Whatever you do, don't oppose them and don't struggle and it should be quite straightforward."

Spiral nodded.

Weaver and Matter glanced at Concept and Maverick as they too prepared to say their final goodbyes, uncertain as to when and if they would ever actually see each other again. Concept leant forward and slapped them both gently on the back as he hugged each one.

"Soon you guys won't even remember who I am." Concept teased. "Soon you'll be back inside your own bodies and your own homes." He insisted. "Don't worry I'll come and find you and then you can buy me a beer."

Weaver and Matter nodded solemnly.

Spiral walked towards the front door of the hallway with Weaver as they both bravely prepared to face the Exterminators situated outside. Matter hung back for a few seconds as he searched Concept and Maverick's faces for reassurance.

"You don't think I'm a coward for leaving this way do you?" He asked curiously slightly nervous about how the two men might now perceive him and the final choice he'd made. "I mean for leaving you here and not leaving the other way."

Concept smiled as he slapped him on the back playfully. "Not at all, someone needs to go with Spiral and Weaver and make sure they're alright." He quickly reassured him. "There's nothing cowardly about that."

His cheerful response was appreciated as Matter smiled and accepted his encouragement, he held Concept in such high regard that his opinion mattered to him and to be considered a coward by Concept would have devastated him. Concept released him gently from any feelings of guilt he may possess as he smiled and nodded at him reassuringly as he encouraged him to go.

Matter took a deep breath, turned to face the door that led to the street and then walked briskly towards it as he joined Spiral and Weaver. Once situated next to them both, he gently took Spiral and Weaver's arms and then led them out of the doorway.

"We have to go now." Matter urged.

The three exited the building and then crept quietly down one side of the side of the street as they followed the Exterminators at a safe distance as Concept had recommended. They continued to follow them until they entered into the next street as they complied with Concept's instructions precisely. The idea was that they should be a safe distance away from Maverick and Concept, before they actually exposed their presence to the Exterminators, which would then allow them an additional few minutes of concealment and provide the two men with the opportunity to clear the street they were currently situated in without actually being spotted. That extra precaution Concept had felt was absolutely necessary, just in case there were any other Exterminators lurking anywhere nearby as it would provide them both with a chance to escape seamlessly.

The two men, Concept and Maverick left the building as they stepped outside and watched Weaver, Spiral and Matter disappear into the distance. They started to creep up the street in the opposite direction as they headed back to the underground hideaway quietly. Throughout their return journey, they contemplated their remaining plans for the day ahead thoughtfully as they walked, Concept was hopeful that the return journey for the three that had departed to their own bodies would be as painless as possible. Three of Concept's group had now gone, one had been lost and now only he, Quorn and Maverick remained as he prayed that Connie was now back inside her own body. She'd, had no choice, she'd had to endure the death Barbelo inflicted upon Skylar's body and the manhandling by the Exterminators without any preparation at all.

Inside the heart of the Mindplant Centre, Barbelo paced the main control room situated on the ground floor aggressively, deeply perplexed by the Exterminator's lack of success. She had deliberately, specifically created a certain number of Randoms inside the Mindplant vacations on purpose, so that she could realize a larger number of death experiences at the same time and her preparations had been elaborate, manufactured precisely and orchestrated to perfection. Her efforts however had been frustrated by the Exterminators sheer incompetence and their failure to capture all the Randoms inside Mindplant once the vacationers had evaded the death exits she'd initially planned for them. However Visual had trained and programmed them, it definitely wasn't sufficient enough to deliver the results Barbelo actually required.

She'd planned to enjoy the multiple deaths concurrently and reside in at least three bodies at the same time, alongside the Mindplant vacationers, whilst they were actually slaughtered which would heighten her death experience. Now however, due their random status and disappearance, it was becoming increasingly unlikely that her goal would ever actually be achieved. The death experience she'd planned would now actually have to be put on hold and the system adaptations restructured again, in order to fully experience the interactions and multiple deaths she yearned to enjoy.

Mindplant itself was much more sophisticated and complex than Brain Break had been and instead of the gruff nature of the mind transfer's she'd experimented with originally, she'd now managed to devise a mind, extraction sensory tool, that was totally unique in form. The tool sensed and locked onto the interior of a client's brain, extracted the contents and then inserted their consciousness into the body of the profile they'd selected within the simulated Mindplant world. The complex program that governed the Mindplant mind transfers had taken her years to develop and she'd actually built it with both Maverick and Visual's assistance, the more complex aspects of Dual Convergence she'd later developed herself with only Visual however as Maverick had been trapped inside Mindplant when he'd become problematic and hence had been unable to contribute.

MINDPLANT: TRIMORPHIA

The Brain Break massacre had allowed her to some witness deaths, but not actually allowed her to also step inside the minds of the participants and experience it herself as they died. Although Brain Break had satisfied her somewhat it had been purely voyeuristic and she'd only experienced the deaths of participants from a purely external perspective which had been slightly unfulfilling. The interactive personal chamber however she'd built in the basement, actually allowed her the luxury to enter inside the Mindplant bodies and experience death alongside the vacationers as she shared their consciousness and experienced their pain. Barbelo was completely fascinated, curious and obsessed with every aspect of death and wanted to experience it as often as she possibly could and Mindplant had provided her with the opportunity to do so. She sat down impatiently in front of a large, wafer thin screen and touched it as she summoned Visual and prepared to brief him.

Her actual fascination for death stemmed back to her childhood as when Barbelo was only six years old, her grandmother had died and she'd known her moment off death was far from serene. It had been filled with terror, pain and anguish as she'd been brutally attacked and murdered by strangers whilst walking in the park alone one evening near her home. The peaceful expression upon her grandmother's face when she'd actually attended her funeral, Barbelo knew was a complete lie. An appeasement to a grieving family and the broken relatives that surrounded her dead body by a memorial company who had made her face and body look as presentable as they possibly could, simply to comfort the people who had not actually witnessed the brutal nature of her murder. From that moment on Barbelo had felt an unquenchable desire inside her to actually understand the contradiction of death for herself and the Mindplant program and her research later in life had provided her with an excellent vehicle and disguise which enabled and allowed her to achieve this goal discreetly. Mindplant furnished Barbelo with the perfect opportunity to not only see death first hand, but also experience it.

Visual suddenly appeared on the screen in front of Barbelo as he faced her and stood to attention in a somewhat regimented fashion. "Chaos and Extinct have found three more of the Randoms and I've flagged their profiles on the system for you." He verified eagerly as soon as he appeared, anxious to appease Barbelo's mind and reassure her that the Exterminators he'd designed were actually capable of delivering what was actually required from them. "Aggress and Riotous are making their way towards them now. Let me know how you wish to proceed."

Barbelo nodded as she smiled. "Tell Extinct and Chaos to wait for Aggress and Strangler to arrive and then I'll instruct them further." Barbelo explained. "I'll start preparing the Accidental Death Initiation Sequence (ADIS), Memory Overwrites and the Awakening Program for each of them now."

Visual nodded in agreement and then evaporated quickly as he disappeared from the screen in front of her and left Barbelo alone once more inside the control room with her thoughts. Barbelo immediately began to load a program onto screen in front of her and quickly flicked through some of the vacationer's profiles until she actually found the three profiles that had been flagged. The word 'CAPTURED' appeared on the screen in front of her against each profile as Barbelo smiled with satisfaction and rubbed her hands together in glee, finally the Exterminators had delivered. She touched a few more commands and allocated each one to the ADIS processes and the screen went blank for a few minutes. Barbelo was extremely excited as she absorbed the reality that this was her opportunity to experience three deaths simultaneously.

A few minutes later the words 'ALLOCATION COMPLETE' appeared on the middle of the screen as Barbelo smiled, today at least she'd actually achieved something. The frustration and worry that had built up inside her earlier that week, she now knew would soon be over. Soon Visual and the Exterminators would capture the rest of the Randoms and any issues regarding a possible threat to the funding renewals would be completely avoided and laid to rest. Now at last Barbelo had a sprinkling of peace.

Inside Mindplant, Maverick and Concept arrived back at the underground station as they prepared to collect Quorn and head towards the other side of the city for the performance of the Mindjolt procedures. When they entered the control room, he quickly stood up and greeted them, anxious to depart and return to the real world as soon as possible.

"Ready?" Maverick asked.

"Totally." Quorn replied as he nodded enthusiastically. "Where are we actually going to do this?" He asked as he followed them outside.

"A building on the other side of the city where I can perform the Mindjolt procedure." Maverick replied. "I've built my laboratory in the basement of a building over the years and it's never been discovered, this control room is just way too basic to perform the elaborate procedures required. I've even built a demagnetizing field around the whole block to disguise the magnetic traces I usually leave behind and hide them from detection completely, which means it's perfectly safe." He explained. "That's why the Exterminators haven't actually found it yet."

The three men quickly gathered up some pieces of equipment they felt might be needed and then quickly left the underground hideaway via the underground tunnels as they avoided the surface entirely and possible further exposure to Exterminators and Watchers. The underground tunnels were a much more discreet means of travelling across the city and would provide them with an ounce of peace as they would not have to scan every inch for possible threats as they walked. Concept, Quorn and Maverick discussed the Mindjolt method of mind implantation as they walked and Concept began to feel slightly relieved inside that Quorn seemed to have perked up a little. He'd taken Connie's capture the hardest amongst the group, possibly because the two had actually met outside the vacation program and had an ounce of reality to their friendship. Concept had suffered as he'd mourned, but Quorn had almost had a complete breakdown.

An hour later when the three men finally arrived back on the surface in the midst of the Unoccupied Zone, they prepared for their actual departure from Mindplant as they passed through the empty streets that surrounded them and walked towards Maverick's hideout. The building itself was rooted in an isolated, remote part of the city and as soon as they arrived outside the building, Maverick quickly rushed the two men inside. They headed quickly through a door situated on the left hand side, just beyond the main entrance, which contained a set of stairs which led towards a basement. The building itself was dusty, completely rundown and showed no signs at all of recent occupation.

"It looks like no one's been down here for years." Concept observed as he walked down each step cautiously as the stairs were broken in places and had bits of debris scattered across them.

"I left it that way intentionally so that the Exterminators, if they ever visited, wouldn't be suspicious and actually return." Maverick explained. "I made sure the building attracted as little attention as possible on purpose. Keep intruders less interested."

At the bottom of the stairs, there was a black, iron door that appeared to be firmly shut and Maverick quickly plucked a device out of his pocket and touched it. Seconds later the door swung open and Maverick quickly invited the two men inside.

"Welcome to my headquarters." Maverick teased playfully as he stood back from the door and allowed them to enter inside the basement room. "The champagne dust fountain is situated directly to your left and the grimy, cobweb spa is just on your right. Just in case you feel the need to relax and poison your pores. There are no mudcakes available today, I'm completely out of those as I've run out of stock."

The two men grinned as they entered inside the large basement room which was made out of stone as they observed it was indeed very messy and extremely dusty. The heavy, black door swung shut firmly behind them as Maverick quickly walked over towards one side of the room and pressed a small hidden button which sat concealed behind a book on a dusty bookshelf. The bookcase slid back almost immediately and the gap between it and the wall, revealed a secret room behind it and Maverick briskly led them inside. Once inside the hidden room, Maverick quickly touched a control panel situated on the wall next to the gap and it prompted the bookcase to slide back in place and return to its usual position.

The hidden room itself was quite large, but clearly not built for comfort and there were very few items of furniture inside it. Maverick quickly offered Concept and Quorn a seat on a worktop situated at one side of the room, which they accepted graciously. The worktop was covered in dust and Concept quickly brushed some of it away, before they both jumped on top of it and made themselves as comfortable as they could. Maverick made his way towards the centre of the room and started to prepare his equipment for the performance of the Mindjolt.

"It's not pretty, it's not very clean, but it is a useful hideaway and it's extremely well equipped." Maverick replied as he smiled. He'd noticed Concept dust of the worktop surface that he'd invited them to sit on and his actions brought a smile to Maverick's face, elegance and cleanliness in this instance had simply been overlooked as keeping his equipment functioning effectively and avoiding detection from the Exterminators was significantly more important and his top priority.

Maverick sat down in front of the large server and a huge screen situated in the centre of the hidden basement room and touched the screen in front of him and it lit up immediately with a bright, blue fluorescent light. He started to initiate some devices as a personal chamber popped out of one of the walls nearby and exposed its existence, Concept and Quorn immediately recognized the personal chamber from their experiences inside the Mindplant Headquarters as they glanced at it quietly.

"What will happen to the bodies we're inside now once when we actually arrive back inside our own bodies?" Concept asked curiously as he interrupted Maverick for a moment and started to imagine what might actually happen to them both when they entered inside the pod.

"Yes and what should we actually do once our minds arrive back inside our own bodies, how do we get out?" Quorn asked curiously as he suddenly realized they might actually be back inside their own bodies, sooner than he'd thought.

The questions posed prompted a smile to appear on Maverick's face as he immediately stopped what he was doing, stood up and walked over towards them. "The bodies your minds are currently inside will disintegrate inside the pod once I initiate the Body Disintegration Sequence (BDS) that starts to occur once your minds are actually reimplanted back inside your own bodies." He replied. "Your minds will be sent back to your bodies five minutes apart and once you arrive back inside your own body, you will lie completely still inside the personal chamber until the other person arrives. You'll have to keep your eyes closed, until I'll trigger a fire alarm which will be your signal to escape. The guard in the Body Preservation Dormitory will then be distracted and leave the room once the fire alarm is triggered and everyone else will vacate the building as per the fire safety drills and then you can leave the dormitory." Maverick explained.

"Don't they remove our bodies from the Body Preservation Dormitory if the fire alarm goes off?" Concept asked Maverick curiously.

Maverick shook his head. "No once the building is cleared, Barbelo will activate a special fire wall that shuts down over the doorway of the Body Preservation Dormitory and protects its contents from being consumed by fire. That's why the whole room is made out of stone, unlike the rest of the building as she fireproofed the whole dormitory. That means you only have a short space of time once the fire alarm is activated to actually leave the Body Preservation Dormitory before she shuts it off from the rest of the building."

The plan Maverick had devised was immaculate and Concept smiled as he listened to him speak. His thoroughness was evident and it seemed, there was absolutely nothing he hadn't thought off at all. Concept quickly concluded that Maverick had probably been planning every intricate detail of his escape for a very long time in the hope that one day perhaps someone would find him and agree to assist him. Finally the two men were providing him with the opportunity to implement a plan Concept could tell he'd put a tremendous amount of effort into actually devising.

A map suddenly appeared on the screen in front of them as Maverick touched a device in his hands. The map detailed the interior of the Mindplant building and had a red line marked upon it that was clearly visible, it seemed to mark a route that led straight towards a fire exit.

"This map will be inserted inside your brain Concept. You'll follow the red route to escape." Maverick explained. "It will lead you towards the back of the building and a fire exit, which you will then use to escape. It will be instinctive and once the map is placed inside your mind, your mind will automatically lead you to the correct path."

The two men observed the map quietly and nodded their heads in agreement as they listened to Maverick.

"Concept I'll be inserting the map, escape instructions and my Mindfile inside your brain. Once you arrive back inside the Mindplant Centre and clear the building, you'll receive an instruction sequence directly from your mind that will outline exactly what you have to do next." Maverick confirmed. "You'll know exactly where to go and exactly what to do instinctively."

Concept nodded as he listened quietly.

Maverick stared at both men quietly for a moment as he paused thoughtfully and then began to pace the room slightly anxiously. "This is your last chance to decide gentlemen." Maverick clarified as he pointed out to them, they could still actually change their minds. "If you want to you can still return the other way through Barbelo's Exterminators and her invocation of death." He insisted as he made one final attempt to seek clarification that both men were perfectly comfortable and happy with the choice they'd actually made.

MINDPLANT: TRIMORPHIA

The two men glanced at each other for a few seconds and then Concept smiled and quickly shook his head. Concept was very sure, he absolutely had to remember everything, he had to help Maverick return and he had to ensure the serum could be administered to Spiral, Weaver, Connie and Matter and to him, this was his final duty as the leader of the group. The rest of the group, who had returned Barbelo's way were now totally reliant upon Concept, Quorn and Maverick to ensure their survival in the longer term and Concept fully accepted that responsibility and duty. He knew the pending brain damage from Barbelo's Memory Overwrite procedure could lie dormant inside their bodies waiting to strike at any unforeseen moment in the future and he had to find a way to neutralize that threat. The feelings he had for Connie and the intimate moments they'd shared he also had to remember as she definitely would not and their romance would then simply die alongside the artificial depths of the false persona's it had started inside.

"I'm totally sure." Concept insisted. "I'm going back this way."

"Great in that case Concept." Maverick replied pleased by his certainty. "You can go first." He stood up, walked over to the nearby personal chamber and opened it and then waited beside it expectantly for Concept to enter inside.

Concept grinned as he jumped down from the top of the worktop eagerly and shook of his nerves. He followed Maverick across the room as Quorn sat and watched them both silently and then immediately stepped inside the pod as the bright, blue light that emanated from inside it, surrounded and engulfed him.

"See you back in the real world." Concept remarked cheerfully.

"Definitely. Then we'll go for a beer." Maverick grinned.

The two men Maverick and Concept smiled at each other and then a few seconds later Maverick shut the transparent lid over Concept's body and walked back towards his screen situated in the centre of the room. Their farewell had been brief as Concept had no desire to indulge in any lengthy, emotional pleasantries as inside his mind he was hopeful that very soon everything would be fine and that farewells were not actually required. He wasn't as overtly emotionally expressive as he'd noticed some other men could be, but he was certain and had confidence in Maverick's ability to get his mind back inside his own body in one piece, relatively quickly and that comforted him as he stood inside the personal chamber fearlessly and boldness filled him inside. Concept prepared his mind to return to the real world and his real body as he hoped that he would also see Connie once again as he stood perfectly still inside the personal chamber and waited for Maverick to perform his magic.

The Mindjolt program was quickly initiated as Maverick sat back down in front of the screen and then touched it. The personal chamber with Concept inside it immediately appeared on the screen in front of him as an orange light filled it and a few seconds later the physical form that Concept's mind was situated inside began to disappear. Maverick and Quorn watched quietly as both the orange light and Concept's body dissolved in front of their very eyes.

A blue light suddenly emanated from inside the personal chamber once more as the orange glow disappeared and shone out into the room as it flooded onto the floor, walls and ceiling around them. Maverick and Quorn quickly covered their eyes as the brightness engulfed them and pierced their vision as it almost blinded them. Twenty seconds later the bright, blue light dimmed and the grey, bland walls of the basement once more surrounded them. The screen in front of Maverick went blank for a few seconds then some words appeared in the centre of the screen that shone out brightly from it 'MIND TRANSPLANT COMPLETE', the verification message read, which prompted a smile to appear on Maverick's face as he accepted that the first Mindjolt had actually been performed and then quickly prepared himself for the second.

He turned to face Quorn, who was still seated on top of the dusty worktop. "Are you ready to go back yet?" Maverick asked.

"I'm ready." Quorn replied decisively as he jumped down from the worktop and prepared to enter inside the personal chamber, just before he reached it however he stopped and paused for a moment as he glanced down at Montgomery's body slightly regretfully. He admired Montgomery's frame and stature for a few seconds as he quietly contemplated that in a few minutes time his body would no longer actually belong to Quorn. "Back to my real self I guess." He joked.

Maverick smiled. "I know, reality can sure be a downer sometimes." He teased.

"What happens to you when we leave?" Quorn asked curiously.

"I'll be here waiting for you guys. You only have seven hours to get me out." Maverick explained. "Any longer than that and Barbelo will probably discover you've escaped and she might even find a way to start destroying my body so that I can no longer return to it."

"I understand." Quorn replied.

"I've programmed the personal chambers that your bodies are currently situated inside to replicate your vital signs for the next seven hours so that the medical dormitory guard won't notice your disappearance for a while." Maverick explained. "There should be no other staff around to notice your disappearance until they arrive at work tomorrow morning, which means we have roughly seven hours to implement my plan."

"I'm a little scared." Quorn admitted as he smiled nervously.

"Everyone gets scared. It's natural to be scared. It's really up to you Quorn you can either embrace tomorrow or live in yesterday." Maverick teased gently. "Barbelo's program represents yesterday's world and upon my return, I'll usher in the world of tomorrow. Her reign will end and her rule will be terminated."

"Do you hate her?" Quorn asked as he speculated how Maverick might feel towards the woman who'd kept him captive for so long.

"The queen I once loved and admired has become cruel and heartless. What I once perceived as innocence has now been revealed as a monstrous inclination. I'm responsible for what she is as I helped create her. I helped empower her and I ultimately enabled her to become the monster she has become." Maverick explained, his voice laden with regret and dismay as he answered the question posed to him sadly and shook his head. "I wouldn't call it hate, but severe disappointment in her and in myself."

"I'm ready now." Quorn replied as he stepped inside the personal chamber. "I have to return this way, for Connie."

Maverick nodded, crossed the room as he followed him towards the personal chamber and then slapped him gently on the back. "You're a good man Quorn. You might not get the girl in the end but you're a good man." He insisted.

"I know. I think she actually likes someone else." Quorn replied as he accepted the underlying truth in Maverick's comments.

The two men smiled at each other as Maverick appreciated Quorn's noble attitude. He respected the fact that Quorn wasn't fooling himself and that he had no false notions that pushed him to act like a hero, simply to have his hopes dashed aside on delivery, reliant on a romance that was unlikely to ever actually happen. Quorn's feelings for Connie had now exceeded romantic leanings and there seemed to be an essence of deep sincerity in his sentiments towards her, he seemed motivated by depths that transcended any sexual desires they may or may not fulfil together and that to Maverick was honourable. His support for Connie was firmly rooted in honesty and so often men simply served their own needs when it came to the sacrifices they made for women and almost always usually had an ulterior motive. He contrasted the two women as he considered Barbelo and Connie for a moment more thoughtfully, he could completely understand Quorn's love for a woman that was so deep, he actually wanted to protect her obvious vulnerability, unlike Barbelo however Connie's vulnerability was actually sincere.

"Did you ever realize the truth about Barbelo before she actually trapped you inside Mindplant?" Quorn asked Maverick curiously. "Did you ever see her for who she really was?"

Maverick smiled at his questions and paused thoughtfully before he responded, Barbelo had disguised herself even to him as she'd furnished her demeanour with innocence, sincerity and pretention and for the most part he'd been completely oblivious to her deception. "At times there were little signs I guess. Things that didn't quite reconcile with the image she actually presented." Maverick explained. "I ignored them and swept them away under a rug of ignorance inside my mind. I was a fool, blinded by beauty and flattered by her attention. I deceived myself perhaps. Barbelo knew I loved her, she knew I was weak. She knew I wanted her and she took advantage of that I guess and I just didn't see it."

Quorn nodded. "Wrong woman." He added in softly as he smiled at Maverick. "Could happen to us all."

"Definitely. Wrong woman and the wrong man." Maverick replied. "If I'd been someone else, I might have walked away, made her listen or perhaps changed something." He shrugged. "Who knows what could have been. People to Barbelo are just objects and tools to manipulate and utilize to fulfil her own agenda, perhaps if I was a different man I would have seen that in time and been able to change that or change her."

"Yeah Connie's definitely different." Quorn remarked. "Nothing pretentious about her. Still, now I know her heart lies somewhere else and that ship has sailed, but we can still be friends."

Maverick smiled and patted him gently on the back. "I'll see you guys soon." Maverick reassured him as he smiled and nodded.

Quorn inhaled deeply and took a huge breath as Maverick shut the transparent lid over his body and then returned to the screen situated in the centre of the room and sat down in front of it. He touched the screen eagerly as the mind transfer was performed and the personal chamber shone brightly with an orange light once more. Quorn disappeared a few seconds later in a similar manner to Concept as Maverick nodded his head in satisfaction, if things had actually gone according to plan, soon his own rescue would be forthcoming and that was something he'd actually waited years for.

The years Maverick had waited years for volunteers had tried his patience and now he'd finally found not just one but two willing participants in one go, well actually they'd found him. Unlike Barbelo, Maverick had avoided coercion and forced manipulation and had waited for real volunteers, people who had sought him out and made the choice to participate in a Mindjolt from their own free will and finally God had rewarded his sincerity. Now Maverick would be provided with a chance to escape the treacherous trap Barbelo had kept him contained inside for so long and now his own freedom actually lay within his grasp. It was a joyful moment not only for Concept and Quorn but also for Maverick as he embraced the thought that very soon he would really be situated back inside his real body and the real world.

Inside the Body Preservation Dormitory, Quorn's mind arrived back inside his body as he aroused from a state of slumber and lay completely still with his eyes firmly closed, just as Maverick had instructed him too. The fire alarm sounded out a few minutes later, just as Maverick had predicted it would and the night guard quickly evacuated the dormitory. Quorn opened his eyes as soon as he heard the night guard depart and then pushed the lid of the personal chamber open as soon as he was sure that the room was clear. He clambered out of the personal chamber quickly and then made his way towards the centre of the room.

Another personal chamber situated at the other side of the room opened up as Quorn watched a man climb out of it and then walk towards him, the two men nodded at each other as they greeted each other politely and then glanced at each other curiously for a few seconds. There was complete silence as they absorbed each other's physical presence quietly intrigued by reality and their real physical forms.

Concept was a slightly younger man as Quorn had a suspected he would be and was somewhere in his late thirties and as Quorn glanced at him, he accepted that Concept had very much been his rival in the battle for Connie's attention and affections. This was the man who'd ousted his position and lain claim to Connie's heart and he'd succumbed to that gracefully as he'd accepted where Connie's interest really lay. Quorn had absolutely no desire at all to be Connie's second choice.

The two men smiled at each other warmly and then stretched out their hands towards each other as they introduced themselves.

"Quorn?" Concept asked.

Quorn nodded. "Concept?" He enquired.

Concept grinned and nodded. "We better get out of here." Concept replied as he gently grabbed Quorn's arm and guided him towards the doorway nearby.

Quorn paused for a moment just before they reached the door and quickly glanced back at the dormitory and the personal chambers as he searched for Connie's body.

Concept smiled. "Connie's probably already gone." He quickly pointed out.

Quorn smiled and nodded slightly relieved and hopeful that she was now back inside her body and perhaps on the way back to her life and world. "Yeah, you're right her body definitely isn't here. Where do we go now?" Quorn asked.

"Just follow me. We're going that way." Concept replied as he pointed out of the door towards a long hallway nearby that led off to the right hand side and towards the very rear of the building.

Quorn nodded in agreement.

The two men exited the Body Preservation Dormitory quickly and made their way briskly down the hallway as they prepared to actually leave the Mindplant building itself. Quorn lagged a step or two behind Concept as he allowed him to lead the way as the two men started to participate in Maverick's plan.

"Do you know who we have to contact, once we actually get outside?" Quorn asked curiously as they walked.

"Yes his name is Troy." Concept replied as he continued to walk briskly towards the back of the building. "Somehow I have his contact details in my mind, Maverick put them into my memories and thoughts before we left Mindplant."

When the two men arrived at the end of the hallway, they found a short passageway which led off towards a nearby fire exit and Concept quickly walked towards it. A few seconds later Concept pushed the fire exit door open and they both exited as they stepped out into the grounds that surrounded the Mindplant Centre and inhaled the fresh air that surrounded them appreciatively. Once they were outside, Concept immediately noticed a huge wall situated directly in front of them and quickly walked towards it. Quorn followed him a few steps behind quietly and when they arrived at the wall, Concept quickly crouched down and put his hands together to form a kind of step for Quorn to actually mount the wall from. Quorn quickly and appreciatively placed his foot into Concept's hand stirrup and then utilized it as leverage to scale the wall as he grabbed onto the top and then jumped up towards it.

Once Quorn was safely on top of the wall, he sprawled across it as he leant quickly back down and assisted Concept who appreciatively grabbed onto his arm and pulled himself up towards the top of the wall. The two men caught their breath for a few seconds as they sat on top of the wall and scanned the other side, which had previously been hidden from sight.

Concept nodded. "Let's go." He insisted a few seconds later.

The two men quickly jumped down from the wall and landed on the ground on the other side and then quickly ran towards a highway nearby. Concept led Quorn fifty metres down the road and then stopped next to a small, silver box attached to a small, black, metal post. The box housed an emergency phone inside it, the type that one would usually find strewn across various highways for emergencies when cars had broken down, it was very basic however and not well maintained as the door hung slightly off its hinges. Concept pulled open the small silver box that contained the phone and then used it quickly to make a call as he picked up the receiver and tapped in a phone number instinctively.

The two men glanced at each other slightly nervously for a moment as Concept waited for someone to actually answer his call. They were both still dressed in the white, clinical robes they'd been wearing since they'd been placed inside their personal chambers and which meant, if any traffic actually passed them on the road they stood next too, they would definitely stand out and be noticed.

Their appearance worried Concept slightly as he feared a member of staff from the Mindplant Centre itself might perhaps actually drive past them as they stood on the edge of the roadside. The building was situated very close to where the emergency phone box was actually positioned and that made him slightly uncomfortable.

The phone rang for a few seconds before the call was answered by a male voice and Concept sighed with relief as he quickly explained to the receiver of the call, exactly who he was and the situation he was actually in. The man who'd answered the call, Troy seemed very compliant as soon as Concept mentioned Maverick's name.

"Stay exactly where you are I'm on my way." Troy quickly instructed him. "Stay out of sight and when I arrive I'll park my car right next to the emergency phone box."

Concept nodded quickly in agreement as he replied. "Ok we'll be waiting for you." He ended the call and then led Quorn quickly towards a nearby bush as he explained the next plan of action to him. "Now we wait." He insisted as the two men crouched behind the bush. "Troy is on his way."

Minutes passed by as the two men sat behind the bush and waited quietly, Quorn began to think about Connie as he deliberated for a moment that he actually didn't even know where Connie actually lived. He didn't even have her phone number, but he did remember that he'd actually given her his business card which had his cellphone number printed upon it. A cellphone which right now he didn't actually have in his possession as it was firmly tucked away inside Barbelo's Mindplant Centre. Deep down inside himself, he prayed and hoped that she would actually find it and call him once he managed to actually retrieve his phone. He might not be her first choice but he could definitely at least be a good friend.

"Once we're done here we'll look for Connie." Concept mentioned as if somehow he could read Quorn's thoughts through the still waters of silence that lapped gently around them like waves that caressed a tropical island beach shore on a calm, peaceful morning.

Quorn nodded appreciatively. "I don't think I'll be taking anymore vacations from work for a while." He commented playfully as he attempted to make some light conversation with Concept as they waited so that the minutes would feel as if somehow they had passed more quickly.

Concept nodded in agreement. "I know me too. Mindplant was enough to put me off vacations for life." He replied. "Perhaps next time I'll just book a fourteen day package holiday at a hotel like everyone else does. Bit safer."

Quorn laughed.

The two men continued to discuss the complexities of the Mindplant system further as they waited patiently for Oasis to arrive and continued to crouch behind the bush. The various memories that had been created, intrigued them slightly as they observed that everything had been induced, planned and controlled by the various programs Barbelo had created to govern the Mindplant environment. The architecture and blend of reality and artificial components that created a comprehensive experience which existed purely to entertain human minds and serve Barbelo's purposes was captivating but also extremely frightening.

"Do you think she'll do what she did to us to other people?" Quorn asked quietly.

Concept smiled. "Definitely. Unless Maverick manages to stop her. Why would she stop? She's on a roll."

Quorn nodded in agreement.

The two men continued to make light conversation to occupy themselves until a silver car pulled up by the emergency phone box fifteen minutes later and stopped just beside it. Troy had kept his word and shown up just as he'd promised. Concept smiled.

A large, heavy built man quickly climbed out of the silver car and glanced around him as he searched for Concept. He was in his early fifties and was what one might call, slightly rounded and firmly placed on top of his balding head was a slate, grey coloured cap. Concept quickly stood up and made his way over towards him, pleased and relieved that the two men could finally leave the bush they'd been crouched behind, a bush that was still in relatively close proximity to the Mindplant Centre. Troy smiled at Concept and Quorn who approached him rather briskly, anxious to put some distance between themselves the building that had plunged them into the nightmare vacation they had just escaped from as soon as they possibly could.

"You must be Concept." Troy asked politely as he stretched out a hand towards him.

Concept nodded as he replied. "Yes and this is Quorn. Are you Troy?"

Troy nodded and smiled. "That's me. Are you ready to bring Maverick back to the world of the living?" He asked cheerfully.

The two men nodded enthusiastically and Troy smiled at them, he then quickly led them back towards his car which was parked just a few metres away from where they'd actually been hiding. Once they were seated inside the car, Troy drove it quickly back towards the Mindplant Centre and then drove straight past the building. Concept held his breath for a moment as he suddenly imagined being taken back inside and entertained the possibility that perhaps Troy was really one of Barbelo's allies and that the final adventure had been constructed deliberately to add further excitement to the vacation package experience. The car headed towards the rear of the building as Troy silently confirmed that this was definitely not the case and that the horrors they'd endured on their vacation were actually very real. The vehicle entered a small, dirt road situated at the back of the building which led up the mountainside directly behind it and Concept exhaled. No, this definitely wasn't one of Barbelo's simulated, planned adventures they really had been trapped and Maverick's plight was definitely and utterly, completely real.

The car suddenly stopped, mid-way up the mountain dirt road as Troy quickly motioned towards Quorn and Concept to follow him and exited the vehicle with a large rucksack in his hands. The two men followed him obediently as he walked briskly towards a rock nearby and then pushed it towards the right and to their complete surprise the rock actually gave way and moved. A tunnel suddenly opened up in the mountainside beside them and Quorn and Concept glanced at it in surprise. Troy led them quickly inside.

The tunnel they entered, led into a large, dark cavern that was icy cold and the three men felt almost as if they were inside a freezer as they entered inside the large space and shivered slightly. Concept and Quorn glanced around the dark interior curiously as they attempted to see what was inside the large cave like room and as their eyes became accustomed to the darkness, they observed a large, transparent like coffin situated in the centre of the room which had a man's frozen body inside it. The body was surrounded by chunks of ice and the man's face was covered with frost and icicles.

"This is Maverick." Troy explained politely as he turned to face the two men and smiled. He walked towards the transparent box and placed his rucksack on the floor beside it and then quickly opened up the top of the personal chamber. Troy touched Maverick's face gently and smiled fondly. "Maverick my friend I've come to resurrect you." He exclaimed affectionately. "It's been a very long time."

Concept and Quorn continued to watch in silence as Troy quickly, opened up the rucksack and removed a heater like blanket from inside it. The blanket like heater had tubes running through it and Troy quickly threw it over Maverick's body. He turned back to face Concept and then beckoned towards him to come closer and Concept immediately stepped forward. Troy handed him a device to place on top of his head and Concept complied immediately as Troy explained to him exactly what he actually had to do next. Concept nodded as he listened to Troy impart instructions to him.

Once Troy was completely satisfied that the head device was actually situated upon Concept's head correctly, he quickly removed a small, holographic device from inside the rucksack that looked very similar to the one that the two men had seen Maverick utilize inside Mindplant. The blanket on top of Maverick's frozen body began to glow a deep, orangey, fiery red as the ice that surrounded him slowly started to melt away as the two men waited and watched.

"Cover your eyes please." Troy instructed them. "Just for a minute."

The two men immediately covered their eyes with their hands and Troy plucked an eye visor out of his rucksack which he then quickly placed over his own eyes. He quickly glanced at the two men situated at the side of the cave, just for a moment to ensure that they had actually complied with his instructions and then satisfied that they had, he quickly touched the holographic device in his hand as he initiated a program. A bright, blue light immediately began to emanate from the device situated inside Troy's hand and from the device situated firmly on top of Concept's head as Troy focused on the device in his hand intently and touched it at regular intervals as he entered further commands.

The operation lasted a few minutes as Troy quickly extracted Maverick's Mindfile from within Concept's brain and inserted back inside Maverick's body as he facilitated the small device he carried in his hand to perform the various functions he required. Once the mind extraction and implant was complete, the blue light began to dim and Maverick, who had by now fully thawed, started to awaken.

"You can open your eyes now." Troy instructed Quorn and Concept as he removed the blanket that had been strewn across Maverick's body and helped him to sit up. "Maverick it's great to have you back in the world of the living." Troy teased as he turned to face Maverick and smiled. "I've missed you my friend."

"Troy thank God you came." Maverick said as he smiled. "I almost thought I'd never see you ever again." He continued as a huge grin spread out across his face. His huge, grin leant upwards slightly towards his eye on one side of his face and was slightly crooked. "I thought I'd never, ever actually get out of there."

Concept and Quorn smiled at each other as they immediately recognized Maverick's smile. His face had changed somewhat but his smile was still very much the same and that crooked grin, definitely belonged to Maverick.

"Come on, someone had to find you and help you out eventually." Troy insisted. "I always knew this day would come. I've waited for it."

The two men smiled at each other as they embraced Maverick's return to life and the human world that he'd been snatched away from, by

Barbelo's cruel claws. They'd both waited years for this moment and it suddenly struck Concept and Quorn as they watched both men, how lucky they had really been in that they had only had to wait a few days before their rescue from Mindplant had actually occurred, whereas Maverick on the other hand, had actually had to wait years and years.

Maverick chuckled as he turned to face Quorn and Concept who were situated at one side of the dark, cave quietly as they waited patiently for the two men to reacquaint themselves. "You must be Concept and Quorn."

Concept and Quorn nodded enthusiastically.

"I'm Concept. He's Quorn." Concept explained politely.

"So this is what you guys look like in real life." Maverick remarked playfully. "Not so ugly after all."

Concept grinned in response, relieved that they had managed to salvage Maverick from the Mindplant program and actually managed to bring him back to the real world in one piece. "I'm so glad you made it back Maverick."

"I sure did." Maverick returned as he grinned. "You got any clothes for me my good man?" He asked politely as he turned to face Troy once more, aware that he was almost completely naked and only had a small, towel like garment draped over his waist. "I don't fancy going outside like this. Not really dressed appropriately for dinner."

Troy grinned and nodded as he quickly pulled some clothes out of the rucksack on the floor nearby and handed them to him. "I brought these for you. They might be a little on the large side but they'll do for now."

Maverick sighed with relief as the thought of walking around in the real world in loin cloth wasn't very appealing, he might frighten someone with his nakedness. He quickly jumped down from the transparent coffin and then quickly started to dress as Troy started to pack his equipment back into his rucksack. Concept and Quorn stood by the wall of the cave silently as they watched the two men prepare to depart.

Once Maverick was fully dressed, the four men rushed back towards the tunnel as they abandoned the mountainside cave as quickly as they could and made their way back outside, fresh air and the car were politely waiting for them and they couldn't wait to embrace both. When they arrived outside the car, Troy quickly opened the door and the four men rapidly piled their bodies inside the vehicle, once they were all seated, he quickly actioned the control panel to close the car door behind them and the vehicle started to gently roll forward. They made their way back down the mountainside dirt road and then entered onto the nearby highway once more a few minutes later. The car passed the Mindplant Centre and then drove away from it and the four men smiled at each other as a wave of relief washed over them.

The journey to Troy's home was reasonably quick and twenty minutes later as the four men sat around inside his lounge, they prepared to eat their first real meal since their escape as he served them some freshly fried bacon sandwiches. They sipped on piping hot mugs of hot chocolate and coffee as they discussed their next plan of action and what had to be done that day as Maverick embraced his physical form and pushed ahead. The day definitely wasn't over yet and Maverick had something else he definitely needed to do.

"We have to find a way to actually stop Barbelo." Maverick insisted.

Concept and Troy immediately nodded in agreement.

"Maverick." Troy began. "If you infiltrate the Mindplant system, hack her files and then send some files, proving the abuse of her research to her financiers, wont that stop her in her tracks?" He suggested.

"Sure it would, but to actually do that, we actually have to go back inside the Mindplant Centre building as the files are absolutely impenetrable from the outside world. I built the security system myself. I designed it that way, which means we actually have to be inside the Mindplant Centre Control Room to do anything at all to Mindplant or to Barbelo's files." Maverick explained.

"Ok that's not a problem Maverick, we can go back there right now." Troy verified decisively as he quickly stood up.

Maverick smiled at his enthusiasm.

"Are you coming with us?" Troy asked as he turned to face Concept and Quorn. "Or would you prefer to wait for us here?"

Concept and Quorn glanced at each other quietly for a moment as they contemplated the implications of the choice they were actually being given. It was extremely risky to return to the Mindplant building and they both knew it.

"I've come this far." Concept confirmed decisively as he finished a mouthful of food and then stood up enthusiastically. "I can't abandon the ship now."

Quorn was quiet for a few seconds before he too nodded in agreement to indicate his participation also. "Sure I'll come along too. Count me in."

"Great that's settled. I'll sort you guys out with some clothes." Troy insisted. "The white robes just aren't very fashionable right now. That look is so yesterday."

"Don't worry about him guys, Troy's just jealous. You have Barbelo's newest collection and he doesn't." Maverick teased playfully.

Concept, Quorn and Maverick smiled as Troy quickly left the room.

Maverick turned towards Quorn and Concept and faced them both as he smiled. "Thank you so much you guys for helping. I really appreciate it." He insisted as he accepted that the two men had actually done more than their duty when they'd actually freed him. Maverick knew stopping Barbelo was actually his own personal mission and he appreciated their willingness to be involved and participate in that additional duty as the two men had absolutely no reason to endanger themselves further in order to help him sabotage Barbelo or the Mindplant operation itself. "You're both good men."

MINDPLANT: TRIMORPHIA

A few minutes later Troy returned to the lounge, his arms laden with clothes which he quickly handed out to both Concept and Quorn. The two men changed as they removed the white, clinical robes that Barbelo's coordinator's had adorned them in, prior to the commencement of their Mindplant vacations as they stepped inside the regular clothes that Troy had provided them with. Once they were dressed in the casual tops and jeans, Maverick quickly urged everyone to depart.

"Let's go." Maverick insisted as he stood up and quickly strode towards the nearby lounge door.

The room emptied as everyone followed him outside the lounge into the hallway and then the four men made their quickly back outside. They headed straight towards Troy's driveway, where his vehicle had been parked just a couple of hours before and then clambered back inside the vehicle as they prepared for the dangers that lay ahead and their entrance once more into Barbelo's Mindplant Centre. No one was looking forward to stepping inside the building or any possible ugly confrontation that could perhaps occur with Barbelo when they actually arrived as glum expressions adorned their faces.

Twenty minutes later, when they arrived outside the building Troy quickly parked his car near the entrance to the Mindplant Centre on the edge of the grounds and the four men quickly climbed out of the vehicle. They crept through the grounds and then entered inside the building through one of the fire exits that Maverick somehow managed to prize open. Once inside the building, they walked down the hallways almost on tiptoe as they headed briskly towards Barbelo's central control room. The morning had by now actually dawned, which meant the building was actually a lot brighter inside and more active than it had been when Concept and Quorn had last left it. Inside the hallways some staff now even wandered around as the four men hid inside maintenance cupboards and skirted around the passageways to avoid them.

Once the four men arrived inside the control room, Concept and Quorn stood inside the room quietly as Maverick headed straight for the main server and started to access the Mindplant system. A large screen on one of the walls lit up in front of them as Maverick sat down quickly in front of it, there was a lot to do and Maverick wasn't sure how much time he actually had to do it.

A few minutes later, Maverick's question was abruptly answered as Barbelo swept into the room, accompanied by a security guard and Gavin. She coughed gently in order to attract the four intruder's attention to her presence and Maverick immediately stopped, turned to face her and froze as her icy stare infiltrated his senses and pierced his flesh.

"I thought you might just show up one day Maverick." Barbelo remarked sarcastically as she paced one corner of the room. "That's why I took the precautions I did." She continued as she laughed mockingly.

Maverick stared at her silently.

Barbelo held a device up in the air in front of her face as smiled at him. "If you touch or sabotage my master files, I'll initiate this device which will then trigger a disease capsule I've placed inside your body. The disease particles will then be distributed throughout your blood stream within a few minutes and will infiltrate all your critical organs and within ten minutes you will die." Barbelo taunted. "If however you chose to walk away now, I'll actually be kind enough to give you the device and then you can decide when you want to die yourself." She explained as she smiled at Maverick sarcastically. "I'll also give you and your new friends, the rite of passage to leave the grounds of my building peacefully."

Her words inflicted wounds upon Maverick's heart as if she had a sword in her hands that she'd plunged into his flesh as he flinched. Troy and Maverick glanced at each other quietly as they both accepted that on this occasion, Barbelo had beaten them both. Maverick slowly shook his head as Quorn and Concept stood completely still, quietly at one side of the room, totally paralyzed and uncertain as they watched the scene in front of them unfold and listened to each and every word that was spoken.

"Leave it Maverick. She'll kill you if you don't." Troy insisted.

"I could die and this could end forever." Maverick debated. "Wouldn't it be worth it?"

Troy shook his head adamantly. "It won't end that way Maverick. She'll just rebuild her Mindplant booby-traps somewhere else like she did last time." He reassured him. "Don't do it Maverick. You'd die and achieve nothing. Your death would be a wasted death, your sacrifice robbed of any substance, a martyr for a cause whose death had no real impact at all."

Maverick sighed as he listened to Troy and accepted his defeat, the observations he made were definitely true and they both knew it. Barbelo had won this time and her victory could not be denied. He stood up slowly and backed away from the system as Barbelo placed the device on the floor next to one of her feet.

"Don't cause trouble for me Maverick and I won't cause trouble for you." Barbelo insisted as she smiled sweetly at him, her sugary smile mocked the poison her tongue and words actually contained. "Let's just live in the world as if we'd never met and don't actually know each other, that way we won't bring trouble to each other's doorsteps."

The hatred Maverick felt towards Barbelo, hit him straight in the gut as he glanced into her eyes for a second and frustration surged through his veins. His blood started to boil with rage as he seethed inside and the anger within him continued to bubble below the surface of his skin as he glanced at her, his eyes full of venom.

A few seconds later, Barbelo kicked the device clumsily over towards the nearby door as she indicated to Maverick clearly that he should collect it on his way out of the room and the building.

"You're not as clever as you once were Maverick." Barbelo scoffed as she laughed. "You're losing your touch."

The four men glanced at each other silently as Maverick stood up and started to walk towards the door. Troy, Quorn and Concept quickly followed him and glanced at Barbelo distastefully as each of them passed her on their way towards the door. On his way out of the room, Maverick leant down towards the floor and retrieved the device as he yielded fully to his defeat reluctantly.

Barbelo smiled happily as she watched the four men depart, satisfied that for that day she'd won the war and triumphant that Maverick had accepted her victory so easily. She revelled in her moment of glee as the room emptied until only Gavin and the security guard, Oscar remained. Perhaps Maverick wasn't such a huge threat after all Barbelo quickly concluded, she'd managed to get rid of him, at least for the time being in just fifteen minutes.

The four men walked down the hallway in complete and utter silence as the truth hit them like a tonne of bricks, they would definitely not be able to stop Barbelo and certainly not that day. Maverick's shoulders were low as if someone was standing on top of them and his body felt weighed down by Barbelo's victory as he walked, a broken shadow of the man he'd once been. Whilst the threat he presented to Barbelo now actually existed inside the real world alongside her, for that day it had been completely overcome and the possible, positive impact he could have had upon the world had been neutralized, extinguished and demobilized.

An awareness crept around underneath Maverick's skin as he suddenly shivered, it was entirely possible that Barbelo may still actually possess more trigger devices than the one she'd actually given him and that implied that she could still activate one at some point in the future, if she was ever again in close, physical proximity to him. That was the one drawback to Barbelo's disease capsule, to trigger and activate it inside someone's body, the holder of the device had to be situated not more than thirty meters away. Maverick knew he'd have to have a full head and body inspection before he could even risk facing or challenging her again. The implications of the capsule meant however that Maverick's life wasn't actually at risk from Barbelo for the time being as long as he kept as far away from her as he possibly could and avoided the Mindplant Centre completely. If he attempted to attack her work again however, there was also a risk that she would actually track him down and kill him. The situation was tricky and it was becoming increasingly apparent, there would be no easy way to demobilize Barbelo's hellish vacation, death experiment as Maverick's life was delicately balanced on the brink of termination inside Barbelo's devilish hands.

The central control room fell silent as Barbelo smiled victoriously at Gavin and prepared to depart. The crude interruption by Maverick, his odd looking giant of a friend and the two vacationers that had escaped alongside him, had now been satisfactorily resolved and they'd all been thrown out of her building like trash. Barbelo strode over towards Gavin as she prepared to vacate the control room and return to her office.

"Ok Gavin now we've sorted that out you can go back to work." Barbelo insisted politely.

"What should I do if they come back?" Gavin asked slightly nervously.

"They won't." Barbelo reassured him. "I have a lot of dirt on Maverick and he really can't touch me. I'll simply remind him of his sins before I even met him."

The two men nodded politely and left the room in total silence as Barbelo offered them no further explanations to the events that had just occurred inside it. Gavin felt quite numb as he walked down the hallway alone and headed back towards his office, he didn't have a complete understanding of the situation but he knew it was far from ideal and definitely edged upon being highly unethical. Guilt began to prick him inside as he walked and questioned himself further as to whether he was actually sacrificing his ethics for his own family's financial wellbeing. Such unethical entanglements crossed a line that Gavin had simply never crossed before, he'd never had too as he'd never worked anywhere that dealt with such experimental, scientific technology. Now however, Gavin had been thrown into the murky depths of unethical, scientific practices and there was very little he could actually do to stop it or limit his involvement, in as much as he wanted to escape his wallow in the muddy, distasteful, sinking swamp of dirt was not over and he was firmly rooted inside it and deeply implicated in every single speck. He needed his job, he needed Mindplant and no matter how murky the depths of compromise actually were, unfortunately he also needed Barbelo. There was no instant solution for him that he could pursue and that meant for the meantime, Gavin was trapped inside Barbelo's web just as the Mindplant vacationers had been and just as Maverick himself had been too. Escape for Gavin would not be that as easy as his wife's pregnancy dictated his financial reliance upon Barbelo for the meantime and a pregnancy was simply not something Gavin could reverse.

Once the central control room was empty, Barbelo smiled as she swept out of it and made her way back towards her office, satisfied that Maverick for that day had been well and truly taken care off. He would not threaten her again or Mindplant at least not at any time in the immediate future. When Barbelo arrived back inside her office, she stood by the window quietly as she watched Maverick, Quorn, Concept and the almost giant man that had accompanied him, actually leave the grounds.

The men's departure from the building itself had been delayed slightly as they'd stopped off to collect Quorn and Concept's personal belongings from the lockers inside the changing room, which meant they'd only just arrived at the exterior main door just as Barbelo had actually arrived back inside her office. The four men rushed through the grounds quickly as they headed back towards Troy's vehicle, grateful that they had managed to escape alive and grateful that they would actually live to fight another day.

Barbelo's body filled with warmth as she welcomed and embraced the joy that collated inside her as a result of Maverick's subjugation.

She had saved her work from the threat of disruption and potential destruction that her most formidable foe Maverick posed. Maverick, simply wasn't like other human beings in Barbelo's sight and she knew she could not afford to underestimate his intelligence. He was her only enemy and he was the only person alive, who actually possessed the knowledge and the capability to sabotage and stop her and it was for that very reason she'd contained him for so long inside the frozen chamber within the mountainside cave. At one time, Maverick's vast intellect had actually complimented her own as they'd worked alongside each other on the creation off Mindplant itself, but now they were engaged in conflict with each other, it had become an obstructive impediment.

Barbelo's fascination and desire to experiment with and experience death subconsciously as she entered inside the Mindplant bodies vacationers inhibited, had created several consequential dilemma's and contingent obstacles over the years for her, but she was determined to continue with her scientific explorations. Her urge to do so was one that no one alive on the face of the earth seemed to understand as she entered inside the bodies of the dying to share their experience and died alongside them, not even Maverick. At one time the two had been close, but even then Barbelo hadn't trusted him enough to reveal the deepest, darkest desires that lurked and resided inside her nature to him. Barbelo trusted no human being enough to do that, except for herself.

The four men clambered back inside the vehicle situated at the edge of the grounds as Barbelo watched them silently and sighed, the day had only just begun and already it had presented her with significant obstacles and problems. This would not be the first or the last time, Barbelo would take such risks with her work as her thirst to experience death in more complex formats was growing and the more she fed and entertained it, the hungrier her appetite seemed to become. She yearned to experience more elaborate forms of death and this desire could not be contained or controlled as her thirst had quite simply become unquenchable. Barbelo's desires had gripped every part of her mind, body and soul as she continued to embrace them and allowed them to rule her whilst they ran riot inside her like an undisciplined child.

Maverick's presence back in the real world presented problems to Barbelo in that it made satisfaction of her internal desires slightly more difficult and meant that she would actually have to be much more careful. Although she had actually prevailed on this occasion, his presence could not be taken lightly as he would be watching her and he would be watching Mindplant, he represented an obstruction of opposition, that had reared it's rebellious head when she'd least expected it to and it was possible he would try to strike again.

The life force of Mindplant had been salvaged on this occasion from the claws of its adversary Maverick but Barbelo knew the victory she savoured was temporary and that the battle with Maverick was far from over. He would continue to be a constant threat to her existence and her work and he would be a prickly thorn in her side for as long as he lived, breathed and walked upon the face of the earth. Maverick had not extinguished the flames of her passion this time, but at some point in the future, he would perhaps try again. Barbelo leant down and opened the drawer of her desk as she continued to watch the four men depart quietly as the vehicle they were situated inside slowly disappeared into the distance. She quickly plucked an identical device to the one she'd brandished in her hands just ten minutes before out of the drawer and smiled, Maverick's life still sat firmly situated inside Barbelo's hands and as much as Maverick now presented a threat to her life, now she also presented a threat to his life too.